Outstanding Praise for the Novels of Timo

SOMEONE LIKE YOU

"Beck's latest crowd-pleasing gay romance resonates with warm fuzzies."
—*Booklist*

"Witty dialogue and one-liners."
—*Envy Man* magazine

"Beck resolves all the plot lines nicely and makes you want to max out your credit cards on some major retail therapy."
—*We the People*

I'M YOUR MAN

"Beck brings a charmingly light touch to life-changing drama in his latest laugh-out-loud romance."
—*Booklist*

HE'S THE ONE

"This second madcap Manhattan romance from Beck has sexy boys, mild comedy, and even a little amateur sleuthing. Beck seems to have found his calling serving up featherweight fun."
—*Publishers Weekly*

"A delightful sophomore novel . . . smart and breezy."
—*Outsmart* (Houston, Texas)

"*He's the One* stands out for good writing and a fairly inventive plot. This book is a good, quick read, just what everyone needs in the summer. You can enjoy it during an afternoon by the pool or an evening when you don't want to go out or watch TV. Pick it up and see if you don't agree."
—*The Bottom Line* (Palm Springs)

IT HAD TO BE YOU

"Might there actually, or finally, be a market for some good gay fluff? If there is, then Timothy James Beck has his finger on the pulse of that change. If you are looking for an easily accessible feel-good read, this is a prime candidate."
—*The Lambda Book Report*

"An entertaining read . . . genuinely both funny and poignant. *It Had to Be You* flows very well and is hugely enjoyable. If Timothy James Beck sticks with these characters, then he may have a series of homebound stories to rival those of Armistead Maupin."
—*Gay Times*

Books by Timothy James Beck

IT HAD TO BE YOU

HE'S THE ONE

I'M YOUR MAN

SOMEONE LIKE YOU

WHEN YOU DON'T SEE ME

Published by Kensington Publishing Corporation

When You Don't See Me

TIMOTHY JAMES BECK

KENSINGTON BOOKS
http://www.kensingtonbooks.com

KENSINGTON BOOKS are published by

Kensington Publishing Corp.
850 Third Avenue
New York, NY 10022

ISBN-13: 978-0-7582-1686-1
ISBN-10: 0-7582-1686-6

First Kensington Trade Paperback Printing: October 2007
10 9 8 7 6 5 4 3 2 1

Printed in the United States of America

Acknowledgments

Thank you, John Scognamiglio, Alison Picard, Tom Wocken, Dorothy Cochrane, Lynne Demarest, Timothy Forry, Greg Herren, Rhonda Rubin, Lindsey Smolensky, and Bill Thomas.

And as always: Alan, Amy and Richard, April and Nick, Carissa, Caroline, Christine and John, Cullen, David, Dean, Denece, Don, Gary, Gene, Helen, Jason and Jeff, Jess and Laura, Jonathan, Larry, Laurie and Marty, Lisa K., Lisa S., Lori and Bob, Marika, Mark, Marla, Michael, Nathan, Nora, Paul E., Rob, Robin, Ron, Sarena, Shannon, Shanon, Sheila, Steve C., Steve V., Steve and Doug, Terry and Allen, Trish, the Carter, Cochrane, Lambert, Rambo, Rose, and Wocken families, Charlie the Unicorn, AOL and LiveJournal friends, fellow bloggers, Yahoo reading groups, Tim Brookover and *OutSmart,* and Paul J. Willis and the Saints and Sinners Literary Festival.

A special thanks to the readers who wrote letters and e-mails and who reviewed and recommended the novels.

Inspiration: Pet Shop Boys and Sisters of Mercy.

Relaxation: Brandi, Guinness, Hailey, Lazlo, Margot, and Rex.

AFTER

take cold steel
make music
use wet ashes for ink
blend fire and smoke
into paint
make number-numbed art
without sense
without reason
express the depths
of holes unfilled
of hearts too still
too soon

1

New York City Boy

I ducked beneath a diner's awning and decided that the city had finally made me her bitch. The freezing rain on an already-frigid February day made me want to lie down in the middle of Madison Avenue and wait for a bus to finish me off. Worse, I was getting a cold. My sinuses were killing me. My throat was starting to feel scratchy. I spat a glob of phlegm on the slushy sidewalk. A woman next to me cringed and ran to the next awning down, freeing space for a guy with dreadlocks and an Army coat.

The shitty weather forced us to stop pretending we were all invisible. Until the weather cleared, we had to deal with each other's presence. There were about fifteen of us crowded under the awning. When someone new arrived, we'd shiver and nod, but nobody said anything.

I peered through the diner's window. It was packed. If someone left the counter, I'd buy a cup of coffee. If I had money.

While I counted the change in my pocket, a guy ran across the street, shielding his head with a newspaper. He bumped into me, rendering me visible, and I dropped two quarters.

"Hey!"

"Sorry," he said, wiping flecks of ice from his glasses.

"Fucker," I grumbled. I grabbed my quarters from an old man who'd picked them up. "Give me those. They're mine."

"Just trying to help."

"He was just helping," a woman said.

Suddenly everyone began talking about me like I wasn't there. It felt good to bring strangers together. Another man ran across the street to join us and started a heated conversation with Newspaper Head. I pocketed my change and pretended to consult a bus schedule that I already knew by heart. I glanced at the two men as casually as possible. Pointless, considering that everyone around us was blatantly staring at their performance.

Newspaper Head's friend was in that vague age range that could be late twenties or early thirties. He was blond and wore Diesel jeans and a beat-up leather jacket. He reminded me of Rocky in *The Rocky Horror Picture Show*. Especially when he glared and sort of grunted at Newspaper Head, who was a sheepish, older guy, definitely in his forties. Total geek. My curiosity was piqued when Newspaper Head's new friend said, "I didn't sign up for this!"

I didn't know why Blond Diesel said it, but I completely understood how he felt. I'd said the same thing a lot. The first time I boarded the wrong subway and wound up in Flatbush, Queens. When I saw the metal detectors on my first day at P.S. 35. And especially after I was mugged, which I'd never told anyone about.

I definitely didn't sign up to catch a cold just in time for moving day.

"Why would you think I'd want to move to Chicago?" Blond Diesel asked.

"It's a promotion. You know how hard I've been working. You know how difficult it's been for me there," Newspaper Head whined.

"What about me? I can't just pick up everything and move."

There was a lull, a stalemate, during which two Hassidic Jews came out of the rain to consult the menu taped to the diner's window. Water dripped from the curls that framed their faces. I sniffled and was overtaken by the smell of their wet wool, until my sinuses clogged up again seconds later.

"I'm not moving," Blond Diesel said.

"Look, this isn't a choice I expect you to make on the spot. I just wanted to bring it up for consideration. Could you think about it?"

"Why? It's obvious you've made your decision. Now I'll make

mine!" Blond Diesel loudly announced. He added, "I'll be at Ed's, if you care," then stormed away into the rain.

"Is this where we applaud?" mumbled a Hassidic Jew, and his friend chuckled. "Is it intermission? I don't know."

"Does anything last?" I asked out loud.

"Death," Hassidic One said, and Hassidic Two nodded sagely.

They went inside the diner. I followed and ordered a cup of coffee. I took a sip, savoring the hot, metallic-tasting liquid, added sugar, and stirred it with a spoon. I tasted it again. Once I was satisfied with the sugar-to-coffee ratio, I nonchalantly dropped the spoon into the pocket of my cargo pants. After I finished, I left two dollars in change on the counter. I discreetly dropped the empty mug into my pocket and tried not to wince when it clinked against the spoon as I walked to the door.

It didn't matter. It was too loud in there for anyone to hear. But as I left, one of the Hassidic Jews caught my eye and shook his head disapprovingly. Then he went back to sipping his matzo ball soup, and I was invisible once again.

Everyone I knew got a family tag as a kid. My fraternal twin, Chuck, who I beat into the world by three minutes, was "the one who breaks things." Toys. China. Vases. Cars. Bones and teeth—his and mine. Anything breakable was at risk around Chuck. It paid off for him, because our parents freaked at what he might do to the vacuum cleaner or the lawn mower.

Our older brother, Tony, was "the one who never shuts up." Also known as "the one who asks dumb questions." Since Chuck and I were a couple years younger than Tony, we missed out on his *Why is the sky blue?* phase. But even when I was a little kid, I knew why Tony came up with gems like *Do dogs have headaches?* He didn't want information, just a reason to speculate out loud about the answers. Uncle Wayne used to offer Tony five dollars in exchange for five minutes of silence. Tony's piggy bank went hungry.

If sibling rivalry was a game, those two shouldn't have been much competition for me. But in all other ways, they were the pride of the Dunhills. Good athletes. Good grades. Good looks. They left me no choice except to be "the one who disappears."

It was Dunhill family lore that my mother repeatedly left me in stores as a baby. She always claimed she was overwhelmed by having three kids in diapers. I thought I was just the victim of a shopping snob. I'd never known my mother to look for a bargain or a sale. Having twins was like some kind of two-for-one affront to her. She ditched me to get rid of the evidence.

As I got older, I tended to vanish on my own. Not just when we went places as a family. Even in our house, I could disappear by not fitting in. My parents didn't know how to deal with an inferior Dunhill, so I tried to make myself invisible.

Where's Nicky? someone would ask, even though I was ten feet away, tucked between the back of the sofa and the den window with a comic book or a sketchpad. *Who knows?* was the standard answer, but it sounded more like *Who cares?* Then Tony the Talker would recap my misdeeds from the day. Eventually, it would end with my parents tracking me down to ask, *Why can't you be more like your brothers?*

All that was years ago, but recently, I seemed to be trying to fulfill their fondest desire. Like Chuck, I kept breaking things. My Discman. My umbrella. My promises. And like Tony, I kept asking dumb questions of an indifferent, possibly even a cruel, city.

Maybe the city hadn't made me her bitch. Maybe it was Mother Nature. Rain hit my neck and ran down my back as I hurried to join a herd of people under a bus shelter. I read the *Village Voice* over a man's shoulder. Then my eyes stopped on an ad that made me turn in disgust. Apparently my favorite Hell's Kitchen restaurant had switched to serving Thai—the third time that had happened to me. I hated Thai food. I again asked aloud, "Does anything last?"

A woman next to me thought I was talking to her. "It wasn't supposed to rain today. Should clear up later, though."

"Great," I muttered, both at her and the bus that stopped to pick us up.

Inside the bus I stared at the floor and felt fried. All I wanted was to go home. I looked up and tried to see out the window, worried that I was on the wrong bus. For a second, I couldn't remember where I was going. Then it came back to me. Home was uptown now. Way uptown.

Some hippie once said freedom was another word for nothing left to lose, a phrase that flashed through my mind when I signed a two-year lease after weeks of searching for an apartment. Of course, my generation torched Woodstock when we learned that corporate America jacked up the price for freedom. My freedom cost two thousand dollars a month, plus utilities. Even though the rent was expensive, there was no way I'd burn the place down. Especially after all I went through to get it.

Finding an apartment in New York City, I learned, was a lot like trying to find a boyfriend. You could search ads in the newspaper, like I did, and realize the descriptions and photos never matched up to the real deal. A studio the size of a closet could look damned near palatial if it was photographed with a good lens. I visited something described as an "EVil, flr thru loft, with fplce and sky-light," which turned out to be the moldering attic of a former fac-tory in the East Village with a hole in the roof. The fireplace was a hibachi with a dead rat in it.

Ads on the Internet were pretty much the same, although most of them were faked in an effort to lure homeless saps to a broker-age firm. It seemed ridiculous to pay an agent thousands of dollars for something I could do myself. Kind of like paying an escort to pose as a boyfriend. However, walking all over the city looking at apartments I couldn't afford, and ones that made me want to bathe in peroxide after I was in them, left me appreciating the idea of paying someone else to do the dirty work.

Uncle Blaine always told me fate brought him and Daniel to-gether. Daniel told me in private that fate had nothing to do with it. He saw what he wanted and went for it. Fate led me to a random coffeehouse in SoHo, where I overheard some dude complaining to his friend that he had to move and hated to give up his apart-ment. From that point on, I went for it and got it.

It was a small, one-bedroom apartment on the fourth floor of an ancient tenement in Spanish Harlem. It was dingy, the four rooms were tiny, and the apartment was in the back, so all the grimy win-dows faced the brick walls of the neighboring buildings, but I didn't care. In my eyes, it was perfect. At any rate, it was good enough to give up the search. It was my freedom, after all.

I'd moved the day before—as soon as ConEd turned on the elec-tricity—and spent the first night on my own. I barely slept since I spent the majority of the night listening to the noises of a strange apartment. It was the first time in my life that I felt really alone. No brothers, parental figures, or anyone to fill the silence between the bumps in the night. Sometime around two in the morning, I heard a man yell in the apartment above me, a door slam, and heavy footsteps on the stairs.

When I woke up, I discovered a cat who seemed to live on the fire escape. He wasn't conversational after I opened the window and tried to talk to him over my steaming cup of tea. I finally left him so I could do a housecleaning job for I Dream of Cleanie: a Midtown loft, which made my new place look even worse.

Still, it was home, so when I got off the bus at my stop, I was determined to make the best of things. I immediately stepped into a small pond. My feet made sloshing noises with every step I took. I crossed against traffic to a deli on the corner and used my debit card to stock up on orange juice and Ramen.

Finally, I entered the ugly brown behemoth of a tenement building I now called home. Even though I'd lived there less than twenty-four hours, I checked my mailbox. I liked writing people more than talking to them on my cell phone. Now that I no longer had a computer and e-mail, anyone who wanted to keep in touch would have to buy a stamp.

I hadn't unpacked anything but a box of kitchen stuff. The rest of my boxes, bags, and other things were piled just inside the doorway of the apartment. I closed the door and rooted through a Duane Reade bag filled with toiletries until I found a half-full bottle of NyQuil, uncapped it, and chugged. A knock on the door startled me, almost causing me to choke.

The first of my roommates had arrived.

I had only the vaguest acquaintance with Kendra Bowers. We'd sat next to each other in a class during my first semester at college, bitched together about the instructor, and found out that we liked the same music. Then we bumped into each other by chance in a restaurant where Kendra was waiting tables. During our conversation, we discovered that we were both looking for a place to live.

Kendra's sunny disposition made her an appealing roommate prospect. Most of the people I knew were creative and seemed to think that cynicism and angst were mandatory traits of an artist.

Kendra was definitely one of those glass-is-half-full people. I figured it wouldn't hurt to have somebody with her attitude in my life.

Kendra's brightness seemed to dim while I showed her around the apartment, a three-minute tour. It was hard for me not to take it personally, and I said, "Maybe you shouldn't have left it up to me to find the place. But since you're working two jobs—"

"It probably looks better when it's not so gloomy outside," Kendra said hopefully. I figured sunlight would only illuminate the apartment's flaws, so I kept quiet. After a minute, she said, "Morgan will be here soon. I guess she and I should take the bedroom. Girls need a closed door."

"Sure, whatever," I said, unable to come up with a decent argument.

Kendra turned down my offer of help. While she rolled her bags into the bedroom, I went to the kitchen and emptied the pockets of my cargo pants, taking inventory of the day's piracy. The spoon and cup from the diner went into the sink. Another pocket held a bungee cord I'd found on the street, and two refrigerator magnets. One for a restaurant, the other for a plumber. Shit in, shit out. I slapped them on the refrigerator and dug in the next pocket. Two pens, a small spiral tablet that I kept to make notes of my boss's instructions about the places I cleaned, and in the bottom, two condoms. With a sigh, I dropped those on the counter and reached inside another pocket, where I found what I was looking for: a bag of green tea that I took from the loft I'd cleaned that morning.

I didn't normally steal from I Dream of Cleanie's clients, but who'd miss a single tea bag? Green tea was supposed to be healthy. I'd done my bit for good karma by wiping down the inside of the client's refrigerator, which wasn't on my list of duties.

I turned on the burner under the kettle and glanced at Kendra as she walked in. She homed right in on the condoms and raised her eyebrows. That distracted me for a second. I'd never noticed that her eyebrows were black, which made me wonder if she was a real blonde. I checked out her roots, thinking about my friend Davii, a genius with hair color who often provided commentary on the hair don'ts of people around us. I figured Kendra's hair color must be real, because even with two jobs, she seemed as broke as I was.

She couldn't afford someone like Davii to make her look naturally blond.

"Is there something in my hair?" she asked, nervously running her fingers through it as if she might find a roach.

"No. Sorry I was staring," I said.

"Are you having those with your tea?" she asked, pointing at the condoms.

I slipped them back in my pants pocket and said, "I don't know where they came from. I guess one of my tormentors." She cocked her head. "My uncle and his friends," I explained. "My friend Blythe calls them my gay mentors. I call them my tormentors."

"Like bondage or something?" Kendra asked, her blue eyes huge.

"Ew. No. Uncle Blaine, his boyfriend, their housekeeper, all their friends. They're always giving me advice and warnings about the dangers of living in a big city. How to avoid being bashed, mugged, or otherwise assaulted. How to have safe sex. I'm sure one of them dropped those in my pants when I was at my uncle's."

"It's sweet that they look out for you," Kendra said warmly, as if I'd restored her faith in humanity.

I was still staring impatiently at the kettle when Kendra's friend Morgan showed up. I stayed in the kitchen while Kendra let her in. I tried to ignore the furious whispers that indicated that Morgan, too, might be finding the place less than luxurious. Then her voice went from whisper to bitch in ten seconds as she condemned her last landlord to eternal damnation and declared that her moving men were know-nothing pigs.

My anxiety about Morgan's desirability as a roommate boiled a lot faster than the kettle of water when she stepped into the kitchen and I saw two snakes wrapped around her arms.

"Uh . . ." I said, trying not to back away.

Morgan was short and dumpy. Her uneven hair was black—definitely an unprofessional dye job—and her skin was pale and doughy. Her eyes were like little black currants set deep in her face, and their expression was hard and challenging, as if the snakes were some kind of initiation I had to pass.

"Lucifer," she said, holding up one arm to better display a yellowish snake. It eyed me with a look that made me remember a fifth grade teacher who'd been pure evil. "Hugsie," she added, pointing a black snake at me. That one began to writhe as the kettle shrieked at us.

I was grateful to have a reason to turn away and said over my shoulder, "Nick Dunhill. I guess you're Morgan."

"Brilliant. If you ever enter my room without my permission, you can kiss your ass good-bye. Which will be easy, because I'll make sure your head's stuffed up your ass, just like every other man in Manhattan."

"I'm pretty sure not every man in Manhattan has been stuffed up my ass," I said, turning around and locking my eyes on hers. It almost seemed like she was going to smile, in that Wednesday Addams if-I-smile-I'll-die way. Then she left the kitchen as abruptly as she'd entered, snake bodies trailing behind her like feather boas. Maybe they were actual boas. I had no idea.

When Kendra came back in, looking a little fearful, I hissed, "What did you say she does?"

"She works for an animated children's program," Kendra whispered hesitantly, as if she knew the probability of that was highly questionable. "I'm sorry. I didn't know about the snakes."

"You're the one who has to sleep with them," I said, adding with sadistic satisfaction, "behind a closed door."

Roberto finally showed up with the clothes on his back, two milk crates full of CDs, and furniture he'd found on the street: a futon, a tiny café table, and two rickety wooden dining chairs. I tried to cover up how lousy I felt when I helped him haul his loot into the apartment. Not that he was paying attention. He answered three calls on his cell phone while we trudged up and down stairs. If it were anyone but Roberto, I'd think he was dealing drugs. But I could tell from his side of the conversations that he was fielding calls from one or more of his brothers. He had four.

I knew Roberto from high school. Although he grew up in the Bronx, we had a few things in common. Mostly our exasperated families. Roberto's mother had hoped that art school would put his skills with spray paint and walls to good use. Even though he pretended he had no interest in school and was just biding time until graduation, Roberto was extremely talented. Our teachers often compared him to Jean Michel Basquiat. Without the heroin habit.

"I'm sorry we're stuck in the dining room," I said. "The girls claimed the bedroom. I get the idea they think the apartment sucks overall."

"This is a room? I thought it was a broom closet," Roberto said. "The futon takes up half the room."

I opened a small door and said, "No. This is the broom closet."

He laughed and said, "I'm just teasin', Nickito!"

"Stop calling me that."

"Who gives a shit what anyone thinks? What matters is, we have our own place, yo!" He high-fived me, then saw Kendra standing in our doorway. "It's got a good view, too."

"I just wanted to give you my share of the deposit, Nick." She took a tentative step into the room and handed me a check. "You know, while I've got it? Before I accidentally spend it on something silly, like food."

"Or the power bill," I said.

She sighed and asked, "How much was it to get the lights turned on?"

"They're billing us. It won't come for another month."

"Not me," Roberto said. "I could pop at any time."

I couldn't tell if Kendra was grossed out or trying to figure out what Roberto meant. I introduced them. When she left and I heard the bedroom door close, I turned to Roberto and said, "Roommates are off-limits."

"We got two honeys in our house and you're telling me I can't—"

He was cut off when Morgan knocked loudly on our door frame and said, "Hey, you."

"Nick," I reminded her, then sneezed twice. "Sorry. I don't know if it's a cold or—"

"Listen, just because we're sharing this glorified shoe box doesn't mean I want to hear your life story, okay? Kendra told me she gave you her share of the rent and deposit. I don't want you thinking I'm some freeloader, so here." She slapped a check on top of my duffel bag. Before she left, she said, "You should get a door or hang up a sheet in this doorway. I don't want to walk by and accidentally see your man-bits or anything."

I stood and breathed through my mouth. Roberto was silent next to me. I wasn't sure what he was contemplating. Probably that one of the "honeys" wasn't such a catch after all. The miracle would be if he tried to catch her and didn't get his ass kicked. As tough as Roberto might be, I'd put my money on Morgan. If I had money.

While I put both girls' checks in my wallet, I sneezed three more times and remembered my cup of tea. It was stone cold, but I drank it in the kitchen while Roberto made a couple more phone calls. Then I went back into our room, trying to summon up enthusiasm for unpacking.

"Let's get out of here," Roberto said abruptly, picking up my hoodie and tossing it to me. I slipped into it, understanding his need to leave. Four people sharing the rent was an appealing idea. Four people inhabiting the same small space at the same time was less so. Plus Morgan's movers were due any minute. Something told me that would entail a lot of drama.

I considered my scratchy throat and said, "Let me get a heavier jacket."

It had finally stopped raining, but the air was still cold and damp. While we walked, Roberto entertained me with a perfect imitation of Morgan. When I realized where we were heading, I wiped my nose with alternating sleeves of my jacket and asked, "What's up? Where are we going?"

"Listen to you, all suspicious. It stopped raining, so I thought we'd get out and—"

"No," I interrupted. "I meant, why are we going to the subway?"

Roberto looked like he was about to deny my accusation, but stopped when he saw me staring at the subway entrance at the end of the block. We could see people descending and ascending the stairs beneath the sign for the 6 train. He glared at me and said, "Suck it up. You can't ride the bus forever, and taxis are expensive. We'll be fine. Trust me."

"Manipulative asswipe. You had to bring trust into this, didn't you?"

"You know I think of you like a brother. For you to doubt me, to think I'd willingly put you in harm's way, is like a slap in the face. A knife in my heart. A snake's fangs in my—"

"Enough! Fine. I'll do it."

We fought our way into the subway against people elbowing their way out. I slumped in a seat still warm from the behind of its previous occupant. I did everything I could to distract myself, so my mind wouldn't think about what could be happening above while we were trapped below. I tried counting the dingy white tiles of the station wall outside, but the train lurched forward and thwarted my plan. I counted sneakers. There were twenty-four; twelve pairs. Then I worried all that counting was a sign I had OCD, so I stared at Roberto and tried to send him a telepathic message: *I hate you for making me do this.* He stood in front of me, obliviously holding on to the bar overhead while staring at some girl's ass. I started counting asses.

When we exited at Sixty-eighth Street, I had to cover my ears because of the noise. Across the street from the subway entrance, behind a tall blue construction fence, a building was being torn down. As part of a brick wall crashed down, I glared at Roberto, who stared straight ahead and pretended nothing was happening. I followed him, wanting to get away from the noise and destruction. Since he seemed to have a plan and I had nowhere to be, I stayed silent until he stopped at the zoo and reached into his pocket to pay.

"You don't have to do that," I croaked.

Roberto looked at me and rolled his eyes. "Forget it, man."

We walked in silence, avoiding the sea lions in the Central Garden. I wasn't sure if the sparse crowd was because it was nearly closing time or because of the weather. I hadn't spent much time there. Or in any zoo, for that matter. It was small. Intimate. It might have been a nice date if I wasn't walking toward death's door with Roberto.

"Here we are," Roberto announced.

I looked around. "The North Pole?"

Roberto ignored me to stare at a polar bear, who took little notice of our arrival. The bear undoubtedly loved winter in New York. I wondered what he did during the summer. Probably spent most of it swimming. Maybe he had a time-share in Greenland.

"What up, iceberg?" Roberto greeted the bear. "What's the fizz, fuzzy?"

"You and the bear are close?" I asked.

"He's not bad for a white dude. I come here a lot when I need to think. Or be alone, you know?"

"You usually have the zoo to yourself?"

"You usually such a smartass?"

"Sorry. It's the cold medication talking."

"No, I don't usually have the place to myself. But even when it's crowded, I can tune it all out. Make everybody invisible, like they don't exist."

"Do you always come to see the bear?"

"Yeah. No. I mean, yeah, I always come to see him, but not always just him. I like to spend time with the sea lions, too. But that's about it. Sometimes I check out other stuff, but mostly just those two, you know? There's other bears, too. Somewhere."

"Interesting." I rubbed my forehead.

"You feel that bad?"

I thought about Morgan and her two snakes back in our apartment. "No. I'm cool."

"Good. I haven't been here for a while. I've been saving up for this apartment thing, so I had to wait until I could spare the coins."

I reached into my pocket to see if the condoms had miraculously turned into money. No luck. "Hey," I said, "as long as you're in a spending mood, why don't you buy me a cup of coffee? I'll stay here and keep your bear company."

"Sure."

Roberto headed off. I leaned on the railing and watched the bear, who was playing with a plastic barrel. He seemed to be having the time of his life. I wondered what Roberto thought about when he came here. I wondered if he wanted me to ask him. Maybe that was why he'd brought me here in the first place.

The barrel flew from the bear's gigantic paws and into the water. Without hesitation, he got up, did a belly flop on top of the barrel, then held it in his paws while paddling around his personal swimming pool.

"Nice job, if you can get it," I mumbled.

"His name is Gus," a voice said.

"Huh?"

"The bear. His name is Gus."

I looked at the man who stood next to me, but not too close. Not bad. Not really my type—a little too neat around the edges. But cute. Maybe in his late twenties.

"I'm Mark."

"Nick."

We shook hands. I sniffed and wiped my nose on the sleeve of my jacket before I could stop myself.

"Got that cold that's going around, huh?" Mark asked. It beat *Nice weather we're having, huh?* Plus it was more accurate.

"Yeah. I guess so."

Mark looked back at the bear and said, "They're becoming extinct, you know. Because we're fucking up the climate and their habitat."

"Figures," I muttered, staring at the doomed bear. "Nothing lasts."

Before Mark could answer, I heard Roberto say, "Here's your coffee. Hot and black, just the way you like your—"

"Roberto, this is Mark," I said. "Mark, Roberto."

"—bears," Roberto finished. The two of them exchanged a look I couldn't decipher. Maybe Mark thought Roberto was my boyfriend. Maybe Roberto was assessing whether he should get lost and leave me with Mark.

"Roberto's my roommate. One of them," I said. Then I sneezed four times in rapid succession, sloshing coffee all over the place.

Mark smiled—he had great teeth—and said, "You really should do something about that."

"It's just a stupid cold," I said.

Except I was starting to wonder, because what happened next made me think I might be hallucinating. Roberto and Mark closed in on me a little, so that when they started walking away from the bear exhibit, it was automatic for me to fall in step between them. It was only when we left the park and Mark hailed a cab that my senses returned.

"Are we going somewhere?" I asked.

"We are," Mark said.

"All three of us?"

Whatever expression I wore made Roberto say, "It's chill."

It was the last thing any of us said until we were in the back of a cab and Mark gave the driver an address. I considered the ache in my muscles and the wooziness of my thought processes. It didn't seem like a good time for my first three-way, even if I did have two condoms in my pocket.

I closed my eyes and let my head fall on Roberto's shoulder, indifferent to a din of mental voices that sounded suspiciously like my uncle and his friends. Wherever we were going, it couldn't be for anything too sinister if Roberto was part of it.

An hour later, I was putting my clothes back on and Mark was dropping latex in the trash. Latex gloves.

"If Roberto wanted to pay for a doctor, he could have just told me," I grumbled, gingerly sliding into my pants because of the penicillin injection Mark had given me.

"He's not paying. It's a free clinic. We avoided the red tape and saved you hours in the waiting room. Just thank him for calling me before that sinus infection and tonsillitis got worse. Since it's bacterial, I'll prescribe an antibiotic. Take the full dose as ordered until the pills are gone. Do you have a job?"

"Yes."

"I'll write you an excuse from work while you're contagious."

I wished he could write me an excuse from Morgan while I was contagious. At least now that I had her check.

"It's useful to have a roommate who knows a doctor," I said. My grandmother the hypochondriac would have been thrilled that I'd met a doctor, if only the doctor wasn't sporting a penis. Following up on that thought, I added, "It's been a memorable first date, anyway." Mark's grin encouraged me. "Will there be a second? Or do I have to be stricken with another disease to see you?"

He slid the prescription into my shirt pocket, patted it in place, and said, "If you happen to take my phone number from the prescription and call me sometime, we can talk about a second date then." My face must have shown that I didn't really believe him, because as he nudged me out the door, he said, "You should rent the movie *Casablanca.*"

"Huh?" I asked, wondering again if I was delirious.

"You said nothing lasts," Mark said. "Listen to the song in *Casablanca.*"

Roberto gave me a quizzical look when I found him outside the clinic. I grunted at him, then sneezed again. "You gonna live?" he asked. When I nodded, he thrust out his arm to hail a cab and said, "You can thank me when you're feeling better."

"People always expect you to be grateful when they run your life," I said. I mimicked his accent when I added, "I ain't your bitch."

"I took you to the zoo," he said, opening the cab door for me.

"I ended up getting a shot," I said, sliding inside.

"I'm paying for your cab fare home," he said, slamming the door.

"To an apartment full of snakes."

"You win," Roberto conceded.

"You know any place we can rent movies?" I asked.

"You got anything to watch 'em on?"

"Damn," I said. We stared at each other a few seconds. "Maybe Morgan has something to watch them on," I suggested.

Roberto pulled my hood over my eyes. I didn't push it back, pretending that it made me invisible.

February 23, 2003

Dear Nick,

It was strange to get back from my trip and find you gone. I knew you were moving out, but it was weird when it actually happened. I hope you're settling into your new place okay.

I know my reaction to all this hasn't been great. I can be stubborn and worse when engaged in a contest of wills. (You hold your own just fine, too.) I've probably been smothering or controlling or overbearing. I've heard I can be that way from time to time.

Fortunately, Daniel reminded me that really, none of this is about me. It's about you making your own decisions. And why shouldn't you? That's part of being your own man.

One thing worried me. You took so little. You left your computer and most of the other stuff in your room. I hope that wasn't because I bought it. Those things are yours, and you can take them any time you want. Maybe you left them here on purpose. Maybe you want to know you've always got a room here. That goes without saying. If you need to use anything here, or come here to crash occasionally (everybody has roommate problems from time to time), you have a key and you're always welcome.

That's all I guess I can say except that I love you.

Uncle Blaine

2

A Man Could Get Arrested

There were many advantages to getting horizontal in bed with a
man. Mainly, I appreciated the way my flaws weren't as notice-
able under covers. If a cop brought a guy to a lineup and asked him
to point to the man who screwed him silly the night before, odds
were good that the person singled out would be a muscular hunk,
not some scrawny twink. I wasn't like my beefy brothers—or my
beefy gay brothers in the larger sense—and it mystified me when
people felt compelled to point out how thin I was. Only the nag-
ging mother of an overweight person would dwell on the obvious.
But total strangers would tell a slender person to eat because he
was too skinny. Or they'd use code words to express their criticism.
Rangy. Lanky. Wiry. Gangly. *Wasting away.*

I wasn't as thin as my height made me seem, and I had big
bones. But even I had to admit that being sick had left me looking
borderline emaciated. Still, no one ever complained about being
wrapped up in my bony arms and legs in bed, Mark included.

I went to see Mark because my boss, Benny the Whiner, wouldn't
let me come back to work without a release from my doctor. I figured the clinic was closed on Sunday, but when I called the number
from my prescription, I got the option of paging Mark. A couple
cell calls and a brisk walk later, and I was at his apartment near
Columbia University.

"I'm not sure you've had enough bed rest to go back to work,"

Mark said after he let me in. He looked more appealing than he had on the day I'd met him. Kind of rumpled. Like he had no plans for Sunday except parking himself on the couch and eating junk food.

"Are you coming on to me? Shouldn't you be worried about doctor-patient ethics?" I asked.

Ethics didn't seem to be an issue. An hour or so later, the sheets were twisted around and between us like Morgan's snakes. Which wasn't an image I wanted in my head at that time. I started to tell Mark about my bizarre roommate, but he already knew from Roberto.

"How do you know Roberto, anyway?" I asked. "Is he a patient?"

"My current breach of ethics notwithstanding," he said, while tracing my sternum with his finger, "if he were a patient, I wouldn't talk about him. He's a friend. How do *you* know him?"

"We went to school together," I said. "Broadway High School for the Arts."

"Right. I forgot how young you are," Mark said.

He didn't look too bothered by it, but if he was beginning to dwell on my flaws, he'd soon be stressing over my weight and shoving food down my throat. To head him off, I said, "I'm not young. I'm nineteen. Why? How old are you?"

"In gay years, I'm ancient. In doctor years, I'm young."

"Gay years," I mimicked. "I hate that. Sounds like dog years." He only shrugged as a response, so I asked, "How young?"

"Thirty-one."

"Ugh. It's like I'm in bed with my uncle."

"I can think of worse things," Mark said.

"Do you know him? Is *he* your patient?"

"Roberto told me that Blaine Dunhill's your uncle. You can't be my age and gay in Manhattan without knowing who he is. Also, I've been part of AIDS and HIV fund-raisers with Daniel Stephenson."

My uncle's boyfriend, Daniel, was a C-list actor who'd been the focus of a very public outing a few years before. Even though it was old news, for a while he and Blaine had been *the* celebrity gay couple, constantly pictured or interviewed in *Advocate, Out,* the *New York Blade, HX,* and for some reason, *Martha Stewart Living* magazine.

"Their fifteen minutes were nearly over around the time I moved in with Blaine," I said.

"When was that?"

"October"—I had to think a second—"of 2000."

"Where's your family? Or is that an insensitive question?"

"They're in Wisconsin. I came out to them that fall. My father was completely not cool with it—he still isn't—and my mother just hoped it would go away. My brothers are big jocks. Actually, my older brother was away at college, but Chuck—my twin—couldn't deal. When our fights got physical, it seemed like a good idea for *me* to go away."

Mark was a good listener, lying on his side and absently running his thumb up and down my arm while I talked. The swing I'd taken at Chuck came after years of dealing with my family's crap. What made it different was that in the aftermath, I'd impulsively blurted out to my parents that I wanted to move in with my uncle.

When they sent me to my room so they could discuss the idea, I jumped online and researched art schools in Manhattan. I downloaded and printed a brochure from Broadway High School for the Arts. Next, I Googled Uncle Blaine. We'd spent a little time together and exchanged e-mails, but I thought it would be a good idea to see what I was attempting to get myself into. I knew he was an advertising executive for Lillith Allure Cosmetics, but I'd never bothered to check out his work.

With a few clicks of my mouse, I found his company's Web site and saw pages of ads with beautiful photographs of models in extravagant settings. It was good stuff. Everything popped. My mind wandered, imagining the effort that went into putting together even a simple ad. The models, props, costumes, lighting, photographers, location, poses, product placement. The final result.

I wanted to be in the middle of that kind of creative buzz, surrounded by artistic energy and innovative people. I didn't think I wanted to get into advertising, but if I was going to be sent away and hoped for a life in art, Uncle Blaine and his friends seemed like the kind of people I needed to be around. Plus they were a thousand miles from my family.

A few weeks later, I was in Manhattan, in public school for a couple months until the new term started at BHSA.

"Then I met Roberto," I told Mark. "Our group of friends stayed tight even after graduation. When I moved out of my uncle's place, Roberto was looking for a roommate, too."

"What are you doing now? Are you in college? Art school?" Mark asked.

"I was at Pratt for a semester. Then I dropped out. Now everyone in my family is pissed at me."

Mark's phone rang, and while he talked a patient through some crisis, I thought about my confrontation with Blaine. I'd chosen to break the news over dinner in a restaurant, sure that my uncle wouldn't make a scene in public.

"What do you mean you dropped out of college? Your second semester started two weeks ago. Are you telling me that you've been pretending to go?" Blaine hissed.

"It wasn't for me," I said in a way that I hoped sounded offhanded, as if I had everything under control. "It was boring. I want to start my life now."

"Oh? How? Do you have a job lined up? A career?"

"Kinda. I got a job with I Dream Of Cleanie."

"The gay maid service? You're going to be a maid?" Blaine laughed and looked around, as if he expected Ashton Kutcher and a cameraman to jump out from behind a ficus. "That's not a career, Nick."

He was right. It wasn't a career. Then again, I hadn't said I intended to slave for I Dream of Cleanie the rest of my life.

Plus—I liked the job. It got me inside some really cool apartments, places I'd never get to see any other way. Not to mention that it gave me surprising insights into the dirty underbelly of human nature. The stuff you found under people's beds. . . .

It was that night, with Blaine at the restaurant, when I'd run into Kendra. She was our server. Her uniform was stained and slightly disheveled, like it realized it wasn't up to par with the ritzy décor and was rejecting its wearer. She'd gotten the order wrong and begged us not to tell her manager.

"You're not a vegetarian, are you? Thank God. I'm this close to being fired, and I really need this job. Even though I also work at Manhattan Cable. I'm looking for an apartment that I can afford in the city."

"You are? Me, too."

My uncle dropped his fork, but I refused to look at him. He could've offered to get me a job in Lillith Allure's art department, but he didn't. Fuck him.

"Sorry," Mark said. "Where were we?"

I wanted to change the subject. "I rented *Casablanca*. Their world was crumbling around them. Their romance was sacrificed for a greater cause." I made air quotes around "greater cause," even though people who made air quotes annoyed me. "I don't get it. How does *Casablanca* prove that anything lasts?"

"Forget the movie. I told you to listen to the lyrics of the song," Mark said. "People will always fall in love. The world always welcomes lovers. You did hear the song, right?"

"The world welcomes lovers if they're straight. The rest of us they'd sacrifice right along with the polar bears." When Mark opened his mouth, I said, "Don't tell me I'm too young to be cynical."

"Actually, only the young can afford to be cynical," Mark said.

"Yeah, you old dudes are always swooning over romance," I said.

Mark attacked me to prove how young and energetic he still was. By the time I finally left, I was feeling less cynical but no older, since I was bearing my permission slip for Benny the Whiner as if I was still in grade school. In a brighter development, Mark and I had scheduled a movie date to see *How to Lose a Guy in Ten Days*. I tried not to see the title as a bad omen.

Especially when I came face-to-face with another bad omen on my walk home.

Even though I shared an island with a million and a half New Yorkers, there were certain people I saw over and over. Sister Divine was one of them. The first time I spotted her, I was with my friend Fred, who'd just paused outside St. John the Divine to light a cigarette. A woman shrouded in layers of dark fabric that resembled a medieval nun's habit appeared in front of us. She pointed at Fred and yelled, "Your body houses twenty of Satan's lieutenants! Cast them out and do God's work!"

I made an effort to act indifferent and not gawk at her, but Fred was the real thing. He didn't even blink. I fell into step next to him as he walked away from her.

"What the hell was that?" I asked.

He shrugged and said, "Twenty cigarettes to a pack, I guess. *Do God's work.* I wonder what God pays. If there's overtime. Just think about calling in sick to a deity. God would be all, 'You're not sick.

You're hungover. Get your ass to work. Stop stealing Mrs. Vela's newspaper. And I wasn't joking about that masturbation thing, mortal.' "

The first boy I dated after I moved to New York was Pete. Pete was also the first person who broke my heart, when he had a fling with Fred. Not because I was in love with Pete. Because I wished I'd gotten to Fred first.

Although I'd jeered about romance to Mark, I wasn't against the idea. I just wasn't the kind of person who constantly sized up the boyfriend potential of every guy I met. I didn't make mental lists of what I did and didn't want. But if I did, it would be easy to think of reasons why Fred *shouldn't* be a boyfriend.

He smoked too much. He was always late. He thought monogamy was outdated. Actually, he practiced serial monogamy. Fred treated boyfriends like most people treated fashion: seasonally. Hot summer love migrated south at the first nip from autumn. And the man who blanketed Fred's bed in winter would melt away like snow in the spring.

Fred was one of my few friends who had no inclination to do anything artistic. A year ahead of Roberto, Pete, and me at BHSA, he'd gone there only because the tuition was free. His uncle was the headmaster. He'd sneered at the school's creative programs. Fred's classes focused on the technical: set design or sound or lighting. He managed BHSA's photo lab, although he had no interest in photography.

Now Fred worked at Starbucks, which in itself wouldn't disqualify him as a boyfriend—after all, I bleached people's bathroom grout—except that he enjoyed brewing java for the evil empire. He said the benefits rocked. He liked leaving the job when his shift was over and not thinking about it again until he went back. And if he felt like it, he could abuse the customers. Fred said they expected it, because most Starbucks employees were miserable and looking for a gig as an actor, musician, model, writer, illustrator—anything, it seemed, as long as it was creative and far from the grind of coffee beans.

Fred's disinterest in all things artistic could be conversationally limiting. And he didn't atone for it by having a flawless face or a great body. He wasn't ugly, by any means. Just an average guy, the kind who played the sidekick in movies or was friends with your girl cousin.

But Fred had one habit that turned me on, even when it wasn't directed at me. In a place where you could see or hear anything, so you tended to tune out everything, Fred paid attention. No cell phone, headset, or handheld anything ever got between him and another person. When he spoke to you, he looked at you. When you spoke to him, he heard you. His ability to completely focus on someone was erotic in a way that was beyond sex.

I never made the mistake of thinking he was flirting with me. Fred was my friend the same way Roberto was. I'd never tell Fred or anyone else how much time I spent thinking about the way his hair sort of curled against the back of his neck when he needed a haircut. Or how sexy I thought it was when he was mixing a Venti-whatever-latte and bit the tip of his tongue in concentration. Or that I once lied for three weeks and said I couldn't find a jacket he left at Uncle Blaine's apartment. I liked having it in the room with me. Maybe that was obsessive, but it was my little secret, and it hurt no one.

After the day Sister Divine accosted Fred, she seemed to pop up everywhere. I saw her outside Lincoln Center. At Seventy-ninth and Broadway. Skirting Columbus Circle. I wasn't sure whether or not Sister Divine was homeless. Maybe she was just crazy. Whenever I saw her, she was skulking along, the same layers of black cloth shifting and settling around her. Until she'd go rigid and fix her gaze on some unwary tourist. Or anyone moving slowly—like a predator assessing the weakest potential prey. Then it would happen.

"Forty-two generals and six thousand lieutenants of Satan are in your body. . . . two hundred field generals. . . . five hundred captains . . . Repent! Cast out your demons! Do God's work!"

Most people ignored her. I regarded her with affection, because she gave me a reason to call Fred. He enjoyed the Sister Divine updates. He'd picked up a transit map and map pins to mark my Sister Divine sightings, sure that a pattern would eventually emerge. Friends began placing bets on it. So far, the face of Jesus was losing to the face of Donald Rumsfeld two to one.

I was a few blocks from Mark's when I saw Sister Divine. Or worse, when she saw me. She stopped, pointed at me, and shouted, "Legions of demons inhabit your body! Drive them out! Find the silver cord. Get inside yourself before it's too late. Do God's work!"

No one paid any attention to her, and I whipped out my cell so I could brag to Fred that I was possessed by more demons than he was.

"Oh, good," he said. "I was starting to worry about her. Where are you?"

"I don't know. Somewhere near Murray Hill."

"Wow, she's spreading faster than West Nile virus," Fred said.

"She's not that far from the first place we ever saw her."

"What are you talking about? She's practically—" He cut himself off with a sigh. "You said Murray Hill. What address?"

I looked around and said, "I don't know. Somewhere near 119th and—"

"Never mind. Right letters, wrong neighborhood. Morningside Heights, Nick. It frightens me how little geography you know after almost three years here."

"At least I know Harlem," I muttered. "How many New Yorkers can say that?"

"Everyone. Harlem's the old *and* the new black. You can't swing a gold chain in Harlem without hitting a once or future president. And you do realize that Morningside—never mind. Where are you going now?"

"Home."

"Good. Hook up with the roommates of your choice and meet us out later."

"Who is us, and where is out?"

He rattled off a list of people from our recurring cast of friends, then said, "Cutter's. Between nine and ten." When I didn't answer, he said, "Oh. It's been so long that I forgot. Maybe Cookie forgot, too."

Cutter's was a dive on the Lower East Side. It was owned and operated by a retired Marine named John Cutter. Everybody called him Cookie.

Even though Cutter's was quite a distance from the Hell's Kitchen apartment where I'd lived with my uncle, I started going there with my friend Blythe not long after I moved to New York. She'd once lived in the neighborhood, so she knew the bar. Blythe was over twenty-one, and although I was only seventeen at the time, I never drank, so it wasn't a big deal. When I started drinking, it still wasn't a big deal. Cookie could barely be bothered to wipe down the bar or keep the toilet working, so he wasn't exactly conscientious about checking an ID. Since several of my friends were underage like me, it was a good place for us.

Most of Cutter's patrons were rough around the edges. Vets. Aging policemen. Ironworkers. We didn't mingle with them, and they didn't pay attention to us. We weren't spoiled college kids. We didn't make a lot of noise. No one got drunk or rowdy. We didn't act like we were slumming. We were grateful to stay at our long table in the corner and shoot the shit. The working men stuck together at the bar or around the pool tables. We maintained a peaceful coexistence.

Blythe was the only person I knew who moved comfortably between the two groups. Blythe was an artist—an actual working painter whose work got shown and made money for her. She was our bohemian fairy godmother. Sometimes people didn't take her seriously because she was around five feet tall and probably weighed ninety pounds. That was a mistake. Blythe had a take-no-prisoners disposition, and you crossed her at your own risk.

Something about Blythe endeared her to Cutter's burly clientele. They looked out for her, but she had a way of looking out for them, too. Like Dennis Fagan, who was part of the reason I'd been kicked out of Cutter's a few weeks before.

"What does that mean?" Kendra asked later, after I told her about Fred's invitation. "Are we going, or aren't we?"

"I don't know," I said. "I'd feel better if Roberto was with us. He's bigger than me. He commands respect from the blue collars."

She shrugged and said, "I haven't seen him today. He's probably at his mother's." She slapped at my hand when I started chewing a hangnail. "What did you do? Get in a fight with this Dennis guy?"

"Um, no," I said. "Do I look dead?"

"So why'd you get kicked out?"

"It wasn't my fault."

"It never is."

"Some guy was running his mouth about us. He was probably drunk. He made a couple comments that bothered me. I said something back. He called me a name, and Dennis clocked him."

"Seems like the drunk guy and Dennis should have been the ones kicked out. Not you. I must be missing a lot of details."

"Yeah, whatever," I said. "I haven't been back since. I don't know if I'm banned for life."

We stopped talking as Morgan walked through on her way to the kitchen. Roberto and I had gotten tired of our lack of privacy in Chez Snake Pit. While I'd been out, he'd finished installing walls made of sheets. Kendra had left me exposed by pulling back a sheet when she came in.

"Interesting portiere," Morgan said, looking up at the aluminum poles that were suspended by chains from the ceiling. She fingered the sheets and said, "Not cheap. And not floral, thank the god of your choice. Are these from Drayden's?"

When we were in school, Roberto's financial contribution to the Mirones family had come from retail jobs—first at Lord & Taylor, then at Macy's. His experience had helped him get his most recent job on the Visuals staff at Drayden's, a newcomer to the department stores on Fifth Avenue.

"We can't afford sheets from Drayden's," I said. "His mother got these from the hotel. And what's a porter ray?"

"Portiere," Morgan corrected. "It's fancy talk for something hanging in a doorway. Roberto's mother steals sheets from Four Seasons?"

Kendra said, "That sounds like *she sells seashells at—*"

"Of course she doesn't," I said. "They probably let the housekeeping staff buy old sheets or stuff that needs mending. I don't know. Ask Roberto."

"You should go out with us tonight," Kendra said and gave Morgan one of her encouraging smiles. I imagined a force field of evil around Morgan that would deflect Kendra's goodness and send it shrieking into the night, like a tranny prostitute with VD. "Nick was just telling me the story of steelworker Butch—"

"He's an ironworker, and his name is Dennis."

"—Cassidy and the Sunflower Kid," Kendra finished. The expression on her face rattled me. Sometimes she seemed more passive-aggressive princess than dumb blonde. "C'mon. It'll be fun!"

"Gosh, I don't know," Morgan said with exaggerated enthusiasm. "I'd go, but I don't have anything to wear!" She pretended to flip back her hair with her hand and a toss of the head. Then she resumed her mask of Satan in human form and went into the kitchen.

"Do you think that means she's not going?"

I looked at Kendra, trying to figure out if she was kidding. Although it was one of the most social exchanges I'd had with Morgan, there was no mistaking her message.

"Yeah. I think that's what it means."

"She can be such a buzz kill sometimes." Kendra unfolded her legs and dramatically flung herself onto the futon. Then she started talking about her hair.

Even if we missed Roberto, we had to get out of there before Kendra turned my night into a slumber party.

It wasn't really cold out, but Kendra and I were both dressed in heavier coats than most of the people we passed. I was trying to avoid a relapse, and Kendra said she needed a heavy coat to go with her outfit. Which made no sense. Nobody could see what she was wearing beneath it. And Cutter's was always warm to the point of tropical, so she'd ditch it as soon as we were inside. Maybe she only had the one coat. Or maybe she felt the need to be buttoned up from head to toe.

"Do you get nervous walking through the barrio?" I asked.

"You make it sound like we live in a Santana video. No, of course I don't get nervous," she said with an anxious glance around. "You know it's longer between buses on Sunday, right? I hate waiting for a bus."

I decided to make a concession for the sake of her mental health. "If you're that worried about it, we can take the subway. What's the problem? Do you think you stand out because you're so blond? So white? So walking like you're spastic?"

"It's the rats," she said, doing another sidestep, although there wasn't a rat in sight. "Anything above Ninety-fifth is rats, rats, rats."

"Rats are everywhere. All you have to do is pay attention and don't take stupid risks."

"You're being naive. We're in Harlem. There's gang graffiti—"

"Street art."

"Trash on the streets—"

"Every street in the city has trash," I protested.

"To be collected. Not to be blown down the sidewalks. Then again, I understand why people don't use their trash cans. Yesterday I saw a chicken scratching around ours."

I laughed and said, "It's winter. No place in the city looks decent until spring. When Harlem thaws, you'll change your mind. Roberto tells me there are block parties. Street festivals. Sometimes they close off streets for kids to play—"

"Yeah, that's another thing," Kendra said. "You don't see so many kids anywhere else. The city is a lousy place to have a family. Families should live in Connecticut or Pennsylvania."

I wanted to ask if her family was Republican. Or I could have told her that the only time I'd been mugged, I'd been outside an art gallery in the Village, which was probably Kendra's idea of a safe neighborhood.

"Why are you so quiet? You artistic types are always brooding," Kendra said.

"Brooding? Who uses that word in real life? I'm thinking."

"You artistic types are always thinking," she amended.

"You do know this isn't a club we're going to, right? We're not having some *Sex and the City* moment. We're not tweakers or club kids. Or even a bunch of overwrought, emo poets—"

"Disliking rats, free-range chickens who live in trash cans, and drive-bys doesn't make me a snob," Kendra said.

I put my arm around her as we walked. Regardless of what Kendra thought, anyone who paid attention to us at all seemed friendly. Older people even smiled, maybe mistaking us for a couple.

"I'm a reverse snob," I said. "I'd rather walk these streets than walk into a loft in SoHo. Or a shop on Park Avenue. Talk about brutal people."

"You don't have to be rich to live where you don't see homeless people sleeping on stoops," Kendra said and pointed.

"You get what you pay—does she have clones? The bitch is every-where."

"Who?"

Sister Divine was sound asleep, and I couldn't stop myself from checking out how she looked when she wasn't screaming about demons. Without the intensity of her waking hours, the creases on her forehead and around her eyes weren't as visible. She looked like a filthy fallen angel at rest.

As I stared at her, Kendra and the neighborhood around me faded. I remembered how I'd felt when I first moved to New York. The city had seemed magical. The crowded sidewalks, the rumble of the trains beneath the surface, the streets jammed with cars, cabs, and buses going places. I was always outside, always carrying my sketchbook. Even though I rarely left Midtown, there was inevitably something—an iron fence, a hidden garden, a bodega, or building masonry and adornments—with details that I couldn't wait to get on paper. And the faces. After the sameness of people in the Midwest—or maybe I was just accustomed to them—I couldn't get enough of the variety.

Sister Divine's face had a childlike innocence as I looked at her, and I itched to have my sketchbook with me again. I wanted to protect her, even though nothing about her sleep showed fear. That comforted me, and I knew why.

There would always be before and after. I'd been in Manhattan for almost a year before September 11. A year when I immersed myself in every day and thought the adventure would last forever. Then came the nineteen months after.

Seeing Sister Divine asleep made it feel like before again. Like I was cradled by the city the way she seemed to be while lying there.

Kendra pulled impatiently at my sleeve, and the spell was broken.

We were greeted with warm, stale air inside Cutter's. I held my breath, not knowing if Cookie would let me stay or make me bounce. Cutter's was the kind of place where your eyes had to adjust once you went inside, no matter what time of day it was. But I spotted the ex-Marine watching us almost as soon as we went through the door. I kept my head low when I walked past the bar, where he was setting a beer in front of a guy with a hard hat hanging from the back of his stool.

"No trouble tonight," Cookie said.

It was more of a decree than a warning. I got the idea that he didn't blame me for what had happened the last time I was there. And I was sure he'd supported Dennis in that battle. I did a quick scan of the bar, but Dennis wasn't with the rest of the blue collars.

I led Kendra to the usual table, where Fred was flanked by Roberto and Melanie. Melanie, who looked like a younger version of Meg Ryan, had been popular at BHSA. I wasn't sure if she was in school anywhere now. A sculptor of rare talent, she could shape stone, wood, or metal into astonishing beauty and motion. It wasn't often that she joined our group, but I always liked it when she did. She had a certain upbeat purity to her, a little like Kendra's sunny disposition. I couldn't quite put my finger on why the two were different. Sometimes Kendra had a childlike quality that I was pretty sure Melanie hadn't had since she was about five.

I'd often thought that unusually talented people were robbed of childhood. It showed up in different ways in each of them, whether in their art or their personality. If Dr. Mark had been there, I could have told him that this was where my romantic streak showed itself. I was a fool for anyone gifted with creativity.

"You're late," Fred said, smiling at me in a way that I found sexy.

"Since you're already here, I must be," I said.

"My own special blend of spiced tea," Melanie said, reaching to fill two empty cups as Roberto introduced her to Kendra. "Unless you'd rather have a beer?"

"Tea's fine until I get warmed up," Kendra said, shaking out of her coat. "My grandmother made her own tea. I was never allowed to have any, though."

Everybody stared at her until I introduced her to the group; then I said to Fred, "You won't believe this, but I saw Sister Divine again on the way here."

"The homeless woman? What was up with that?" Kendra asked. "I thought you were going to kiss her or something."

While Fred explained about Sister Divine, I sipped my tea, wondering why Cookie put up with us. He couldn't make any money selling us hot water. I saw Roberto staring at me, but before I could ask him how he'd known to join us, I felt a presence swoop in behind me, and then two strong hands fell on my shoulders. As Blythe loudly pulled out the chair next to me and straddled it, I turned to see who'd taken possession of me.

"Davii! Aren't you supposed to be on some remote island styling Lillith Allure models?" I asked.

"I needed him," Blythe said, running a hand over her new spiky haircut. It was colored mostly dark red, with just the tips of the spikes hot pink. "He had to give me good luck hair."

With one last squeeze of my shoulders, Davii slid into a chair between Melanie and me. More introductions were made for Kendra's benefit, and Fred and I exchanged a glance. We both thought that Davii was possibly the hottest man we knew. Tall. Slender build. Icy blue eyes that contrasted with his nearly black hair. We competed to be the focus of his good energy, because it was calming and stim-ulating at the same time. As far as we knew, Davii was single, but Fred had never gotten any farther with him than I had.

"I only repaired what she did to her hair," Davii was saying. "Then I escorted her to her opening." He turned to me and added, "The photo shoot was rescheduled. Although I think they should do it here. How could a beach in Puerto Rico be more fabulous than Cutter's?"

"Opening? Are you a performer?" Kendra asked Blythe.

"She's the most amazing artist ever," Melanie said.

"Ever?" Blythe asked and tried to look modest. "That may be stretching it."

"Pay no attention to her false humility," Davii said. "When we left, the Rania Gallery had already sold a half dozen of her paint-ings."

"It was four," Blythe said.

"Not that you noticed," Roberto said, and I could sense the envy under his joking tone.

I understood his frustration. Roberto was happiest when he was consumed by his art. As a little kid, he'd been intrigued by stories about the Quetzal, a rain forest bird that was part of Latin American mythology. He'd gotten in trouble for drawing the bird on the walls of his bedroom. He shared the room with his brothers, so he tried to pin the blame on them. His childhood misbehavior had fore-shadowed the times he'd gotten busted for defacing public prop-erty as a teenager. But when an artist didn't have money for materials or a space to work in, tenement walls, dirty buildings, and sidewalks became a canvas for creativity, anger, and beauty.

Although Roberto's art had become more abstract, I still saw ev-idence of the quetzal in his paintings. A bit of wise eye. A trace of wing. The colors of tail feathers. The bird was his muse, totem, and guide. But because Roberto had to work at Drayden's to pay rent and to help his family, he wasn't painting. It wasn't surprising that he envied Blythe's ability to support herself with her art.

However, at least he had a job that allowed him to express him-self creatively. Drayden's windows and displays were extremely elab-orate and always changing. What kind of creative outlet did I have with my job? Sometimes I wrote my name in the cleanser before I started scrubbing.

Roberto had a unique vision and knew how he wanted to express it. When he did paint again, everything would probably just explode out of him. I envied him the way he envied Blythe. I could sketch anything. I could paint and get good grades in art classes. But everything I did was derivative of someone else's work, and it bored me. Studying art or being expected to imitate the styles of other artists seemed like a sure way to extinguish whatever creativity I had. No matter what my uncle thought, dropping out of Pratt had been my first step toward self-preservation. I didn't have a quetzal to inspire me, but there had to be something in the world that would help me develop an original vision.

I only half listened as the others talked about Blythe's installation. I shifted my focus from Roberto to Melanie. Her sculptures had begun selling when we were still in high school, sometimes even before she finished them. I didn't think she was making as much money as Blythe, but sooner or later, she probably would be. In the meantime, her parents paid for the Chelsea space where she lived and worked. She had a few neighbors who looked out for her. She was always trying to get Fred or me to hook up with them. A lot of our female friends seemed to share Melanie's delusion that all single gay men were in desperate need of a boyfriend.

At least Kendra hadn't tried to be my marriage broker. She was too focused on her own problems, and was struggling financially even more than I was. Even though she worked two jobs, I assumed she was always broke because she was putting herself through college. But Kendra wasn't an artist. Her goal was to produce television shows, so going through Pratt's Media Arts program made sense for her. Not only did she need to learn her craft, but she needed to make contacts.

As for Fred . . . I could stare at him as much as I wanted, since he was preoccupied with Davii. It was fun to watch him flirt. Fred lived the way most of us probably would if we believed fate was our guide. Things just worked out for him. Right now he might be pulling coffee at Starbucks, but I was sure that one day he'd luck into the perfect life for himself. Just like he'd gotten into art school through his uncle.

Or the way he'd gotten his apartment. A teacher from BHSA was on a yearlong yoga retreat in Okinawa, so Fred was living in his apartment, rent-free, to take care of his two cats. Being Fred, he'd almost turned it down because he couldn't smoke there; then he found out it had a private rooftop terrace. The phrase that best applied to Fred's life was one I'd learned from Aunt Gretchen: He could fall in a bucket of shit and come out smelling like a rose.

A wave of nausea washed over me, and all I wanted to do was leave. I felt selfish. Blythe was obviously in the mood to party, but I found it hard to celebrate her good fortune. When was I going to have good news to share? When would people be able to say, "Hey, Nick, that's great news. I'm so happy for you." I was tired of congratulating other people on their luck and was ready for some luck of my own.

The others didn't notice how quiet I was. Or maybe they thought I was in a bad mood and wanted to give me space. I alternated between feeling sorry for myself, being angry for feeling sorry for myself, and being angry with everyone who was making me feel sorry for myself.

I mumbled something about getting a beer and left our table. Cookie tore his gaze from the basketball game on the TV over the bar when I slid onto a stool. He leaned forward with narrowed eyes, almost like he was mad at me. It was possible that I'd been wrong and he was holding a grudge.

"MGD, please," I said.

"I told you before," he said, "no ID, no drinks."

"Huh?" Maybe he'd gotten me mixed up with someone else. He'd never asked for an ID from me. I glanced toward the men at the pool table, the only cops in the place. But they were off duty and weren't looking our way.

"I can't serve you without seeing an ID," Cookie repeated.

"Fine." I took out my wallet and handed him my fake ID.

"I'll need to see that ID, too," a man seated on the bar stool next to me said.

"Wh-wh-wh-what?" I stammered.

"Sorry," Cookie said as the man reached over and took the ID from him.

I was such a dumbass. Of course Cookie hadn't given a shit about my ID; he'd been trying to warn me. I should have just said I didn't have my license with me and walked away.

"Peter?" The man squinted at the ID. "Would you care to step outside with me?"

"Outside? It's cold outside. My coat's over there. With my friends."
I tried to sound innocent. I glanced toward our table, unsure what
they could do to help me, but at least Blythe, Davii, and Kendra
were all of legal drinking age. Unfortunately, everyone at the table
was oblivious to what was happening to me. I felt like I was in one
of those nightmares where I screamed and no sound came out.
"What are you, a cop?"

"Something like that," he said. He gripped my arm and gave me
a little push. I glanced again at my friends, but they still hadn't noticed that I was being manhandled. I wondered why Fred had chosen this night to stop paying attention. But of course, he was. To
Davii.

"Am I being arrested?" I asked.

"We'll let them decide that at the precinct," the man said. Then
he repeated with sarcastic exaggeration, "Peter."

The cold air blasted us as we went through the door, giving me a
moment of clarity.

"Peter's my friend," I said. "I must have picked up the wrong license. Mine's probably at home."

"Like I said, we'll let them figure that out at the precinct."

He walked me to a van, where a uniformed cop opened a door
so I could get in. Three other people barely glanced my way as I sat
down. Two of them were girls with black-rimmed eyes and dye jobs
as bad as Morgan's. One of the girls was putting on dark lipstick,
and the other was on her cell phone.

"Just tell Daddy to get there," she snarled into the phone before
snapping it shut.

"Hey, can I use that?" the only other guy asked. He was short,
even thinner than I was, and covered with acne. Why had he imagined anyone would think he was old enough to drink?

The girl tossed him her phone with indifference. She looked at
me and said, "You can use it, too. If they're too stupid to take it
away from me, I figure we can call whoever we want, right? I'm sure
as shit not sitting in jail."

"I've got my own," I said, reaching into my pocket for my cell
phone. I stared at it for a minute, realizing that more than anything
in the world, I didn't want to make my call.

I dialed the number and waited.

One ring.

Two.

Three.

"We're not here. To leave a message for Daniel, press one. For Blaine, press two. For Gavin, press three. For anyone else, hang up and dial your number again."

I pressed 2 and began, "Uncle Blaine? It's Nick."

Too bad I hadn't specified *good* luck when I'd wished for some luck of my own.

A couple hours later, I was a free man, wondering how much Uncle Blaine had spent to buy my way out of being charged with anything. He hadn't waited around to give me answers. I didn't want the cops to change their minds, so I just walked out of the Ninth Precinct. Someone had brought my coat and left it for me. I buttoned it against the cold night air and splurged on a cab to take me home.

March 5, 2003

Nicky,

I was surprised to call my brother and learn that you moved out of his apartment and dropped out of Pratt. My check that was meant to cover your tuition cleared. Is that the money you used to get into your own apartment? Don't you think that's something we should have talked about first?

I suppose it's too late for me to reason with you, but I'm very concerned about the choices you're making. I assume you're getting a job and suggest that if you plan to return to school in the fall, you save enough to pay your tuition. I'm not going to give you money again unless you can prove that you're more responsible and committed to your education.

Dad

3

The Sodom and Gomorrah Show

The beauty of working as a housekeeper for I Dream of Cleanie was that I usually didn't have to work until after 10:00 AM. The downfall of living in a microcosm with three other people was that my roommates made a lot of noise in the morning. Because my room was off of the kitchen, I heard it all. I lay in bed and listened to the same dialogue each morning.

"Can't I go first?"

"I'll be five minutes. Ten, tops."

"Hurry up. Don't use all the hot water, like yesterday."

"Give me a break, Morgan. When you get out of the bathroom, it looks like a steam room."

"At least I hang up my towels."

"At least I don't hang my panties to dry over the curtain rod."

"Where do you dry your panties, Roberto?"

"Shut up."

Roberto slammed the bathroom door behind him. I finally got out of bed just as Morgan turned her wrath on Kendra.

"Is that my cereal you're eating?"

I pulled back the sheet in my doorway and saw Kendra perched on a stack of boxes in the corner of the kitchen. She sat cross-legged, a bowl of cereal in one hand, a spoon poised midair between the bowl and her mouth, looking guilty as sin. Through a mouthful of cereal she mumbled, "No."

Morgan, her back to me, folded her arms and said, "It is. Why are you eating my cereal? I clearly labeled everything that's mine."

"It's mine," Kendra insisted.

Morgan opened a cupboard and pulled out a Raisin Bran box. She shook it for dramatic effect and said, "This is your cereal. The one with three flakes and a raisin inside."

"Sounds like our apartment," Roberto yelled from the bathroom.

Morgan ignored him and said, "Mine was practically new, but now it's half-full."

"Or it's half empty," I said, moving past her to make toast. "Depending on your worldview."

"Stay out of this," Morgan demanded.

"Don't mind me. I'm just waiting for my toast. Carry on with your interrogation." Morgan sneered at me and over her shoulder, I could see Kendra cringe. I added, "Do you have time for this? Don't you have to be at work soon?"

"I can manage my schedule on my own, thank you," Morgan said. She turned to Kendra, glanced at the clock on the wall, then made a noise of exasperation as she went into her bedroom, obviously giving up.

"Thanks," Kendra whispered.

"Don't thank me. I just want peace and quiet. I don't know why I have to wake up to this insanity every day." My toast popped up and I caught it before it hit the counter. Even though I bleached it daily, I knew the counter was a roach playground in the middle of the night. When Kendra hopped from the boxes to the floor, I pointed at them and said, "I thought you guys were going to find a place for all your crap."

Kendra rinsed her bowl in the sink and replied, "We will."

"That's what you said last week."

"Most of it's Morgan's. You try getting her to do anything."

"You got me there."

Roberto passed through on his way to our room, a towel barely wrapped around his waist. "Yo."

"Yo," I replied to his retreating backside.

Kendra blushed, stammered something about it being her turn, and scampered into the bathroom. I took my tea and toast to the living room, the best place to avoid the others' morning routines.

Roberto poked his head into the room, tossed my cell to me, and said, "Your phone just vibrated. I think you have a message." While I listened to my messages, I heard the front door slam. A few minutes later, as I was dialing, it slammed again. Kendra meandered into the room and sank to the floor in front of me. She opened her mouth to speak, but I cut her off by holding up my hand.

"Benny, it's Nick. I got your message. I'm sorry, but Chelsea? I don't think I can—"

"What do you mean? Nick, I need you. Deshaun is sick. He covered for you when you were out sick. Besides, weren't you the one who was begging me for more hours?"

"I wouldn't say I was begging," I protested.

"I'm really in a bind, Nick," Benny whined. "I know you don't like to work below Fifty-seventh Street, but there's literally nobody else who can do this job. Anyway, the client's a neat freak. You'll hardly have to do anything. A little dusting, that's all."

I knew that was bunk. While it was true that our more anal retentive clients had cleaner apartments, they were also far more demanding. The smallest spot on a water glass, or a speck of dust on a bookshelf, sent them into fits of rage. But as a substitute, I wouldn't have to break my back. If my work wasn't up to snuff, Benny could apologize and promise I'd never darken their doorstep again.

"This is a one time thing, right?"

"Of course. You can fit him in between your ten and four o'clock clients. Please, Nick. You have to do this. He's a very important—"

"Fine," I relented. "I'll do it."

Benny gave me the address, and I groaned after I disconnected the call.

"Bad news?" Kendra asked. I'd almost forgotten she was in the room. Before I could answer, she said, "Roberto and Morgan are gone. Call in sick. I don't want to go to my classes. Let's goof off."

"I can't afford to goof off. I have bills to pay. So do you."

"They don't pay me to go to class," she said. "Besides, I'm just talking about ditching class. I'll go to work this afternoon."

"Let me get this straight. You want me to miss work and not get paid, so I can keep you company and entertain you. But later, you're going to ditch me, so you can go earn a living?"

"Uh, yeah," she said.

"Nice try. Go to class," I said. "I have to get ready for work."

By the time I arrived at the temporary cleaning gig in Chelsea, I was already exhausted. My ten o'clock had been a single mother, which meant several loads of laundry. Of course she didn't have a laundry room in her building. I had to schlep everything three blocks away, running back and forth between loads to wash dishes, vacuum, dust, and bleach everything her precious baby could possibly put in her mouth. Right before I left, there was a diaper incident that made me want to call in a hazardous waste crew.

The address Benny had given me led me to a condominium high-rise. I rechecked the numbers, hoping I'd read them wrong. Unfortunately, I hadn't. I stood outside, staring up, trying to count the floors. Across the street, the half-finished steel skeleton of a similar building rose from behind a blue barricade. Signs were posted along the fencing, urging pedestrians to keep back. Returning home to Spanish Harlem seemed a safe distance. But I didn't want to lose my job. With any luck, the apartment I'd been sent to clean would be on the third floor.

In the lobby, the concierge handed me a key to one of the two penthouses. He called after me, "Don't forget to water the plants on the terrace."

I turned back to smile and nod. When he looked away, I flipped him off and reluctantly summoned the elevator. Inside, I closed my eyes and screamed the chorus to "What Have I Done to Deserve This?" by the Pet Shop Boys, until the doors opened again. I willed the key not to work, but it did. Everyone and everything was against me.

The penthouse was easily four to five thousand square feet, with a mezzanine loft providing extra acreage to thwart my plan to get in and out as quickly as possible. The vast space was heightened by the minimalist décor. The few pieces of furniture were arranged in small groups, making a guided tour irrelevant. The black leather sofa, two chairs, and barren glass coffee table seemed to exclaim, "Hi! We're the seating area. If you sit down, please don't touch the table." And so on through the apartment.

As promised, the owner was compulsively neat. The kitchen was cold and sterile. The stainless steel island begged for an emergency appendectomy to be performed on it. The glass table in the nearby dining area suggested that its owner's motto might be *Tables should be clean and not seen.* The mirror in the guest bath had one finger-print on its center. I laughed and wondered how many other strate-gic hairs or crumbs were left to test me.

I emptied the trash can, but ignored the mirror entirely.

The bedrooms were just as sleek and modern. I was grateful for the black lacquered platform beds, because I didn't have to clean under them. Not that I would've. I'd already made up my mind that I didn't like the apartment's owner. I didn't want to care for his apartment, either. I didn't like modern high-rise buildings. They sometimes looked interesting and different from the norm on the outside, but inside, the apartments were always the same cookie-cutter formation. Kitchen, living area, bedroom, bath, all arranged in rectangle after rectangle, box upon box. The owner of this penthouse had to be king of the banal.

I tried to water the plants on the terrace, as instructed. But when I felt the wind rush past my ears and saw how high up I was, I heaved into a potted palm and went back inside.

I found some aspirin in the master bathroom medicine cabinet. I washed it down, leaving water droplets on the granite sink, sat down on the bed, and opened a nightstand drawer. Parker D. Brooks owed fifty-six thousand three hundred twelve dollars and eighty-two cents to American Express. And I thought I had problems. I spent the next half hour looking through his closets and opening draw-ers, sometimes trying on his clothes.

I was accessorizing with a pair of sunglasses when I heard the un-mistakable sound of a pistol being cocked. A voice behind me said, "Drop the shades and raise your hands slowly! Wait. Don't. Carefully place the Armani sunglasses on the dresser, then raise your hands slowly."

I followed instructions and willed myself not to pee in his pants.

The guy I assumed was Parker D. Brooks patted me down with one hand, then said, "What the hell do you think you're doing?"

"Cleaning?"

I slowly turned around. He looked like he was only a few years older than me, which was surprising. I'd imagined Parker D. Brooks as being in his forties, with a chiseled body underneath his expensive suits. This guy looked like he spent all day at the tennis courts—so he could watch.

He squinted at my crotch and asked, "Are those my pants?"

"They're a little big," I said defensively.

"Take them off!" he demanded. "And hang them up. I don't believe this. Who are you, anyway, and where's Deshaun?"

"I'm William," I lied. "Deshaun's sick. I'm just filling in."

"This is unacceptable." He tossed the gun into the bedside drawer on top of the American Express bill, muttering that it wasn't loaded anyway. He pulled a vial from his pocket, cut two lines on the night-stand, then snorted them up his right nostril while I pulled on my jeans and thought about running for the fire stairs. I'd never seen anyone snort cocaine. "This has never happened to me before. I'm not a bad person. Why would you do this to me? I don't deserve to be treated like this. If you were me, what would you do?"

Wipe my nose off, I thought. Instead, I said, "I don't know."

"Genius answer," he said. "Do you do this to all your clients?"

"No."

"Just me? I don't even know you. Ask me anything, and I'll tell you whatever you want to know. You don't have to snoop through my things."

"Are you going to call my boss?" I asked.

"I should," Parker D. Brooks said. "Unless you can give me a reason not to."

Before I knew what I was doing, I heard myself stammering and whining about how I needed my job, how I had rent and bills to pay, and how I wouldn't know what to do with myself if I got fired. I sounded weak and pathetic.

I was almost grateful when Parker D. Brooks held up his hand and said, "Okay. I get the picture." He thought for a minute, looked me up and down, then said, "William, I won't call your boss. Your friend Deshaun and I have an arrangement, and since you're filling in, maybe you'd like to fill in on that end, too."

"What end?" I asked, willing my eyes not to look at his pearlike butt.

"I run a company. Videos."

Of course you do, I thought.

"Sometimes I direct. What do you say I set up my camera, turn it on, lie on this bed, and you and I—"

"I don't think so," I interrupted. Then I remembered the gun and added, "No, thank you."

"You're sure? I'd pay you. Two thousand. Five, if you let me screw you."

I didn't really know Deshaun, or where he lived, but I wanted to find out immediately so I could smack him around.

"Really, no. Thanks anyway," I said and turned to leave.

"Then I have no choice but to speak to your boss and tell him what I caught you doing," Parker D. Brooks called after me. He spoke in a singsong tone, as if that somehow made it okay to blackmail me.

"Okay," I answered. "'Bye."

I barely realized that I rode down in the elevator. I felt like ants were crawling up my arm. I remembered having the same creepy feeling after I was mugged. The helplessness, fear, and nervousness that lingered after the fact. At least that time the only thing taken from me was twenty dollars. This time, I was going to lose my job. I hadn't asked to be mugged, but I'd pretty much begged to be fired. Why did I try on his clothes? Why did I look through his drawers? What was I thinking? Rent was due again soon. So was the ConEd bill. Would I have enough to cover that? Would giving Parker D. Brooks a blow job really be so bad? How long could that take? A half hour?

The doors opened at the lobby and a woman got in the elevator with me. Seconds later, when I realized she'd asked me something, I said, "Huh?"

"I asked which floor you want."

"Penthouse."

"Really? You don't live here, do you?"

"I'm the maid," I said. She smiled and nodded. What else could I be doing there? I added, "I was about to go home for the day, when it dawned on me that I forgot to give the master his blow job. Silly me, huh?"

"Gross!" she exclaimed. When we reached her floor, she said, "Next time, use the service elevator."

As the doors were closing, I said, "Good idea. We haven't done it in there yet."

After I rang Parker D. Brooks's doorbell, I tried to pretend I was somebody else. An escort. But not all escorts put out, right? A gigolo would. But the word *gigolo* sounded stupid. Nobody talked like that anymore. I'd be a rent boy. A rent boy named—

"William?" Parker D. Brooks said when he opened the door. "What are you doing back here? I thought you left in a snit."

"No. I left in a huff. I came back on the elevator. Can I come in?"

"No," he said. "Why would you want to?"

"I changed my mind," I said. Although I still wasn't sure. I felt icky.

"So have I. Get out of this building, or I'll call security. I already phoned your boss. If you give me your home number, I'll call your parents, too."

I felt sick the rest of the day. I went to my last client's apartment and tried to lose myself in work. But I couldn't stop thinking about what I almost did. Was that what life was all about? Money? Greed? Blow jobs?

I cleaned the toilet relentlessly because I kept seeing Parker D. Brooks's face in the bowl. No matter how many times I tried, the scrubbing bubbles wouldn't take him away so I wouldn't have to.

My cell phone began to vibrate against my leg while I was walking home. I answered it by saying, "Benny, I told you I didn't think I should take that client in Chelsea."

"What happened, Nick? Come in to the office and tell me your side."

"No. What did he tell you? Whatever he said is a lie."

I heard Benny sigh. "He said a guy named William stole from him. I can only assume you're William."

"I didn't take anything."

"He claims he has it all on video. Do I need to see that? I don't want to think of you stealing. Don't make me watch it," Benny begged. "I'm so disappointed in you. I thought you were a nice kid. This is the age of surveillance, Nick. Mr. Brooks has nanny-cams all over his apartment. I didn't think I'd have to explain things like this to you, of all people."

"What can I do to keep my job?" I asked warily.

"If you pay him back—give back whatever it was you took from him—I won't have to fire you. Or you can quit."

I nearly dropped my phone. I hadn't taken anything. But Parker

D. Brooks had video of me riffling through his drawers and closets. It was my word against my actions. Parker D. Brooks didn't have to screw me. I'd already screwed myself stupid.

"I didn't take anything," I repeated. "I guess I'll have to quit."

"I'm sorry, Nick," Benny said mournfully.

I didn't want to be a snitch, but I decided to take someone else down with me. "Deshaun is sleeping with Mr. Brooks."

"Sweetie, I know. I've bought all their videos. Good-bye, Nick."

When Roberto came home, he found Kendra and me in the living room. She was plying me with hot tea and telling me about the times she'd been fired. She had a lot of stories.

"Half the town got botulism. Could you just die?" she was saying. "Did they?"

"What's going on?" Roberto asked.

"Poor guy lost his job," Kendra said. She patted my hand and I snatched it away. I didn't deserve coddling.

Roberto sat down. I told him what happened, without using names, and he said, "I'm glad you didn't do it. You would've hated yourself afterward. Or you would've hated yourself if you got a disease from him. Where does this pig live? I'll kill him."

"I was propositioned once," Kendra said archly. We waited for more, but she just stared at the table and nodded.

"What now?" Roberto asked.

"I guess I look for another job."

"You'll get one. Something better," Kendra predicted.

"I hope so. I don't want to have to borrow money from anyone."

Of course that was the moment Morgan walked in. Why wasn't she as noisy coming home as she'd been when she left that morning? Her eyes narrowed, as if she was willing a truth-seeking laser to fire at me, and she asked, "Why would you need to borrow money? More importantly, where are those boxes that were in the kitchen?"

Roberto exclaimed, "I knew something was different around here."

"I needed something to do, and those boxes were annoying the crap out of me," I explained. "I put your stuff in your room. I lost my job."

Morgan said, "That sucks," then went into her room.

"Was that her being comforting?" Roberto asked. "She probably had to lie down after being so warm."

"She probably meant it sucks that you went in our room," Kendra said.

"No," I said. "She meant it sucks that I went in your room and the snakes didn't kill me."

March 26, 2003

Hey, Nick,

Hope you don't mind that Blaine gave me your address. I had to send you this brilliant drawing from Emily. She was at the office with me, and my assistant gave her markers and paper. When I admired the drawing and asked what it was, she said it was from the day she was with you at the "buseum."

Isn't it good to know that your day at the buseum to show Emily the Picassos wasn't wasted? I can't believe she remembers. I think it's because she wants to be an artist like Cousin Nick. Not that I'm implying that your work looks anything like the enclosed!

Hope you're doing well.

Love,
Gwendy

4

Nervously

"I don't like men who dress as women," the waitress said as she slammed our salads on the table in front of us.

When she walked away, I noticed that Martin was looking down at himself with bewilderment. Although he'd once made his living as a female impersonator, tonight he was just Martin, dressed in black from his cashmere sweater to his faux combat boots.

"Did I overlook a spot of stage makeup?" he asked, tilting his head to the right, then to the left so I could examine him. When I shook my head, he called after her, "I'm a dancer!" Then he shrugged and pushed his lettuce around with his fork.

I didn't know if the waitress had put him off his food or if my choice of cheap restaurants made him feel like he was slumming. I'd secretly hoped Martin would suggest a better place, giving me the opening I needed to tell him that I was now jobless and nearly broke. Even if Martin didn't offer me a loan, he talked to Daniel several times a week. The news would eventually get to Uncle Blaine. Considering that our most recent contact had been my appeal to be kept out of Fake ID Jail, Blaine probably needed time to cool down before he and I actually talked.

"And you dance so well," I said to Martin. "Thanks for the ticket."

"The show is crap," Martin muttered. "I always swear I'll never let another aspiring choreographer persuade me to dance in a fresh, steaming pile of it. Then I do."

I pretended I couldn't talk because of a mouth full of tomato, but I agreed with him about the gloomy musical I'd just squirmed through. *Asphalt and Battery* was the story of Edward J. de Smedt, a Belgian immigrant who invented asphalt. Among the places it was first used was Battery Park, and according to the show's *Playbill*, Edward's ghost felt guilty about his role in the "proliferation of automobiles, urbanization, pollution, and global warming." Most of Martin's time onstage had involved a dance in which he unrolled bolts of black fabric until it covered the floor, the backdrops, and the props, before he finally smothered all the actors with it. The last had gotten the most enthusiastic applause of the night.

"What's that?" Martin asked, looking at my wrist.

"This bracelet? Do you think that's what the waitress was talking about? It's a man's bracelet," I said defensively.

"It's gold. You're not a gold person. Silver or platinum. I shouldn't have to explain these things to you."

"It isn't mine. The clasp broke, and I had it fixed for my roommate."

"Julio?"

"Roberto."

"What happened to Julio?"

"There was never a Julio. His name is Roberto."

"I remember when I was the new boy in town," Martin said, staring into the distance as if watching a newsreel of the olden days. "I crashed anywhere I could and had a constantly changing cast of roommates. And jobs. I was always broke."

"Me, too," I said, thinking that was as good a segue as any.

He focused on my face and said, "Maybe you should let your roommates pay for their own jewelry repairs."

"It wasn't much," I said, on the defensive again. "Besides, Roberto buys all the groceries, especially since I lost—"

"Maybe Julio was one of *my* roommates," Martin cut in, his eyes glazed over again. "He was allergic to MSG and swelled up like a puffer fish whenever we got Chinese takeout. Wait. That was Wing Lee."

"Someone named Wing Lee was allergic to Chinese food?" I asked. I could never tell when Martin was serious.

Instead of answering, he continued to reminisce. "Wing Lee's boyfriend, Yu, also lived with us. It made answering the phone problematic. 'It's for Yu!' 'Me?' 'No, Yu!' Or I'd yell to Julio, 'It's for you!' and Yu would pick up the extension. It was like Abbott and Costello."

"Who?" I asked.

Martin glared at me and said, "Is that some kind of age crack? I'm only twenty-six."

I knew for a fact that Martin was at least thirty, but I said, "I thought you were twenty-two."

"Yes, four years ago I was twenty-two, but aren't you sweet for thinking so? Maybe I should tell people that. If I thought I could pull it off, I would." He paused. Then his face cleared and he said, "I'll just say I'm twenty-three."

It seemed cruel to distract Martin from his favorite topic: himself. But these were desperate times, so I said, "I wouldn't normally ask you to meet me on a Thursday night, but I'm in kind of a bind, and—"

"Is this *Thursday*?" Martin interrupted with a horrified expression. "I think I had a date tonight." He jumped up. "I'll take care of the check on my way out." He mimed the "call me" signal as he backed away from our booth. I saw him thrust cash at the waitress. Then he was out the door. As a frantic tactic to avoid being hit up for money, it was still a more graceful dance than the one he'd performed earlier onstage.

The waitress stopped at my booth, looked around, then scooted into Martin's place. After I blinked at her a few times, she said, "I'm guessing he wasn't leaving me a huge tip for two house salads and water, so he must want you to have the change."

"How much did he give you?" I asked.

"A fifty. You made out okay, even if he dumped you." She pushed the fifty across the table toward me.

"He didn't dump me. We weren't on a date. He's a friend. How come you insulted him?"

"It's not an insult. Lots of good men dump their dates."

"We weren't on a—I mean when you said you don't like men who dress as women."

"Oh, jeez, him?" When I nodded, she rolled her eyes. "Everybody thinks everything's about them. It was the end of a story I was telling the busboy. He was right next to your booth and I was *staring at him* while I spoke." She looked at someone behind me and blared, "I'm on a break!"

"Lucky me," I said. Since she showed no sign of leaving, I asked, "What was the story?"

"If you can believe it, it was about a time *I* got dumped." When she saw my face, she said, "Yeah, I know. He didn't dump you because it wasn't a date. Mine was a boyfriend and a Halloween party in college. Barry went as my roommate, Holly Waisenhaus. She had long, lanky red hair and nerdy glasses. She always wore a green-and-brown-striped sweater. She looked like a beetle. Barry got a wig and some glasses, and I snuck the sweater out for him. He was a big hit at the party. Why didn't I get it? Why didn't I know that imitation is the sincerest form of 'I want to ditch my girlfriend and fuck your brains out'? They live in Connecticut now. They have a duck pond and three kids, and I try to make decent tips in a diner. Bastard."

"I lost my job," I said. "Plus I almost got arrested for using a fake ID."

"Oh, I see," she said, looking irritated as she slid out of the booth. "You're one of those guys who only pretends to listen to other people so they'll feel obligated to listen to *your* problems. I don't need a tip that bad."

"Why are people always doing that to you?" Roberto asked later as we lay in the dark. Or what would have been the dark if there weren't two or three cop cars at the entrance to the alley behind our building. Our room was bathed in flashing lights. If we'd had a disco ball, we could have danced the night away.

"Doing what? Getting pissed off at me?"

"Confiding in you."

"It's the way I look."

"Like you've got a face that says, 'Free therapy'?"

"More like a body that says, 'I can't outrun your story of devastation and ruin.' I should put on weight. Work out. Get muscles and look menacing. Like you. Nobody ever tells you hard-luck stories."

"Except you," Roberto said and giggled at himself. His giggle was endearing because it was so at odds with his virile appearance. "You didn't have to get my bracelet fixed."

"I'm the one who stepped on it," I said. "Martin rebuked me for wearing gold."

Roberto laughed again and said, "It's my Guido bracelet."

The bars on the windows provided a shadowy contrast to the flashing blue and red lights. In Eau Claire, that kind of show would have lured the entire neighborhood out of their beds. People in robes and slippers would have gathered in groups until everyone knew every lurid detail. Now I couldn't be bothered to get up and look out the window to see what carnage lay at the end of our alley.

"You know I can cover your part of the rent," Roberto said.

"I've got money for rent," I assured him.

What I couldn't tell him was that I didn't have the money to cover Kendra's part of the rent, because she was short a few hundred dollars. I didn't want him to think that I'd asked him to move in because he was my only financially solvent friend. Besides, Roberto's extra money went to his mother to help feed and clothe his younger brothers.

I heard him sigh, always the last thing he did before he fell asleep. One long sigh; then his breathing would deepen and keep the same rhythm for the rest of the night. He never snored. He never snorted himself awake. Sometimes when I couldn't sleep, it pissed me off the way he could just drop off and stay that way until his alarm woke him. But mostly, it made me feel comfortable. Like a sleeping giant lay between me and whatever was out there.

The drama in our alley finally played itself out, and the lights went away. I closed my eyes and focused on breathing the way Gavin had taught me. Gavin was not only the man who took care of Uncle Blaine's household; he was a massage therapist who was big on the proper way to breathe. And on drinking water.

I tried to remember if I'd drunk my mandatory eight glasses of water for the day. My throat felt dry. My skin itched. I held off as long as I could, but I finally got up to slink into the kitchen. I wasn't afraid of waking Roberto, but I didn't want to draw Kendra or Morgan out of their room.

I drank a bottle of water, then made it back to my bed without having to deal with my roommates. A half hour later, still wide awake, I got up again to go to the bathroom. Kendra waylaid me in the miniscule hall.

"Did you get the money from your friend?" she whispered. "Because if you didn't, I'm totally screwed. I wrote a bad check today."

"I didn't have a chance to ask him," I said. Her face fell. "Don't worry. I'll think of something."

"No, it's not your problem. Maybe I can get my boss to loan me money."

According to Kendra, her slimy boss at Manhattan Cable was always making passes at her, so I didn't think that was a good idea. "He'll take it out of your paycheck. Then you'll end up short the next time rent is due. Just give me another day, okay?"

She nodded and furtively dissolved into the Snake Pit.

After crossing Martin off my emergency loan list, I decided to call Jeremy. As Daniel's ex-boyfriend, he'd be just as effective as Martin in getting the news about my destitution to my uncle. I'd only hesitated to call him in the first place because Jeremy's opinion mattered to me more than any of Blaine's other friends.

Jeremy shared a big farmhouse with his lover, Adam, in Eau Claire. It was hard to believe my parents lived in the same town; their worlds couldn't have been more different.

My father worked long hours to be able to afford golf and alcohol on the weekends. My mother worked to be anywhere but with him. Neither of my parents was ever at home. The last time I'd gone back to Wisconsin for a holiday, I'd overheard Tony making fun of Chuck for living at home while he was in college. Chuck explained how sweet the setup was. He and his buddies had the run of the house and all its features. The monster TV, DVD player, stereo, computers, pool table, fully stocked kitchen, and my parents' housekeeper to pick up after them. Girls came in and out, and kegs were set up on the deck. My parents generally steered clear as long as Chuck didn't break too many things. It was like living in a frat house without the hazing or the lumpy mattresses.

Adam and Jeremy, on the other hand, both worked from home. Adam owned his own business and put in as many hours as my father, but he was always doing things for other people. He designed free Web sites for artists. His computer company sponsored stuff like AIDS walks or breast cancer benefits.

Jeremy was an actor. He'd even starred in a sitcom in the nineties. But when he moved to Wisconsin to be with Adam, he went to graduate school so he could be an instructor in UW–Eau Claire's theater department. He also took classes in counseling and mentored teenagers.

That was how I'd met him, when I was still in high school. I was part of an acting workshop that gave peer support to at-risk teenagers. The only way I was at risk was possibly dying of boredom in Eau Claire. I hadn't turned into an actor, but I had eventually come out to Jeremy. He was the first adult I trusted with the truth, and he'd never let me down. I didn't want him to think I'd turned into a big loser.

Unfortunately, when I called the farmhouse, I only got Adam's assistant. Adam and Jeremy had escaped Wisconsin's winter to go to some friend's wedding in Acapulco. Great for them; bad for me.

I muttered a few vile things about Kendra under my breath and began gathering up my dirty clothes. For the cost of a cab ride to Hell's Kitchen, I could use Blaine's washer and dryer and get that bit of drudgery out of the way. By the time my uncle got home from work, maybe I'd be mentally prepared to throw myself on his mercy. Again.

Blaine and Daniel lived in an apartment in an eight-story building on Fifty-seventh. It was actually two apartments combined—one on the seventh floor, and another directly above it. There were two bedrooms upstairs: the master bedroom where Blaine and Daniel slept, and the room that Blaine's daughter, Emily, used when she stayed with them. The dining room had been converted into their shared office. They rarely used the kitchen, unless they entertained. A terrace garden that had originally been accessible only from the master bedroom could now also be reached from their living room. The area provided the ideal setting for the small dinner parties they sometimes had.

I preferred the downstairs area. My bedroom had been there, as was Gavin's. That living room had been turned into the entertainment room and included theater seating and a stereo system with speakers wired to every room on both floors. Gavin and I cooked meals in the downstairs kitchen, and Blaine and Daniel ate with us whenever they didn't have other plans. The dining room table was the hub of the apartment. It was where everyone caught up, where all of us read over coffee or hot tea in the mornings, and where everyone but me had cocktails in the evenings. Even though there was a desk and a computer in my bedroom, I'd often done my homework or sketched at the table to keep Gavin company. His boyfriend, Ethan, was there a lot. It was fun to watch them flirt with each other, and they both spoiled me, so we were all satisfied.

"But it's not real," Fred had once said to me after we spent a Saturday afternoon battling each other on the PlayStation 2.

"That's why they call it a game."

"Not Ultimate Ninja. Your big gay family. The men are flawless. Their smiles gleam. Their eyes sparkle. The apartment is fantastic. Nobody's broke. Everybody's buff and healthy and white."

"Ethan's Native American."

"You know what I mean. You never see anyone paying an over-due bill or taking a crap. It's like a TV show about two gay couples and their rebellious teenage son. Except your rebellion is mostly limited to multiple ear piercings and slouching around in clothes they wouldn't be caught dead wearing. Every problem will have a happy resolution in less than thirty minutes."

Fred was wrong. We had problems, and they didn't get worked out to a laugh track. But living with Blaine was still a million times better than my life in Wisconsin, right up until I told him I was moving out.

I walked into the lobby of his building with the duffel bag of dirty clothes slung over my shoulder. The concierge, a big hulking Greek named Stratos, smiled and waved me toward the elevator. At least Blaine hadn't told everyone to keep his bad-news nephew out of the building.

When I reached for the number pad, my finger hovered briefly over the THREE. That was the floor where my little cousin Emily lived, and I hadn't seen her since before I moved out. Then I chose EIGHT. Blaine and Daniel were never home during the day, and I could get the lay of the land before I went downstairs and faced Gavin.

As I shut the apartment door behind me and heard the synth-pop music pulsing through the apartment, I wondered if Stratos had called Gavin to let him know I was on my way up. I leaned against the wall and listened for a few seconds to what our house-hold of men with very different tastes had called our peacekeeping music.

Daniel liked the classic divas: Cher, Madonna, Barbra, Judy, Bette, and Liza. They'd provided the soundtrack for his gig as a female impersonator when he was younger. Blaine preferred music without words. Techno, drum and bass, classical, jazz. Music that he could work or work out to. Only Blaine would endure Gavin's tendency to put on New Age music. Even Ethan, who'd made a career of doling out spiritual advice and wisdom, preferred to indulge his inner sister and wail along with Aretha, Mary J., Queen Latifah, Oleta Adams, and Erykah Badu. Unlike Gavin and Blaine, Daniel liked Ethan's music, but could barely tolerate anyone else's.

Then there was me. When I'd first moved in, none of them wanted me to control the tunes, because they hated Eminem, Marilyn Manson, and Ozzy. Later, they refused to let me play Gorillaz. I could barely even get away with the Foo Fighters, White Stripes, or Bush.

The only music all of us ever agreed on was the Pet Shop Boys, and it was their *Behaviour* CD that Gavin was playing when I went in. It made me happy. Relaxed enough to put down the duffel bag and walk through the apartment. Blaine's screen saver, the Lillith Allure logo, was the only thing moving. Daniel's favorite coffee cup was on the table, but other than that, everything was immaculate. Parker D. Brooks would have loved it.

I went down the hall and glanced into Emily's room. The marks she'd scrawled with her Crayons were still on the far wall, but she had new Hello Kitty bedding. This was apparently a recent interest and had replaced the original Beatrix Potter nursery furnishings. I thought of the years ahead and wondered if Emily and Blaine would go head-to-head about her tastes. Maybe she'd like the Pet Shop Boys, too.

It seemed rude to go inside Blaine's and Daniel's room when neither of them was there. And since I had no desire to go on the terrace, I walked back into the living room. Gavin was leaning against the half wall that hid the stairs, his arms crossed over his chest.

"Hello, Attica," he said.

I scowled and said, "They didn't put me in jail for the fake ID. They didn't even arrest me."

"That may change if you're starting a new vocation as a cat burglar," Gavin said.

"Did I scare you?"

"I recognized the laundry bag." He smiled, uncrossed his arms so he could hug me, and said, "Come on down and let's get it started. Are you hungry?"

"No."

I followed him down the stairs. Then I had to forcibly take the bag to stop him from doing my laundry. "You don't get paid to take care of me anymore."

"I never did it for pay in the first place," Gavin said.

After I started the first load, I went back to the kitchen, pulled out a stool, and sat down. Gavin was filling pastries with some concoction. I didn't want to break his concentration, so I studied him for a few minutes.

Fred was wrong. The men in Blaine's apartment weren't flawless. People who didn't know Gavin might not even think he was handsome, especially if they didn't like the features that went along with having reddish hair. Light eyebrows. Some freckles. Fair skin. He did have a good body, toned more because of stretching and doing yoga than putting in time at the gym.

I thought it was Gavin's personality that made him attractive. He was always upbeat. Friendly. I liked it when he teased me because I knew it came from a good place. I watched the gentle way he nudged Dexter, Blaine's cat, away with his foot so he wouldn't step on him. Gavin took good care of everyone he loved, as I knew firsthand.

I watched him slice mushrooms and finally said, "Can I help you with anything?"

"It's under control. What's going on with you? Tell me about your roommates. Your new place. Your job. I hope I've been a great role model for your career as a domestic."

I slid off the stool and opened the refrigerator. I wasn't really hungry, but I couldn't face Gavin. I didn't want to lie to him, but I wasn't ready to tell him the truth about being fired. He was being so nice. It made me feel guilty for staying away until I needed money.

I took out a container of yogurt and got a spoon before I sat down again. I told him about Kendra and what a sweetheart she was. Then I quickly launched into tales about her evil alter ego, Morgan. She and her snakes were always a good diversion. Plus it was satisfying to know that she'd hate being useful to me.

Gavin laughed about Lucifer and Hugsie and said, "My first boyfriend had a snake."

"Is that the beginning of a dirty joke or the truth?"

"Truth. A boa constrictor named Squeeze. One thing I learned. Nobody fucks with a gay kid in the Baltimore suburbs when he walks around with a big snake."

"That's the stuff of after-school specials," I said, scraping out the last of the yogurt. "Instead of trying to turn your kid straight, just let him pack a snake in his book bag."

"Soon every school would have a snake detector at the door."

"Too bad my apartment didn't," I said.

"Maybe Morgan's like my first boyfriend. The snakes keep away people who might hurt her."

"I don't think Morgan can be hurt," I said.

Gavin turned to stare at me and said, "I don't mean to sound like Dr. Phil, but *everybody* can be hurt, Nick."

"Don't make me feel guilty about Morgan," I said. "Let's hear more about your first boyfriend."

Gavin washed his hands, got a different knife, and talked while he chopped onions. "Allen came from Florida. That seemed exotic to me at the time. He was all attitude, tan, and sun-bleached hair. We were fifteen. Freshmen. He was out and proud from the first day he walked into our school. I'd never told anybody about the feelings other boys gave me, so even though I admired Allen, he scared me. If I hung out with him, people might figure out the truth about me."

Gavin stopped and tilted his head toward the stereo speaker. We both grinned as the Pet Shop Boys sang "Nervously."

"Is that the way it was for you?" I asked. "Two boys from different places, too shy to talk about it?"

"Oh, that first kiss," Gavin said. "It's always a killer, no matter the circumstances. On the weekends, everybody used to drive out to this abandoned chromium mine to drink or get high. Even kids too young to drive, like me and my friends, still managed to show up, hang around, pretend we were as cool as the seniors. One night, Allen was there with Squeeze. I don't know what it is about girls and snakes." He made a resigned gesture with his hands. "But Allen was surrounded by them. I knew that one way or the other, I was getting some alone time with him. I shunned offers of rides home. Outlasted my friends and the snake-loving girls. And finally it was just Allen and me and die-hard couples off doing what couples do."

"Did you do what couples do?" I asked when Gavin paused to wash his hands.

"As it got later, the night turned cold. Allen was wearing a denim jacket. He took it off and sort of stretched it across both our backs. Which meant we had to sit close. I have no idea what we talked about. I doubt I made any sense. I was too dazed by being in such close proximity to Allen, with Squeeze covering our laps. When we both turned our faces at the same time and nearly bumped foreheads, he kissed me."

"With tongue?"

"He had no choice. I was practically eating his face," Gavin said and blushed. "That's the first time I kissed a boy."

"I was sixteen," I said. "My stupid brother wasn't outside when my mom came to pick us up from school. She made me go to the boys' locker room to look for him. I never went near that place because I valued my life. But I knew she'd just keep sending me inside until I found Chuck, so I forced myself to go there. I caught Keith Lindblom, one of the track coach's student aides, um, *adjusting* himself while he watched my brother and his friends horse around in the showers. I didn't say anything to him. Other than could he tell Chuck our mom was waiting. But it freaked him out. He knew what I saw, and I guess he was afraid I'd tell the jocks."

"You weren't out yet?"

"No. Keith started making a point of speaking to me in the hall between classes. Forcing me to meet his eyes. Being all friendly. I worked in the audiovisual department of the library, and he came in one afternoon when I was putting up some equipment. He was acting all jocklike and shit, trying to pretend we were friends, hitting me on the arm. He was too gutless to ask me to keep my mouth shut. That provoked me. I trapped him against a shelf of videotapes and kissed him."

"What'd he do?"

"He shoved me away and burst into tears. I felt like shit. For about ten seconds, until he grabbed me and kissed me back. Then he walked out, and we never spoke of it or went near each other again. Especially when Shelley Creighton told the whole football team I was gay a couple weeks later. I think your first kiss went better than mine. Especially if it led to better things."

"I wouldn't be a teenager again for a million dollars," Gavin said. Then he looked at me and said, "Oh. Sorry."

"Don't be. I'd give a million dollars to skip nineteen. It's good that no one can make that happen, because I'm too broke to pay up."

"I thought you might be," Gavin said. "Is that why you're here? To ask Blaine for a loan?"

"Guilty. Do you think he'll raise hell at me?"

"Not likely," Gavin said.

"Really?" I asked, feeling more hopeful.

"It would be hard, since he and Daniel flew to L.A. this morning."

"Fuck me," I muttered. "I lost my job. I can cover my rent. It's my roommate who can't. I promised to help her."

"The snake woman?"

"No. Kendra. Morgan is the snake woman."

Gavin frowned. "You lost your job?"

"I wouldn't put out for a client," I said without elaborating, even though it made Benny the Whiner seem like a jerk.

"How much do you need?"

"Kendra's part of the rent is five hundred."

Gavin stared at me a few seconds, then said, "I'll cover it. On one condition." I'd known there would be conditions, so I just nodded and hoped it wouldn't be too bad. "Be careful about who you trust, Nick. People aren't always what they seem."

"You mean like . . . Who do you mean?"

Gavin frowned again and said, "Never mind. Hey, I've been thinking about piercing my ear. Can you do that for me? Painlessly?"

I laughed and said, "Yeah, sure. It'll cost you five benjamins."

April 10, 2003

Dear Nick,

Gavin told me you came by and pierced his ear. He said you have the hands of a surgeon. Have you considered med school? (That's a joke, I swear.)

Daniel and I have had crazy busy schedules lately, which is why I didn't get your message about being at the Ninth Precinct until a couple of hours after you called. By the time I stormed the justice system on your behalf, you'd already been released with no charges filed. According to Blythe, a couple of cops from Cutter's took care of whatever the problem was. Glad it all worked out.

Let me know if you need anything. Hope to see you soon.

Love,
Uncle Blaine

5

It Always Comes As a Surprise

I'd just cracked an egg into Kendra's frying pan when the apartment door opened. I winced at the sound, knowing I was busted.

"If that's one of my eggs, consider yourself dead," Morgan said. She pushed past me and took an egg carton from the refrigerator. Her name had been boldly written on it with a black Sharpie. She opened it and started counting her eggs. Each one had an *M* scrawled on its shell.

"I didn't use your eggs," I stated. "The eggshell is in the trash can. Check it, if you don't believe me." She didn't. She put her eggs back without saying a word, then pushed by me again on her way to her room. Before she left the kitchen, I said, "Why are you such a bitch?"

"Excuse me?" she said, slowly turning around.

"I—I mean . . ." I stuttered. I'd pushed my luck. "You're always accusing us of using your stuff or taking your food. You must've had shitty roommates in the past, or something."

"You've been out of work for a month, Nick. Where did you get the money to buy that egg, if it's yours? Or any of the other food you've been eating, for that matter?" She didn't wait for an answer. "Do you have money saved? Are your parents giving you cash? Maybe your uncle, or one of his rich friends? It's the middle of April. Rent's due in a couple of weeks, Nick. I think I have a right to know if you're going to be able to pay your share."

"I will," I insisted. Even though I'd finally received my last paycheck from I Dream of Cleanie in the mail, I wasn't too sure. If I ate store-brand spaghetti and sugar wafers for the rest of the month, I figured I'd save enough of it to cover rent.

"Right," Morgan said. She sounded doubtful, as if she could read my mind. "If stealing my food is part of your budget, you can nix that plan right now. I've got a job. I've got responsibilities. You're not one of them."

"Fine," I said. "Who asked you?"

"You did," she said. "I left my last situation because my roommates were freeloaders. Your name is on the lease here, not mine. I can move out just as quickly as I moved in."

I didn't have anything to say to that, because I was suddenly envisioning my rent increasing. As annoying as Morgan could be, I couldn't afford to lose her as a roommate. I flipped my egg with a spatula and repeated, "Fine."

After she closed the bedroom door, Kendra came out of the bathroom in her waitress uniform and whispered, "It's the middle of a weekday. What's she doing here?"

"She heard me break open one of her eggs from her office in Midtown and flew up on her broom to make me pay," I guessed.

"Don't use her food," Kendra insisted. "It's not worth the pain. I told you, my food is your food. Help yourself."

I rolled my eyes. Kendra's current rations were a loaf of moldy bread, an unopened can of baking powder, and a Diet Coke. She ate at the restaurant, where the staff was given a free meal at the beginning and end of their shift. When she could be bothered to remember, sometimes she'd bring home a bag of leftovers from work.

I pointedly took out her Diet Coke and said, "Here's to your health."

Kendra cringed and said, "That's not mine. It was here when we moved in."

"At least it's not mine," Morgan said, coming out of their room. "For once."

"What are you doing here?" Kendra asked her. When she saw Morgan's expression, Kendra added, "I mean, uh, did you come home for lunch?"

"I forgot something I need for work," Morgan answered. She

nodded at me and added, "You should be asking him why he's home, and not out looking for a job."

"If she did," I said, "I'd tell her that I intend to do just that after I eat this delicious egg."

"My delicious egg," Morgan said.

"Guys, please," Kendra said, holding her hands over her ears.

"What about you? You can't expect him to cover your rent again, since he's out of work. You'll have enough for rent, right?"

Kendra put her hands down and said, "What?"

"Leave her alone," I said. "You act like you're our mother, or something."

"No. I act like the only one around here with a real job."

"That's not fair. Kendra has two jobs and manages to go to school. Roberto has a real job."

"I can't stand listening to you two argue," Kendra said. "I'm out of here."

"Speaking of Roberto," Morgan said, "is he sick?"

"What?" Kendra said, shutting the door and returning to the kitchen.

"He seems fine to me," I said.

"Now that you mention it, he's been looking really tired," Kendra said.

"He works hard," I said, "and he sometimes looks after his brothers while his mother's at work."

"He looks like he's lost weight," Kendra said. "Maybe he's bulimic. I never see him eat."

"Bulimics eat and hurl," Morgan said. "Anorexics don't eat."

"I've seen him eat," I declared. "A lot. He never pukes. And he's not losing weight."

"I once knew a girl who was anorexic," Kendra said. We waited for more, but after a long pause, she said, "What do you think is wrong with him?"

"Nothing!" I exclaimed. "He's fine."

"Thank you, Dr. Dunhill," Morgan said. "That was a brilliant diagnosis."

"He always takes care of himself," I said, thinking about when Roberto took me to see Mark. "He's got a doctor."

"Oh?" Morgan and Kendra both said.

"Maybe he's got Lou Ferrigno's disease," Kendra guessed.

I snorted and Morgan said, "Yeah, that's it. He's going to get mad and turn into the Hulk. Lou Gehrig's disease, you idiot."

"What *is* Lou Gehrig's disease?" Kendra asked. I shrugged. Morgan looked at the floor. "I see. Anyway, we shouldn't be talking about Roberto behind his back."

"Thank you," I pointedly said to her. "Besides, it's not like Morgan really cares about Roberto. She's probably just worried he'll kick it and stiff her with the rent."

"I think he's positive," Morgan stated.

Kendra and I were quiet and stared at Morgan as if she'd just announced that she was leaving to fill Mother Teresa's vacant sandals.

"But he's not gay," Kendra said. She turned to me and asked, "Is he?"

"You don't have to be gay to contract HIV, you ninny," Morgan said.

"I know that!"

"He's not," I said.

"Gay? Or positive?" Kendra asked.

"Neither. Both," I said, even though I couldn't be sure. I didn't want to think about either scenario. "You can be a real bitch, Morgan. Would it matter to you if he was positive? Or if I was?"

"It's not like I'm wishing anything bad on him. People with HIV are still discriminated against. The world can be a sucky place. I'm concerned. That's all."

I didn't buy it.

"Don't you have to get back to work?" I asked. "Thanks for stopping by and spreading sunshine on our day."

Morgan shook her head and quietly left. As I finished my egg, Kendra said, "I don't think he's positive. Roberto looks fine to me. A little tired, maybe, but who isn't? He's still hot. He's always flirting with me. I think it's cute. Don't you?"

I wanted the conversation to end, so I just nodded and quietly washed my plate. Kendra turned to leave, then jumped back when the apartment door opened. Morgan stuck her head back in and said, "Hey. That's my plate you're using. You'd better . . ."

Her tirade trailed away when I held up the dripping plate, then did my best to rub away the plate's pattern with a dish towel. I grunted a few times to make it seem like I was using Herculean strength to make her plate shine. I asked, "Anything else I can do for you?"

She ignored me and said to Kendra, "Come on. We'll share a cab downtown."

As the sun was setting, I sat outside on our fire escape with Roberto and told him about Morgan's egg tirade. He laughed in all the right places and said, "Wasn't it always eggs that dragons guarded in medieval times?"

"I thought it was treasure."

"Maybe eggs are all she has left."

I disagreed. If Morgan left, our apartment would be empty again. She was the one with all the furniture, the appliances in the kitchen, the television and DVD player, and the good stereo in the living room. We used her things all the time, because we had nothing. I knew the main reason she annoyed me so much was that she seemed so in control of her life. I always felt like there was something inside me that was defective. Maybe the decision-making part of my brain. I was a factory reject. Any day now, someone was going to knock on our door and inform me that I was being recalled.

"Roberto!" someone yelled from below. "Open up!"

"Why can't he use the buzzer," Roberto asked while crawling through the window, "like a normal person?"

A few minutes later, Roberto's brother JC was in our apartment. I watched through the window as they playfully smacked each other around. JC—Juan Carlos—was an even beefier version of Roberto. He was five years older, solid, and almost menacing looking. Except when he smiled; his dimples made him look like an angel on steroids.

After a few minutes, I crawled back into the apartment. JC pointed at me and said, "You still hanging out with this piece of trash?"

"He keeps following me around," Roberto said. He shrugged, as if to say, *What are you gonna do?*

Suddenly I was being crushed by JC's arms and lifted off the floor. I gasped for breath, and all I could smell was cigarettes, sweat, and cheap cologne. None of which smelled bad on JC. He put me down, pushed me away, and said, "Punk."

"Asshole," I muttered.

Roberto and JC locked eyes and both said, "Ooh, snap!"

JC threw his jacket on a chair, looked around, and said, "This place isn't half as bad as I thought it would be."

"It's worse, right?" Roberto said, grinning.

"You got that right. Your mom would go apeshit if she saw this place."

"At least I don't still live with her," Roberto said.

In a flash, they were rolling on the floor. I sat on the windowsill and watched them wrestle. I wondered how much money I could make if I videotaped them. If only Morgan had a camera. When JC put Roberto in a headlock, I said, "If you guys need it, I'm sure I have some lube."

JC pushed Roberto away. They both lay on the floor panting for a few minutes. JC reached into his jacket, pulled out a folded-up brown paper bag, and tossed it to Roberto. It hit him in the middle of the chest. Roberto's eyes lit up. He opened the bag, peered inside, and grinned.

"My brother's the bomb, yo," he said to me. "Didn't I tell you?"

I'd never been one of JC's biggest fans. He was pigheaded, overly macho, and sometimes rude. But he always scored the best weed in the city. From what I'd heard, most cops did. We passed around a tightly rolled joint, and JC filled Roberto in on their youngest brother's latest exploits at school. I tuned them out and followed the cracks in the ceiling with my eyes. They formed a spider-web around a dusty glass light fixture, which looked on the verge of giving in to gravity. Maybe one day it would fall on Morgan's head.

"What are you giggling at?" Roberto asked me.

"Nothing," I said. I hadn't realized I was laughing.

JC pointed at me and said, "This kid's crazy. One day, he's gonna snap."

I snapped my fingers and flipped him the bird. We all started laughing, until we heard the apartment door open. Kendra walked into the room and said, "Why does it smell like my grandmother's house in here?"

"It's him," I said, gesturing to JC.

"Uh-oh," JC said. "Mom's home."

"Your brother?" Kendra asked. Roberto nodded. She turned to JC and said, "Nice to meet you."

JC stood and took Kendra's hand in his meaty paws. In a low voice, he said, "Hello."

"Hey, Kendra, I forgot to tell you about something earlier," I said and dragged her into the kitchen.

"What?" she asked, pulling her hair behind her ears.

I looked around the room, then took a jar of mayo from the refrigerator. "Is this yours?"

"No." She pointed to the label. *Hellman's* was crossed out and replaced by *Morgan's*. "Are you stoned?"

"Why? What have you heard?"

"I don't care if you are," she said. She pulled me into the bathroom and shut the door. "I've got a problem."

"Oh God. Is this a female thing? Why do women feel compelled to tell their gay friends everything that happens *down there?*"

She blushed and stammered, "Oh. I guess you're right. You probably don't want to—I'm sorry."

I sighed. "Go on. What is it? Does it burn when you pee?" Kendra looked as though I'd just slapped a scarlet *P* on her crotch. "Really? Gosh," I said. "I was just kidding."

"Believe me, it's not that funny," she whispered.

"Does Morgan have any cranberry juice? Isn't that supposed to help?"

Kendra folded her arms and said, "Right, Nick. It burns when I pee, so I'll drink something that's going to make me pee even more."

"I don't know! I'm not a doctor!" I shrieked.

"Shut up!" she hissed. "I don't want the whole building to know. This is so embarrassing. What am I going to do? I don't have insurance. I can't afford to see a doctor. I don't even know if I can pay rent. Again. I still owe you for last time."

"It's okay," I mumbled. Suddenly I didn't feel as bad about my life as I had earlier. "My final paycheck from I Dream of Cleanie arrived in the mail the other day. I'll float you a loan until you get paid again."

A knock on the door made us both jump. I nearly fell off the toilet seat. Kendra cautiously opened the door. Roberto's hand came into the room, holding a slip of paper. As Kendra took the note, I heard Roberto say, "They're open for another hour. It's not far, but if you get a cab, you'll get there in plenty of time for someone to see you."

"Okay," Kendra mumbled. Roberto's hand popped into the room

again, this time offering a twenty-dollar bill and a condom. Kendra stuffed them both into her pocket and weakly said, "Thanks."

"I'll go with you," I offered.

Halfway down the stairs, I realized that I'd forgotten my wallet. I told Kendra I'd meet her on the corner and ran back for it. Roberto and JC were watching a game on TV. As I searched a pile of dirty jeans for my wallet, I heard JC say, "That chick you live with's hot. You hittin' that?"

I stopped what I was doing and waited for the answer.

"Nah," was all Roberto said.

I found my wallet on top of a milk crate by the futon. I stuffed it in my back pocket and ran downstairs.

The address Roberto had given Kendra led us to a clinic near Columbia University. It wasn't a free clinic, but they charged on a sliding scale. Kendra tried to haggle with them, but changed her tune when they referred her to the free clinic and said it wouldn't be open until the next day. She mumbled something about it being a burning issue and followed a nurse into an examining room.

I flipped through the magazines in the waiting room. A picture of Sheila Meyers caught my eye. Sheila was one of my uncle's best friends. I read the box of text and smiled.

> *Sheila Meyers, the spokesmodel for Lillith Allure Cosmetics who's currently filming scenes for a movie version of That Girl (Meyers will portray Ruth Bauman during the first half of the movie. Tina Yothers continues the role in the film's second half.), on recent rumors that she's a transsexual: "Nobody wants to hear a model say she was born in the wrong body. That's a step beyond 'Don't hate me because I'm beautiful.' Maybe I am a transsexual. Would it matter? We're all human. Sexuality doesn't demand a cure."*

"Nick?"

I looked up, expecting to see a nurse or doctor who'd come to inform me that Kendra's condition had taken a turn for the worse. They'd have to operate, but needed the consent of Kendra's family. Which, of course, would be impossible, since I knew nothing about her family. Kendra would lapse into a coma and—I shook my head clear of *ER*-induced fantasies and said, "Hey, Mark. How've you been?"

"Okay," he said. He looked concerned. "How are you?"

"Oh. I'm waiting for a friend to come back out," I said. "I'm fine."

"Good," he said and smiled. Then he asked the dreaded question. "What's new?"

He looked good. As bed buddies went, Mark was the best. He could be sweet and gentle, or rough and hot. Whatever I wanted. But out of bed he was Dr. Mark: successful, organized, together. Everything I wasn't. Who wanted to look at a bed buddy and see a role model? I wanted the two of us to be on an even plane. Out of context—out of bed—we were in different universes. Judging from his anxious expression, Mark felt it, too. I wished I had good things to tell him. I wished we were in bed, so I could tell him everything that was bothering me. Instead, I said, "Fine. Hey, this isn't the clinic where I met you."

"That clinic was a real zoo," Mark joked. "No, you're right. I'm meeting—"

"Mark, hi," a man in a white coat called and interrupted our boring conversation. When he was near enough, his hand reached for Mark's shoulder, but when he noticed me sitting there, he shook Mark's hand awkwardly. "I got held up in the lab. Sorry."

"It's okay," Mark said. He introduced me to David, a radiologist, who didn't have much to say to me. David said he'd change and meet Mark outside. He then speed-walked away with the long strides favored by eight out of ten New Yorkers on a time schedule. When we were alone again, Mark said, "That was David."

"I see. I mean, I saw. He came and went so fast, I wasn't sure. Are you sure he's not an illusionist?"

"He's definitely a radiologist."

"How long have you guys been dating?"

"Oh, we're not—" Mark broke off and collapsed on the seat next to mine. "Shit, I guess we are. We call each other a lot. We've had three dates. There was talk about a share in the Pines."

"You're dating," I said seriously. "I could prescribe something for that. An injection, maybe? If you'll step into the bathroom for a few minutes and drop your pants—"

"I don't think so," Mark said and grinned.

"Right. You're the doctor. I guess you know what's best." I added, "Besides, he really likes you."

"How do you know?"

"He obviously wanted to touch you. He didn't like me being near you at all. He couldn't wait to get out of here and have you all to himself. And he's pacing outside now, glancing through the window and staring at you like you're a puppy he wants to play with."

Mark turned, saw David through the window, and said, "Whoops. I guess I'd better go."

"I guess you'd better."

"Look, I—"

"We've had fun," I said quickly. "You're a great friend. See you later, right?"

"Right," Mark said.

I had a good view of Mark and David as they greeted each other outside, all smiles. David hailed a cab, opened the door for Mark, and touched his back as they maneuvered inside. They reminded me of Uncle Blaine and Daniel; how they always found ways to make contact like that. To the untrained eye it seemed casual, but I knew it was much more. It was love.

When Kendra returned to the waiting area, she could barely look me in the eye. She mumbled, "Can we get out of here?"

There was only five dollars left over from our earlier cab fare, so we bought big cookies at a deli and walked home. After a few blocks, Kendra finally said, "It's NGU."

"I almost went to school there," I joked. "What's that mean?"

"It's an infection of the urethra brought on by chlamydia."

"Hot," I said.

She glanced at me and shook her head. "Not so much."

"No, it's not," I agreed.

"Go ahead," she said. "After hearing about your uncles and their endless safe sex speeches, I'm sure you have quite a bit to say."

"Nope. It's your life."

"That's it? That's almost worse than a lecture."

If she knew that Roberto was probably cured of his need to flirt with her, Kendra might have thought that was worse. But I didn't say anything. Instead, I gave her the other half of my cookie and held her hand the rest of the way home.

April 18, 2003

Nicole,

    Your uncle and I were having dinner with Sheila and Josh recently. As usual, I went digging through Josh's pile of photos to see if I could find any of "former soap actor Daniel Stephenson" that needed to be destroyed. Instead, I found an old one of you and Blaine standing side by side at Rehoboth Beach. Normally I'd say you look nothing alike, but your expressions are identical here. The two of you seem so disapproving. I have no idea what you were staring at when Josh took the picture, but I hope you didn't make anyone's head explode. I thought you might like the photo, so I'm enclosing it.

    Come by sometime. I have no one to torment.

Yours,
Danielle

6

Opportunities
(Let's Make Lots of Money)

I quickly learned that trying to find a job in New York City could be as bad as finding an apartment. I combed all of the ads in newspapers, but was beaten to the punch by people who read them first on the Internet. I took to wandering the streets of random neighborhoods, looking for HELP WANTED signs in windows. I asked friends, hoping that word of mouth would come through for me again, but nobody knew of anyone hiring. Fred couldn't even get me on at Starbucks because no one was leaving. Apparently actors and musicians were having trouble finding work, too.

After two weeks, I started to take it personally. Maybe I was dressed wrong. I made it a point to dress in my most boring clothes: plain black pants and a button-down shirt. Whenever I'd talk to store owners or managers, I could always see their eyes quickly drop and scan me from top to bottom when they greeted me. I had a feeling they were looking for labels and mentally calculating how little I spent on my appearance. My family had long since given up on trying to take me shopping. I knew nothing about fashion. I only cared about expressing myself creatively. Not following some trend like a mindless sheep.

Unfortunately, the East Village thrift stores I frequented weren't hiring, either.

I hid from reality in movie theaters. Sitting in a dark, frigid theater and avoiding my problems with a box of popcorn was better than dealing with rejection. So was playing pool. Or reading in bookstores. Unfortunately, escapism wasn't cost-effective for the unemployed.

That was when I started leaving the house in the mornings, pretending I was going to spend another day looking for a job. I'd wait in the Korean deli across the street until I saw Kendra leave for school. She was always the last to go, so I knew the coast was clear. I'd have the apartment all to myself until she returned around two to change for her waitress job. Originally, I ducked out for an hour while she was there. Then I got daring and just stayed quiet in my room until she left again.

Staying at home was better than roaming the streets because I was afraid of running into someone I knew. I quickly learned that the unemployed were like lepers. All conversation would turn to the dreaded question: *Any luck with the job search?* My negative reply would always receive sympathetic looks, as if my ear had just fallen off, followed by their assurances that I'd find something soon.

It would've been fine to be out of work if I was painting. But even sketching bored me. I could barely bring myself to doodle in the margins of job applications. I felt dead inside, creatively.

"Stop worrying about it. You're putting too much pressure on yourself because you don't have a job," Davii said to me one day while he was cutting my hair. We were in the kitchen of his apartment, a small loft in the fashion district. "It's hard to be creative when you have outside forces putting demands on you. Once you find a job, I'm sure you'll start working on your art again. It's like this apartment. I grabbed it when I first moved to New York, assuming I'd trade up once I got established. But I'm hardly ever home, so what's the point?"

"What *is* the point?" I asked.

"It's easy to get stuck in a rut," he answered.

"Maybe. The only outside force putting pressure on me is my roommate, Morgan. The dark force."

"Problems in paradise?"

"I'd settle for purgatory."

"I think you're already there. I think you enjoy being tragic." A chunk of hair slid down the back of my neck, and I shivered. Davii pushed my head lightly and said, "Hold still."

"Sorry."

"You should be," he teased. He moved in front of me and started snipping my bangs. His face was inches from mine. The intense look on his face and the way he bit his lower lip while he worked was sexy. Luckily, I had on a black smock that covered my crotch.

"You're so lucky. Your job fell into your lap."

"Maybe. But I paid my dues, Nick. Beauty school, barbershops, mall salons." He paused and visibly shuddered. "I guess I was in the right place at the right time. I suppose Sheila did pluck me out of nowhere. But ultimately, I had the skills and made them work to my benefit."

I thought about that. What skills did I have? I could draw, sure. But how could I make that work for me if I was creatively dead? I felt like I was caught in a trap and I couldn't walk out. I frowned and pointed to the radio on the windowsill. "Do we have to listen to Elvis?"

"Yes. I'm going through an Elvis phase. It's all about the King." I sighed loudly. Davii stopped cutting and said, "Fine. Brat." He switched from the radio to the CD player, and suddenly Howard Jones was assuring me that things could only get better.

"I hate you," I said.

"No, you don't," Davii said, laughing.

"I do. I'm going through an I-hate-everyone phase."

"You're too old for that now. Grow up. You're the one who wanted to live in the real world. Welcome to reality, my friend. It's not all fun and games."

"This is what I get for confiding in my hairdresser," I said. "Lectures and advice. Your hotness is fading fast."

Davii stopped working and grinned. "What? You think I'm hot?"

My mouth fell open, but I couldn't speak. If I'd been a leper, that would've been when my dick fell off.

"Anyway," Davii segued, "what's with this Morgan chick? What's her deal?"

"She's a cartoonist, I think," I said. "I'm not really sure. But her main job is to make my life miserable. She's always ragging me about something. Rent, bills, food. She's evil."

"That's a shame. I always got along great with my roommates. Why don't you get rid of her?"

"I don't know. At least she's got a job. She pays everything on time. Finding someone else would be too much of a hassle."

Davii stood up and squinted at me. He reminded me of Johnny Depp in *Edward Scissorhands*. He pushed a lock of hair from my eyes and said, "There. You're done."

He led me to his bathroom. I stared at my hair in the mirror. It was cut in a modern shag style and had blue highlights.

"I asked for give-me-a-job hair. This is form-a-new-garage-band hair."

"No," Davii corrected, "it's appreciate-me-for-who-I-am hair. Whether it's prospective employees, your roommates, your family"—he raised his eyebrows pointedly—"they all need to appreciate you for the unique and wonderful person that you are. But you can't expect them to do that unless you can do the same thing. Trust me, I know that can be tricky sometimes. Especially when you're having a run of bad luck. But—"

"Things can only get better?" I guessed.

"You're such a brat," Davii said. He pulled me to him and hugged me quickly. Then he let go and said, "Get out of here. You've got a haircut. Now go. Get a job."

I had to admit that my new hair gave me confidence. I walked down Eighth Avenue and could hear the Bee Gees playing in my head, as if I were in *Saturday Night Fever*. But I wasn't a woman's man, so I pulled out the iPod I'd borrowed from Roberto and listened to Rammstein. While I was passing the Chelsea Hotel, a hand grabbed my shoulder, causing my earbuds to be yanked from my ears. I shouted, "Hey!"

"Sorry, man," a guy my age said. "Nick, right?"

He looked like half the guys at Pratt: baggy jeans, sneakers, a T-shirt with some random slogan printed on the front over a long-sleeved shirt. He had bad posture and smelled like a tomato. He seemed familiar, but I couldn't remember his name or how I'd met him. I dumbly said, "Yeah. Hey."

"I haven't seen you in ages. Did you drop out?"

"Uh-huh."

"Bummer. Got a job?"

Instead of screaming like I wanted to do, I said, "I got fired recently."

"That sucks! That happened to my friend, Steve, back home. Only he quit."

Suddenly I remembered him. Random Rick. He was constantly telling random facts about his supposed friends from back home. I always guessed that he was homesick and couldn't wait to go back since he talked about it so much. He was kind of pathetic.

A guy driving by in a truck suddenly yelled, "Hey, fag! Nice hair!"

"Sit on my face!" Random Rick shouted back, and threw his bottle of Coke at the truck. It bounced off the back bumper, and the driver hit the brakes. There was a loud noise when the cab behind it ran into the truck's rear bumper.

"Uh-oh," I said.

"Run!" Random Rick needlessly said, pushing me to the nearby E subway entrance. We dashed down the stairs, and I grabbed Rick's jacket to stop him from jumping over the turnstile. I jerked my head toward a group of armed guards and pulled out my MetroCard. Rick said, "Good call."

Only after we were on the E train and it began lurching uptown did we heave a sigh of relief.

"Man, that was crazy. It's like this one time, back home, Justin and I were cruising the main drag, and—"

"Dude," I interrupted, "I don't care."

"What?"

"I'm sorry, but I really don't give a shit," I said. "Nobody does. We don't know these people back home that you're always talking about. It's not that interesting. What are you doing here?"

"I'm on the subway," he said stupidly. "With you."

"No. You don't get it. It's like you're stuck. Are you going back there? Or are you going to accept that you're here and move forward? Make up your mind." We both sat silently. We watched the Thirty-fourth Street station come and go. Finally I said, "Dude, I'm sorry. I didn't mean to—"

"No, it's cool. I get it." Rick pulled a notebook from his backpack and scribbled an address on one of the pages. He tore it out and handed it to me. "Go here. It's a design firm. A friend of mine told me about a job there. They're looking for someone to run errands, or something. I was going to apply, but you need the job more than I do."

"Hey, thanks. But I couldn't—"

"Yeah, you can. Do it," he urged. "You're not in Ohio anymore, right? Isn't this city all about grabbing opportunity by the balls and taking advantage of situations? Using your friends and connections? Go right now, though. Someone might beat you to the punch."

I didn't bother to correct him about where I was from. Instead, I smiled and thanked him. He got off the train at Penn Station after saying, "See ya round, Nick."

I surfaced on Fifth Avenue and Fifty-third, because I wasn't sure if there was another stop after that and didn't want to end up in Queens. After walking a few blocks I gazed around at the corner of Central Park and the Plaza Hotel. I flashed back in my mind to the first time I'd seen this part of Manhattan. All the white buildings, ritzy stores with things I'd never be able to afford, and stone-faced people stalking the sidewalks like they owned the city intimidated me.

They still do, I thought, as I darted out of the way of a woman with too many shopping bags.

The address was for an office building a few blocks away on Third Avenue. It was across the street from a gaping hole in the ground surrounded by a chain-link fence. In the lobby, I struggled with Random Rick's handwriting and tried to match it with the directory on a wall near the elevators. Wamsley & Wilkes, I learned, was on the first floor. I took that as a good omen.

The reception area looked like someone's living room. There were bookcases lining the walls, their shelves crammed with books, plants, and various picture frames and other trinkets. The portraits on the walls were of smiling people in suits. I assumed they were people who worked at Wamsley & Wilkes. Instead of being arranged around a television set, the various love seats and chairs faced a desk. A woman dressed head to toe in pink sat behind it, knitting while talking into a headset. She looked like somebody's grandmother, in concert. When I stepped tentatively forward, she winked, smiled, and held up one finger, as if to say she'd be with me in a minute. Then she gestured with wide-eyed enthusiasm at a plate of cookies on the edge of her desk. I took one and nibbled at it. It tasted like chalk.

She put down the phone and said, "Hi! Welcome to Wamsley & Wilkes. How's that cookie?"

"Great," I lied.

"I baked them myself this morning. They're sugar-free," she said in a low voice, like it was a state secret. "I'm Eileen. What can I do for you?"

"A friend of mine told me there's a job opening here," I said.

"You haven't finished your cookie," she said darkly. She brightened again when I said a silent prayer, then stuffed the whole thing into my mouth. "Are you an interior designer?"

"No," I answered. A few crumbs flew out of my mouth.

"Furniture designer?"

"Um, no."

"Carpenter?"

I shook my head again.

"Contractor? Design intern? Accountant?"

I thought about running for the door. Instead, I meekly said, "Afraid not."

"Good! Those positions are all filled," she said. "Another cookie? No? The partners are looking for a—well, I guess you could call it a gofer. Or a runner. Someone to run errands, help with deliveries, and that sort of thing. I'll tell you now, it's drudgery."

"I don't care."

"Good boy. Fill out this application while I see if someone can interview you today."

I filled in the boxes on the form with robotic precision. After submitting hundreds of others, it became like breathing. But as usual, I paused at the space for notification in case of emergency. Sometimes I put my parents. Other times, Uncle Blaine. Or Gavin. This time, I filled the blanks with Roberto's name and his cell phone number.

Just as I finished, a toy poodle with a pen in its mouth pranced through the reception area as if it had an appointment down the hall in another office. It was dyed crimson, and I took that as another good omen.

"Alrighty then," Eileen suddenly chirped. Then she said to me, "You're in luck. Both partners have time to meet you. Down that hall. Behind the walnut door on the left is the conference room. They're in there."

"Great. Thanks, Eileen."

"Have another cookie. I insist."

"I couldn't. Crumbs," I said. She nodded, as if crumbs were the devil.

I found the conference room and knocked. After the door opened, a blue poodle ran through my legs and scampered down the hall with a swatch of fabric in its mouth. I looked up and saw a woman smiling at my puzzled expression. "Was that the furniture designer or the carpenter?" I asked her.

"Close. That's Ottoman," she said. "Come in."

"So the gofer position has already been filled?" I asked. My eyes quickly swept the room. I took in a long, dark table, leather chairs, plants, and an older man in a dark suit standing by an enormous globe. I half expected him to spin it, point to a random continent, and announce plans for an invasion while laughing maniacally. I figured I'd end up being rejected again, so with nothing to lose, I added, "Would it help if I came back as a Shar-Pei?"

"No. Maybe a mastiff," the man suggested. He didn't sound evil at all. His tone and expression reminded me of Mr. Rogers. Or Fred Rogers meets Dr. No. "We need a working dog. Now, the kuvasz is a fine dog. Please, have a seat. Nick, is it? I'm Thaddeus Wamsley, but you can call me Mr. Wamsley."

"Okay," I said. I sank into a leather chair and added, "Mr. Wamsley."

"I'm Bailey Wilkes," the woman said. She leaned across the table and firmly shook my hand. She looked young, maybe a few years older than me. Her suit was immaculate and hid her flaws, if she had any. Her hair was honey blond, with a dark streak in her bangs. She wore a pair of nerdy glasses, favored by nine out of ten business-women and female solo artists. "Please, ignore my partner. Mr. Wamsley is an old man whose idea of new and exciting design is Martha Stewart's Kmart collection. I only keep him around because he's the money behind our organization."

"And Ms. Wilkes is nothing but a hotshot fresh out of design school who blew a couple of rock stars, replaced some pillows on their beds, and was lucky enough to snap a few photographs before they kicked her out, which she then got printed in *Town & Country*," Mr. Wamsley said. "If she wasn't so good at drumming up business and making sure we're mentioned in every publication dedicated to our craft, Bailey would be at home where she belongs, selling homemade pillows on eBay."

Bailey's mouth dropped open, feigning shock; then she grinned and said, "Good one."

Mr. Wamsley picked up my application from the table, glanced at it for a few seconds, then dropped it. It skimmed the table's polished surface and landed in front of me. In a bored tone, he said, "I could go on and on about how we're looking for a team player, someone with an upbeat attitude and good people skills, and all that crap . . ."

He trailed off and Bailey picked up his patter, as if I'd stepped into a scene they'd rehearsed without me, and said, "The truth is, Nick, we need someone to do what he's told, and to do it without question."

"You make it sound like I'm auditioning to be your slave," I said.

Mr. Wamsley's left eyebrow rose. "In a word, yes."

"I wouldn't go that far," Bailey hastily disagreed.

"Don't be such a nanny," Mr. Wamsley growled at her. He turned to me and said, "Nobody's going to ask you to wash toilets with your tongue. You'll help with deliveries, assist the designers with installations, perhaps nail together a table, fax, file, and maybe get coffee. Is that so terrible?"

"No," I answered. "I can do all that."

"I'm sure you can," Bailey said warmly. "You'll be great."

"Does that mean I have the job?" I asked.

Bailey picked up my application again. Her eyes skimmed the page and her forehead wrinkled. She looked up and asked, "You're going to Pratt? Good school."

"I dropped out," I admitted. She continued to stare at me, which made me think she wanted more of an explanation. "I wasn't sure what I wanted to do. What area to focus my studies on, you know? It seemed like a waste of time and money, so I figured—"

"Look," she interjected, "I don't need to know everything that happened before you walked in here. I just wondered if you plan on going back. This is a full-time job. We need you here."

Her change in attitude was startling. It jarred something in my memory and I felt as though a fog had suddenly lifted, allowing me to see Bailey more clearly. The trim figure, chic clothes, salon-bought hair, enhanced features—she looked like an upgraded version of Morgan. Morgan 2.0. I hardly ever thought of Morgan as human, much less as someone who might have a living and breathing family. I just assumed she stepped out of a pod, or was hatched from an egg buried in sand. Were she and Bailey related?

My mind flashed on Morgan's rent checks. Morgan Adams.

Bailey Wilkes. Different last names, but the physical resemblance was eerie. Maybe they were cousins.

I suddenly realized Mr. Wamsley was staring at me as though I'd just loudly farted. I asked, "What? I mean, no. I don't plan to go back any time soon."

"Good," Bailey said. She shrugged, as if my application had no more interest and asked Mr. Wamsley, "Any more questions?"

"We could check his references," he said. "I didn't recognize any of the names he put down. Frankly, I don't care."

"Me, either," Bailey agreed. She smiled brightly at me and said, "It's your hair. I like it. You're hired."

"Rock on," I said. "I mean, thank you."

Mr. Wamsley shook my hand firmly and said, "I don't care about your hair. If you're not here at eight sharp, you're fired."

"I'll be here, sir," I promised.

"Sir," he repeated, obviously pretending to savor the sound of the word. "I like that. Bailey, call me 'sir' from now on, okay?"

"Only if you refer to me as 'high priestess of everything fabulous and my personal queen.' "

"Oh well," he said, "so much for that idea. See you both tomorrow."

"Score!" Roberto shouted that night after I told him my good news. He gave me a bear hug and jumped up and down, carrying me with him around the living room. My feet nearly clipped Kendra's head, causing her to jerk backward and drop the magazine she'd been flipping through.

"Watch it!" she shrieked.

"Will you guys shut up?" Morgan hollered from the bedroom. "I'm trying to work in here!"

"What's up with Countess Crab-a-lot?" Roberto asked. He'd just come home from work. None of us ever came home and relaxed. First, we had to figure out if Morgan was home and assess her mood. If she was in a bad mood, the three of us would go out, or hang out in my room. If she was in a good mood—

I supposed we'd find out someday.

"She came home and locked herself in there," I said, gesturing to the bedroom, "grumbling about her bosses, work, and men in general."

"Her boss is a general?" Kendra asked, lost in her magazine.

"Yes. General Whyareyousuchadummy," I answered.

"What a strange name. Is it Polish?" she murmured. "Should I get capri pants?"

"Will they make you smarter?" Roberto asked.

"What a silly question. Of course not."

"Then, no," Roberto said.

"Speaking of names," I began, but stopped when I realized Morgan was suddenly in the room, standing like a pissed-off statue with crossed arms and a stony stare.

When she had our full attention, she came to life. "Is it too much to ask for you guys to be quiet? I was forced to bring a ton of work home with me tonight, and it all has to be done by tomorrow. I can't concentrate with the three of you chattering like a bunch of magpies in here. I can hear every word you say, you know." She glared at Roberto and added, "*Every* word."

"Nick got a job," Roberto said brightly, as if he hadn't heard a word she said. "It's a happy day."

Morgan closed her eyes for five seconds. I imagined that she was willing herself not to kill us in our sleep later that night. She came to and asked, "Where are you working?"

"Wamsley & Wilkes," I said, enunciating clearly. I waited for a reaction, but if the name meant anything to her, she didn't let it show. "It's a design firm."

"Do they make—"

"Interior design," I said, interrupting Kendra. She frowned and went back to her magazine. "I'll be doing shit work, but it's good pay."

I told them everything that Eileen had told me while I'd filled out tax forms. I'd get ten dollars an hour to start, a two-dollar raise after three months, with health insurance, dental, and an optional 401k program.

"I should be working a lot of hours, so I'll finally make some real money," I said. "Plus it's in a creative field. It's not art, really, and it's fulfilling someone else's vision, but still . . ." I trailed off, unsure where I was going with my train of thought.

"As someone in a similar situation, I know what you mean," Roberto said.

"Way to go, da Vinci," Morgan said blandly. Before she went back into her room she added, "Now keep it down, please."

Kendra looked up. "Did she just say please?"

"This would be a good time to consult Nostradamus," Roberto said.

"I used to date a psychic. His predictions have been accurate so far," Kendra said. We looked at her, but she was already reading her magazine again.

Roberto ran his hand over his eyes like he had a headache, and I bit my knuckles to keep from laughing.

May 1, 2003

Dear Nicky,

Thank you for finally responding to the many messages I've left on your voice mail. I'm sure it was just luck that you managed to pick a time to call back when my phone was turned off. I would really like to speak to you soon.

As for the cell phone bill, it's all part of a package that includes the entire family's phones. So no, there's not a way to separate your bill out. Did you ask because you want to pay for your own phone, or because you're worried that we'll have a record of your phone calls? All of that's handled through Dunhill Electrical. Only the bookkeeper there sees the bills. I don't even know if the calls are itemized for each number. Neither your father nor I is interested in spying on our sons. So please don't give the bill or your privacy another thought.

I'll keep trying to reach you at a time when it's convenient for you to talk.

Love,
Mom

7

Do I Have To?

I arrived promptly at 8:00 AM on my first day as an employee at Wamsley & Wilkes, but I was the only one. At half past, Eileen drifted down the hall toward me. I could see something blue sticking out of a canvas bag. I thought it might be Ottoman the dog, but it was a skein of blue yarn for what I assumed would be that day's knitting project.

After Eileen unlocked the door, I made coffee while she unloaded her bag. I was relieved to see there were no cookies.

"Now what?" I asked, bringing her a cup with two sugars, no cream, as requested.

"You wait for our driver, Isaiah," she said. "Sometimes he's late because he comes from the Bronx. Then he has to pick up the van from the garage." She peered at her computer monitor while it booted up.

"Is there anything I can do to help you?" I asked, eager to make a good impression. I sat on the chair in front of her desk and heard a loud squeak.

I jumped to my feet, certain that I'd killed a poodle when Eileen also squeaked, "Otto!" Fortunately, it turned out to be Ottoman's toy pork chop in the chair. "I wish those dogs could be trained to put their toys away," Eileen complained.

"What's the other dog's name?" I asked, gently placing the pork chop on Eileen's desk.

"Tassel. They come in with Bailey. She's late this morning."

The door opened and a barrel-chested black man walked in. It didn't take a genius to realize this was Isaiah, since he was in a navy shirt with a badge on one pocket that said *Isaiah.* At least no one had suggested that I wear a similar shirt. I wasn't above wearing one, and I was often attracted to men in uniforms. But the shirt made me think of Dunhill Electrical, my family's company where I hoped I'd never have to work in my life.

When Eileen introduced us, Isaiah wore a dubious expression. I didn't blame him. I probably looked like a scrawny kid to him, even though he didn't seem much older than I was.

"Twenty-five," Isaiah said later when we got into the van and I asked him. "You?"

"Nineteen."

He consulted the clipboard Eileen had given him and said, "You're in luck. Light morning." Then he lurched into traffic in a way that made me grab the oh-shit handle above my window. I hurriedly fastened my seat belt while a man in a black Lexus stuck his hand through his sunroof to flip us off. Isaiah seemed oblivious as he attempted to find a station on the radio.

"I can do that," I volunteered when he nearly clipped a cab.

"Good," Isaiah said and reached for his coffee. "I'm off to a sluggish start this morning."

I hit the first preset station and left it on 50 Cent. I thought my prayer as Isaiah cut across two lanes to make a right turn was only in my head, but I must have sounded like I was patiently waiting for disaster right along with 50 and Eminem, because Isaiah turned to stare at me. Fortunately, he was stopped at a traffic light.

"You know this song?" he asked. It sounded like an accusation.

"I like 50 Cent," I said defensively.

"Ah ha ha haaaaaaa." He threw back his head when he laughed. "I take it you don't?"

"I hate that gangsta shit. If you're trying to impress me—"

"I started listening to Tupac and Snoop when I was a kid," I said.

"Your parents should have been arrested. You like 50 Cent. Ah ha ha haaaaaaa." The light changed, and his foot was heavy on the accelerator. "Nick, huh? Like nickel. I guess I have to call you 5 Cent till you grow up."

"Shut up," I said without animosity. He made me think of the torment I endured from Roberto's older brothers. "You do realize that you nearly took out two pugs and an old woman just then?"

"Pugs are ugly, anyway," Isaiah said. "I'll only get fired for killing poodles and greyhounds."

"Greyhounds?"

"Mr. Wamsley owns five." He whipped the van into the loading zone of an office building and said, "First stop. We deliver that."

My gaze followed the direction of his thumb, and I said, "That looks like something my grandmother has in her house. What is it?"

"That is an antique washstand," Isaiah said. "There's a pitcher and bowl to go with it. Because people want the strangest shit in their offices."

After our fourth delivery of the morning, Isaiah jumped a curb to pull into a McDonald's. We were eating our Quarter Pounders on the loading dock in the garage when I pointed up and asked, "What's the story on the people at Wamsley & Wilkes? Is there anyone extremely evil I should stay away from?"

"No. Everyone's cool here."

Isaiah's answer lacked detail, but turned out to be extremely accurate. I spent the rest of the day assisting Jisella, Wamsley & Wilkes's master carpenter. Everything about Jisella was large. She was tall, with large hands and feet. Her hair was a thick mass of wiry curls, which were twisted and bound into a huge knot. Jisella's head contained what I assumed was an enormous brain; she casually mentioned in conversation having a degree from MIT.

"I could've geeked it up with the best of them, I guess, in Silicon Valley or at NASA. But I'd rather build a table than the next supercomputer," she said. "Keep sanding. It's possible to listen and sand at the same time, you know. If you do a good job, I'll show you how to plane a door."

I was getting some coffee in the break room when a man in jeans and a Sex Pistols T-shirt under a black suit jacket stared at me and said, "You're Nick."

He pulled a pencil from behind his ear and used it to stir sugar and cream into his coffee. He glared at me over the rim as I said, "Yeah. I don't know who you are."

"Nigel," he said. First he offered me his cup. Then he switched and firmly shook my hand. "I'm a designer. The one they'll never promote."

"Oh," I said.

"It's no big deal," he assured me. "I've had offers from several top firms in town. But I like it here."

"That's good."

"I need you," he suddenly said.

"What?"

He laughed and said, "No. Not like that. I just finished some sketches for a job we're doing on a—well, just come look."

I followed Nigel to his office and looked at several drawings of various rooms. They looked like Aphrodite's summer home in the Hamptons, and I said as much.

"I know. The client just vacationed in Greece. She wants her place to look like a villa in Athens."

"Do they have villas in Greece? I thought that's Italy."

"A temple, then. Whatever. Greece is so played out. We want to be original, but what can you do with a concept like Greece that hasn't been done a million times before?"

A fact from one of my classes at Pratt suddenly reared its ugly head and made my mouth move. "Coins were invented in Greece. In Lydia." I realized Nigel was staring at me with an expression that I was sure I used daily, whenever Kendra opened her mouth. I quickly added, "What if you used coins in the bathroom as a tile? Kind of like a—"

"A mosaic," Nigel interrupted. "That's not bad."

I watched as he began scribbling notes on one of the drawings. I tentatively suggested, "A lot of people automatically associate white-figure pottery with Greece, but black-figure pottery was very popular in Ancient Greece. It had black lines over red clay, which would look great in—"

"In the study!" Nigel exclaimed.

"I was going to say the kitchen, but okay." I liked that Nigel was listening to my ideas and taking me seriously. I boldly added, "I was going to suggest scrolls for the study. Like in the—"

"Library of Alexandria?" Nigel said. "That might be a little too literal, don't you think?"

It took me a minute to realize that he thought he'd made a clever pun. I laughed, but it seemed painfully obvious that I hadn't gotten the joke. Luckily, the awkward moment was ancient history when Mr. Wamsley unexpectedly entered the office.

"Nigel, I met with Crepsky and Turner this morning. We got the account."

"That's great."

"That's crap," Mr. Wamsley said, pointing to one of the drawings.

"Nick was just helping me with that," Nigel explained. I detected a hint of terror in his voice, and wondered if he was about to pin the blame on me. But he didn't. He told Mr. Wamsley my ideas and how they could be incorporated to enhance the client's overall vision. "He's right, earthen tones will work a lot better in the grand scheme of things."

"Fine. But make sure you have some marble in there," Mr. Wamsley advised. "Nothing says Greece like marble. Nick? Terry needs your assistance."

Terry's unofficial title was Fabric Bitch. Her office looked like a fabric outlet. There were yards of prints in rolls leaning against the walls. Swatches littered every surface in the room. Two chairs stood in the center of the chaos, half covered in a red-and-gold-patterned silk.

"I need you to hold. I'll staple," she said. Somehow she managed to speak while gripping several pins between her lips. I made a mental note to dress as Terry for Halloween.

A girl my age walked in and dropped three bags on the floor. She crossed something off a list and said, "Your organza, Madame."

"Thank you, Susan," Terry said. Three pins flew across the room. She said to me, "Susan's our buyer."

"Hi," I said. I jumped as a staple missed my pinky by a millimeter.

"Hey," Susan replied. "Want to go buy a piano?"

"Uh, now?"

"He's helping me," Terry said.

"I'm not blind," Susan stated. Terry shook her head and muttered something unintelligible through the pins. "I'm supposed to meet some friends in an hour. We're going to a concert, and I'm worried I'll be late if—"

"You can't make Nick pick up your slack," Terry admonished. "Just because you suck at budgeting your time—"

"Who asked you, Terry?"

"Or, maybe you were shopping for yourself again, instead of—"

"I don't mind. Really," I insisted. "I've never bought a piano before. Could be fun."

"You're not authorized to use the company cards," Terry said. "Put your finger here. Don't move, while I get the glue gun."

"She's right," Susan said and sighed. "Oh well. Thanks for offering. Stupid piano."

"That girl thinks time stands still for her," Terry said, once Susan had left the room. "Wait until she's my age. She'll see that it all zips right by you. Time waits for no—hey!"

I laughed as she chased Ottoman, who'd grabbed a yard of organza and run from the room.

I didn't mind getting up early every morning to go to work. The job was a little like I Dream of Cleanie, in that I got to go inside people's residences as well as businesses. But the stays were of shorter duration, and it was a lot more fun to deliver a piece of furniture, or hang a painting, or even drop off boxes of tile, than to clean someone's toilet.

As long as I got enough sleep, I found that I was actually cheerful in the mornings. It was fun to see what Eileen was up to at her desk, dodge her offers of food, and be greeted by the poodles. I continued to enjoy getting to know my coworkers. And Isaiah was an interesting, if hazardous, pilot, who apparently not only woke up happy, but stayed that way no matter what the day dealt us.

However, even with my new schedule, I planned to sleep late on Saturday morning, my first work-free day. Apparently, Morgan had other ideas. I opened one eye to see the sheet pulled back, allowing me a clear view of the living room. Morgan was poised at the stereo, watching me, and as soon as she saw eyeballs, she began noisily opening and shutting empty CD jewel cases.

"Look," she said. "Not here. And nothing here. Wow. Nada. And yet another empty case. Where are my CDs?" When I just stared at her, trying to remember how to speak, she went on. "I know how this works. I've been taken before. First you use my TV, my DVD player, my stereo. Then you eat my food. Then you lose my CDs and my books. Next you'll be wearing my clothes."

"Well, no," I croaked.

"It's not going to happen this time, you understand?" She jabbed her finger in my direction. "These CDs better be back in their cases when I get home tonight."

She swooped out of the room, and I heard the apartment door slam shut. That was usually the moment when Kendra came out of hiding and Roberto emerged from the bathroom. But I seemed to have the place to myself. Rare. I let out a sigh that I felt I'd been holding for weeks.

I'd hoped that having a job would get Morgan off my back. Of course, it would take a while for me to get my cash flow adjusted. Especially since more cash had flown from me to Kendra than I liked to think about. But I hadn't told Morgan or Roberto that. As far as they knew, everything was fine.

The sound of a key in the lock alerted me that someone was home. I was betting on Kendra and jumped up to put on clothes. She had an annoying habit of crawling on the futon, forcing me to stay under the covers or flash her.

I was pleasantly surprised when Roberto rounded the sheet into our room.

"Yo!" He jumped back a little. "Make some noise next time, will ya? I just about took you out." He peered at me. "What's wrong with you?"

"What makes you think something's wrong?"

He looked at me like I'd just asked if he knew the alphabet. "Don't waste our time with guessing games. You need to jump in the shower. We got stuff to do."

"I was gonna hang out here today."

"You've already been hanging out here."

"I just woke—"

"Time to take the act on the road. It's a great day outside. I won't even make you take a subway."

"I hate it when people who wake up earlier than everybody else think it's their business to get the world moving," I said.

"Squeaky clean boys get a cup of hot tea," Roberto promised.

"Yeah, whatever."

From the patch of blue I could see through our window, it did seem like a nice spring day. But after I showered and drank my tea, I grabbed a sweatshirt just in case. I had no idea where we were going or for how long.

"Hey," I said when we were on the street, "we have to stop by my bank. As long as I have to be out at this ridiculous hour, I have junk I can take care of, too."

"It's almost eleven."

"I didn't fall asleep until after four. I'm tired."

"It's all about you," Roberto said.

"Don't you forget it." Roberto stuck out his arm for a passing cab.

"What are you doing? Where are we going? I can't be throwing a bunch of money around for a cab."

"I'm paying."

He gave the driver a Lower Manhattan address and ignored my frown. We rode in silence. Occasionally, I saw a branch of my bank come and go past my window, each time thinking, *Oh, we have to stop there. . . .*

When the cab dropped us, we walked for a while down Lafayette Street until Roberto paused in front of a building.

"What?" I asked.

"You wanted to come here."

I glared at him. "To SoHo?"

"No, to the bank. Right? Citibank? Isn't that you?"

"Oh." I felt my face turn red. "Yeah. Give me a minute, will you?"

I went inside and looked at the unfamiliar lobby. After wandering around a few minutes, I found a customer service telephone. I took out my wallet, found the Visa card that I had in case of emergency, and looked at it.

Emergency. It was a word that could mean different things. Some people would call not having any cash at their immediate disposal an emergency. Others would say it was an emergency to need a pair of Prada shoes. It was all relative.

And relatives were on my mind as I followed the directions on the Bat Phone. I'd never actually used the card, knowing my parents would be the ones paying the bill. No emergency was worth having to explain myself to them.

But thanks to Kendra . . .

The computerized voice told me that I had fifteen hundred dollars available. I felt light-headed. Then I got in line behind other customers. Unfortunately, the line moved slowly, allowing time for an internal debate to kick in.

Was I really about to rip off my parents for fifteen hundred dollars? Of course not. I wouldn't max out the card. That would be stupid. I'd only withdraw what I could afford to pay back.

Like five hundred. Five hundred dollars was nothing to my parents. And I *would* pay it back. I'd even call my mother and let her know the bill was coming, so she could prepare my father. Everything would be out in the open.

"May I help you?"

"Yes," I answered, fumbling for the card that I'd held only minutes before. I found it sandwiched in my wallet between my Social Security card and my Wisconsin driver's license. I pulled it out and placed it on the counter.

"I need a cash advance on this, please. Five hundred dollars."

The teller looked at the card, then back up at me. She picked up the card and examined it. "Unless you're a lot older than you look, honey, you can't collect on this one for quite some time. If ever." She handed my Social Security card to me.

"Oh, sorry." I went back into my wallet, producing the Visa card. "This should work better."

"How much did you say you wanted?"

I hesitated. Odds were this would be a one-shot deal. My father might hit the roof. Maybe I should ask for a thousand. Or blow the whole wad. Screw 'em.

"Five hundred, please."

The teller's pen flew over her paperwork with the efficiency of a machine, and she turned the slip around for me. "Sign here, Mr. Dunhill."

It gave me a creepy feeling to be addressed like I was my father. I signed my name, then stuffed the hundreds and twenties the teller counted out in my pocket.

Roberto was leaning against the building with his arms folded. "Are you okay? I was about to go in and see if you were holding up the place."

"Yeah, yeah, c'mon. Let's go take care of what you wanted to do. Then we can get something to eat. My treat this time."

"You so robbed that place. I know you're broke."

"Don't sweat it. Just let me do this, okay?"

"Fine."

We continued to walk up Lafayette Street toward Houston in silence, until Roberto stopped and said, "This is it."

I stared at the window of the Pop Shop and said, "This is why you dragged me out of bed? You're kidding, right?"

"I need a Radiant Baby T-shirt. My old one has paint all over it, and I want one for a date."

He danced in place for a few steps before entering the store. I wasn't sure what that was about. Maybe he was boxing the ghost of Keith Haring. I shook my head and followed him inside.

I'd always liked the shop. Every time I came in, I saw something I hadn't noticed before. Or I got lost in the floor-to-ceiling murals. I loved the paintings of Keith Haring the way Roberto loved Basquiat. But as far as I knew, there was no Basquiat shop.

"Hey, how you doing?" A man appeared next to me with a box of merchandise to put on shelves: mugs, buttons, notebooks. He looked about my age, with dark hair, very carefully messed up. He had a couple tattoos on his forearms and a ring through his eyebrow. His eyes were the same bright blue as mine, and I couldn't stop peering into them, almost squinting. He smiled. "You looking for anything special?"

"I'm here with him." I gestured in the direction where I'd last seen Roberto, who had of course moved on. It wasn't like me to be such a geek in reaction to an appealing face. I shrugged and said, "I'm just looking."

"You ready, Nick?" Roberto asked.

I looked at Eyebrow Boy. "Thanks."

"No problem. See you next time." He flashed another smile.

When we were outside the store, Roberto said, "Were you cruising him? Do you want to go back?"

I regarded him warily. "If anything, he was cruising me."

"Oh, I see."

"I wasn't cruising him. He totally wasn't my type."

"Okay, that does it. We're going back." Roberto turned and started toward the Pop Shop.

I lunged, grabbed his arm, and spun him around. He was laughing.

"Damn," I said. "I can't take you anywhere."

"Were you taking me somewhere? I got us here."

"Yeah, well," I said, "I'm feeding us."

We walked for a while, watching for possible places to eat. I started to point out a diner to Roberto when I realized he was no longer next to me. I turned around and saw him looking in a shop window. Instead of going back, I waited. After a few seconds, he approached me.

"Here's one for you," he said. "What do Basquiat, Keith Haring, and Roberto Mirones have in common?"

"You're all amazing artists who started on the streets?"

"I cannot deny what is, but that's not what I was thinking."

"What were you thinking?"

"AIDS will kill us all."

He made it a simple statement of fact, but I felt like he'd knocked the wind out of me. I thought of Morgan and Kendra gossiping about him. I remembered Mark telling me that he was Roberto's friend, not his doctor. And Davii saying that I enjoyed being tragic.

No, fuck no, I do not, I thought.

I stared at Roberto, keeping my eyes locked on his rather than checking his appearance for evidence. I wanted him to take it back. I wanted to yell at him. I wanted to sit on the sidewalk and bawl like a lost child.

"Nothing good ever happens below Houston Street," I said and turned to keep walking.

He grabbed me from behind, his arm tight across my chest, and pulled me back against him. Like a lover. Or a mugger. Which was probably the thought of the woman who'd been walking toward us. She stopped and frowned at Roberto.

"Don't you hurt him," she said.

"I'd cut out my own heart first," he promised her.

It made me smile. Even though it was probably the smallest smile in New York, it reassured her. She nodded and walked on, but Roberto wouldn't let me move. His mouth was against my ear, and he made a fist of the hand that was over my heart.

"I told you this," he said in a tone so low that I had to strain to hear him, "because you're the only one of my family that's strong enough, that I trust enough, to tell. JC doesn't believe in AIDS. Leo thinks it's a government plot to kill the gays and anybody not white. Ernie and Santo—they look up to me."

"*I* look up to you," I said.

"*Hermano*, it may kill me, but I never said I'd die young. I'll die when I'm seventy-two. Then Leo can say, 'See? The AIDS killed him. I told you they were out to get us.' " I laughed, because he wanted me to. He pushed his chest harder against me and said, "I've got your back. Always."

"Me, too," I said.

"I know."

He let me go. I turned around, looked him in the eye, and repeated, "Always."

For just a moment, he allowed his brown eyes to get soft. "No questions?" he asked, his tone a little surprised.

"No," I said. "None of that matters."

We were at a place on Spring Street with a board out front that advertised pizza by the slice. I had no appetite. But many months before, Roberto had taught me something.

Just pretend like everything's normal. Do the same things you do every day, like it's any day. Soon it will be normal again, and you'll be okay.

Eating was normal. Anyone could eat pizza, no matter what time of day or night. Pizza was always right. We'd eat it, everything would seem normal again, and we'd be okay.

"Here?" I asked.

"You read my mind," Roberto said. "Pizza is always right."

May 14, 2003

Dear Nick,

I could barely read your letter about being fired from your cleaning job because I was laughing so hard. I'm sure it all seemed horrible at the time, but it's good that you have a sense of humor about it now. I imagine that's because you got another job that you like better. It's funny how things work out, isn't it?

We did have a great time on our trip, thanks for asking. I'm enclosing photos of the two of us looking like typical sunburned, stupid tourists on the beach. Adam wanted me to point out that it's only the camera angle that makes my biceps look bigger than his. Always competing.

One thing Adam and I agree on. If you need anything, just ask. I know you aren't crazy about flying, and Adam's the same way. We'd drive to Manhattan to get you if you wanted to visit Wisconsin. Otherwise, I'm not sure when we'll be back in the city, but I'll definitely call you when that happens. You know my mother won't let me stay away from Brooklyn forever.

Take care of yourself and call any time. Collect if you need to. And nothing you say ever goes past me, as usual.

I love you,
Jeremy

8

Bet She's Not Your Girlfriend

My friend Adalla and I "met cute." If we'd been in a romantic comedy, the audience would have known immediately that we were destined to fall in love and get a happy ending. It was a movie-perfect afternoon. A brief cloudburst, which would have made the day sopping in winter or steamy in summer, left everything feeling refreshed in May. Leaves were green. Flowers were blooming. An upbeat soundtrack played through my mind.

Or maybe that was the salsa music on the supermarket's sound system. I was trying to pick a checkout lane by mentally reviewing Nick's Rules for Fast Shopping. These were roughly similar to Nick's Rules for Picking Up Men While Shopping, but I was after only groceries on this particular day.

Rule One was, *Never get behind elderly ladies.* Despite a few unhappy times with my Dunhill grandparents, I didn't dislike old people. But old ladies tended to trap cashiers, unwary bystanders, and managers in pointless—and endless—conversations. Avoiding them was the best option whether I was picking up guys or soy milk.

Rule Two also applied to both situations: *Stay away from people on cell phones.* Most cell phone users couldn't do two things at once. Since the phone was their first priority, they did anything else in slow motion. In fact, Roberto had stayed on the sidewalk while I shopped so he could continue one of his many phone conversations with a random Mirones brother without annoying me.

Rule Three was, *Avoid the coupon bearers.* There was nothing they wouldn't do to use a coupon. They'd tear off an expiration date, slip in coupons for items they weren't buying, and thumb through dozens of tattered slips of paper hoping for fifteen cents off Clorox. Occasionally, my mother's distaste for a discount reared its ugly genetic head and made me see anyone with a coupon as a menace.

Rule Four worked no matter where I was or what I was doing: *Avoid lines with any person under four feet tall.* Especially if there was candy in the area. Children and shopping always ended in tears, and I was determined that they wouldn't be my tears.

The best line to be in was all male. Men were practical. Efficient. Miserable in any situation that involved standing in line and spending money that didn't also include placing bets or watching porn. Men weren't interested in having a *shopping experience.* Unless they were also picking up men. Then they might want to get out of the market quickly with me. A win/win situation.

So there I stood, fourth in line, with only men in front of me. No one was using a coupon, talking on a cell phone, or chasing kids away from Mr. Goodbar.

I scanned tabloids and made up translations for their Spanish captions until something made me look behind me. An approaching girl either stepped in something slippery or turned one of her high heels. She was holding a toddler and a huge container of orange juice. Both went flying. I had the presence of mind to ignore the orange juice and grab the kid, who was all big round eyes and big round mouth as I caught her.

Then we were both drenched in a geyser of orange juice as the container burst.

"*Dios mio!*" the girl gasped, reaching for the child with a horrified look. "I'm so sorry!"

"Me, too. This orange juice has added pulp," I said. I held up a palm to ward off Senorita Stiletto before she stepped into the puddle of orange juice. The toddler suddenly realized she was in the arms of a stranger. She let out a piercing wail, and various people came at me like I was snatching her.

Roberto was still on his phone by the time I walked out of the market. I was sort of cleaned up, thanks to a store clerk. I had my single bag of bread and shaving gel, and the little girl was still yelling while Senorita Stiletto continued to apologize as they followed me out.

Roberto raked the two of us with his eyes, snapped his phone shut, and said something that provoked a rapid conversation in Spanish. I understood nothing. Then I heard a word I recognized. I'd once thought the boys on the corner were calling me "American" until Roberto corrected me.

"Don't tell her I'm a fag," I said indignantly.

"He didn't say it the way you think," Senorita Stiletto said, extending a hand past the baby. "I'm Adalla."

"I'm Roberto Mirones. He's Nick Dunhill. *Mijo*, you have pulp in your hair."

We ended up walking her home. I was allowed to carry the child. Roberto carried the replacement orange juice. I gave Adalla a lecture about treacherous shoes and told her to get a baby sling like the one I'd once used to haul my cousin Emily around. Roberto tried to get her phone number. Adalla spent most of the walk laughing at the two of us.

She had big white teeth in a great smile that made her look prettier than she was. Her eyes were a little close-set and her ears stuck out, but for some reason, I found everything about her adorable. She was one of those people I immediately liked and felt comfortable with.

She said she was twenty-three, and Isleta, her daughter, was eighteen months old. Adalla had a short, slightly plump body, but she made the best of it. Although Roberto had turned on the Mirones charm, I was the one she watched. I wasn't sure why, since Roberto had so quickly labeled me *maricon* so she wouldn't think I was boyfriend material.

The building on Lexington where she lived was ugly. Only four stories, it was dwarfed by the surrounding buildings. But the three people we met at different times on the stairs all smiled and spoke. It seemed everyone knew Adalla and Isleta.

They lived with Adalla's mother, who wasn't home, although her presence pervaded the apartment. At least I hoped it was the mother who was responsible for every surface and corner being crammed with plaster saints, candles, and rosaries. Seeing Mary—whose woeful expression made her look like she could use a dose of Wellbutrin—wherever I turned made me feel guilty, and I wasn't even Catholic. Roberto, too, had the look of a man whose collar was too tight, and he was wearing a muscle shirt.

Not long after we got there, he seemed to decide that Adalla wasn't going to succumb to his charms, so he made an excuse and left. I was content to stay put, with Isleta on my lap and a bottle of water at hand.

"You crushed him," I said.

"What are you talking about?"

"He was flirting with you."

"He's Latino, I'm a female. It's expected. But I'm years older than he is, and I have a child. He's not interested in me. He only stuck around long enough to make sure you'd be okay with me."

"What are *you* talking about?"

She shook her head and said, "You don't speak any Spanish?"

"I have no aptitude for other languages," I said. "I even have that in writing from my sixth grade teacher. I understood enough to know he called me a fag."

"No, he didn't. He told me if *I* was the kind of person who'd call you a fag, I needed to high-heel myself away from you. He's protective of you."

"Oh. Anyway, you shouldn't be wearing high heels."

I found out a lot of things about Adalla that day. Her mother had come to the States in the 1960s, and later became a citizen. Adalla was born in Texas and grew up in Corpus Christi. She was finishing her courses at a community college when she met Isleta's father, who was Cuban. When she got pregnant, he split. She thought he might have had a wife in Sarasota, where he was from.

Adalla and her mother moved to New York when her uncle Jorge, who owned a cleaning service, offered them jobs. His company only cleaned offices, so Adalla had never heard of I Dream of Cleanie. Her mother helped supervise a crew that cleaned a tower on 125th, and Adalla worked in Uncle Jorge's accounting department.

Even though she talked a lot about herself, Adalla's eyes, when she wasn't watching Isleta, seemed to be assessing me. Finally she said, "Have you ever been with a girl?"

"Have *you*?" I countered.

She laughed and said, "I like you, Nick Dunhill."

The feeling was mutual. Once she had my cell number, Adalla called me at odd times. Since she was new to the city, she surfed the Web at her office, looking up interesting factoids to share with me. If she called while I was out with Isaiah, I'd put my cell phone on speaker. That way he could hear her, too, as he rocketed the Wamsley & Wilkes van through the streets.

"Did you know the guy who designed the Statue of Liberty used his mistress and his mother as models?" she'd ask, and "Twisted," Isaiah would answer. Or, "The Harlem Globetrotters originated in Chicago!" was delivered in an indignant tone, and I answered, "Posers."

I spent my free time with her and Isleta. Since I was less stressed about money, I splurged on a baby sling and gave it to her. She wouldn't stop wearing impractical shoes, so I took charge of Isleta whenever we went places. The weather was great, and we did things outside that didn't cost money. Watched street performers. Went to free concerts. Explored Harlem together, something I could never do with Kendra. We passed hours people-watching in various parks and talking about nothing in particular.

Adalla's mother, Inez, was usually at home when I went by for Adalla and Isleta. Inez rarely spoke and seemed to regard me with suspicion.

"Why does she hate me?" I asked Adalla. "It's because I'm gay, isn't it?"

"She doesn't hate you. She's afraid you're my boyfriend."

"Would that be bad? Is it because I'm white?"

"No. It's because you're gay."

"But you just said—"

"She doesn't care if you're gay as long as you're not my boy-friend."

I was waiting for Adalla to get ready one Sunday—she tended to go overboard with her hair and makeup—when Inez came home from Mass to find me feeding Isleta sections of a pear.

"How come you're so good with kids?" Inez asked. "You got brothers and sisters?"

"Two brothers. But we're about the same age. I used to spend a lot of time with my cousin Emily. She's a year older than Isleta."

Adalla must have overheard our conversation. I was almost asleep later, stretched out on a blanket in Ralph Bunche Park, when she said, "Where does your cousin live?"

"You mean my uncle?" I asked. "Blaine?"

"I don't know. Is Blaine Emily's father?"

"Yes. They both live in the city. Midtown. Hell's Kitchen, to be exact. But in different apartments."

"Blaine's divorced?"

"No. I mean, yes. But not from Emily's mother. It's confusing."

"I know I'm not a gofer for some hotshot design firm, but if you speak very slowly, maybe I can follow."

"Shut up," I said, sitting up and yawning. "I was half asleep."

"Now that you're awake, tell me about your uncle's complicated life."

"He got married in college. Then they got divorced when Blaine figured out he's gay."

That prompted a flurry of questions about gay men and their sexuality, as I knew it would. I answered as best I could.

"It's not easy being the ambassador for gaydom, even in the shadow of the United Nations," I finally said. "I'm not the one who slept with women and got married. Do you want to interview Blaine?" She smacked my leg. "He moved to New York, met Daniel, they fell in love, and now they live together. Daniel's sister, Gwendy, is a lesbian. Don't start hounding me with questions about that, because I've never been a lesbian, either. Gwendy's partner, Gretchen, wanted a baby. Blaine agreed to be the sperm donor. Emily was born in December of 2000. She lives in the same building as Blaine, but not with him."

"I can't believe I comprehended all that," Adalla teased.

"It's actually a lot more complicated and involved. It could fill entire books. I gave you the condensed version."

Adalla looked thoughtful for a few minutes and finally said, "I was brought up to believe family is the most important thing. But I'm not so traditional, either. A single mother who's never been married. I want Isleta to have male role models, but my brothers live in Texas. I think it's good that Emily's mothers and fathers can live in the same place."

"I'm in the mood for ice cream," I said. "Do you want to go somewhere else? Or should I just grab something from a vendor?"

"A vendor. Can you get me a bottled water?"

"Sure," I said, waving her away when she reached inside the diaper bag for money. "I've got it."

When I came back, I'd barely settled on the blanket when she said, "You should bring your cousin with you when we hang out like this."

"Emily's social calendar is pretty busy," I said vaguely. Adalla gave me a sideways glance, then looked away. She seemed miffed, so I said, "What?"

"Why don't you want your family to meet us? It's because I'm Mexican, isn't it?"

I finished my Dove bar, stared across the grass, and finally said, "I wonder if Isaiah's ever been here. To the Isaiah Wall." Then I looked at her. "I have a hard time being around my family these days, okay? It's not them. It's my problem. I don't want to talk about it. Don't take it personally. I don't want to talk to *anyone* about it."

"I can deal with that," she said. She picked at a speck of dirt on Isleta's shoe with an iridescent fingernail. Isleta offered her stuffed duck to me with a beatific smile. I took it and smiled back at her.

My cell phone rang. Roberto and Fred had just seen *The Matrix: Reloaded.* When they found out where we were, they decided to join us.

"How was the movie?" I asked when they showed up. I tried to ignore the way Fred scrutinized Adalla and Isleta, as if trying to figure out how they fit into my world.

"Sucked," Fred said.

"Didn't suck," Roberto disagreed.

"I'd love me some Keanu Reeves. He's wicked handsome," Adalla said.

The four of us ended up walking to a nearby restaurant that Roberto said had bistro tables on the sidewalk. Fred watched the way I took charge of Isleta and pushed her stroller. "You look like a little family," he said, falling in step next to Roberto behind us.

"*Cállate,*" Roberto said softly.

Fred started talking about why the movie was bad, and I slid my eyes toward Adalla.

She grinned, and in a voice even softer than Roberto's, translated, "It means 'shut up.' See? He always looks after you."

By the time we got our drinks and appetizers, Isleta was asleep in her stroller. I watched an elderly man across the street who was walking two golden retrievers. They made me think of Otto and Tassel. Which made me think of Lucifer and Hugsie. Spending more time around Bailey Wilkes had left me convinced that she was related to Morgan. There was just something about the two of them . . . It was the same with Tony, Chuck, and me; people could tell we were brothers. Much to Chuck's discomfort, they also often asked if we were twins even though we didn't look alike.

"Nick and I were still in school at the time," Roberto said.

I'd zoned out and lost track of the conversation at our table.

"I'd already graduated. We all went to BHSA," Fred said for Adalla's benefit.

"What's that?" she asked.

"Broadway High School for the Arts," I said.

"For performing and visual arts," Fred added. "I was off work that day. I was asleep. I didn't even know anything had happened until my mother called me and told me to turn on the TV."

I realized what they were talking about and looked at Roberto. He was staring down at his iced tea.

"How scary for you guys," Adalla said. She looked at me. "But you probably didn't know either, since you were at school. Or did they close the schools?"

"We knew," Roberto said, drawing her attention back to him. "There were TVs all over our school. Some students couldn't go home. It's not like a public school, where everybody lives in the neighborhood. There were students from the outer boroughs, too. The subways and buses finally started running again in the afternoon, but the bridges were closed until that night. My oldest brother came in with a bunch of other cops from the Bronx to volunteer for rescue and recovery. He told me to stay at Nick's until I could help my mom get home. She was working at the hotel that day."

Adalla looked at me and said, "Where did you live then?"

"Midtown. With Uncle Blaine. Roberto and I went there."

"And our friends Pete and Tyrone," Roberto said. "We watched TV news all afternoon with Daniel and Gavin."

"Gavin?"

"He works for my uncle," I said. I wished we could talk about something else, and I signaled Roberto. He looked uncomfortable, too.

"Was your uncle at work?" Adalla asked me.

"He was out of town on business. He was supposed to fly back from Chicago that afternoon, but of course his flight was canceled." When I stopped talking, Adalla stared at me, expecting more. "The first time he called, they were saying flights would start back on Wednesday. But he didn't want to take a chance. He rented one of the last available cars and got back to Manhattan as soon as he could."

"You must have been worried about him."

"I was okay once he got home," I said.

"Can we not talk about this?" Roberto asked.

"Sure," Adalla said, looking from me to Roberto. Her eyes widened. "But your brother was okay, right? The cop?"

"Yeah," Roberto said. "JC was fine."

"You're not yourself today," Isaiah said.

"I'm not? Who am I?"

"I don't know. Are you feeling okay?"

"You know what? I'm not. I think it's allergies or something. Spring fever."

"You mean hay fever."

"Right. Hay fever."

He picked up the clipboard when a traffic light stopped us. "Two more deliveries—just small pieces—then measuring for some shelves in an apartment near Sutton Place. I can handle that. Why don't I drop you here? Go home, pop a Benadryl, and sleep through your allergy attack."

"As long as you tell Eileen I cut out early. I don't want anybody to think I'm lying about my hours."

"Take off," Isaiah said. "Eileen won't care, as long as the work gets done."

I didn't give him a chance to change his mind. I could make up the time later in the week. As I walked toward Fifth, I noticed a guy in front of me. I was overcome by longing, but not for him. I—

haunter of thrift stores, patron of all that was secondhand and therefore cheap—couldn't stop staring at his Helmut Lang jeans.

I picked up the pace until I was next to him. Then I violated the code of acceptable sidewalk behavior by saying, "Did you buy those jeans downtown?"

He didn't break stride or even blink as he said, "Barneys."

"Thanks," I said and peeled off.

I thought of my uncle when I went inside Barneys. The store was his mecca. Since I was his surrogate son, he'd tried to give it to me, but I'd resisted. Until now. A man on a mission, I found the jeans. Tried them on. Looked at my ass in the mirror and overcame whatever small alarm the price tag caused. I'd finally become my mother's child. I stayed in the grip of Helmut Lang right up until the moment that my emergency credit card didn't work.

"But . . . I mean . . ." I didn't know what to say to the sales associate.

He made it easier by not being an asshole. He just politely asked if I had another card. I stared at my version of the Holy Grail for a moment. Was a pair of jeans really worth emptying my bank account?

"No," I finally said.

His smile was so kind that I had to get out of there fast before I started feeling emotional. Block after block, as I walked up Madison, I had an internal debate with my father. No, the jeans hadn't been an emergency. But what if there *had* been an emergency? What if I'd been bleeding to death from a head wound in the emergency room when I found out the card was no good? Couldn't he have told me I was cut off?

Was I being punished for the five-hundred-dollar cash advance I'd taken? He'd probably gotten the bill for that, hit the roof, and canceled the card. But again, couldn't he have told me? Or at least called and asked why I'd needed money?

I stopped at Marcus Garvey Park, took out my cell phone, and called Eau Claire.

"Let me speak to Dad," I said when Chuck answered.

"He's not here."

"Then Mom."

"They left this morning for Hilton Head."

"Golf?" I asked. "Mom, too?"

"No, him and the dog. That's who 'they' would be, moron—your parents."

That seemed to be all either of us had to say to each other, although we didn't hang up. I listened to him breathe and realized we were synchronized. Had that begun in the womb? How could two people who'd started out together be so different? Or have nothing to say to each other?

"Are you working this summer?" I finally ventured.

"I'm working for Grandpa. Dunhill Electrical now installs home security systems. I help set up the computer stuff. Did you finally get a job?"

"Yeah," I said. "I work for a design firm."

"Like Tommy Hilfiger?"

I couldn't help but smile and said, "Not a designer. A firm that does residential and corporate renovation and decorating."

"So you're an interior decorator? Nothing like being a stereotype."

"I'm a runner. Or just—whatever they need," I said. "The firm contracts most of our interior decorators. The ones in-house are either women or straight men. Sorry to crumble your illusions. Could you tell Dad that I called, and—"

"You could always call his cell phone."

"It's not important," I said.

"Did you move back in with Uncle Blaine?"

"No. I have an apartment in East Harlem," I said. Then an imp took over my mouth in a way that would have had Sister Divine screaming that I was possessed. "Did you want me to give Blaine a message? I'll probably see him soon. Maybe at the *gay pride* parade."

"This is where you hope I get all worked up so you can pick a fight with me," Chuck said. "But I honestly don't give a flying crap. As far as I'm concerned, you can put on a wig and a formal and ride down the street in a convertible. Just thanks for not doing it here."

"You warm my heart," I said, feeling tired. "So listen, I need to—"

"What I'm wondering," Chuck interrupted, "is what you have to be proud about. You dropped out of school. You have a shit job. And you live in Harlem. Isn't that like the *worst* part of New York?"

"I've got another call," I said and snapped the phone shut. Then I flipped it open and dialed Adalla's number.

A few minutes later, I was headed north again after promising to pick up burgers and a movie. A romantic comedy, Adalla had said. Apparently her day hadn't been much better than mine.

June 2, 2003

Nickster,

We love the little illustrated story called "Nick's Day" that you sent to Emily. When we take walks, she points to all the white delivery vans and says it's Cousin Nick! She's learning so many new words and putting sentences together all the time now.

She very much wants to see the blue and red dogs. There's nothing abnormal about that to her, as we often meet a woman in the elevator who has a Maltese with pink highlights. Very chic.

Last night something was on TV with a character named Isaiah. Emily informed me that Isaiah is a "very big man with a very big laugh." Then she yelled "ah ha haaaaaaa" just like I'd read it to her from your story. She likes this laugh a lot. It's very disconcerting to say, "Did you finish going potty?" and hear "Ah ha haaaaaaa" echoing from the bathroom. Thanks for that!

Much love,
Gwendy

9

Only the Wind

After the third time the sales associate at Drayden's asked if she could help me, I realized that I probably looked like the classic shoplifter. Loitering. Picking up stuff I had no interest in buying and quickly scanning the area.

"I'm waiting for someone. He works here," I said.

Roberto chose that moment to show up and say, "Don't let him fool you. Thievery is his superpower."

"Yeah? Yours is mendacity," the woman said as she walked away.

Roberto looked puzzled and said, "Should I be proud or ashamed?"

"Proud," I answered with a little mendacity of my own. "Dinner? Movie? Staten Island?"

"Like I'd get you on a ferry."

"Stranger things—" My cell phone rang, and I frowned at the display. It was a 715 area code, but I didn't recognize the number as belonging to anyone in my family. "Hello?"

"You need new clothes," my mother said.

I looked around with paranoia and said, "Mom? What? What phone are you calling from?"

"This is my new cell number," she said. "It's a long story. At least you finally took my call."

"I wasn't dodging your calls."

"Let's don't argue about that," she said. "I want to see you."

"I can't come home. My job won't—"

"I'm here. In Manhattan."

I gave Roberto a panicked look and he mouthed, "What?"

"She's here," I mouthed back. He looked as surprised as I felt. "Are you at that same hotel? The Park Savoy?"

"I'm at the Four Seasons," she said.

On her other trips to Manhattan, she'd wanted to get in and out as quickly as possible and spend as little money as she could. Now she was staying at some of the priciest real estate in Manhattan, only minutes from where I stood. And her hotel happened to have Roberto's mother on its housekeeping staff. It made me uncomfortable.

"Are you with Dad?" I asked. There was no way my father would spring for the Four Seasons unless he was trying to impress somebody. He'd never do it just for her.

"I'm alone. When can I see you? Have you had dinner?"

"Mom, it's only eight." Then I remembered at home, dinner was never later than six. I hoped she didn't suggest that I join her in ordering from room service. I'd be trapped without distractions or other noise to fill the empty spaces. "I was supposed to have dinner with Roberto tonight."

He began shaking his head violently at me. He'd never ditch *his* mother. I was a shitty son.

"I really want to see you, Nicky."

"Of course you do," I said. "I need to change my plans. Can I call you back at this number?"

"You will call, won't you?"

"Yes." I hung up and looked at Roberto. "She's staying at the Four Seasons. Did she rob a bank?"

"Runs in the family, I guess," Roberto said. "She's spending, bare minimum, six hundred a night. I wouldn't pay that much to see you."

"Go with me."

"Nickito."

"I know, I know. Fuck. Tell me somewhere to meet her. I'm not dressed for the restaurant at the Four Seasons."

"You could get a jacket right here at Drayden's," Roberto said.

"Now you sound like her."

"What's her favorite food?"

"She loves seafood."

"Call her back. Suggest Oceana. Fifty-fourth between Park and Madison. Not our kind of place, but the food's good. Tell her it's safe to walk and you'll meet her there."

After I made the call and snapped my phone shut again, I said, "She seemed surprised that I called her back. I hope she's not going to act wounded all night."

"Come with me to the personal care counter," Roberto said. "We gotta get you flossed."

By the time I walked into Oceana, I was sprayed, spritzed, and sporting a new blazer courtesy of Roberto's Drayden's card. I knew it would be worth paying him back when my mother spotted me, looked me up and down, and smiled.

She'd already been seated. As I crossed the room toward her, I was struck by how attractive she was. She wasn't beautiful. She was too thin and her facial features were too sharp. But she'd always known how to look put together. She'd developed an intense grooming ritual from her work as a consultant for Clinique Cosmetics. From the time I was a kid, she worked at the Eau Claire Drayden's. When Roberto was interviewing with the company, I was able to tell him about it because my mother was a Drayden's junkie.

She stood and hugged me, which wasn't as awkward as I'd feared. For a moment, I knew what it felt like to be Chuck.

"I guess I shouldn't have worried about your clothes," she said. "You look cute."

"Cute?"

"I like the jeans and those shoes with the blazer. It's a good look for you."

"Thanks," I said. She was making me nervous. I glanced around at the crisp white tablecloths, subdued lighting, and sea-themed murals. I didn't think much of the murals, and the décor was what I imagined a cruise ship would be like. Why would people want to eat in a place that made them think of being seasick? "I've never been here. Roberto suggested it."

"I met him once, didn't I?"

"Yes. He's the one who ended up at Drayden's. Actually, we were there tonight when you called." She looked at the blazer and smiled faintly. "Why didn't you tell me you were coming to New York?"

Our waiter arrived to ask what I wanted to drink. I glanced at my mother's cocktail, and she said, "Go ahead, if you want one."

"I hardly ever drink," I said. At least that was the truth. I had an appealing vision of the waiter holding a tray of expertly rolled joints toward me, telling me the merits of each blend. And the day's special, something like Deep Sea Weed or Great Coral Reefer. "I'll just have water, please."

Before he could leave, my mother handed him our menus and said, "Why don't you just choose for us? There's nothing on your menu that doesn't look good to me." She looked at me. "Unless you'd rather—"

"It's fine," I said, my nerves going up another notch. She always pored over menus and gave detailed instructions about how she wanted things. Maybe she'd already had a couple cocktails at the Four Seasons.

After she and the waiter finished talking and he left, she said, "It was an unplanned trip. I'm here on Drayden's business. At their expense, obviously. You don't care about that."

"Tell me," I said. Anything was better than talking about me.

"Several Drayden's locations opened spas in their stores this year. Manhattan Drayden's has the flagship spa. I came to organize training classes for our midwestern managers."

"Are they Clinique spas?" I asked.

"I'm not a Clinique consultant anymore. I'm overseeing Drayden's spas at eight different stores."

"That's a big promotion, right?" I asked. She nodded. "That's great. Good for you."

"Thanks." She talked for a few minutes about her new position. Our salads came. I started to relax. Then she said, "About the clothes comment I made on the phone. I'd just—I heard some news that upset me, and I was being silly. I'm sorry."

The assault on my nerves moved to my stomach, and I said, "What's wrong?"

"Do you remember Maddie Monroe?"

"Uh-huh," I said. Maddie had dated my brother Tony in high school.

"She's on a scholarship at Wellesley. She'll be a senior next year. She just came home for the summer, and she's changed. She's really weird. She's goth or emo or whatever it's called these days. She wears those black outfits and black makeup, like you used to. She buys all her clothes from thrift stores."

"That doesn't make her weird—"

"Yesterday, she emptied her parents' medicine cabinet, went to their cabin on Altoona Lake, and tried to kill herself."

"Is she okay?"

My mother rolled her eyes and said, "I don't think she noticed what the prescriptions were for. High cholesterol. Acid reflux. Diarrhea. Oh, and there was some Viagra. Anyway, she earned herself a date with a stomach pump and a bad summer. But it made me think about all those gloomy clothes you wear and how depressed you were—"

"I'm fine, Mom," I said.

I could have told her that none of the Monroe girls had ever seemed all that sane. Or that some of Maddie's problems started when I, just a week after I got my driver's license, had to drive her to Madison to get an abortion. Tony had already broken up with her by then and wouldn't return her phone calls. In the area of parent-child relations, I still adhered to the us-against-them code, although if our situations were reversed, Tony would have ratted me out. Anyway, Tony and Maddie were ancient history.

I didn't feel like answering a lot of uncomfortable questions, so while we ate, I talked about Wamsley & Wilkes, from the partners to the dogs. I talked about places that Isaiah and I had seen. Clients we'd worked with. I tried to sound as upbeat as possible, all the time wondering what judgments she was making. Our salads were removed and our entrees delivered, but I never took a breath. Her expression was so intense that I knew she was listening for things I wasn't saying.

She suddenly put down her fork as if she'd been using it to hold up the last of her hopes for me. "*Are* you fine, Nicky? Really?"

I took a deep breath. "I know it seems like a crap job. I know it looks bad that I dropped out of school. Moved out of Uncle Blaine's. But I'm doing okay."

"If you need anything—"

"Why does everybody say that?" I asked, sounding more hostile than I'd intended. Her face fell. "I'm sorry. But do you expect me to fail? Do you expect me to end up dead on a park bench with the needle from my last dose of heroin sticking out of my arm?"

"Nobody thinks—"

"I'm not emptying out anybody's medicine cabinet. I've got friends. I'm holding down a job. I'm not starving. If you guys were so concerned about me, why'd you cancel my Visa card?"

She stared at me, and my sick feeling came back. She hadn't known.

"He canceled your credit card?" she asked quietly.

"I don't know. I guess. It doesn't matter."

We'd arrived at a familiar place. I didn't want to cause problems between them. She wouldn't say anything bad about him to me.

Then she abruptly changed the rules and said, "I asked your father for a divorce last month."

Our waiter cleared his throat, his face conveying an apology for showing up at that moment. "Can I bring you anything else?"

"No," my mother said. Our eyes met, and we both smiled as he practically ran from our table.

"Are you getting divorced?" I asked.

"No. I mean . . . He's cut back on his drinking. We're trying to do more things together."

I didn't know what to say. I noticed that along with our waiter, other people—the owners? Managers? I wasn't sure—kept circling our table. Maybe they were afraid we'd make a scene and disturb the other diners. If so, none of them were midwesterners. Midwesterners didn't make scenes. We pushed everything down and smiled and borrowed from our parents' medicine cabinets.

"They're like sharks," my mother murmured.

"It's part of the theme," I said. "Wait'll you see the mermaid show." She smiled. "Is that why you went to Hilton Head? To work things out?"

"How did you know we went to Hilton Head?"

"Chuck told me."

Her face lit up and she said, "You and Chuck have been talking?"

"Not really," I said. "I called home to ask Dad about the credit card and got Chuck. He was an asshole. As usual. He's such a cretin."

Her face got the weary look I hated, and she said, "I don't understand how this happened. How the two of you could go from being best friends as little kids to this."

"We were never best friends," I said. "They always knew there was something different about me. At least Tony did. It was like some British boys' novel you read in high school. Tony moving in, making an alliance with Chuck. Chuck hero-worshipping Tony and always willing to sacrifice me. I know it sounds stupid. It sounded stupid to you back then, too. You thought it was normal little kid stuff. But they fucking terrorized me on purpose, and you and Dad let them." I realized belatedly that I'd just said "fucking" to my mother.

"Do you ever put yourself in Chuck's shoes?" she asked.

I wished the waiter had the balls to come back with our check.

"I understand Chuck," I said.

"Do you remember doing your homework together when you were kids? Everything was easier for you. You caught on fast, and once you'd mastered something, you wanted to move to something else because you were bored. Chuck had to work harder at everything. He'd get so frustrated that you could do things he couldn't. He'd compare himself to you and—"

"Are you joking?" I interrupted. "Chuck was every teacher's pet. He was bright and funny and outgoing. Who didn't love Chuck?"

"It's true that Tony and Chuck never got in trouble at school. They never rebelled against the dress code. They never skipped class, or at least they never got caught. They made good grades. They were good athletes and good sports. They didn't break curfew. They went to church on Sunday. They volunteered to do things with our youth group."

"Yeah, I know, Mom. Like I said, who didn't love Chuck? And Tony. The pride of the Dunhills."

"And you," she went on, as if I hadn't spoken, "how many times did you get sent home from school? Dress code. Smarting off. No hall pass. Cutting class. Writing sarcastic papers and answers on tests. Your grades fluctuated wildly. You stayed locked up in your room all the time. Were grounded every time you pierced an ear, then did it again, just for spite. Didn't want to do anything with the family. If you had to be with us, you made sure we all knew we were imposing on you."

I stared at her. Back to familiar territory.

"What about dessert?" the waiter asked, and we both jumped. He wouldn't look at me.

"No, thanks. We're not done here." She waited until he was out of earshot. "You think I don't understand how miserable you were? I know they picked on you. I know how bad it was, Nicky. That's why I brought you to New York in the first place. But to Chuck, it's as if all your bad behavior was rewarded. You disrupted our home. Kept things in turmoil. Then you got to go away to a private art school and live in New York City with your uncle. There were no athletic or academic scholarships offered to you the way there were to Tony and Chuck. Your father had to pay the full amount of your tuition to Pratt. Buy all your supplies. We sent you money, clothes, whatever you needed. Then, without a word to us, you decided it wasn't for you and dropped out."

"Okay. I know. I suck."

"You don't suck. I told you I understand. I'm an adult. I'm your mother. I love you and want to protect you. I know all that acting out came from your fear and unhappiness. But Chuck was a kid, just like you. How was he supposed to understand?"

"You just don't get it, Mom."

"No, *you* don't get it."

"This is where we always end up. Tony hates me because he's like—" I stopped myself. It was pointless to say that my father hated me. She didn't want to hear it. She'd never agree with it. "Chuck is scared that since I'm gay, he could be, too. He does whatever it takes to distance himself from me. For that matter, who in our family doesn't?"

"Blaine doesn't."

"Of course not. He went down this road before I did."

"All I wanted was for my children to be happy and healthy. Would I rather you weren't gay? I used to feel that way. But the point came when wishing for that was like wishing you away. I can't do that."

"I know I'm a disappointment—"

"*Please* stop putting words in my mouth. What do you want from me? It's as if our family has been hemorrhaging for years. How do I stop the bleeding?"

"Can we please get out of here?"

As soon as she looked around, the waiter rushed up with our check. It was okay, though. It made us smile at each other again, which broke the tension.

Outside Oceana, she paused, and I realized she was disoriented. I took her arm and began walking in the direction of the Four Seasons.

"When do you go back?" I asked.

"I have meetings tomorrow morning and fly out midafternoon. You'll be at work, I suppose."

"Right."

"So I guess we won't see each other again this trip."

"Guess not."

We were quiet until we got to the hotel and she said, "Do you want to come up? See my room?"

"Roberto's mother works here," I said. "I've been all over the hotel with him. Don't tell hotel management that." She smiled again, but she looked sad, too. "I'm sorry about . . . I probably sound like I hate you all, or blame you for my miserable life. But it's not miserable. I'm fine. I didn't want to waste your money on tuition when I'm not sure what I want to do. Working is the best thing for me right now, okay?"

"Whether it's okay or not, you can make your own decisions."

I hugged her again. She felt too thin. We'd always been alike that way. Two people who couldn't eat when they were tense or scared. Maybe sometimes she felt invisible, too.

"So, if I call you, will you answer?" she asked, pulling away to look up at my face.

"Yes." She wouldn't look away. "I promise."

"I'll check on that credit card—"

"Noooo," I said. "I don't need money."

She heard what I hadn't said: *I don't need his money.* But all she said was, "Let me know if you do."

"I will."

I waited until she was inside the hotel; then I walked back to Park Avenue. I looked south for a minute, then glanced toward Lexington. It would make sense to take the 6 home. I'd get there faster.

A crashing noise made my entire body jerk around. Then I saw the offending garbage truck and tried to convince my pounding heart that I was fine. After a minute, I began walking up Park Avenue.

*   *   *

Roberto finagled permission for us to watch the Puerto Rican Day parade from a window at Drayden's. Roberto's sixteen-year-old brother, Ernie, and two of Ernie's friends, along with Adalla, Isleta, and me, tucked ourselves in among the mannequins. I figured the boys would much rather be in the crowd on the street, but I was grateful to be two floors above the madness. Huge gatherings of people seemed like a target to me. I'd skipped parades for the last couple years, though I had to admit it was fun to have a bird's-eye view of the brightly colored floats and cars. Plus I liked watching Adalla get excited about her first New York City parade.

"I don't understand a word they're saying," Adalla whispered to me as Ernie and his friends joked around. "I'm old."

"It's not just you," I assured her. "I've only been out of high school a year, and I've already lost all street cred. I don't know if they even say 'street cred' anymore."

"We never did," Ernie smarted off, but it only made me grin at him. Typical Mirones cockiness.

"See anyone familiar?" Roberto asked as he slipped up behind me.

"You gotta be joking," I said.

He nodded toward the street and said, "Look, a group from the Department of Corrections. You must recognize someone."

"Smartass."

"You're so sensitive," he said, ruffling my hair. Then he looked at Ernie, said something in Spanish, and left.

"What's that green froggy-looking thing on those flags?" I asked Adalla, who was using a cookie to bribe Isleta to sit still.

"It actually is a green froggy thing," she said.

"*Coquí*," Ernie said, forgetting for a moment to pretend he didn't know us. I nudged the pack of cookies toward him. "I said *coquí*, not cookie. That's the sound it makes when it sings."

"What makes?"

"The tree frog."

"What tree frog? What are you talking about?"

"The frog on the flags," he said. His tone showed he was out of patience with me.

"I believe Puerto Rico is the only place you can find the *coquí* frog," Adalla explained, drawing from her wealth of all things trivial. "Maybe that's why some people put it on the flag."

"Oh," I said. I scooted next to Isleta and leaned forward until my forehead touched the glass. For a moment I felt dizzy, even though we were only on the second floor. I reminded myself to breathe the way Gavin had taught me. A mounted policeman looked up at our window. I gave him a halfhearted wave, and he winked at me. Then he lowered his head, and his helmet hid his eyes.

"Doesn't New York have a gay pride parade?" Adalla asked.

"One of the biggest," I said. "Although technically, it's called a march."

"Oh. Is it on Fifth Avenue?"

"Yeah. It starts at Fifth and Fifty-second and eventually ends at Christopher Street. There's also a festival and a dance."

"Do you go?"

"I went in 2001. Not last year," I said.

Adalla was quiet for a while, and I thought she was engrossed by the scene outside, until she said, "When is it? Can anybody go?"

"Three weeks from today. You can go if you take your pink card." I turned to see her frowning at me. "Oh, that's right. You don't have a pink card because you're straight. Maybe you could get together with Kendra and watch it on public access cable or something."

"I'm not watching anything with your freaky roommate," she said.

"You're getting them mixed up," I said. "Kendra's the one we like."

"I'm not getting them mixed up. Kendra's the blond flake. Morgan's all right, though."

"Morgan's the one with the snakes!"

"You sound like those people who say to me, 'You've got a *kid?*' So Morgan keeps strange pets. And she isn't cute and perky like the other one. I like her." She noticed that I was gaping at her. "I do! Kendra is sweet on the surface, but underneath . . ."

"Kendra's nice," I insisted.

"You know what Kendra reminds me of?" she asked, glancing down at the street. "Those people who sit in their big houses with a BMW and an Expedition in the garage. They work at companies like my mama cleans. They bitch all the time about somebody maybe getting something they don't deserve. Immigrants taking jobs. Black mothers getting free milk for their kids. Like anybody's ever taken milk from *their* refrigerators to give to somebody else's kid. They act like any time somebody gets something, it takes something from them."

"You just described my parents," I said. Then I felt guilty. "My grandparents. And my father. Anyway, Kendra works all the time, and she knows what it's like to be broke. She's not like you think."

"Give her a few years. What do you mean, I can't go to the gay pride parade because I'm straight? I'm not Puerto Rican or Irish, either, but—"

"I was kidding," I said. "Of course you can go."

"Are you going?"

"I don't plan to."

"Huh," was all she said.

Over the next few days, I couldn't stop thinking about what Adalla had said. Not her opinion of Kendra, which was irrational and inaccurate. I wondered if there was something wrong with me because I had no interest in the upcoming Pride festivities.

During my first June in New York, Blaine and Daniel were still the darlings of the gay press, even after Daniel lost his job as the bad guy on *Secret Splendor*. They said his exit was "storyline-dictated," but everybody knew it was because he'd come out. He stayed employed long enough to keep his producers from looking like assholes. Then his role got smaller, until finally he was written off the show. Everybody's favorite villain became everyone's favorite victim, and Daniel's schedule was filled with a new round of interviews and appearances, especially during Pride month.

I'd had my own friends to be with and places to go during Pride. I was barely aware of what Daniel and Blaine had going on, either then or the rest of that summer. Then it all became irrelevant in September. I still hadn't felt much like celebrating in June of 2002. Plus I avoided crowds the way I did the subway, skyscrapers, and Lower Manhattan.

I didn't have to explain any of this to Roberto, who wasn't surprised when I told him I'd decided to shun Pride again this year.

"Maybe you could take Adalla if she wants to go," I said.

"Are you trying to hook us up?" Roberto asked.

"No. But she hasn't lived in the city long, and being at a parade with half a million people—"

"Adalla can take care of herself," Roberto said. "I'll see what everybody else is doing. Once I know the plan, I'll invite her. If you change your mind, you can always go with us."

"Not likely," I said.

As far as I was concerned, that was the end of it. Apparently, however, I'd caused a disturbance in the force, as I first realized from Kendra.

"You're not going to Pride? That's awful. It's worse than when I decided not to go to the prom with the Shermans' grandson."

She impatiently twisted her hair into a knot, as if a little air against the back of her neck might blow away a traumatic memory. I still hadn't learned my lesson and waited for the rest of her story. Of course, it never came.

"Plenty of people don't go to Pride," I finally said. "It's hot. It's crowded. You either have to get there hours early for a good spot, or you get stuck watching it with the haters near St. Patrick's."

"What are you talking about?" Morgan asked as she walked in. She did a quick scan of the kitchen. Morgan, like the Terminator, saw the world through infrared sensors that triggered stolen food alarms even when she didn't catch us in the act.

"He says he's not going to Pride," Kendra said.

"No!" Morgan gasped. She was wearing a shapeless black dress with big pockets on the front. She reached into one of these and took out a business card. "This guy writes a column for the *Village Voice*. He'll probably want to interview you."

It was easier to ignore Morgan than my friends. I felt like I was part of an experiment on peer pressure. The more pressure I got, the more I resisted. Only I knew how guilty that made me feel, until I confessed to Isaiah.

We were delivering a ceramic pink flamingo to a town house near Sheridan Square. No one was home, but the owner had left a key with his neighbor. When we went inside, both Isaiah and I recoiled.

"*Dios mio,*" I imitated Adalla and looked around at ten thousand tchotchkes and a wall that was covered by a mural of Barbra Streisand. A rainbow flag fluttered from the ceiling. "So this is where 1970s San Francisco has been hiding."

Isaiah pushed aside strands of beads to glance in the kitchen. He turned around and said, "Trust me, you don't want to look in there. Gently dock the flamingo, then exit the apartment. Make haste, young man."

Once we were back in the van, we burst out laughing, and he said, "I am one proud motherfucker! How 'bout you?"

"Really proud," I said. "Now I can stop feeling guilty about skipping the parade this year."

"It's not mandatory," Isaiah said, flipping off a cab driver who took offense when Isaiah intimidated him into another lane.

"You're the first person who's said that. You're not going either?"

"Are you kidding? I'm marching with the Full Gospel Gay and Lesbian Choir. We're gonna win the award for outstanding musical contingent." He laughed when he glanced over and saw my expression. "Yeah. You may as well turn in your queer credentials now."

"I'm queer. I'm here. Fuck you," I said.

July 4, 2003

Dear Nick,

Today Adam and I are at this huge PFLAG cookout at his parents' house. Every gay, lesbian, and bisexual person his mother knows is here, I think. I'm so disappointed in Aggie Wilson; she wasn't able to find anyone transgendered this year, but she sure tried.

You know how she is. Her theme: No One Is Free Until All Of Us Are Free. And to illustrate, her Weimaraners have been forced into costume: thus the American flag stovepipe hats and rainbow vests they are wearing in the enclosed photos. Usually I'm more than willing to indulge Aggie in her shenanigans. And so are the dogs, if there's food involved. But have you ever seen two dogs look more embarrassed?

Anyway, I made the mistake of telling her that you work with red and blue poodles. She immediately downloaded these photos and made me print them for you. Keep them if you think Sadie and Marnie may run for office in the future and they'll be useful to you. God knows if I were a dog, I'd do anything to conceal these.

And oh yeah—happy Independence Day. Now that we're halfway through the year when Nick Dunhill declared his independence, I hope you're celebrating!

Love you,
Jeremy

10

Young Offender

Growing up in Wisconsin had taught me that cream of chicken soup, not variety, was the spice of life. Wamsley & Wilkes taught me that one spice, or one kind of soup, wasn't enough. Because I was always doing something different, I loved my job. There was never a moment to feel bored. There was always something to do, or someone who needed an extra pair of hands on a project. Most importantly, I was always learning something new.

I'd never used a sewing machine in my life, but I quickly learned how to thread a machine and follow patterns. I started to see the beauty in custom draperies, pillows, and upholstery. Terry, the self-proclaimed Fabric Bitch, lauded my newly acquired ability to identify fabric from twenty paces.

I almost couldn't wait to talk to Chuck on the phone again, because Jisella had taught me how to use a band saw. I still had all my fingers, to boot. Chuck had almost failed shop class in high school. So had I, but I decided that the teacher hadn't made class interesting. Working with Jisella had become my favorite activity. If they needed me, everyone knew to find me in her workshop. Anytime there was a lull in my day, I'd walk in and she'd toss me a pair of goggles and say something like, "Okay, kid. Ever made coopered doors? No? Let's get to it." Or, "Okay, kid. Ever milled your own lumber? No? Pass me that six-quarter."

Helping Jisella build custom pieces of furniture for Wamsley &

Wilkes's clients became like assisting a postmodernist sculptor. At first I had trouble reading her blueprints. Every piece she made was carefully planned out to the finest detail. To me, it was like another language. Nothing but lines and numbers on paper. I never liked math. But the more pieces we made, the more the plans made sense. It wasn't long until I felt brave enough to question the plans and wonder aloud if they fit the design scheme.

"I know they asked for a scrolled base for this end table," I said one day, "but wouldn't bracket feet fit the overall scheme better? A parquet top would be really cool, too. Don't you think?" I realized Jisella hadn't answered and turned around to see her staring at me with a glazed look in her eye. "Paging Jisella. Jisella, please return to earth immediately."

She blinked and looked around, as if she'd just woken up and expected to find herself home, in bed. She glanced at the riffler in her hand and looked like she was trying to remember why she'd picked it up, and when.

"Are you okay?" I asked.

"Yeah. Fine. Just tired." She sat on a stool at the workbench and used the riffler to scratch the middle of her back. "Ever get lost in a moment?"

"Huh?"

"Close. But not that kind of lost," she joked. Jisella placed the riffler on the workbench and said, "When you were talking about the table, you sounded just like Lou."

"Who's Lou?"

"He used to work here. With me, here in the workshop. Lou was always challenging other people's ideas. He wasn't afraid to take risks, or of pissing off architects or designers if he thought he could do better. He usually could, too. The man was a genius. He made furniture look like art."

"Why'd he leave?" I asked. "Did he get a better job?"

"He died," Jisella said. "Liver and renal failure and PML."

I didn't know what to say, so I said nothing but "Oh."

Jisella spelled it out for me. "He had AIDS."

"But—"

I felt stupid as soon as I said the word, and stopped talking. I felt even more stupid when Jisella seemed to know what I was thinking and said, "The inhibitors don't work for everyone. Lou had strong reactions to them. He had all the side effects. It was awful."

I thought of Roberto. Ever since he'd told me that he was positive, I was hyperaware of how I acted around him. I didn't want to treat him differently. I didn't want it to matter that he was positive. But if I was in our room when he took his meds, the sound of pills rattling in bottles would seem amplified a thousand times. I'd catch myself staring at him and wondering what life would be like without him. If he sneezed, I almost expected his head to explode. Worse, if I sneezed, I felt like I should check in to the nearest hotel.

"I'm so ignorant," I complained.

"I find that hard to believe," Jisella said.

"It's not that I think I'm invincible, like most people assume my generation thinks. I practice safe sex, but mostly because it's like . . ." I struggled to find the right words. "Sort of like following a set of instructions."

"Step one. Arouse partner," Jisella said and laughed.

"Step two. Magically produce condom at the right moment," I added. "It's weird how safe sex is ingrained in my mind, but I really haven't thought about what HIV is, or what it does to a person. That's the best way I can explain it."

"Do you think about cleaning products on a daily basis, and what effect they have on the environment?" Jisella asked.

"No."

"How about breathing? Do you dwell on carbon dioxide and how plants need it to live?"

"No."

"You're not a bad person, Nick," she stated.

After a moment of silence, I said, "I'm sorry about Lou."

"Me, too," Jisella quietly said. Then she stood up and said in her normal booming voice, "Ever hand tooled a table leg? No? Let's get to it."

My review after three months of employment lasted fifteen minutes. Bailey and I sat in matching Parisian Deco leather chairs and sipped cappuccino in her office. She tossed my file onto a nearby oak Parsons table and said, "There's nothing for me to say, really. Everybody here raves about you constantly. Cinnamon?"

"No, thanks," I said. I really didn't like cappuccino. I only accepted it because I wanted to seem gracious.

"You work hard. You're polite. You help everyone," she said. "I assume you want to keep working here."

"Of course," I said. I replied quickly, as though she'd suddenly scream, *Too bad, sucka!* if I paused too long.

"Good. Isaiah threatened to quit if you left us."

"Isaiah rules," I said.

"Yes, he does," Bailey agreed. "Your salary increase will be reflected on your next paycheck. Your benefits kick in now. Be sure to get all the information from Eileen about the HMO. I don't understand a word of it, but she can tell you everything you need to know. Is there anything else?"

I thought she might be talking to herself, so I waited and thought about how nice it would be to buy actual Cheerios, instead of the generic brand. When she cocked her head slightly and raised her right eyebrow, I said, "I can't think of anything. Do I need to speak with Mr. Wamsley?"

"I don't know. Do you?"

Her answer was obviously meant to be humorous. But I couldn't help but grimace, because her choice of words was eerie. Just that morning I'd asked Morgan if I should replace the sheets hanging in the doorway of my bedroom with something nicer. Now that I had a steady income and a job that was all about fine furnishings, I kind of wanted to bring my work home with me. I couldn't imagine anyone from Wamsley & Wilkes seeing the rat hole we called an apartment. Morgan hadn't even looked up from her Alpha-Bits when she blandly said, "I don't know. Should you?"

As I had for months, I squinted hard and tried to blur Bailey's edges and see Morgan somewhere in her features. The nose was all wrong. But her mouth, even without the blackberry lipstick, was close. I couldn't tell if they were the same height, because Bailey always wore high heels. But even if they seemed dissimilar, I still got a feeling about them. I was reminded of something Jisella had said: Even though two mass-produced end tables seemed the same, they were always different. Even if it was the direction of the wood's grain. Or sometimes, a millimeter of difference in height could make a piece feel different.

"Do you have a sister?" I suddenly asked.

Bailey's nose wrinkled and she set her cappuccino on the Parsons table, a foot away from a waiting coaster. "Why would you ask me that?"

"Just curious, I guess." I tried to sound casual, even though I was suddenly worried about getting fired. "I have two brothers. They live in Wisconsin."

"That's nice," she said. The way she said it told me she didn't care. "Nick, I'm sorry, but I only talk about work at the workplace. I find it cuts down on the sexual harassment claims. Okay?"

Just a few days before, we'd had a long conversation that went from Broadway musicals, to Jekyll and Hyde, and then to her secret crush on Sebastian Bach. None of which had anything to do with work.

"Yeah, whatever," I said. "Sorry."

There was a tapping on her door. Eileen stuck her head in and said, "I hate to interrupt, but Sheila Meyers is here."

"It's okay. I think we're done. But you could've called," Bailey said. "I'll be right out."

"She's not here to see you. She's asking for Nick."

Both women stared at me with curious expressions, as if the reason why a famous model would visit me at work might be stitched on my shirt or tattooed on my arm. Eileen was smiling, as if she'd known from the moment we met that I'd be full of surprises, like a spunky child in a Disney movie.

Bailey's expression, on the other hand, didn't need interpreting, because she said, "How do you know Sheila Meyers? Why are we just finding this out now? Who else do you know? But more importantly, how do you know Sheila Meyers?"

"You already asked that," I said.

"You haven't answered me."

I decided to take a risk. "She's a friend. It didn't seem appropriate to bring her up in workplace conversation."

Bailey smirked and said, "Good one."

I found Sheila caressing the leather armrest of a wing chair in the waiting area. A Yankees cap covered her blond hair. She wore white shorts and a tank top emblazoned with a crown, obviously the insignia of a designer I knew nothing about. Her sneakers were gleaming white, as if they barely ever touched the ground. I stared at her white purse and wondered if Jisella would go for the idea of an alligator ottoman.

"Like that?" I asked. Sheila started and her sunglasses fell from the tip of her nose, bounced off the chair's seat, and fell under an Art Nuevo end table. I found them for her and said, "Sorry."

"I'm such a klutz," she said. She banished them to her purse and then looked at me as if we were starting over. "Hi! You're so thin. Are you eating?" Before I could answer, she hugged me. Over her shoulder I could see Eileen and Bailey staring at us from halfway down the hall. Sheila released me and said, "I'm mad at you."

"Why?"

"Because I haven't seen you since—"

"I know," I interrupted.

"It's been a long time," she said. "I know I've been busy. But you know that I'll always make time for you."

Sheila took my hand, as if sealing a deal. Jisella walked by, saw us holding hands, and grinned wickedly. She mouthed the words "hot stuff" at me, behind Sheila's back, then gave me the thumbs-up and walked on.

"I know you would," I said to Sheila.

"And you've moved. You haven't invited me to your new place. Or any of us, for that matter."

"I wouldn't. The place is disgusting. Trust me, you don't—" I stopped talking when I noticed Terry and Susan standing near the elevator and holding a yard of printed silk charmeuse between them. They were having a very quiet and overly animated discussion, like extras in a soap opera. I turned my attention back to Sheila and said, "You don't want to see my apartment."

"I do. By not inviting me, you're denying me my right to bring you a casserole," Sheila joked.

"Trying to feed me? Out of everyone, I never expected you to jump on the bodyweight bandwagon."

Sheila cringed and said, "Ugh. I did that earlier, didn't I? I didn't even realize it. Sorry."

As I waved away her apology, Tassel trotted up to Sheila, sniffed her sneaker, and sneezed. He pulled on her shoelace until it was untied, barked once, then left the waiting area. Sheila propped her foot on the wing chair so she could retie her laces and said, "Cute dog."

"He had an appointment to get to," I explained. "There's another one around here somewhere, in blue."

"Speaking of appointments," Sheila began, "what does a girl have to do around here to get one?"

"You need a designer?" I asked. Nigel, who'd stopped walking by long enough to stare at Sheila's ass while she tied her shoes, suddenly looked up with a hopeful expression. "One of my bosses, Bailey Wilkes, was very excited when she heard that I know you. I'm sure she'd love to work with you. She does amazing work." Out of the corner of my eye, I could see Nigel frown. "If she's not available there's this other guy, Nigel. He's pretty good."

"Whoever," Sheila said.

Nigel took that as his cue, cleared his throat, and introduced himself. While they talked, Eileen returned to her desk. Five seconds later, Bailey walked up to her with some files. She frowned at Terry and Susan, who both looked embarrassed as they folded the charmeuse and slunk to their offices. I worried that I was about to be lectured for talking to friends on company time, but Sheila's hand landed on my shoulder and I heard her say, "That sounds great, Nigel. I really appreciate your doing this on such short notice. Can Nick come with us?"

"It's up to him," Nigel answered. To me he said, "I could use you. Taking Polaroids and cataloging items, that sort of thing. That is, if you're not helping anyone else right now."

I glanced at Bailey. Her wide-eyed expression and frantic nodding prompted me to say, "Sure. Let's go."

Ten minutes later we were in the air-conditioned comfort of a black car that was on loan to Sheila. I was surprised when she gave the driver an address on Central Park West. She noticed my puzzled stare and said, "I'm moving."

I thought of the town house apartment she and her husband, Josh Clinton, rented. It was a cozy duplex on the ground floor with a small garden behind it. "Are you outgrowing your apartment?"

"I thought we weren't commenting on each other's bodies," Sheila said. Before I could say anything, she added, "My career is outgrowing the old place. Everyone is telling me I need to be in a building with security."

"The San Remo is supposed be like a fortress," Nigel said.

"That's what I hear," Sheila said.

I always confused the San Remo Building with the El Dorado, so I didn't say anything. I couldn't hear an address and automatically know which building it was. I felt out of my league.

I felt out of my body while we were in the elevator, until we exited and followed Sheila as she led us to her new apartment. She fumbled with the obligatory key ring of a true New Yorker. It looked like one of those key rings jailers in cartoons always seemed to have, comically crammed with hundreds of keys. She figured out which ones worked the locks and opened the door. I prepared myself for the mandatory celebrity apartment: one worthy of a very special episode of *MTV Cribs*.

Instead, we walked into an apartment that almost resembled a typical college dormitory. Each room deserved the suffix "ette" attached to it. A small kitchenette adjoined a living roomette. There was no dining area, so I tried to imagine Sheila and Josh eating on TV trays. The bathroom was the size of a Honda Accord. Surprisingly, there were two bedrooms.

Sheila and Nigel were talking about the apartment in admiring tones. They praised the light, the neighborhood, and the view of the park, all without taking more than ten steps. Their voices echoed in the empty space. I felt like we were in a recording studio instead of an apartment, and wondered if carpeting the walls would make the place look bigger.

"Why?" I suddenly asked without meaning to.

"What?" Sheila asked. Behind her, Nigel's eyes grew wide.

"I mean," I began, "for some reason I thought this place would be bigger."

"I'm not a girl who worries about size," Sheila quipped. Nigel laughed. I rolled my eyes. She looked around the room and absently said, "I know it's not much, but it's all we need. Besides, we got a good deal." She laughed and added, "I remember when I first moved here. I lived with Blaine in this dump of an apartment. It was probably no bigger than this place."

"I know," I said. "I lived there. I slept on the couch, because Gavin had your old room."

"Oh," Sheila said. "That's right."

There was a short silence, which Nigel killed by asking if we could see her current apartment. Sheila sent the car and driver away, saying she'd rather walk the short distance to the town house. Her newfound need for security seemed unfounded, because the people we passed along the way seemed barely to look at her. One woman even bumped into Sheila and called her a bitch.

Once inside her real apartment, Sheila ran around, straightening piles of magazines on tables, picking up discarded shoes from various corners of the living area, and asking us if we'd like something cool to drink. I waved her away and got myself and Nigel glasses of ice water, while Sheila grabbed a basket of dirty laundry from the kitchen counter and ran to her bedroom while muttering something about not having enough hours in a day.

While she was gone, I showed Nigel around the apartment and pointed to several pieces of furniture in the living area that I'd always liked: an apothecary cabinet, a set of ladder-back dining chairs, a Noguchi coffee table, and an enormous oak bookcase with intricate scrollwork and gargoyle heads carved along the edges.

Sheila returned just as Nigel was running his fingers along the edge of the bookcase and said, "After Josh and I got married, I begged him to get rid of that thing, but he refused. I don't think it's going to fit in our new place."

I didn't think anything would fit in their new apartment, but I didn't say it out loud. Instead, while Nigel asked Sheila about her favorite colors, I slipped away from them and went downstairs to the den. I stared through the French door at the garden behind the brownstone, remembering different times I'd sat outside with my uncle and his friends while Sheila and Josh told us stories about their travels. Those nights were always fun. But I couldn't remember the last time I'd been a part of one of their garden parties. Was that my fault, or had they stopped inviting me because I'd moved out of Blaine and Daniel's place? Was I being punished somehow? Why?

I hadn't noticed that the red light above the door to Josh's darkroom was lit until he stepped out with a set of prints in one hand and closed the door behind him. When he saw me standing in the den, he grinned and said, "Hey, stranger. How goes it?"

"It goes. I go with it. What's that?" I asked.

Josh grimaced and said, "I guess you call it Josh Clinton's greatest hits. They're just proofs, highlights from my career, for a book of my work."

"A book? Cool."

"My agent fished around and found a publisher who's interested. It really wasn't my idea. I can't imagine who would buy the thing, but what do I know? I'm just going along with it and seeing what happens. No skin off my nose."

"Can I see them?"

He handed me the photos and said, "Knock yourself out."

I sat on a nearby sofa and started flipping through the photographs. Josh sank down on the cushion next to me, and I felt myself blush. He was supposed to be like a member of my family, but he was more like that hot second or third cousin that you probably shouldn't think was attractive. The fact that he was so passionate about art didn't help, either. As he explained why he chose each picture, and pointed out various lines, shadows, and focal points, I kept concentrating on his hands as they moved through the air, through his shaggy brown hair, or thoughtfully rubbed his chin.

When I was done looking at the last picture, a shot of the back of someone's head with a shoe balancing on top, I said, "They're all really cool."

"Thanks," he replied. He put them into a manila envelope and said, "Is my wife home?"

"Yeah. She's upstairs with Nigel." When he looked puzzled, I added, "This dude I work with."

"Oh, right. I forgot about that. No offense, but I told her we should just have a huge tag sale and start over from scratch. What did you think of the new apartment? Glamorous, huh?"

"Seems really cozy," I said diplomatically.

Josh laughed, then said, "That's a good word for it. The place in L.A. is a lot bigger."

"What place in L.A.?"

"We just closed on a house in Beverly Hills. Okay, technically it's in West Hollywood—nothing fancy by any means—but it's a cute place. And I can see by the look on your face that this is all news to you, isn't it?"

"Yeah. Sheila didn't mention the house in Los Angeles part."

"A while back we rented movies, one of which was that movie

with Jodie Foster where guys break into her town house and terrorize her. From then on, Sheila wanted to move. Her manager thought it was a good idea. Because she's apparently too high profile now, she needs a place with a doorman, and all kinds of other reasons. We started looking for a place to buy. Which sucks, I might add."

"I can imagine," I said, remembering how much I'd hated looking for a place to live.

"Then we stopped and talked about our long-term career goals. Sheila's taking acting lessons and trying to get more movie roles. Most of the commercials she does are shot on the West Coast, and she's always flying back and forth. It just makes sense to get a house out there and keep a small place here."

"But what about you? Aren't you still working for *Ultimate Magazine?*"

"It folded."

"What?" I exclaimed.

"Yup. The last issue comes out next month. Couldn't compete with the Internet. It's a blessing, really, because I have enough work as it is. Most of which is on the other coast."

"Oh."

"We'll be back a lot, though. You haven't seen the last of us. I promise." His cell phone rang. He answered it and said, "It's my agent. I have to take this."

I nodded and watched as he bounded up the stairs. Then I frowned at the envelope on the coffee table for a while. I heard footsteps and didn't look up until Sheila said, "I'm sorry I didn't tell you that we're moving to Los Angeles."

"It's okay," I mumbled.

"I didn't want anyone else to tell you, and I wanted to tell you in person."

"Should I tell Nigel the gig is over, since it was just a ploy to get me over here?"

"No! Look at this place. It looks like a used furniture shop. Nigel's already making big plans for our house in L.A., so don't ruin that, please. We need his help."

"I always liked this apartment," I said.

"Yeah, so did I," Sheila said. She sighed and sank onto the sofa. "We've had some good times here. We'll have more. We're not going away forever."

"I know," I said, even though I didn't.

"Are you mad at me?"

"No," I said.

"Then what's with the surly teenager bit?" I glared at her, but she spoke before I could. "I don't know why, but you've completely bailed on us, Nick. You're an adult now, you're in your own apartment, you're living your life. That's great. That's how it should be. I did the same thing when I was your age. But I didn't cut myself off from the people who care about me. I don't know why you're doing that. I don't even want an explanation, because I'm still your friend and I'll always care about you. No matter what you do." Sheila thrust her face in mine and said in a demonic voice, "You can't get rid of me, Nick Dunhill!"

I laughed and said, "You're nuts, lady."

She pulled a set of keys from her pocket and said, "Here. These are keys to the new apartment."

"Why?"

"Because you'll need to get in and out whenever Nigel starts moving stuff, won't you?"

"Oh, right," I said, feeling dumb.

"And if you were to make a set for yourself, Josh and I won't mind. You never know when you might want to get away from whatever madness is going on in your life. Plus I'd love it if, when we're gone, you'll check on the place every now and then."

"When are you guys moving?"

"Pretty soon. I'm starting a new movie in a few weeks. It's an action-adventure film and I play a model—big stretch, I know—but I get killed. I'm getting big bucks to play dead. I can live with that. It beats hawking fried chicken," she said, referring to her most recent commercial. She'd portrayed a model voraciously attacking a bucket of fried chicken between walks down a fashion show runway.

"No. That was funny," I protested.

"Thanks. Are you still mad at me?"

"I never was," I said. "I'm just—I don't know, sad, I guess."

"You don't like change," Sheila stated. "I understand. But I thrive on it. I'm lucky to have the career that I do, because I'm never in one place for too long. Josh is the same way. We're a good fit. We go with the flow. You do it, too, though. You came here, you lived with

Blaine, you tried college, you dropped out, you moved into your own place. You're going with the flow, too."

"I guess so," I said. "I've never really thought about it."

"Are you happy? Healthy?"

"I guess I am."

"Haven't really thought about it?" she said and smiled.

"I'm fine. Everything is good," I assured her.

"Good. I'm proud of you, Nick. You're starting a new life for yourself. It's exciting."

Before she could ruffle my hair or pinch my cheeks, I stood and said, "Thanks. I should probably get back to work."

Sheila went to the office with us to sign paperwork authorizing Nigel to do whatever it was he planned on doing to the Meyers-Clinton homes. When we walked in, Eileen looked up from her knitting to tell me that Bailey wanted to speak with me. I promised Sheila I'd see her again before she and Josh moved, then went to see what Bailey wanted.

When I entered her office, Bailey said, "Did you have fun hobnobbing with the rich and famous?"

"Did I do something wrong?" I asked, pointedly ignoring her question.

"No. Did Nigel get the account?"

"I think they're signing paperwork now."

"Good." She opened a desk drawer and removed two dog leashes. She held them out to me and said, "I need you to walk Ottoman and Tassel."

"Can Eileen do it? I was hoping to get back to the workshop. Jisella and I were going to—"

"Eileen has more important things to do," Bailey interjected. "What's your job title?"

"I'm a runner," I said.

"Right. Now, run along."

I took the leashes from her and walked away, muttering, "Yes, Morgan."

"What did you call me?" she asked before I could close the door.

I stuck my head back in and said, "I said, 'Yes, Bailey.' "

"No, you didn't. You called me Morgan."

"I did? That's my roommate's name. That was stupid of me. I'm sorry."

"It's not a big deal. Walk the dogs," she said in a distracted voice, then pointedly added, "Please."

"She's related to Morgan. I'm sure of it now," I said to the dogs as they sniffed a mailbox on the corner. If I hadn't been walking two obviously pampered poodles on the Upper East Side, people probably would've thought I was just another New York crazy talking to himself. Few people looked in my direction. Those who did either smiled at the dogs or openly laughed and pointed. I knew how that felt, so I ignored them all.

"Did you see the way she reacted when I called her Morgan?" I asked Tassel, who sniffed Ottoman's butt and then turned away from both of us. "Oh yeah. You weren't there. You guys must know something, right? Why won't you tell me anything?"

Ottoman looked up at me and started to poop.

"That sums it up, I suppose." I pulled a plastic bag from my pocket and cleaned the mess from the sidewalk. "Fine. Don't tell me. I'll figure it out on my own. Who needs you two, anyway? Stupid poodles."

"I guess you told him," said a guy who'd been waiting for the light to change. I wasn't sure if he was talking on a cell phone or to somebody else. The only other person waiting for the light to change was dancing to the beat of whatever was playing through his headphones. The guy who spoke looked familiar. I looked at him again, noticing that his dark hair had some curl to it, and how that helped the strategic messiness of its style. He had blue eyes and a ring in his eyebrow . . .

"Hey!" I turned with sudden realization. "Keith Haring!"

He looked around quickly and said, "Yeah, but keep it down. Everyone thinks I'm dead."

"Very funny," I said, thinking about when I'd seen him a couple of months before at the Pop Shop. Roberto had accused me of flirting with him.

"Well, you thought so," he answered. The light turned and we stepped off the curb in unison. "So, whatcha got there?"

"Huh? Oh, just walking my boss's dogs. I work at a design firm nearby."

"Are you a designer? That's cool."

"Me? No. I'm an artist. Kind of. I mean—I've studied art. Briefly. But I'm not really doing anything now. Other than walking dogs and odd jobs at work."

"Yeah, but you're artistic. It's in your soul. I can feel it."

"Yeah? What else can you feel?" We continued to walk down the sidewalk, turning a corner and heading toward Park Avenue.

He smiled and said, "I can feel that you'd like to go out with me tonight."

I couldn't help but smile back. I was a sucker for cockiness. "Are you sure about that?"

"Oh yeah. You know, nothing fancy. Maybe coffee? Or we could grab something to eat? Maybe just walk, like we're doing now?"

I did my best to play it cool; then I realized I'd been holding a bag of poodle poop the entire time we'd been talking. It smelled, too. I hoped he didn't think it was me. I wanted to discreetly throw it away, but the nearest trash can was at the end of the block. I held the bag behind me and replied, "Sure. That sounds good. I'm Nick, by the way."

"Nick Bytheway. Interesting name."

"Ha."

"I'm Brian. Brian Taylor."

"Nick Dunhill. I'd shake your hand, but . . ." I nodded at the dogs, who were winding their leashes around my legs.

"Not a problem. I'll shake it later. How about we meet around seven? Where do you live? What's convenient?"

We exchanged information, agreed on a place to meet, and walked in opposite directions. I tossed the bag of poop in the garbage on the corner, then herded the poodles back toward Wamsley & Wilkes. While I walked, I congratulated myself on following Sheila's advice: I was going with the flow.

Since Brian and I hadn't discussed dinner and I was starving when I left work about half past six, I grabbed two dogs from a hot dog cart on my way to True Brew, the coffeehouse on the Upper West Side where we'd agreed to meet. The barista gave my food a stern look and shook his head. After a quick glance around to make sure Brian wasn't there, I went back outside. I hurriedly ate my hot dogs while perched on a planter that had little white lights woven into its tree. Then I took a bottle of water and a breath mint from my bag, glad that I'd gotten all that out of the way before Brian arrived.

I needn't have rushed. I watched as couple after couple, and even single after single, went inside True Brew. Several came out right away with various beverages: hot, cold, foamy, steamy, and iced. The drinks were as varied as the people who carried them.

Occasionally, I looked inside again to check whether Brian was already there. Maybe I just hadn't seen him.

"Why are you so late?" he'd ask.

"Late?" I'd respond. "I wasn't late. I've been waiting outside for you the whole time."

We'd both laugh about what losers we were. . . .

I looked at my watch. Actually, only one of us was a loser: the one who'd been sitting outside a coffee shop for more than an hour, refusing to acknowledge that he'd been stood up.

"Hey, Nick, right?"

I looked around eagerly and tried not to let my face fall when I saw a man who had to be at least forty smiling at me. I had no idea who he was, and it felt creepy that he knew my name.

"You probably don't remember me. I'm Jack."

I wondered if my face conveyed what I was thinking: *Don't remember you. Don't want to.*

"We had a class together at Pratt. I think it was Introduction to Photography."

"Jack! Right. Sorry I was—how are you? What's up with you?"

"Not too much. Just saw you sitting here and realized I never saw you at school after fall term. Where've you been? Is everything okay?"

"Yeah, everything's fine. I just needed to take a break, you know?"

"So you're not in school right now?"

I felt like he was about to give me one of my uncle's lectures. "No, I'm not in school right now."

"That's too bad. But I understand."

"You do?" I asked. Since I rarely got that response, I decided to savor the moment.

"Yeah, you seemed a little ragged when I knew you. I worried about you."

So much for savoring the moment. I knew he was just trying to be nice, but it would be refreshing occasionally not to be treated like I was on the verge of a breakdown. Next he'd be offering to take me to his place, feed me, and fuck me. I didn't want to hurt his feelings, but there was no way that was happening.

"I did the same thing," he was saying. "Dropped out. Only started back last year."

The last thing I wanted to hear about was some old guy who'd wasted his youth working a string of fast food/grocery clerk/pizza joint jobs to make ends meet. "What'd you do in the meantime?" I feigned interest while trying to figure out how to make my exit.

"I started school when I was your age, but I got tired of being told what to do. I guess I have a bit of an independent streak. I'd been working part-time as a delivery person and thought I could do a better job than the people I was working for. So two other guys who worked there left with me to start our own business. I'm one of the owners of a very successful courier service. Crazy how shit like that works out, huh?"

"Yeah," I said. Now he had my attention.

"So all this time, I've been working. And it's fine, because I did what I wanted to do. Sort of. I mean, it's all cool. It's all for a reason, you know? But I finally thought to myself, *Jack, it's time to go back and revisit that passion for photography.* So I am." He shrugged. "If you're enjoying what you're doing, you keep doing it. If you're not, it's time to make a change. But you just need to do things on your own schedule, you know? Everything happens when it's supposed to anyway."

I stared at him and considered the way Sheila and Josh kept themselves flexible, grabbing opportunities as they arose. I'd thought I was doing that with Brian, but maybe he'd only been the means for me to run into Jack. Maybe . . .

"Oh, hey," Jack said, looking at a woman who'd just emerged from a cab. She was somewhere between his age and mine and was, as Roberto would say, a honey. She was smiling at Jack like he was Brad Pitt.

"This is Penny," he said, presenting her to me. "This is Nick. I know him from Pratt."

"Hi, Nick," she said, and her smile was warm. The two of them radiated that happy couple thing. I felt like a jerk for all my bad thoughts about Jack, especially my suspicion that he'd been trying to pick me up. "Are you joining us for coffee?"

"Yeah, you should," Jack said, quickly masking his surprise.

I smiled and said, "No, actually I have a date. You two have fun. See you around, Jack. It was nice to meet you, Penny."

"You, too," she said. I walked away but just before the door of True Brew closed, I heard her say, "What a polite young man."

"Yeah, he's great," Jack said.

I stopped feeling like a jerk.

August 2, 2003

Dear Nicky,

I've done a lot of thinking about things since I saw you a few weeks ago. There are things we never say, and that's probably my fault. I never wanted to treat my sons like friends. I know people who do that, and it seems unfair to their kids.

But I probably went too far in the other direction. Maybe I seemed too aloof or like I didn't care. I'm sorry, because the truth is, I love you, love all my sons, so much. I'm not very good at confiding in people or telling anyone my problems. And don't worry! I'm not going to make you the person I dump on. I just can't forget what you said about feeling distant from your family. If there's emotional distance between you and me, it's my fault. I'll work on it.

Meanwhile, enclosed is one of the perks of my raise and my determination to do a few things that I want to do for a change. The only person who'll ever see the statement for this credit card is me. The account is in my name. This card is in your name. The limit is five thousand. You can get up to a twenty-five-hundred-dollar cash advance. I completely trust you with this. And you know what? I've always trusted you, even when I didn't always understand you. You're a good person, Nicky, and I'm proud to be your mother.

Love,
Mom

11

It Couldn't Happen Here

"**A**re you getting some?"

This question from my occasional Saturday afternoon date didn't really surprise me. I was sure he wasn't expecting a detailed answer. He'd asked the question as an opening for something he wanted to talk about. I doubted that it had anything to do with my sex life.

"Not so much," I said, hoping this didn't give him a reason to offer me unsolicited advice.

I didn't take my eyes off the backgammon board, where his hand hovered as he tried to decide whether to bear off two checkers and leave a man vulnerable, or keep his man safe in case my next roll was a lucky one.

It didn't bother me to wait. I liked looking at his hands. They were strong, a little veiny, and a lot callused. Workingman's hands, like a man who'd spent most of his life doing roadwork for the city of Harrisburg, Pennsylvania, should have.

That had been Kruger Schmidt's job. He was my cousin Emily's maternal grandfather. I met him when he moved to Manhattan in the winter of 2001. A widower of several years, he'd found that retirement didn't suit him. He got tired of living alone in his three-bedroom house in Harrisburg. Sick of shoveling snow in the winter and mowing a yard in summer. He stored a few of his belongings that might one day have sentimental value to Emily. Then he sold the rest and moved into what would have been the live-in nanny's room next to his granddaughter.

In time, he became something of a babysitter to Emily, although she had a real nanny who came to the apartment every weekday. There was no lack of adults who could take care of her. Wanted to take care of her. But as her grandfather, Kruger had a stronger claim than most.

Emily probably couldn't remember a time when Kruger hadn't been there. I understood the feeling. I'd gotten attached to him and our occasional backgammon games over the past couple years.

"What about you?" I asked. "Are *you* getting some?"

He took a chance and bore off his two men, returning his hands to his knees and sucking in his breath when I rolled my dice. Double sixes, and since I had a man out, and he had his six point blocked, he was safe. I rolled my eyes, and he looked pleased. Kruger took his backgammon seriously.

"I suppose you think I'm too old for all that," Kruger said. He grimaced as he worked out his possible moves and realized he'd have to leave a man open.

"You're the youngest sixty-five-year-old I know." I couldn't help but grin when my roll allowed me to bump his exposed man, buying me the time I needed to get back in the game.

"Do animals still fool around after they stop making babies?" Kruger wondered aloud.

"I don't know," I said. "Don't some of them mate for life? Is mating just about sex? I should have paid more attention in biology."

He grunted when I blocked all the points on my home board; then he said, "You can learn just as much watching the Discovery channel."

"That's not much of an endorsement of public education."

"The best education is life."

"Yeah, I used that line when I dropped out of Pratt. It didn't go over well."

He shrugged, scowled at my continued luck with the dice, and said, "You're old enough to make up your own mind about your education. My problem is, I can't pick a girlfriend."

I won the game, and as we repositioned the checkers for the next one, I asked, "You can't commit?"

"I've got too many choices."

WHEN YOU DON'T SEE ME

"Am I supposed to feel *sorry* for you?" I asked. "You're like James Bond's father. Who are all these women that are after you?"

"There's Miss Goldman." His tone indicated that I should know who he was talking about, but I was drawing a blank. "At the dry cleaner's."

"Uncle Blaine's dry cleaner? The woman who does alterations?"

"Yes."

"I've never heard her say a word," I admitted. "How did you get to know her?"

"We're both German," Kruger said. "She suggested we do genealogy together. She's sure we'll find ancestors in common."

"I've never understood that," I said. "Why does it matter? It's just names on paper."

Kruger rolled the dice. I assumed his preoccupied frown came from trying to decide how to move, until he said, "Maybe Miss Goldman would rather research distant generations than think about this life."

"Maybe Miss Goldman hasn't had much of a life to think about."

He looked at me over the top of his eyeglasses and said, "She's a Holocaust survivor. She lost her parents and her brother in death camps."

My stomach churned, and I quickly asked, "Who are your other girlfriends?"

"There's Mrs. DeSalvo," Kruger said. "She treats me to spicy cooking and invites me to Knights of Columbus senior dances. She loves to talk about her Aldo. They bought their little deli with a loan from their fathers, and it was the center of their lives. They could never afford good help, or wouldn't trust anyone, so they opened the store every morning and closed it at night. Her children did their homework on barrels in the back. That store put five kids through college. They all make a good living, and they wanted their parents to retire to Florida. Aldo and Bella wouldn't even consider it. Leave New York? Leave the store? That was crazy. Then Aldo died in his sleep one night, and Bella had no husband and soon, no store. But I've never heard her complain. She talks about Aldo, wipes her eyes, then dances with me."

"She sounds fun," I said. "I think you should pick her."

"I haven't told you about Mrs. Bostany," Kruger said. "Her husband was a firefighter. He died on the job back in the eighties, so she's been a widow nearly twenty years and has a half dozen grandchildren, but you'd never know it. She can tell a dirty joke, throw back a few shots of whiskey, and still be every inch the lady who knits scarves and hobnobs with mayors."

Kruger won the game with a flourish and smiled at me.

"You've got your own League of Nations," I said. "What country is Mrs. Bostany from?"

"Brooklyn," Kruger said. When I squinted at him, he said, "Her parents came here from Lebanon. That doesn't matter to you, right, since they'd just be names on paper?"

"We all came from somewhere else," I said with a shrug. "I happen to think it's the here and now that matters."

Kruger leaned against the back of his chair, lighting a Camel to let me know we were taking a break from backgammon. I could tell I was about to get a story, so I settled in to listen.

"When I was a kid," Kruger said, "many of the men in my family went away. World War Two. Some of them fought in the Pacific. Most of them were in Europe. But we were all German, so they were fighting people who'd been their neighbors a generation or two before."

I watched two Rollerbladers in the distance as Kruger talked. I hadn't skated in years, and I'd never done it with the agility these two were showing. They mirrored each other's movements, like a skater and his shadow. Like twins.

"Our parents told us not to speak German outside our houses. When our mothers walked to the market, people who knew they had German names would cross the street to avoid them. My grandfather's two dogs were poisoned because they were *German* shepherds. People threw red paint on my uncle's bakery or painted swastikas on the brick walls, with slogans like 'Nazi, go home.' "

"That's horrible," I said. "Didn't they know you were Jewish?"

"It was a crazy time. We were being persecuted in Germany for being Jewish, and persecuted here for being German. My father was risking his life for *both* his countries." Kruger shook his head. "When our fathers and uncles and their friends started coming home, they didn't brag about what they'd done. They barely talked about the war at all. Unless they talked about friends they'd made in the ranks. Or places. Not battlefields, but little towns or farms. Castles or great cathedrals."

The Rollerbladers looked like birds: swooping, dipping, making wide, graceful arcs.

"But the women—they had stories. When Gretchen was little, she'd sit on her *grossmutter's* lap in the kitchen and listen. To what it was like when the men were away. To endure rationing of food and gas. To have a husband or son that never came home. To be treated like dirt because you, or your parents, or your grandparents, had come from Germany. I used to worry that was what turned her into such an angry adult."

"Angry?" I asked. That didn't sound like the Gretchen I knew, who was always laughing or celebrating something.

"She was so serious all the time. I expected her to turn into a boy-crazy teenager, but instead, she was always signing petitions or organizing something." Kruger lit another Camel and grinned at whatever memories were playing through his head. "It seemed her mother and I were to blame for everything. Vietnam. Watergate. Race riots. Discrimination against women. She turned our dinner table into a battlefield. She and I were on opposite sides, with her mother in the middle trying to make peace between us. But even Miriam gave up when Gretchen told us she was a lesbian."

"Did you think she was telling you that just to get your attention?" I asked. "That's what I got accused of."

"I thought it was a phase," Kruger admitted. "By then, she was putting herself through college. Then she started working here in New York, making money hand over fist. She seemed nothing like that little girl who used to listen to the women's stories in the kitchen. She stopped going to Pennsylvania, even on holidays. It was too much of a strain for all of us to be together."

"How did things get worked out?"

"Miriam was diagnosed with cancer. I was almost afraid to tell Gretchen. I didn't want her to break her mother's heart again. What if she wouldn't come home? What if she stayed mad at us?"

I didn't have to ask how Gretchen had reacted. I knew she'd never disappoint anyone who needed her.

Kruger briefly talked about the progression of his wife's disease, and how their daughter came home as often as she could. "Gretchen was standing next to me at her mother's hospital bed when Miriam died. I wanted to comfort her. Instead, she hugged me and repeated a saying of my mother's. 'With faith, there is love. With love, there is peace. With peace, there is blessing.' It was weeks later before I realized that Gretchen had said it in German. She hadn't turned her back on her family after all."

"It's not fair how much you've lost," I said after a pause.

"That's not the point," Kruger said, grinding out his Camel. "When I was first widowed, I thought I'd spend the rest of my life lonely. I'd have my daughter and later, my granddaughter, but romance was for young men."

"And now you've got too many girlfriends."

I watched as he repositioned the game pieces on the board for another match. We were quiet for a while, concentrating on our strategy.

"I moved to New York, and life started over," Kruger finally said. "I made a new family, but that doesn't mean my other family was less important."

I glanced up as he rolled the dice. I understood the little smile that vanished almost before I saw it. It had nothing to do with the fact that he was winning our game. I'd been tricked. He wasn't talking about himself after all.

It was dusk by the time I closed the backgammon board while he threw away our coffee cups and his little pile of Camel butts. His hug was brief but heartfelt.

"Same time in a couple of weeks?" he asked, taking the game from me.

"If you don't elope with Mrs. DeSalvo."

I stopped at Bethesda Terrace on my way out of the park. I stared at the fountain and thought about families. When Chuck and I had turned fifteen, my mother wanted to have a family portrait done. She made an appointment at a local studio. The plan was that we'd all dress up, get the photo taken, then have our birthday dinner at Fisher's White House, a restaurant in Eau Claire. My mother wore a black dress and her pearls. Like my father, Tony and Chuck dressed in blazers, but instead of ties, they kept their collars open. They looked like the healthy young animals they were.

When I came downstairs, I was wearing jeans with a thrift store black leather jacket over a black T-shirt. My father hit the roof.

"Why do you always have to ruin everything? Let your mother have one goddamn picture of us looking like a normal family."

Before I could answer, Tony said, "He can't, 'cause he's not normal. He's a freak."

When my father told me to change clothes, my mother said, "We'll be late. In twenty years, when I look at the picture, I'd rather see him dressed this way than remember everybody fighting. Let's just go."

It didn't matter that I hadn't done it to piss them off. I'd had a different opinion of what made a picture-perfect family. They wanted to look like something out of a catalog. I thought we were supposed to look like who we really were. Later, at the restaurant, when the waiters sang "Happy Birthday," they put the cake in front of Chuck. The glow of the candles made him look like Mr. Golden Boy. No one in my family bothered to mention that it was my birthday, too. My leather jacket made me invisible.

I walked out of the park onto Fifth Avenue, but instead of turning toward home, I went the other way. I had no particular destination in mind. I just didn't feel like another unfinished story from Kendra or a confrontation with Morgan. Roberto was still at work. I hesitated when I got to Drayden's, then kept going.

I thought about the surprise birthday party Gretchen and Gwendy had thrown for Daniel in their Tribeca loft when Emily was nine months old. Gretchen loved to host a crowd. The reflection of the candle flames danced in her eyes when she brought in the cake, singing off-key until Uncle Blaine took over the tune. Josh snapped pictures, and Sheila handed out slices of cake after Daniel blew out the candles.

Then Blaine sat with Emily on his lap, his arm draped across Daniel's shoulders. We all listened to Gretchen's stories of the days before Blaine had known Daniel. Now and then, she'd slap Gwendy's greedy fingers away from the cake frosting with warnings about processed sugar. We stayed up late that night, long after Emily was put to bed, talking and laughing while Daniel and Gretchen reminisced. Gwendy shared stories about growing up with Daniel as her big brother. Everyone seemed lazily content to sit there while Daniel got his moment in the spotlight.

Blaine finally insisted that it was time to go. He went to Emily's room to take a last peek at her. Then he and Gretchen hung on each other while everyone else hugged Daniel good night and repeated their birthday wishes, put on jackets, and gathered up purses and cameras.

That Saturday was the last time we'd all been together *before*. Before the Tuesday in September when everything changed.

With faith, there is love. With love, there is peace. With peace, there is blessing.

But there was no peace. Only questions that stuck in my throat like tears that wouldn't come out.

I was all the way to Washington Square Park before I realized what I was doing. I stopped, looked down the avenue at the empty sky, and said, "I don't think so."

I walked east until I stepped inside Cutter's. I didn't see Cookie, so I sat at the bar and ordered a beer. No one asked for an ID. No one paid any attention to me. At least that was what I thought until Dennis Fagan slid onto the stool next to mine.

"Been a long time," he said, tipping his beer toward me.

"Well, you know," I said.

He didn't smile, but his eyes wrinkled a little. "Yeah."

He watched a baseball game on the bar's TV. I thought about nothing in particular. Neither of us talked. I finished my beer and, not wanting to push my luck, waved the bartender away. Then I turned and stared at Dennis until his cornflower blue eyes met mine.

"Okay, then," he said. "We're outta here."

There was no conversation while we walked. I didn't look at the sky. I didn't really even pay attention to where we were going. We ended up on a street near Wall Street, but I had no idea which one.

Inside my head, I counted off *red building, white building, brown building, red building, red building* . . . Until Dennis stopped at a door next to a deli, opened it, and led me to the second floor, where he unlocked an apartment. Tiny kitchen behind a living room; bathroom and small bedroom to the left. I didn't look at it with the eyes of a Wamsley & Wilkes employee. In fact, I didn't see much at all. I took a swallow of the beer Dennis brought from the refrigerator. Then he stared at my face for a few seconds before gently pulling me to him.

We made short work of undressing. His bed was a jumble of sheets, but they felt good and smelled of laundry detergent. Nothing perfumed, just clean. For a man with massive muscles, Dennis was a surprisingly tender lover. He was furry—manscaping was an idea that would never have occurred to him—warm, and strong. We

both knew he was in charge. From the timing, the place, the circumstances, the provision of condoms and lube—it was his show,
and that was how I wanted it.

We lay side by side later, beers propped against our bellies. His
open window faced an office building across the street. The building was dark at that hour on a Saturday night. The August air was
hot and still, allowing street noise into the apartment. I liked it. It
reminded me of Harlem and felt like home.

"I used to have a better view," Dennis said. "A fifth floor walk-up
near Battery Park. My bedroom window framed a clear picture of
the twin towers."

I looked at the hard hat on a scarred desk across the room and
said, "You worked on the site after—"

"Yeah, but that's over. It's good to go back to building things."

"What are you working on now?"

"A job at the Financial Center atrium." He took a pull of his
beer. "You'd think after months of cleanup, I'd want to get as far
away as I could. But it's been my place since I was a kid. My father
and uncles helped put up three of those seven buildings. My brothers, cousins—we're all in the trade. As long as there's work, we'll be
there."

I nodded. We were quiet for a few minutes, until I said, "The
night you got in that fight at Cutter's because of me. I didn't know
you were gay."

Dennis laughed and said, "Gay? Gay is coffeehouses and sushi.
Madison Avenue. Chelsea. Abercrombie & Fitch or whatever you
boys decide is the next right thing. I fuck men. I'm not gay."

"But—"

He gave me a look that shut me up and said, "There's a difference. That's all."

"Okay," I said, realizing he didn't mean he was one of those men
who pretended to be straight and to lust after women. He was
right. There was a difference between his world and the world of
men like my uncle, who identified themselves with the word *gay*.
"Why'd you take up for me that night?"

"Too many questions," Dennis said. He put down his beer, set
mine on the floor next to his, and wrapped me up in his body. It
wasn't sexual, although I had a feeling it would be again. It was
more brotherly. Not like my own brothers, but like Roberto.

"Okay," I said. "I'll shut up."

"Did I say shut up? No questions, but talk if you want. I heard most of it from Blythe anyway."

"She told you about me?"

"She told me about *her*," he corrected. "You figured into *her* story. But it's *your* story, if you want it to be."

Did I want it to be? Hadn't I been doing it Dennis's way? Wasn't that the better choice? Wasn't that why I sought the company of people who didn't talk everything to fucking death?

I thought about Miss Goldman, sitting in her corner at the dry cleaner's. With ignorant people like me thinking she hadn't had much of a life. Would that be me? Never finding a way to release something toxic that churned inside me until finally I was leached clean? Or else, after it destroyed my insides, would it spill over onto other people?

I was walking to the men's room in Cutter's when the drunk's words registered and I realized he was talking about us.

"Fucking punk kids," he said. "Everything handed to them. Don't appreciate any of it."

It stopped me. I stared at him. I noticed his bleary eyes and realized he was just a stupid, tired drunk. I turned back toward the restroom.

"They oughta be fighting like real men their age. Instead of sitting on their asses, getting drunk. Just walking on blood and ashes, not giving a shit."

I froze for a few seconds. My ears were roaring. I turned around. I wasn't sure what I thought I could do, but I never had a chance. Dennis exploded out of a group of men standing nearby. He was on the drunk, hitting him, and he didn't stop until he was pulled off by two men as big as he was.

"Just get out of here," Cookie said, shaking my arm.

I couldn't stop staring at Dennis, the drunk's blood splattered across his face and chest. A beast inside me thrilled with recognition of the same animal inside him. It took hours for me to settle down after Fred dragged me from the bar.

Had I cried that night? Probably not. I used to cry at sitcoms. Insurance commercials. A dog without a collar. Losing a favorite graphite pencil. I'd been dry as a bone for longer than I could remember.

"One of my roommates has two snakes," I said to Dennis. "She feeds them mice. Live mice. She gets them from a pet store."

Dennis pushed his thumbs into the muscles around my shoulder blades. His hands were strong, and the pressure was so intense that it silenced me for a minute. I could almost hear Gavin saying, *Breathe!* I breathed.

After a while, I went on. "On one level, I understand that snakes have to eat. And they eat mice. It's the choosing that bothers me."

"Your roommate choosing. Like she's playing God," Dennis said.

"Exactly. Why this one and not that one? And why do I fucking care? Why do I even think about it?"

His thumbs went down either side of my spine in the same rhythm he'd used on my shoulders. Press, release, move. I felt like I was shivering inside.

"You tell me," he said.

"It's like she's God playing a game," I finally said. "The way I play backgammon. But a game has strategy. Rules. There's a reason for what you do in a game. It's arbitrary shit that makes me crazy."

Press. Release. Move.

"A woman wakes up one morning, drinks her coffee, kisses her partner and her nine-month-old baby good-bye, then goes to work. Not to her own office, where she goes every day. To somebody else's office. Why that office, on that floor, in that building, on that day? It's so fucking random."

"Right," Dennis said. His voice was tender. I wanted to crawl inside it and never leave.

He reached over to turn off the light, then put his arms around me again. I knew I could talk as long as I wanted, street music in the background, and he'd keep holding me.

I knew something else, too. Dennis would listen to me because he did belong to that world where things went unsaid. *When our fathers and uncles and their friends started coming home, they didn't brag about what they'd done. They barely talked about the war at all.* Like Kruger, Dennis came from a place where silence was part of being a man.

Maybe we both needed for me to talk.

I felt like something clicked inside my brain. Dennis's silence was part of how he'd been taught a man should be. But my silence—had that come from my mother? The person who didn't want to burden anyone? So instead, she left people—left *me*—feeling helpless and inadequate. Did I make people feel that way, too, with my silence?

Not Roberto. I never had to explain things to Roberto; he just *knew*. It was like he was the twin I was supposed to have been born with.

But just because I had Roberto, did that mean I never had to talk to anyone else? Maybe sometimes people needed to hear things. Maybe I needed to say things to them. Like with Dennis and me.

Tonight, I answered Kruger's earlier question, *I'm getting a lot of some. And I don't mean just sex.*

Feeling safe, I curled against Dennis, sighed, and began.

"Her name was Gretchen Schmidt. She was my cousin's mother. That morning, she left early for work because she had a meeting in the North Tower. . . ."

September 4, 2003

Dear Nick,

I'm so glad you called, because you've been on my mind a lot. I didn't realize how much I needed to hear your voice until after we hung up. I agree with what you said. This anniversary seems harder than last year's. I think that's why Daniel and I decided to go ahead and make the trip to Europe, just to get away from everything that will be on TV here.

Gwendy said she isn't interested in going to any of the memorial services. She and Kruger are going to Wisconsin and will be there on the eleventh. This eases my mind, because I know the Stephenson family and Adam's family will make sure there are a lot of happy things going on for Emily, Gwendy, and Kruger.

I know you said you can't get away from work, but if you change your mind, I've got your passport. All we have to do is buy a ticket and you can go to Spain with us. Or if you want to go to Wisconsin, that's fine, too. I'm enclosing our itinerary and all our phone numbers if you need to call me for anything. Even if just to talk. You can always charge any calls to our home account. Just in case you don't have that card anymore, I'm dropping in a copy.

I love you, Nick. I probably don't tell you that enough, or let you know what a comfort you've been to me over these last couple of years. I've never had one moment's regret about the way I borrowed my brother's son three years ago and kind of forgot to give him back. You're the best.

Love,
Blaine

12

Tonight Is Forever

"You know, this place wouldn't be so bad if you guys hadn't turned it into tent city," Fred said. He cleared a place on the futon so he could sit down. When he moved stuff around, I caught a faint scent of soap and aftershave from Roberto's clothes. It was one of my comfort smells, even more than freshly brewed tea. Or Isleta and Emily after their baths. Probably a scent that evoked childhood wasn't all that comforting, in my case.

It struck me that I no longer noticed the things that had once bothered me about my apartment. The cramped space. The lack of privacy. The noisy fat guy upstairs. Morgan's snakes.

Fred watched while I tried to decide between two T-shirts. One had *Marvin the Martian* on it. The other had a publicity photo of my uncle-in-law, Daniel, with Tina Yothers at a fund-raiser called Bottle Blondes Benefit HIV/AIDS.

"Strange," Fred said, staring at the second T-shirt. "On our TV set, she looked like a redhead on *Family Ties*. And now her hair's black."

"It was meant to be ironic," I said. "They're both natural blondes. Should I wear Marvin?"

"It'll make you look more like a kid," Fred warned. "You don't want to go back to jail."

"I was never in jail," I said, pulling the Blondes T-shirt over my head. "Anyway, we're going to Club Chaos. We know the owner. Plus I won't be drinking."

"You quit drinking?"

"You make it sound like I had to go through rehab."

"At least you only *wear* Tina. Where's Roberto?"

"He'll meet us there. He had to set up a display after Drayden's closed."

"Anything exciting happened at work lately?"

"What's with all the questions? Am I being interviewed?"

"Touchy. Must be the hormone shots."

"You take hormone shots?" Kendra asked as she parted the sheets and joined us.

"So much for privacy," Fred said.

"No. I take wolfsbane injections," I said. "To protect me from Morgan when the moon is full."

"I heard that," Morgan said from the kitchen. She didn't sound miffed, though. Maybe, after seven months, she'd also become indifferent to annoying things about our apartment. Things like me and any other human who breathed her air.

"You should have gotten the soundproof sheets," Fred said.

Kendra turned her back to me so I could lace her up. "This dress is hot," I said.

"There's not a lot to it, though, so I figure I won't get too sweaty—"

"No, I mean *hot*. Sexy."

"Thanks." She sounded surprised, and it occurred to me how rarely she got a compliment from any of us. "I bought it a couple of years ago when I went to a party for Hugh Jackman."

"Speaking of things wolflike," I said. I pitied Fred for the expectant expression on his face. He hadn't learned that it was pointless to wait for Kendra's rest-of-the-story.

"And?" Fred finally asked.

"I don't know which shoes to wear with it," Kendra said.

Adalla arrived sporting lots of hair and makeup. She went immediately to the kitchen to talk to Morgan. Kendra tried to eavesdrop, but they kept their voices low.

"Maybe they're lovers," Fred whispered.

"I think they're witches," Kendra said. When she saw my frown, she said, "I mean real witches. Like casting spells or cursing people."

"If Morgan knew witchcraft, she'd have turned us all into toads long ago," I said.

"Snake food," Fred said.

I brushed my hair back with my fingers, put in another earring, threw a leather blazer over my T-shirt, and declared myself ready. Kendra still had to agonize over her shoes. Then we walked two blocks before hailing a cab so Fred could smoke a cigarette. He slid in next to the driver, and the girls and I had to sweat it out in back. Adalla whipped out a man's handkerchief and blotted her face. Kendra shifted uneasily between us and scratched at the laces on her leather dress.

"Where's this place we're going?" Kendra asked.

"Club Chaos," Fred said. "They put on the best drag show in town."

"I remember the first time Blythe took me," I said. "I didn't act impressed enough. She then took me to several bad shows in other bars and clubs so I could understand the difference."

"What's the difference?" Adalla asked. "If you've seen one cock in a frock—"

"Not true," I said. "It's not just about a wig, dress, makeup, and a bitchy attitude. The performers at Club Chaos really get into their stage personas. Some of them lip-synch, but most of them dance and sing their own stuff."

"And the stage patter is good," Fred said. "They're funny."

I didn't mention that Daniel and Martin had once performed at Club Chaos, long before their careers in television and theater took off. There were photos of them in drag in the lobby of the club. Daniel's sequined attitude surfaced now and again, especially when he was in a bad mood. But sometimes when he was affectionate, too. Blaine pretended to ignore us when we called each other Nicole and Danielle, but I thought he secretly liked it. Daniel had been known to tell Blaine to pull the stick out of his ass. Daniel was the only person I knew who was never intimidated by my uncle.

While Fred described some of the performers, I thought about the club's owner, Andy Vanedesen. Aunt Gretchen had been one of his best friends. He'd fainted at her memorial service. The rest of us had held our breath, expecting Daniel and Martin to jump on him for the drama. But Daniel propped him up. Martin borrowed an oriental fan from another of their friends and waved it furiously in front of Andy's face.

When someone offered him a cane in case he felt wobbly again, Andy pushed Martin's hand away and said, "Stop it. I just got a little *light-headed*. I'm *not* an old lady."

"You're right," Daniel said. "Nobody would ever call you a lady."

I'd once heard someone say that Andy was a silly old queen, but I thought he was sweet. After Gretchen's service, I'd caught him sobbing into a dish towel in the pantry downstairs. Normally something like that would have sent me running in the other direction. Instead, I sat with him until he felt better. I almost envied him for being able to cry so hard.

Two years later, I still envied him. I looked down the avenue at the twin columns of light pointing skyward. I was glad Daniel and Blaine were in Spain. And I'd been relieved when my uncle told me that Kruger and Gwendy had taken Emily to spend a few days with Gwendy's family in Wisconsin.

"Wow," Adalla said. "When you get closer, you can see that it's not just two lights."

"It's over eighty, I think," Fred said.

"Do any of you ever go to Ground Zero?" Kendra asked.

"Nobody calls it that but journalists and politicians," I said.

"I went once," Fred said.

"Not me," Adalla said. She seemed mesmerized by the lights. "How many nights will they be lit up?"

"They'll turn them off at dawn," I said. "Until next year." When Adalla opened her mouth, I headed off what I was sure would be a suggestion that we go there. "The lights aren't set up at the World Trade Center site."

"Where are they?"

"Battery Park."

"I love the Village," Kendra said as she watched a group of people cross the street. "I wish we lived here instead of Harlem."

Adalla gave me one of her Kendra's-a-snob looks, but I pretended not to see it.

Andy himself hurried across the lobby to greet us when we went inside the club. He air-kissed me, bussed Fred on the cheek, and wiggled his fingers at the girls.

"Your friend is upstairs in Cybeeria with his date," Andy said. "He said you'd all wait there before the second show."

"Roberto has a date?" Kendra asked with a pouty look.

"He means Isaiah," I explained as we took the stairs to the club's cyberbar. "Roberto may not make it before the show starts."

We were still sitting upstairs when Andy joined us with a bottle of champagne. His eyes did a quick scan of the table to determine who was drinking alcohol. He'd probably heard about the night I got in trouble at Cutter's, something I would apparently never live down. Kendra, Adalla, Isaiah, and his date had drinks, but they were all legal. I'd been surprised that Fred hadn't ordered a martini. My stomach had been floopy all day, so I was sticking to water with slices of lemon.

"Just a little taste for each of you," Andy said, motioning for a waiter to bring glasses. He sat down at the table with us. "Tell me who's who?"

"You know Fred," I said. "Kendra's one of my roommates. Adalla's my weekend-in-the-park friend. Isaiah and I work together, and this is Isaiah's date, Luis. He's from Santo Domingo."

Isaiah and I exchanged smiles as Andy purred over Luis, who was a striking man. Isaiah and Luis had met at church, where Luis was a tenor in the Full Gospel Gay and Lesbian Choir.

"Hi, everybody," Melanie said as she came in and fell onto a chair. "It's so hot. It sucks the life out of me." She waved away the champagne flute that Andy offered, looked at the hovering waiter, and said, "A glass of ice water and a Sprite, please."

"What's the verdict?" Fred asked. "Did The Donald buy the sculpture?"

I'd always loved Melanie's bashful smile, and she flashed it now as she said, "You are looking at the proud creator of a metal sculpture that will be in some unspecified Trump office in some undisclosed Trump building."

"Where none of us will ever be allowed to see it," Adalla said.

"Nick and I will," Isaiah said. "We've got friends in high places."

"You make deliveries in high places," Fred said.

"Or we're high when we make deliveries in places," I said.

"I don't want to know," Andy said. He stood, told us to enjoy the show, and spoke to other groups of patrons on his way downstairs.

"Anyway," Melanie said, "I'm not the only one with big news. Don't you have something to share with the group?" She looked expectantly at Fred, who seemed puzzled. "Don't be modest. Dr. Mills told me about the offer." Dr. Mills was Fred's uncle, BHSA's headmaster.

Fred's confused expression changed to discomfort, and he said, "He wasn't—that's not public knowledge yet."

"We're not really the public, are we?" Melanie asked. "I mean, if you can't share good news with your friends . . ."

"What good news?" I asked.

Melanie ignored Fred's shaking head and said, "Fred got a book deal."

"What?" I asked as everyone else at the table murmured some form of congratulations. "What do you mean, a book deal? Fred doesn't write."

"Fred never told us that he writes, but Fred writes," Melanie said. "He just got offered a fat advance—"

"Can we not talk about this now?" Fred asked. He absently patted the pocket that held his cigarettes. I could see he wanted nothing more than to have a smoke. I figured the only thing keeping him in his seat was worry about what Melanie might say if he left the table.

"My friend Josh Clinton has a book deal, too, for a collection of his photographs," I said. "He's like you, all modest about it."

"Modest," Melanie repeated.

"But I think it's huge!" I went on. "I can't believe you, always pretending like you aren't creative. How did it happen? Did you send it to publishers, or—"

"It's his blog," Melanie said.

I heard some tone in her voice, almost like she was mad, and I looked from her to Fred and back again. "Am I missing something?"

"Can we talk about this later?" Fred asked.

"For the past couple of years, Fred has been writing stories online. He has a Web log called baristabrew-dot-com. He writes about his job and his customers at Starbucks. Only he calls it 'Brewbucks.' The blog is his own little blend of stories about New Yorkers, tourists, and people he knows."

"That's great! Why didn't you tell us? I'm so proud of you."

Melanie laughed, but it was a joyless sound. I looked around the table at everyone else. They seemed as confused as I was by Melanie's hostility and Fred's embarrassment. He'd obviously wanted to share the news in his own way at a time of his choosing. Although I didn't understand what the big mystery was, I didn't like seeing him uncomfortable.

"Congratulations, Fred," I said, leaning over to hug him. "We'll talk about it later. We should go downstairs before somebody steals our table."

Somewhere along the way Fred, enslaved by nicotine, faded out. He came back after we'd settled at a large round table near the stage. I smiled at him, but he still looked a little grim. Kendra leaned over and said something to him, and they traded seats. It left her next to the empty chair that Roberto would sit in if he ever showed up.

The show always opened with a parade of celebrity impersonators called "A Rainbow of Divas." They periodically changed their musical number and their outfits, and Daniel said that Andy updated the divas from year to year, but the act was still familiar to me. Nonetheless, I was more than willing to lose myself in the antics of the faux Madonna, Gwen Stefani, Pink, Mary J. Blige, and Queen Latifah as they belittled a hapless Jewel, who only wanted to sing a soft folk song with excruciatingly bad lyrics. Kendra and Adalla laughed so hard they had tears streaming down their faces. Melanie and Fred seemed preoccupied. I assumed they were still thinking about Fred's book deal. Isaiah and Luis were roaring at the divas' take-no-prisoners behavior. Luis's laugh was so loud that Queen Latifah stopped the show and made them turn the spotlight on our table.

"Security, security!" she called in that voice that all men in drag seemed to automatically adopt. Maybe it had something to do with how they were tucked. "You have exceeded the limit of allowable handsome men at your table. I'm afraid this one has to come with me." She expertly whipped a long feathered boa at Luis. He reacted with another of his booming laughs.

Whatever Queen was going to do next was lost in a rush of air that passed me. I watched, shocked, as Roberto cleared the table and landed on Fred. Everything became a confusing mix-up of screams, feathers, sequins, and fists as our table started a bar brawl.

"Stop that!" I heard Andy shriek from somewhere behind me.

I looked over to see the waifish Jewel, white dress pulled up around her waist, straddling a bouncer as he danced around our table. She tried to hit Roberto and Fred with her guitar, but they were rolling all over the floor and she couldn't get a good shot at them.

"This," said Mary J. from the stage, "is why we call it Club *Chaos*, baby."

"You never see shit like this back on the kibbutz," Madonna said.

Three hours later, I walked back to Club Chaos from the edge of Lower Manhattan. I was tired and a little depressed. I had no idea what had happened to my friends. I'd left the club before it all got sorted out. I knew that whatever had made Melanie annoyed at Fred was magnified several times over in Roberto's reaction.

"You fucking betrayed your friends!" Roberto bellowed at Fred when the bouncers finally pulled the two of them apart.

Fred's nose was bleeding, his shirt was half ripped off, and he sounded just as furious as Roberto when he said, "It's fucking fiction, Roberto. Can you not understand—"

"Don't talk to me like I'm stupid. Tell Nick. Tell Nick it's fiction, you cocksucking—"

That was when I'd walked out. I didn't do drama. Or maybe I did, because in spite of all my intentions, I'd gone to the one place I knew I shouldn't. I hated the way it had been made to seem like a tourist spot.

But when I was actually there, standing with other people who stared up at the columns of light, it was different from what I'd expected. Quiet. Respectful. I hadn't felt good exactly, but I hadn't felt awful. I was able to think about Gretchen without the usual quivering that overtook my stomach. I thought about her friendships with my array of well-meaning parental figures. I almost wished I could see Blaine and Daniel. Martin. Gwendy. Kruger. Jeremy and Adam. Gavin and Ethan. Sheila and Josh.

The one person that I could see was Andy, so I walked back to Club Chaos. It was way after closing, but when I tapped on the lobby door, one of the bartenders was passing by with a case of liquor.

"I need to see Andy," I yelled through the glass.

"We're closed."

"Please tell him Nick Dunhill is here. He'll let me in."

A few minutes later, I was hustled upstairs, where Andy sat at a table in Cybeeria. He was drinking a cup of coffee and organizing receipts.

"I wanted to apologize," I said miserably as he stood up and gave me a hug. "I'm sorry my friends caused trouble tonight. I shouldn't have walked out and left you to deal with it all."

"Oh, honey," Andy said. "That was *nothing*. We've had bigger fights backstage over *wigs*. Everything was under control within minutes. Your friends were in cabs, Pink had an ice pack on her elbow, and the show went on. The show *always* goes on."

"You're not mad?"

"No. Silly thing. You want a drink? A cup of coffee or tea? Any-thing?"

I glanced behind me at the bank of computers and said, "What I'd really like is to use one of your computers."

"Help yourself," Andy said. He picked up the receipts. "I'll be in my office. If I leave before you're finished, I'll tell my security guard you're up here. He can let you out. Take all the time you need, he's here all night. He's had to be ever since that *shocking* episode with Whitney Houston. I don't know *why* the crazies always end up impersonating Whitney."

"Me, either," I said.

When Andy was gone, I sat at a computer and typed in the site baristabrew-dot-com. *An anonymous blogger offers a brew of stories about the trials of a coffee-chain barista and the characters in his Gotham life.*

I began reading backward. I didn't get it. The tone was funny, sometimes sarcastic, and generally entertaining. I could see why Fred's blog would be popular. He was a good writer. If someone wasn't from Manhattan, they'd feel like they were getting a glimpse of it from him. Anyone familiar with the city would recognize its flaws and virtues. Fred's—or rather, the Barista's—attitude toward his customers depended on how they behaved in "Brewbucks."

"What am I missing?" I asked out loud. There was a search func-tion on the blog, so I typed in *Nick*. Nothing came up. Same with *Roberto, Melanie, Pete*, even *Davii*. I tried to think of any conversa-

tions Fred and I had shared that would be blog-worthy. On a whim,
I typed *Sister Divine.*

Bingo. I went to that entry.

> *My friend Stick is obsessed with a homeless woman that he
> sees all over the city.*

Stick? I wondered.

> *Sister Divine, as he calls her, thinks we're all possessed by
> demons. Our souls vacate our bodies and the demons move in,
> making us nothing more or less than any other typical Gotham
> real estate. Mind you, in Stick's case, I'm not so sure she's
> wrong.*

"Thanks," I said aloud and kept reading.

> *I'd say Stick's worst demon is fear. Granted, he has his rea-
> sons. His aunt died on September 11. She wasn't one of those
> people who called anyone to say good-bye. She was at a
> meeting in the north tower that morning. Nothing proving her
> existence has ever been recovered. She just disappeared, leav-
> ing people to move on without her. Which they've done pretty
> well. And I'll give Stick credit. He doesn't openly talk about her.
> He doesn't invoke her name or memory to get pity or attention.
> He's more subtle. Stick's afraid of buildings. He's afraid of ele-
> vators. He doesn't want to fly anymore. He doesn't like taking
> the subway. He watches the landscape with the wary eye of a
> refugee who just arrived from some third-world country. Gotham
> has become the enemy, and Stick has become a collection of
> neuroses. Maybe this began as a bid for attention. Or maybe it
> began genuinely. I don't know. But he's not even twenty yet,
> and Stick is a fucked-up mess. I guess this is the cue for the
> asshole chorus to say, "The terrorists win." I hate that fucking
> phrase.*

I stared at the monitor. Then I read it again. I felt numb. I put
Stick in the search field and found a blog entry titled "They Think I
Don't Know."

Have you ever heard of the daisy chain of desire? When everyone wants the wrong person? I'm suddenly a crazy daisy. The Blond Con wants my friend, Macho. Macho says he's straight, but he's half in love with our friend, Stick. Stick wants me. Does that sound arrogant? I see the signs, although Stick thinks I don't know. When we were in school together, he lied about having a certain article of my clothing for about a month. I mean, come on. That's so Brittany Murphy in Clueless. So Stick wants me, and I . . . I've got my own Daisii to pursue. I don't know who he wants, but it's not me. Yet.

I was starting to get why Roberto had been upset. Had he read this? Who was the Blond Con? Kendra? What did that mean, *Con* . . . That she was scamming us in some way? I knew she had a crush on Roberto, so he must be Macho. But Roberto had no romantic interest in me. We were brothers.

Admittedly, I'd had a crush on Fred forever. It was embarrassing to find out that he'd known all along. And Daisii was clearly Davii.

And none of this should have become reading material on the Internet.

I was starting to feel squeamish, but I tried using *macho* as a tag. There were a lot of entries about "Brewbucks" customers. There was something about "Macho's" older brother the cop that was fairly harmless. Then I found an entry called "They Think I Don't Know, Part 2."

Macho is HIV-positive. I'm not sure who knows other than Stick. I'm not supposed to know, so I can't talk to him about it. I found out by accident. I don't understand how any informed person can get infected. Maybe it happened a long time ago. I don't have anything else to say about it.

I wanted to stop then, but I looked for another Stick entry and found "Unbalanced."

Yesterday, a Famous Personage from Washington, D.C., visited Brewbucks. Secret Service guys were outside the store as well as inside, all talking on their little gadgets with serious faces just like in the movies. Famous Personage, who's as fa-

mous for her constant scowl as much as anything, is in a chain coffee shop. She knows how it goes, that we have a system worked out INTERNATIONALLY. But in order to feel that she's the Bitch in Charge—clearly, she has control issues—she has to instruct Barista 4 on how she wants her drink made. It must be a layered thing with chocolate syrup, cream, coffee, caramel syrup, cream, coffee, whipped cream. It's all about balance, she says. There aren't too many customers in the shop, and we're the mellowest little Brewbucks on the island, so Barista 4 humors her and makes the blend to her specifications.

But that day is over, Bitch in Charge won't be back, and she doesn't deserve to be brewed. Today I'm brewing my friend Stick.

Stick is unbalanced. I don't mean mentally. Or metaphysically. He may need a shrink or an aura fluffing, but that's not the point.

Stick is a twin. Let's call his twin, who's trapped in his little midwestern mentality in one of those flyover states, Stuck. Stick and Stuck don't get along. Do you know why I call him Stick? He's tall and thin. Very thin. Why? You never see Stick eat an entire meal. Something is always pulling him away from food. Does he have an eating disorder? I think he does. I think he came to Gotham with that eating disorder because his family is composed of a little group of total assholes. His parents are middle-class losers who never planned on a queer son. His two brothers are both athletes, the pride of the family. Stuck and the older brother—what the hell, let's call him TONY, because that's his name—bonded. Even though Stick and Stuck are twins, Stuck is like TONY'S butt boy, though of course, no butts are involved because that would be GAY, right? Like Stick.

Stick is unbalanced because he's missing the other half of himself, his womb mate, since his family basically kicked him out when he was sixteen. He moved in with his uncle. The uncle is gay, so it seems like the ideal solution, right? Yeah, in Perfect World. But this is Gotham, never a perfect city.

In many ways, Stick's Gotham family has also abandoned him. They've left him in near-poverty to figure out a way to work *through his nervous breakdown caused by grief, fear, para-noia—*

I'd read enough. I pushed away from the computer and walked downstairs. I was dimly aware of the security guard's polite good night. I must have answered him. He didn't act like I did anything abnormal.

I walked north a few blocks before I realized that I couldn't make it. I'd already covered too much territory during the night. I was mentally, physically, and emotionally drained.

I paused at the stairs that led down to the subway. *Stick is afraid of buildings. He's afraid of elevators. He doesn't want to fly anymore. He doesn't like taking the subway.*

"Fuck you," I said.

There was almost no one on the train with me. Hardly anyone on the streets as I walked through East Harlem. I felt like one of the last people on the planet. Unfortunately, I wasn't. I was a person whose life had been reinterpreted and recorded in a public way. A way that could be read by anyone with a computer, which was everyone but me.

It could be read by Uncle Blaine, who'd been nothing but kind and generous to me from the time we'd started e-mailing each other a few years before. He'd let me move in with him. He'd had no room in his old apartment. No room in his life, really. But he made room. And now Fred was publicly criticizing Blaine. If Blaine read that, would he think I felt that way? Would he think Fred was speaking for me? I didn't feel that way. Did I? In any case, I'd never said anything like it to Fred.

The apartment was dark and quiet when I went inside. I slid as noiselessly as possible through the wall of sheets and peered toward the futon. I listened for the steady breathing that would mean Roberto had made it home safely. Was sleeping soundly. Had made some kind of peace with Fred.

There was no one lying there. There was nothing breathing in the room. My stomach hurt. I was glad I hadn't drunk alcohol, because I'd be throwing up.

You never see Stick eat an entire meal. Does he have an eating disorder? I think he does.

The window in the living room was open. I walked through the room and climbed through it to the fire escape. Before I stood up, I caught a glimpse of the alley below. I tried not to think about how far I'd fall if the rusty metal I clung to decided to pull away from the building. I turned to my right and, instead of Roberto, I stared at a half-dead potted palm our neighbor must've left outside. I didn't want to look down again, so I looked up and noticed the ladder connecting the fire escape to the rooftop.

I quietly climbed the steps, past the windows of other apartments in the building, hoping nobody would notice me. Or worse, mistake me for a burglar and shoot me. At the top, I grasped the rung of the ladder and started chanting to myself, "You're not going to fall." Over and over, until I reached the roof.

"Yo," Roberto said softly.

He reached over and pulled me against him. I breathed in the soap. The aftershave. The sweat and anger. The loyalty. The love.

The two of us sat in silence, unmoving, and watched the twin columns of light disappear as the sun rose.

October 3, 2003

Dear Nick,

You are something else. I just got a letter in the mail letting me know that you'd made a donation to the Anti-Defamation League in Gretchen's name. This is the kind of thing that made Gretchen love you so much. It's a reminder of what a fine young man you are. Emily is fortunate to have a cousin like you, who wants to make a positive difference in the world she'll grow up in.

Thank you from the bottom of my heart for remembering my daughter in this way.

Love,
Kruger

13

We All Feel Better in the Dark

Ijumped into the waiting van and Isaiah screeched away from the curb, barely giving me time to fasten my seat belt. Sometimes I felt like Manhattan was a giant pinball machine. I was the unlucky ball, and Isaiah manned the controls. I never knew where we were going next or if we'd get there in one piece.

"Hey, look," he said, pointing toward a bus. Which was unnerving, since his other hand was reaching for his Pepsi.

"I hate to whine, but could you keep one hand on the steering wheel?" I turned to look at the bus and read the ad on the side. Next to a network logo, it was just black letters on a white background that said ANGUS REMINGTON IS BACK, AND YOUR AFTERNOONS WILL NEVER BE THE SAME.

"Is your Uncle Daniel on *Secret Splendor* again?" Isaiah asked. His tone was hopeful. I'd heard from him many times how Daniel was the best actor in soaps and should go back because the show was lousy since he'd left.

"Not that I know of," I said. "They probably recast."

"Fuck that. Daniel Stephenson is the one-and-only Angus Remington," Isaiah said.

"He was like the third or fourth Angus Remington."

"He was the best Angus Remington."

"Can we use 'Angus Remington' in every sentence we say for the rest of the day?" I asked.

"Yeah, like you can tell me how that guy just Angus Remington'd you in the service elevator."

"I never get screwed and tell."

I knew he wasn't sure whether or not to believe me. "Why are you such a sex fiend lately? Is Morgana slipping Viagra into your hemlock?"

"Morgana," I repeated and laughed. "It's the weirdest thing. I'm actually starting to like Morgan."

"Damn, you *are* horny."

"Not that way. She just doesn't bug me the way she did. Maybe I got used to her."

"Olive sheep syndrome," Isaiah said.

A test of wills ensued. I knew he was dying for me to ask what that was. He knew I was trying not to. As usual, I caved and said, "Is that some kind of Italian slur? I'm not Italian."

"No. Nothing wrong with being a black sheep. Black is beautiful. But you ever noticed all our clients hate olive? The olive sheep must feel unwanted. You're the olive Dunhill. You think Morgan is an olive sheep, too, because Bailey's the good twin."

"You and your theories," I said.

"You're the one who says Bailey and Morgan are related," he pointed out.

"They have to be," I insisted. "They're too weirdly alike. To answer your question, I don't know. About the sex thing, I mean. Maybe I'm just getting more offers lately."

Too much sex would never make my list of things to complain about. I felt like some inner switch had been flipped. Everywhere I looked, there was another man who saw and came toward the light.

"Do you still see that doctor? And the construction worker?"

"He's an ironworker, and I talk too much," I said. "No wonder I have friends who put my business on the Internet."

"Quick. Write that down."

"What?"

"First almost-humorous thing you've said about Fred in the last month. You talked to him yet?"

"Nope," I said.

Fred had left a single message on my cell to tell me that he was willing to discuss things whenever I was. I still didn't want to. I missed him. A lot. But I was afraid if we talked too soon, it wouldn't go well for either of us. Every time I thought about his blog, I got pissed off again.

"Where to next?" I asked.

"Rug delivery to a high-rise in Chelsea," Isaiah said. "Maybe we can find you a rich boyfriend."

"A boyfriend is the last thing I'm looking for," I said.

When Isaiah pulled into the building's loading zone, I stared upward with an attack of nerves. "This delivery isn't to a penthouse apartment, is it?"

Isaiah consulted the clipboard and said, "Fourth floor."

"Ah. Not a problem."

"You need to get over being afraid of heights."

"I'm not worried about the height," I said. "I'm more worried about a man with a gun and a grudge."

Isaiah was practically wetting his pants by the time I finished the story of Parker D. Brooks and the loss of my I Dream of Cleanie job.

"White people are so fucked up," he said. *"Carefully place the Armani sunglasses on the dresser, then raise your hands slowly.* Ah ha ha ha haaaaaaa."

"Shut up."

We delivered and placed the rug without incident. After a few more stops, Isaiah drove me as far as Marcus Garvey Park. I walked the rest of the way home, pausing only long enough to pick up a bottle of water. It was a beautiful fall afternoon. I was pretty sure I had an unread paperback. Everybody else should be at work, so I could lie on the futon with the window open and read. Or jerk off. Whatever my mood called for.

The apartment had an eerie silence when I stepped inside. The hair on my arms and the back of my neck stood up. I wondered if we'd had a break-in. Maybe the burglar was still there. No, that was crazy. He'd have heard me come in and gone out the window. Or rushed me in the hall. Unless he was waiting to jump me.

I stood frozen for what seemed like hours. Condensation ran down my bottle of water and onto my hand. I needed to pee.

"Hello?"

Nice going, I thought. *You think the burglar will call hello back? Maybe you can have a conversation about the weather.*

I couldn't stand there forever. The cramped hall was dark, as always, and I reached for the light switch. Nothing happened. Which was when I finally understood why everything seemed spooky. The refrigerator wasn't rattling. Morgan's air purifier wasn't on. And the heat lamp over the snakes' aquarium, which sometimes made a buzzing noise, was silent. Everything was quiet the way it had been during the blackout in August.

"Fuck me," I said. "We've got no power."

I stepped back outside and listened. I could hear TVs, music playing, a high-pitched whine that might have been a hair dryer. So it wasn't a blackout. It was just us. It must be a fuse or something. Unlike the rest of the Dunhills, I didn't know about that stuff, but I knew we'd paid our power bill.

I went back inside and thought about the heat lamp. If the bedroom windows were open, would the cool air be bad for the snakes? The last thing we needed was dead reptiles. Morgan would turn into something out of a Greek tragedy. Empires would topple. Civilization as we knew it would cease. My sex drive might even vanish.

I walked into the bedroom and ducked under the taut rope that separated the sloppy side—Kendra's—from Morgan's immaculate part of the room. Then my heart lurched because there were no snakes in the aquarium.

I jumped, searching the floor around my feet. Then I rushed out of the room and slammed the door, my heart pounding. But Lucifer and Hugsie could be anywhere.

No way was I staying there alone with snakes on the loose. It was every viper for himself, and I was out on the street in seconds.

Then guilt set in. The longer they were free . . . And if there were windows open . . . Or they got into someone else's apartment . . .

"Why me?" I moaned.

"Why not?" a dreadlocked guy said and stepped around me.

I admired his ass as he walked away, then remembered my dilemma. I flipped open my phone and found Morgan's cell number.

"This better be important."

"Is that how you always answer your phone?"

"Only when it's one of my loser roommates," she said.

"For some reason, our power's off. I guess we blew a fuse. Lucifer and Hugsie are missing."

"How do you know? Were you in my room?"

"I was checking on the snakes," I said. "God. I'm doing you a favor—"

"We didn't blow a fuse," she interrupted. "Our power's been cut off because the bill wasn't paid."

"No way. Wait. You knew about this?"

"It went off while I was home. I called ConEd. We're behind two months. And we ignored a shut-off notice."

"Did you tell them it's a mistake? We paid the bill," I argued.

"We *thought* we paid the bill," Morgan said cryptically. "The snakes are with me. The electricity is not my problem. I gave you my part, so it's on you. Deal with it, Nick."

"But—"

I shut up when I heard dead air. She'd hung up on me. I flipped my phone shut. Then I opened it again and called Drayden's. When Roberto answered his page, I repeated my conversation with Morgan.

"Let's think about this," he said. "What'd she give you, cash or a check?"

"She always gives me cash for everything but rent. Same as you."

"Did you pay it in person, or—"

"I usually pay it at the check cashing place. Maybe I forgot? But I wouldn't forget two months in a row. And I'd have all that cash, and—wait. Now I remember. Kendra needed cash before she went out one night. I gave her the money I'd gotten from you and Morgan for the power bill. She said she'd swing by ConEd the next day and write a check for the full amount. She was going to pay my part, too, because she owed me money. When was that?"

"Wish I could tell you," Roberto said.

"Sorry," I said. "You're busy. You know what? I'll figure it out."

I stayed on the sidewalk and tried to remember. It must have been August when I'd given Kendra all that cash. After a few more minutes of mind-torture, I had a hazy memory of writing a check for the September bill. I left it on the kitchen counter with Morgan's cash. I also left a note telling Roberto and Kendra to add their part. Then it was all gone, and I assumed one of them had taken care of it.

I went back upstairs and called ConEd, only to get a repeat of what Morgan had told me. We were two months delinquent.

I wrote down how much we owed and where I could pay the bill to get everything turned back on. Unfortunately, that couldn't happen before the next day. At least the weather was good. But that wouldn't help me face Morgan and Roberto.

"The hell with that," I said. "I'm not the one who screwed up." I flipped open my phone again.

"How can I work if you call me incessantly?" Morgan complained.

"We won't have power until tomorrow," I said. "You and the kids might want to stay somewhere else tonight."

"I'd already planned to. Stop calling me. Unless it's to tell me we have electricity. And you'll have to replace anything I have in the freezer and refrigerator that spoils."

At least Roberto was nicer when he suggested that I stay in the Bronx with him.

"Nope," I said. "I didn't say anything to Morgan, but Kendra's the one who took our money. I'm ambushing her tonight."

Roberto laughed and said, "Sure you are." He adopted a falsetto and said, "Oh, Nick, I'm sorry. But I got fired when I wouldn't put out for my boss. Then I had to pay rent, and I got syphilis after that night I spent in the harbor on the yacht with you-know-who."

"Who?" I asked.

"I was being Kendra," he said in his Roberto voice. "We'll never know."

There wasn't much daylight left, so I tore through Kendra's side of the bedroom as quickly as I could. I found my check and the two unpaid bills under a pile of dirty clothes. Once the evidence was in hand, I lit candles, poured myself a glass of Morgan's wine, and sat in the living room to wait.

Kendra finally came home smelling of grease and looking like she'd detoured through Iraq. She was holding two carry-out boxes. She gave the candles a puzzled glance. "Am I in the right apartment?" she asked, wearily kicking off her shoes.

"You are," I said. "I know you're tired and dirty, but the power's out. If you want to shower, there's hot water. But you'll have to do it by candlelight."

"Ew," she said. "What's if there's a roach in the bathroom? You know they come out when it's dark."

"Sorry," I said.

"I'll just wash my hands," she said. She dropped the food on the overturned crate that served as a coffee table, though it was mainly used for rolling joints. "Maybe by the time we finish eating, the electricity will be back on."

I let her complain about her shitty day while we ate. Then I poured her another glass of wine.

"Is this Morgan's wine?" she asked, peering at the label in the candlelight. "Wait a minute. Where is Morgan? We need to hide this bottle."

"Yeah, we could hide it under your dirty clothes. Along with the unpaid bills."

"Huh?"

"It won't work, Kendra." I recounted what I remembered about the last two months' power bills and finished with, "I found the unpaid bills in *your* room under *your* stuff."

"I might have forgotten—"

"You didn't forget. You basically stole from us. Don't lie about it, too." I paused. "The worst part is that suddenly I sound like a parent, but you're four years older than I am."

"Five," she said. When I stared at her, trying to get back my train of thought, she said, "I had a birthday last month. No one mentioned it. But now I'm five years older than you are."

"Don't play the birthday pity card. You didn't tell anyone it was your birthday. Or we'd have stolen Morgan's wine then, too." That made her give me a tentative smile, like she hoped the worst was over. I pushed a slip of paper toward her. "If you go there and pay that amount tomorrow morning, they'll have the power back on before close of business."

"I don't have that much money!" she yelped.

"Not my problem. By the end of this week, you'll also need to pay back all the money I've loaned you."

Her mouth fell open. She finally sputtered, "That's like—it must be—like—nearly a thousand dollars."

"Eleven hundred," I said.

"I didn't know you were running a tab."

"I wasn't running a tab. I really never gave a shit if you paid me back. Until I found out you were using me and lying to me."

"You know why you're being so hateful? You're making me pay for what everyone else has done to you. You're being mean to me because you're mad at Fred and your uncle."

"I'm not being mean to you. And I'm not mad at my uncle."

"You're starting to act like Adalla and Morgan. They've never liked me."

"I liked you, Kendra. I still like you. I just don't like being used by you."

"Fine," she said. She grabbed her purse and stomped out of the apartment. It would have been a lot more impressive if she hadn't had to come back inside for her shoes after she slammed the door.

The electricity was back the next day, but Kendra wasn't. I still hadn't seen her by the end of the week, but when I got home from work on Friday, I found a sealed envelope on the futon. I opened it and counted eleven hundred dollars. I felt guilty, wondering what she had to do to get it.

I stuffed the bills in my cargo pants and took a cab to the bank. There was no reason to invite disaster.

I felt like I'd gotten a bonus. After I made my deposit, I stood outside the bank and tried to figure out a way to treat myself. I remembered those Helmut Lang jeans I hadn't bought, but that moment had passed. A woman walked by me doing something with her iPod. I thought of all the technology that was beyond me now that I didn't own a computer. I could get a laptop. Or buy art supplies. Or use the money for a trip to the dentist.

I hated being practical.

I was looking down the block as I crossed a street on my way home when I noticed the dingy sign for Doug, Ink. I picked up my pace, wondering how late the tattoo studio stayed open.

"Hey," Doug said, looking up from a customer when I walked in. "Did you finally decide on a tattoo?"

"No," I said. "I was wondering if you'd seen Kendra lately."

Doug gestured with his head to indicate that I should sit on the other side of the barber-style chair where his client was reclining. I watched for a few seconds as he applied the last bit of blue-green color to a shark silhouette above her anklebone.

"Why a shark?" I asked the girl. She looked like she might weigh ninety pounds soaking wet. She was more like a minnow.

"I'm taking back my power," she said. "This will remind me to stop being such a doormat."

I met Doug's eyes, but his expression was serious. Doug never made light of anyone's reasons for getting a tattoo or what they chose. I liked that about him, so I didn't make a joke about how I'd just gotten my power back, too, thanks to Kendra and ConEd.

I waited while he gave the girl instructions on how to take care of her new tattoo. Then he walked her to the dramatically over-pierced woman at the cash register. I stared at her for a minute and ran my fingers over my ears. But I already had four piercings in one ear and three in the other. Maybe my eyebrow. Or a nose pin . . .

"You sure you don't want a tattoo?" Doug asked as he came back. "I'm the best."

"I know you are," I said. "If I could think of anything I wanted to look at the rest of my life, I would. But nothing's come to me."

"Kendra stopped by a couple of days ago," Doug said. "She told me about the power bill crisis. Poor Kendra. She's a disaster."

"Did she borrow money from you?"

"When I saw her, she said she'd already taken care of everything. Why? Is your power still off?"

"No. She paid the bill."

"I wonder where she got the money," Doug said.

He shifted his attention to a guy who asked him about a Celtic knot tattoo. Then he wanted to see Doug's back, which was amazing. He had a feather tattoo that began right above his butt crack, then went up his back, just to the right of his spine, with the very tips of the feather brushing his bones.

"I had it done in L.A.," Doug told his customer. "This ancient Japanese guy did it with little needles instead of the machine. It took forever. But the inks have never faded."

"What does a feather symbolize?" the man asked.

"Purity and strength," Doug said. "For the Celtic knot, you want to book an appointment with Pamela. It's her specialty." He nodded at a woman who came in and said, "I'll be set up for you in a second."

"I'm sorry," I said. "You're busy."

"It's fine," Doug said. "Give me a minute to get things set up. Then we can talk. It relaxes people to listen to conversations while they're getting inked."

He moved efficiently as he cleaned the chair and brought all new, sealed supplies to prepare for his next tattoo. I'd been impressed by how sanitary things were whenever I'd come in with Kendra. The grimy exterior of the shop was misleading.

I walked around and looked at photos of tattoos I liked: dragon, phoenix, lion, gargoyle, rooster. But none of them had any meaning for me, any more than Betty Boop, the Nike Swoosh, or the Tasmanian Devil.

"C'mere," one of Doug's employees said. She was wearing a necklace that said CYNDI, but I was afraid to call her that, in case it was her girlfriend's name. "Check this out," she said.

She was working on a woman lying facedown on a massage table, getting a gypsy tattoo on her lower back.

"The colors look great," I said.

"See?" Cyndi or Cyndi's girlfriend said. "I told you I could do it from the photo."

"You're gonna love it," I promised.

"My mother calls it my tramp stamp," the woman said.

"That's a good enough reason to do it," I said, and both women laughed.

By the time I went back to Doug's chair, he'd started on his client. I looked at the pattern he was working from: a heart with vines around it and the name Josh in the middle. I wondered if she would eventually come to regret that.

"So I was thinking," Doug said, "Kendra's been my friend for at least three years. And I just realized that I don't know that much about her. Other than her jobs, or places she's lived, or an occasional story about a roommate or a professor. I guess I just always thought of her as one of those people who lives in the moment."

"She definitely doesn't live in the past," I said. When he gave me a curious look, I said, "You haven't noticed? She'll say something that sounds like the beginning of an interesting story. But then she never tells the story."

He thought it over for a few minutes, then grinned and said, "You're right. She does do that."

"In my experience, mysterious people always turn out to be kind of boring," Heart Woman said.

I was distracted by a man who took off his shirt before he sat in the next chair over.

"I just want it darkened, man," he said to Jeff, another of Doug's employees. Jeff was big and hairy and looked like a Hell's Angel. I'd be scared to let him tattoo me.

"Is that what I think it is?" I asked, peering at the customer's biceps.

The man looked over and said, "It's called an ouroboros. A snake eating its own tail. It's all about cycles, man. The circle of life."

"Not exactly the tattoo for you," Doug said. Kendra and I had told him about Morgan's snakes.

"You're trying to decide on a tattoo? You should get an Eye of Ra on your shoulder," Heart Woman said.

"Or get two matching snakes," Ouroboros Man said. "In a circle eating each other's tails. If I could get a do-over—"

"You can't go wrong with a Muppet, I always say," another woman interrupted as she walked past us.

"Too many ideas," I said, covering my ears. "I can barely decide what direction to take when I get out of bed. I can't pick a tattoo."

"You just did," Doug said.

"I did?"

"Cyndi—oh, she's busy. Somebody bring Nick my book!" Doug yelled.

Muppet Woman brought me one of those old-fashioned three-ring binders, saying, "Kermit. Elmo. Big Bird."

"Nick's not a Muppet type," Doug said. "Flip to, like, the third or fourth page. Yeah, that's it."

"What is it?" I asked.

"It's a nautical star, but it has more points. It's based on Polaris. That's the star used on the north point of a compass. A lot of my maritime tatts have to do with voyages. This is one I designed a couple of years ago to symbolize a safe journey home. I've put a fleur-de-lis on each of the direction points, but I'd personalize it for you. Kendra talks about your big heart, so maybe the four points would be hearts. Like it's your inner compass. A reminder that you only have to look inside to know what direction to take. If you get lost, you'll have an adventure, but the North Star will always bring you safely home."

I stared at it a long time and finally said, "I'd want to keep the same fleur-de-lis on the east, west, and south points. But on the north point I'd want twin hearts joined together. Could you do that?"

"Of course. That makes it yours. Nobody else will ever have one like it."

"Where will you put it, though? My arm's too skinny for a decent-size tattoo."

"Nick, have you looked in a mirror lately?" Doug asked.

I glanced at the one behind us and said, "Yeah. So?"

"Dude, check out your arms. You've got muscles."

I frowned at my reflection, then took off my thin sweater and pushed up the sleeves of my T-shirt. He was right. How had my biceps arrived without being noticed? I should have thrown a block party. Invited all the neighbors. Made Roberto show me some respect.

"It must be all that shit I haul around for work," I mused, still admiring my biceps.

"This would look great on your upper arm, just below your shoulder. Right side, I think."

"I guess I could make an appointment."

"Buy my dinner, and I'll do it after I finish Gail here."

"Gisele," Heart Woman said.

"Right. Gisele. Sorry."

"Poor Kendra," I said. "Her money's going on my arm."

"It's *your* money."

"You have a point," I said.

Gisele laughed as I flexed my muscles at my reflection.

From somewhere in the back, I heard a soft voice muttering, "Gonzo. Animal. Cookie Monster. Fozzie . . ."

October 19, 2003

Dear Nick,

Hot tattoo! Thanks for the photos. Adam wants to know if you're working out. He says you look good enough to—you know, you don't need to hear that. Adam's a dirty old man.

You didn't ask for my advice about Kendra, but as you know, none of the old men—dirty or otherwise—in your life is ever short on advice. We all make mistakes. You can look back and think that Gavin tried to warn you about trusting people, or that Fred seemed to have her number. But you're the one who lives with her. There's nothing wrong with being willing to forgive, forget, and move on. I don't think that makes you stupid. I think it makes you a good person.

If she takes advantage of you again, however, I've got a couple of old roommates we can hook her up with. Then we can have vengeance all the way around. I'm kidding. My point is, we all go through roommate drama. Let's hope this is the end of yours.

Talk to you soon.

Love,
Jeremy

14

My October Symphony

During my first months in New York, when Blythe was introducing me to the city, she also shared some of her philosophy with
me. Not about art. According to Blythe, she had no philosophy about
art. At least not one she wanted to share. She never liked talking
about her own creative process and refused to analyze anyone else's.

Instead, she liked to talk about friendship, love, and romance.
Looking back, I saw that as funny, because no one, including me,
knew anything about Blythe's love life. I wasn't even sure she had
one. That may have been her point.

"Most people fall in love badly," Blythe warned me. She always
punctuated her sentences with cigarette smoke. Roberto called her
Little Dragon. "People undervalue themselves. They're thankful
that someone wants to spend time with them"—puff, puff—"and
they mistake gratitude for love."

I hadn't really been interested in love at the time. For one thing,
I was only seventeen. For another, I was busy trying not to be overwhelmed by a new home, new school, and new city. Sex, on the
other hand, was a different matter. Sex I was interested in, and
Blythe had opinions about that, too.

"Never fall in love with the first man who makes you see God,"
Blythe warned between rapid exhales. "Good sex and love are not
the same thing. In fact, my advice is to have all the good sex you
can"—puff—"safe sex, of course"—puff—"either with friends or with

people who can be friends. Friends with benefits." Long exhale. "Good sex and good friendships will protect you from bad love."

It was easy to agree with a philosophy that could get me laid well and often. It took a while for me to improve my early awkward attempts at seduction; then I met Pete. We learned together, and things went fine for us, until people started treating us like a couple. Neither of us saw it that way, so I understood when Pete ditched me for a quick romance with Fred.

It didn't bother me that I wasn't interested in finding a boyfriend or falling in love. I knew men could love each other and form committed relationships. I saw that with Blaine and Daniel, Jeremy and Adam, and Gavin and Ethan. But I wasn't in any hurry to get there. I just wanted uncomplicated physical enjoyment.

It had been a little weird to actually agree to a date with Pop Shop Boy. I'd already forgotten his name, but I hadn't forgotten the way he looked: a little like me. Maybe narcissism had prompted me to say yes. But being stood up made me feel like the old way was better. Get laid, then move on or become friends. I wasn't ready for dating. Sex was easy. Dating was complicated.

It seemed most of my friends felt the same way, even the girls. Melanie was too busy seeking success as a sculptor to focus on a boyfriend. Morgan—I had no idea what her deal was. For all I knew, the cartoon gig was a front for something seedy. Maybe she was a hooker. There had to be *some* men who were attracted to women who never made an effort to look good or to play well with others.

Adalla was Morgan's opposite. She tried new hairstyles, was forever on a diet, and spent any extra money from her paycheck on clothes and cosmetics. However, Isleta's father had soured Adalla on men, at least for the time being, so she insisted she was doing all those things for herself.

Only Kendra seemed to want a boyfriend, and unfortunately, she'd set her sights on Roberto. Roberto had offhandedly told me that a decreased sex drive was a side effect of his medication. I wondered if that was a convenient excuse for not having sex. I was sure Roberto would be able to find any number of willing partners who could deal with his HIV. It seemed more likely he was trying to get his own head around being positive. But that was just my take on it.

Roberto and I didn't sit around analyzing ourselves or our choices. After all, we had Fred to do that for us.

I'd tried several times to make myself call Fred, but I never did. My inaction hung over me, especially after the incident with Kendra and the power bill. If I could forgive her for stealing money from me and lying to me, I wasn't sure why I was so hard on Fred for his stupid blog, or why I didn't want to talk to him.

Then again, Kendra and I didn't really talk, either. She'd avoided me since skulking back to our apartment. I didn't know if Roberto or Morgan had given her any grief, but I was done with the whole episode. I could tell her that if she ever stopped dodging me.

I wondered what Fred would say if I ever stopped dodging him. The problem was, I didn't think it would make a difference. I was starting to figure out that I'd always thought of Fred as a boyfriend in reserve. As if maybe when I was ready for a boyfriend, Fred would be ready for a relationship that had a longer life span than the average housefly's. Confronting him could bring the end of something I wasn't ready to give up yet.

Work became not only my opportunity to explore new creative urges, but to forget about the problems in my various relationships. I was starting to understand why Uncle Blaine and my mother worked all the time.

I got to Wamsley & Wilkes one day to find Bailey waiting for me with a digital camera. "Battery Park," she said.

"Aw, have a heart. It's chilly outside, it'll be colder by the water, and I don't like Lower Manhattan."

"Stop ranting," she ordered, sounding so much like Morgan that it made me shudder. "Why would I want photos of Battery Park? It's an *apartment* in Battery Park. I need you to meet with"—she paused to look at her desk calendar—"Janet Templeton. At this address." She slid a piece of paper across her desk toward me. "I don't know. Something about decorating a corporate apartment. She didn't give me many details on the phone and—"

Bailey broke off when Tassel landed in her lap with a skein of yarn. Someone was going to be in trouble with Eileen, but I didn't blame Tassel. He was obviously getting ready for the coming Christmas season. The cherry red yarn was a nice contrast to his current green dye job.

"So you want me to shoot the apartment?" I asked.

"Yes, and find out what she wants. It doesn't sound like that big of a job, but her budget was impressive, so maybe it's more than decorating. Maybe the bathroom and kitchen need updating. Get a feel for it, and report back to me. She knows you're not a decision maker with the firm."

"Sure thing," I said.

She reached inside a desk drawer for some money that she held toward me. "Take a cab. I don't want some lowlife on the subway stealing my camera."

I couldn't stop myself from glaring at her and saying, "Do you want to pin my name and address to my shirt, too? You must think I'm a total moron."

"I know how it can be on the subway. The way a person can get lost watching bands of light fall across someone's tweed jacket. Or noticing the way the dark color of something spilled and stepped in has made an abstract of the floor. How you can stop paying attention to the camera and bam! It's gone."

"Oh. Someone stole one from you already?"

"And a cell phone. Go. And discreetly drop this yarn in Eileen's vicinity on your way out."

I stopped at a deli near the office and grabbed a bottle of orange juice and a dry bagel, which I ate while I walked several blocks before finally hailing a cab. The driver was on his cell phone, so I took a paperback from my bag and read, successfully ignoring the view of the financial district on our trip down the West Side Highway.

The building was nine stories and probably around twenty years old. It was a block from the Hudson River. I remembered a summer day when I'd gone to Battery Park with Blaine and Emily to wait for Gretchen to get off work. We'd stared at the Statue of Liberty in the distance. Blaine talked about wishing he could suspend Sheila from Liberty's torch for a Lillith Allure print ad.

The doorman motioned me in, and the concierge told me Ms. Templeton was waiting for me in a fifth-floor apartment. She seemed a little flustered when we introduced ourselves. She was the kind of person I'd probably forget as soon as I left. No humor in her eyes. Meek. Wearing a gray sweater set over gray wool pants. Everything about her was drab, from her limp, dull brown hair to her sensible flat shoes with scuffed toes.

The camera seemed to make her nervous, and I reassuringly said, "Since my boss can't be here, the pictures help her see the apartment's size, features, colors, and furnishings."

"We don't want anything in the apartment changed or replaced," Janet said. "It just needs to look lived in. Homey."

"Uh-huh," I said, not really paying attention to her as I shot the bathroom. Boring. Like her. I hated apartments like this. No wonder the owner wanted a decorator.

"We need to furnish it with things that make it look like someone actually lives here," she said, as if I hadn't gotten it the first time. "Artwork on the walls. Furniture that's interesting. Maybe some antiques."

"Okay," I said, moving on to the bedroom. Decent view. Small closet. Nothing special.

"Some photographs that give the illusion—"

"That someone lives here," I interrupted, and she nodded vigorously, pleased that I'd finally caught on. I hated being treated like I was stupid. "I'll tell my boss. I'm only here to take pictures and measure the space. I'm not a decorator."

"Oh. Right."

She got a weird, almost sad expression on her face. Maybe she just wanted to talk. So I said, "Most people don't like to put anything too expensive in a rental. Tenants who are just passing through—"

"It's not that kind of corporate apartment," she said. She turned to stare out the window.

I watched her a few seconds. Maybe the reason she seemed so lifeless was that she was doing something she didn't want to do. I tried to picture her at a table in a club with her friends. Would she be more animated? Less monochrome?

"Decorators are a little like bartenders. Or hairdressers. They end up knowing private stuff about you. You want to be smart when you choose one so your business doesn't end up on the street. You'll like working with Bailey Wilkes. She's talented. And trustworthy. She'll keep your secrets."

"Have you ever met a bartender you wanted to confide in?" Janet asked. "Because most of the bartenders I meet are jerks who act like they're too good to talk to customers."

"I haven't actually gone to a lot of bars," I admitted. I thought about Davii. "But I can tell my secrets to my hairdresser."

"I don't have a regular hairdresser," Janet snapped. Then her eyes sent me an apology. Her body language was making me as miserable as she seemed to be.

"I can be a good listener, too," I said. "I'm not a decorator, but I can keep a secret."

Her shoulders slumped. "I did something at work a while back," she said dully. "Something wrong."

"Haven't we all?" I said. Although I'd come to regard Parker D. Brooks with affection after all the times I'd used him to make people laugh, I said, "I ended up fired."

"The person who caught me was really nice. He told me not to worry about it. Boy, was I stupid. In politics, no bad deed goes unexploited. People keep your secrets because it gives them power."

When she stopped talking, I prompted, "So now this person wants something from you?"

"This isn't a corporate apartment for out-of-town visitors to use. I guess it's what people used to call a bachelor pad. Only the four men who'll be using it—not at the same time—aren't bachelors."

"Oh," I said.

"They have homes on Long Island or in Brooklyn. Nice homes with wives and kids. This is the place where they'll bring their girlfriends. The girlfriends know about the wives. But they aren't supposed to know this isn't where each guy stays when he has to spend the night in the city. I mean, the men have apartments for that, too, but their wives know about those apartments. So they can't exactly take their girlfriends there."

"I understand," I said. "You need a decorator who can keep the apartment generic enough to look like it belongs to each of these men, but comfortable and lived-in enough to look real."

"You got it," she said.

"Men."

"Suck. I feel like I'm helping them cheat on their wives. This is so not me. I'm just a Jersey girl working as a secretary and I made one stupid mistake."

"Maybe you should get a different job."

"Maybe you've never worked for prominent people. There's nowhere I can go if they decide to retaliate. Of course, if you tell your boss all this, and she tells my boss, I'm probably screwed anyway. One way or another, these guys are always screwing women."

"Not me," I said. "Not in any sense of the word."

"Uh-huh," she said listlessly.

I finished taking pictures. Before she walked me out, I had to try again.

"My uncle always says that power's an illusion. They've only got power over you if you give it to them. If you get a new job, they'll probably just forget you. I mean, how bad was your mistake? You didn't kill anybody, did you?"

She almost smiled when she shook her head. Neither of us said anything else before she closed the door between us.

I felt thoroughly depressed. When I got back to the office, I left Bailey's camera on her desk and went to see Jisella.

"Give me something physical and mindless to do," I begged.

"Grab your safety goggles, mask, and a sander," she ordered. "I can use your help with these shelves."

Out of kindness to me, she put in a Pet Shop Boys CD and we worked without conversation. Over the next couple hours, I took breaks only for water. At least until Bailey came looking for me.

"What the hell?" she asked. "Weren't you supposed to give me a rundown on the Battery Park place?"

I pulled down my mask and said, "The pictures are in your camera."

"I can't write up a bid based on a few stupid photos. Did you measure? Did you do an information sheet on the client? Did you—" She broke off and frowned when Jisella cranked up a drill. Then she yelled, "My office. Now."

She walked out, and Jisella's eyes through her goggles were sympathetic. I got cleaned up and went to Bailey's office, but I didn't sit in the guest chair when she pointed to it.

"Listen, you can fire me if you want to," I said. "But all I wanted was to get out of that place. Janet Templeton is like the most pathetic person in the world, and I can't . . . I don't want . . ."

When I trailed off, Bailey just stared at me with no expression. After a few seconds she said, "What? I can't read your mind."

"I know you don't want to know shit about my personal life, but here it is. Everybody in my hometown except my mother knows that my father cheats on her. Because he works in the electrical trade, he gets inside a lot of houses, and in those houses are women. Some of them are lonely or horny or whatever. He gets all the action he wants. And not just with customers. I'm pretty sure he once screwed someone at my dentist's office while my brother and I were getting our teeth cleaned. You don't know what it's like when people look at your mother with pity because they think she's stupid. Or when someone picks a fight with your older brother because your dad screwed his mom. Or when a friend's parents end up divorced because of your dad."

Bailey looked stunned at my outburst, but she merely said, "I might understand more than you think. What does this have to do with Battery Park?"

"Janet's setting up an apartment for four men who sound like they're big deals at City Hall. Four married men who need a place to take their mistresses. I don't want any part of it. If that gets me fired, so be it."

Bailey's face turned bright pink, and I waited to hear the words that would mean I needed to clear out my stuff. Instead, she dug through papers on her desk. I watched while she dialed her phone.

"Hi, Janet, this is Bailey Wilkes. I'm sorry I missed you. Apparently, the job is much smaller than our firm's usual projects, so we won't be submitting a bid. If you need recommendations for a more appropriate firm, give our office manager, Eileen, a call. She can give you some referrals. Thanks so much for considering us." She hung up and stared at me. "Satisfied?"

"You didn't have to—"

"One of the perks of owning my own business, Nick, is that I can turn down jobs that aren't right for me. You can stop looking at me like you admire my integrity. I really don't want the name of Wamsley & Wilkes to be splashed across the city's news rags one day when somebody gets hauled into court on ethics charges. We won't be the firm who's known for decorating a love nest for the commissioner of something or other."

"So I'm not fired?"

"Don't make drama where there is none." She paused, then added, "And where there is drama, walk away. You'll be a lot happier."

When I told Roberto that it was time for me to talk to Fred, he nodded thoughtfully. Then he said, "I want to be there."

"I don't need you to fight my battles."

"It's not just your battle. How long before someone finds his stupid blog and tells the wrong person that I'm positive? Like maybe one of my brothers. Or my coworkers."

"People who know us know I didn't have a nervous breakdown. Maybe they'll think Fred's lying about the HIV thing, too." When Roberto didn't comment, I said, "Did I have a nervous breakdown? Am I the last to know?"

"Just because you make me laugh, *mijo*, doesn't mean I'll change my mind. We deal with Fred together."

"Fine."

We had to decide on a neutral meeting place. I asked that no food be involved. Fred asked that no art be involved. Roberto asked that no crowds be involved. It was like setting up a summit of world leaders as we text-messaged back and forth, since none of us wanted to actually talk before we *talked*.

"Sweet bride of Satan!" Morgan shrieked from her bedroom one night as Roberto and I strategized in the kitchen. We waited, but when no more oaths were forthcoming, we went back to our endless debate about a place to meet. Both of us were ready to scrap the entire idea and leave Fred hanging.

Morgan whipped into the kitchen and threw a business card at Roberto. As he bent to pick it up, she said, "That's an address for a spa on the Upper East Side. The owner said you can use their Tranquility Room for two hours on Sunday night. It's a little lounge where their clients relax before their massages or whatever. No one will bother you. Sunday nights, they do a class for a group of hearing-impaired yoga addicts. But don't yell because the staff can still hear you. Since the owner's providing the room for free as a favor to me, don't break anything. Just stop talking about it and fucking *do* it, before you make me bat-shit crazy."

"Too late," Roberto said.

Her eyes got even beadier, and she said, "You know, that body won't always help you charm your way through everything."

"You've been peeking," Roberto said and gave her his most winning smile.

"God," she huffed and went back into her bedroom.

"Did you hear that?" I whispered. "She thinks you're a god."

*   *   *

After Fred agreed to our meeting, I used Eileen's computer to check out Structured Serenity Spa. Everything about it sounded enticing. I called my mother and made her look at their Web site, too.

"Looks great. Are you trying to give me ideas for Drayden's spas?" she asked.

"I thought I might do some research for you."

I could hear the smile in her voice when she said, "It's fine to use the credit card, Nicky. Knock yourself out."

I'd never really gone to a spa before, and I felt a little embarrassed. But every time I thought about dealing with Fred, I got too keyed up to eat or sleep. I hoped spa services of one type or another would settle my nerves.

Without telling Roberto, I booked several appointments for Sunday afternoon. My spa guide was Pascal. He smelled deliciously of rosemary, spearmint, and lemon. I recognized the scents because of Gavin, who used aromatherapy in Uncle Blaine's apartment. It was really just the spa smell picked up by everyone there, but they weren't all as cute as Pascal. I tried to flirt with him, but he was all business and didn't respond to my innuendos.

Pascal's job was to take me from one place to the next. Our first stop was to an aesthetician who gave me a facial. While my cucumber-and-mint mask was drying, a stylist clipped my hair in the same spiky cut that Davii usually gave me. Then Pascal led me to the detox room. I was covered with clay and wrapped in plastic, except for my hands and feet. After a manicure and pedicure, I showered off the clay before getting a full-body massage. The therapist wasn't as good as Gavin, but the massage still melted my muscles.

I tried to let go of my anxiety about seeing Fred. Maybe I'd have been better off following Blythe's wisdom. Instead of doing all these things that were making me more aware of my body, I should have just gotten laid. Then the feelings formerly known as a crush might not make me say or do anything stupid when I saw Fred. Maybe that was the reason Roberto had insisted on being with us: to save me from myself.

After my massage, Pascal helped me into something called a flower-infusion bath, where I nearly fell asleep while I soaked. I finally got out and wrapped a clean towel around my waist before Pascal took me to a dry sauna.

I balked when he opened the door and said, "It's so dark in here."

"It's a one-person room," he said. "Just lie back and sweat out the toxins released by your massage. I won't let you stay longer than you're supposed to."

I did as I was ordered. The warm wood under my body was soothing. If I could afford that kind of pampering all the time, I'd never suffer from insomnia. I began to drift, imagining my room-mates' reactions if I tried to stay in the bathroom long enough for an infusion bath.

I heard the door open, but it immediately closed. I figured someone hadn't known the room was occupied. I was half asleep when it happened again a few minutes later. When I didn't hear Pascal telling me it was time to leave, I drifted again.

Then I smiled when I felt a warm hand grip my thigh. Maybe Pascal wasn't *all* business. I didn't resist or react. I was too relaxed, and I wanted to know what would happen next.

He removed my towel. When I touched his arm, he grabbed my hand and moved it to my chest. Then he placed my left hand on top of my right and held both of them down. His breath was warm as he kissed his way down my stomach. He stimulated me with his tongue, then let go of my hands so he could use both of his hands to explore more flesh below my waist.

I knew he didn't want me to touch him or talk, so I didn't. The only sound in the sauna was my ragged breathing. After I came, we were both still for a few seconds. Then he gently used my towel to clean me up. I felt him place a warm, folded towel on my chest after he shifted away from me. I thought his lips brushed the top of my head. Before I realized what was happening, he'd opened the door. I turned to look at him in the dim light from the corridor, but he was already gone.

I lay back and closed my eyes. I was so drowsy that I wondered if I'd dreamed the whole thing. But I could still smell him. It had definitely happened, although I didn't think it was one of the services the spa was meant to provide.

I'd dozed off when the door opened again and Pascal said, "Nick? Come with me, please."

I got up and went outside, trying not to be obvious about searching his face for any sign of a connection between us. But he was the way he'd been all afternoon. Professional. Polite. A little distant.

"What's next?" I asked.

"While you take a cool shower, I'll bring your clothes to you. Then I'll take you to the reception area. Tara will complete your paperwork, and you'll be finished. I hope you've enjoyed our services."

His speech went on, but I wasn't really listening. I stared down at the floor while we walked, trying to figure him out. Was I supposed to pretend like it never happened and just leave a big tip for him with Tara? Wouldn't that be insulting?

"Do you ever go out with your clients?" I asked.

He looked surprised, either by my question or the interruption. After a few seconds' hesitation, he said, "I only work on the men's side of the spa, so I don't have any women clients."

I frowned. Who was he kidding? Straight men might occasionally drink too much as a reason to absolve themselves of guilt for a little man-on-man action. But they didn't give hand jobs to other men when they were stone-cold sober.

"Sorry," I said. "I thought you were gay."

"No big deal," he said. "It's not the first time someone's made that mistake. But no, I'm definitely straight."

He seemed unfazed, and it dawned on me that I had no proof that it had been Pascal with me in the sauna. I'd just assumed. It could have been someone else on the staff. It could have been another client who'd seen me go in. Since we hadn't exchanged a single word, for all I knew I'd been with one of the deaf yoga people.

Several of the showers were in use. Pascal ushered me into an empty one and said he'd be waiting in the dressing area with my clothes when I was finished. The cool water felt great as it washed away my sweat.

I shrugged into the thick terry cloth robe that was hanging just inside the stall door, and ignored the slippers. As I stepped out, I came face-to-face with Fred, who was also wearing a robe and running a towel over his wet hair.

We stared at each other until he finally said, "The whole meeting thing stressed me out. I thought a massage was a good idea."

"Right," I said. "Me, too."

"I'll see you in a few minutes," he said and hurried out.

I held back, wanting him dressed and out of there ahead of me. I was taken off guard by seeing him earlier than I'd planned, but that wasn't what was making my stomach do flips. Could it have been Fred in the dry sauna with me?

That was crazy. But what was crazier was the mixture of feelings the possibility stirred inside me. I'd had a crush on him for so long and had fantasized about something like that with him a thousand times. But after weeks of being furious at him, the thought of being sexual with him was disorienting.

Fred, like me, wasn't fixated on a grooming routine, so he was already gone by the time I went out and took my clothes from Pascal. Pascal and I exchanged only a few words while he took me to Tara to settle my bill. I added all the appropriate gratuities, wondered what my mother would think of the total, then followed Tara's directions to the Tranquility Room.

"So," Fred said when I walked in.

I'd taken two bottles of water from Tara. I drank about half of my first bottle to buy time. Then I said, "We should wait until Roberto gets here."

Fred shrugged and went to look at a mirror in a mosaic frame, as if he gave a shit about things like that. I couldn't study him, since he could see my reflection, so I stared at the floor. I was still trying to deal with my mixed emotions when Roberto came in. He stopped short, obviously having thought he'd be the first one there, and Fred and I stared at him.

"Is it raining?" I asked. When Roberto gave me a blank look, I said, "Your hair."

"Is wet," Fred added.

"I got here a couple of hours ago," Roberto said. "I took a spin class. Then I needed a shower." He gave me a curious look when I laughed.

"I came early, too, for a massage," Fred explained.

"I had an entire afternoon of beauty," I said.

"Didn't work," Roberto and Fred said together. They frowned at each other, then at me. I frowned back.

"Why are we even doing this?" Roberto finally asked. "Are you going to apologize? Because if you think what you did is okay, we've got nothing to talk about."

"When I started the blog," Fred said, "I never thought anyone I knew would read it. It was a way for me to vent about work. Or talk about what it's like living in New York. Or whatever else was on my mind. I never used people's real names."

"You used my older brother's name," I disagreed.

"Yeah, and he's the only Tony living in the Midwest."

"I'm just saying."

"I don't know how people began finding the blog. Or why they were interested in it. It just took off. My editor says—"

"The fact that you can even say 'my editor says' is fucked," Roberto said. "I don't give a shit about the history of your blog. I don't care how innocent your motives were. I. Don't. Care. Got it? You told secrets you had no right telling. You fucking told the world I'm HIV-positive. In the first place, you don't know whether or not that's true. If it is true, it's not your place to announce it. My little brother's freaking live on the Internet."

"That's why I don't use real names," Fred said. "Only a handful of people know who the Barista is, and *they* wouldn't have known if Melanie had kept her mouth shut."

"Is the author of your book also going to be called the Barista?" I asked.

"Of course not. In case you haven't checked it lately, I've pulled a lot of posts from the blog. Anyone in my book will be composites of several people. No one will be identifiable."

"Not the point," I said. "Even if no one knows who I am, you trashed my family. Both my families. You talked about my brothers. My uncle. You talked about some of the most private stuff in my life. It doesn't matter whether or not people know that 'Stick' is Nick Dunhill. It doesn't matter whether or not you're accurate or full of shit. You violated my trust. I used to think the reason you listened to me, paid attention to me, was because we were friends. All that time, I was just material for your blog. And you still haven't apologized."

"I'm sorry."

"That means so much now that it was dragged out of you," Roberto said. "I know how Nick feels. I thought we were friends, but we're not, are we? I'm just Roberto, the dumb Latino kid who paints on walls and manages to get infected even after being *informed* about the risks. By the way, did you do my lab work? And do you plan to publicly diagnose all your so-called friends, or just me?"

Fred stared at him a few seconds, then said, "I knew you were HIV-positive because I saw you at Duane Reade one night. You didn't see me. The pharmacist was telling you stuff about your medication. I looked it up online and found out it's an HIV drug."

"Maybe he was picking it up for a friend," I said. "Maybe he was getting it for one of his brothers. Or for me or Kendra or—"

"You know what made me sure?" Fred asked, turning back to me. "Because of the way you suddenly fixated on Adalla and her little girl. That's what you did with Emily when Gretchen died. After that happened, you fucked around at school. You stopped hanging out with the rest of us. You got that hollow look in your eyes. It was over a year before you started acting normal. Or as close to normal as you'd been in a long time. Then, for no apparent reason, you dropped out of Pratt. You moved out of your uncle's place. You avoided people who care about you. Same pattern, so I knew something bad had happened. It wasn't much of a leap to figure out that Roberto must have told you the truth."

"You're wasted on us, you should be working for the FBI," Roberto said. "Actually, you don't know shit. And you were wrong to blog about it. I'm done here."

Fred and I watched him walk out. Then I said, "You really, really suck."

"I apologized," Fred said. "I'll do everything I can to mask your identities in the book. It's not like it's all about you anyway. You're just a tiny part of a big picture of life in New York. The book is about the challenges of living here."

I stared at him and thought of all the times I'd imagined being the one he finally fell for. Of his being the one I could fall for. It was sad to let go of that possibility. It was even sadder to feel like there was an exact moment when I could pinpoint the end of a friendship.

"I think you just clarified things," I said. "To me, the city's a tiny part of everything that's big. Friendship. Trust. Loyalty. You were a huge part of my little picture. I'm not mad anymore. I'm just . . . what Roberto said. I'm done."

"Yeah, that's what you do when people let you down. You walk away."

"If your book isn't a big success, at least you've got your degree in Starbucks psychology to fall back on. I can't control what you write about my family. But I won't be giving you any new material."

Roberto was sitting on the edge of the futon when I got home. The girls weren't there. The TV was off. He hadn't even turned on music. He was staring down at his hands when I walked in. He gave me a little smile, then looked down again.

I sat next to him, nudged him with my shoulder, and said, "Okay, so it was you who gave me a hand job in the sauna, right?"

He kept staring down, but I could tell he was intrigued. Finally he looked at me and said, "Seriously? Somebody did that?"

"Come on, admit it. You wanted me bad."

"If I wanted you bad, I could have you any night of the week in this bed," he said.

"You think I'm that easy?"

"Yes." A pause. "Maybe it was Fred with you in the sauna."

"The thought crossed my mind. I guess we'll never know."

"Unless he blogs about it," Roberto said.

I gave him a dirty look. After a few seconds, we both cracked up.

"It's not funny," I insisted.

"I know."

"Why are we laughing?"

"What else can we do?"

"Fred said I always walk out on people who let me down. Do I? Is that what I did with Chuck? With Uncle Blaine?"

"Don't let Fred fuck with your head," Roberto said. "You left Wisconsin before you and your brother could kill each other. You left your uncle's to figure out what you wanted to do with your life. There's no door you've walked through that isn't still open."

"You're kind of sexy when you talk smart," I said and nudged him again.

"Never gonna happen," Roberto said.

"It's because you're straight, isn't it?"

"It's because you're a sauna slut," he said. "I've got my principles."

November 3, 2003

Dear Nicky,

Let me know if you want to come home at Thanksgiving. You can charge a ticket on the credit card, or I can charge one from here. But it would be a good idea to do that soon. The airlines are always crazy during the holidays.

As far as I know, there are no plans here yet. But you know how your father and your grandparents are, so that could change. I'd love to see you, but I don't want to pressure you about it. If you have other plans, I understand.

I love you,
Mom

15

It's a Sin

"Crap," I muttered and dumped everything from my bag onto my bed again. I'd repacked it three times already, because the sweaters took up too much space. I only wanted to take one carry-on with me. The less time spent in airports the better. The thought of standing and waiting for a suitcase to arrive on a slow-moving carousel made my knees weak.

Stupidly, I'd decided to go to Wisconsin to see my family. It was a spur-of-the-moment decision I'd made after Mr. Wamsley informed us that the office would be closed for a week at the end of November. Not because of Thanksgiving, but because of a rodent problem in our building. The entire place was scheduled to be gassed, and Mr. Wamsley decided it would be the perfect time to go to the Bahamas. I made the mistake of letting it slip that I'd have the week off while talking to my mother. It was her duty as a mother to drop a guilt bomb on me, so she did.

"Are you having Thanksgiving dinner with your uncle?"

"I doubt it," I said. "I haven't seen much of Blaine. We've both been really busy, and he's out of town a lot."

"That's a shame. He's been good to you."

"Yeah. I guess. What are you guys doing for Thanksgiving this year?" I asked, hoping she'd tell me she had plans to run off to Greece with a shipping tycoon who'd feed her olives while she lounged on his yacht.

"Whatever your father wants to do, I suppose." She sighed and added, "I'd rather see you. I miss you, Nicky."

I pushed my anxiety away and said I'd come home. I hoped the visit would be one of those impulsive schemes that could turn out okay for everyone. I had a picture in my head of a Hollywood Thanksgiving: the family surprised and happy to see me when I got there. They'd drop everything to give the prodigal son a hug. Eyes would brim with tears and we'd all have a good laugh. My dad would clap me on the back. Then I'd sit in the kitchen while my mom put the finishing touches on Thanksgiving dinner. Later, when we sat down to eat, I'd say a blessing while a light snow fell on the quiet night.

I threw two sweaters into the corner of my bedroom and said, "Yeah, right."

A *blessing?* Who was I kidding?

I missed my family in a weird sort of way. I wanted to be around them, but I couldn't figure out why. Maybe to let them know that I was okay. Maybe to prove that I was making it on my own. I always felt like their expectations of me were being dashed. If they could see how well I was doing, hopefully I'd get their respect.

I stuffed clothes back into my bag and again said, "Yeah, right."

I knew what would happen. I'd go home and my mother would be the only one to greet me. My brothers would have been out late the night before. They'd have gotten up early to join people from church delivering Thanksgiving dinners to shut-ins. This would earn them hours of being slugs in front of the TV with my father. Unless he was out on an "emergency call" for work. Funny how those always happened on holidays. My mother would have ordered food from one of the two or three area restaurants that did a complete Thanksgiving meal. She'd stay in the kitchen warming it all up while drinking a bottle of wine. I'd hide in my room until my grandparents and Uncle Wayne arrived for dinner, return there afterward, and pretty much stay there the entire time I was home to avoid confrontation.

"I must be crazy," I muttered as I zipped my bag closed.

"I could've told you that," Roberto said, coming into the room. He laughed when I jumped and said, "Didn't mean to startle you. But you're cutting it close if you're gonna make that flight."

"Right." I looked around, wondering if I'd forgotten anything.

"Have you seen my sanity? It's been missing for a week. Ever since I let my mother book that ticket."

"If you don't want to go, then don't."

"You make it sound so easy."

"It is."

"No. I have to do this."

Roberto sat on the futon and said, "You don't *have* to do anything but remain true to yourself."

"What's that supposed to mean?" I asked, annoyed.

He shrugged and said, "I don't know. It sounded good. Forget Wisconsin. Come home with me. You know my mother's cooking is better than anything you'll get in Dairyland. We'll have fun. We'll get high. We'll eat good. Whatever you want to do, we'll do. Come on, man. Cancel the flight. You know you're going to, anyway."

Roberto had always been the brother I wished I'd had, but suddenly he sounded like the brothers I already had. His words seemed like a challenge. Worse, they were almost taunting, as if he was implying that I was weak. In my heart, I knew that wasn't what he meant, but I instantly thought of my brothers, Fred, Morgan, and everyone else who'd picked on me or thought I was crazy. I grabbed my bag and walked out of the room.

"Aw, Nickito, come on!"

"Have fun with your family, Roberto."

"*Estúpido,*" he muttered. I decided he was talking to himself and didn't respond.

Kendra stumbled from her room and into my path. Her hair was a rat's nest. She squinted at me. "What time is it?"

"Five in the morning."

"Good. I still have time." Whatever else she said was lost in a loud yawn. "Shouldn't you be gone?"

"I'm on my way out. When does your bus leave?"

"Eight. There's another one at noon, if I don't make it on time. As long as I get home by dinner, it's cool. I have to make the salad. It's a tradition in my family. My parents would be so disappointed if I didn't come home. I almost didn't make it last year."

"Do you guys have to have this conversation outside the door while I'm trying to sleep?" Morgan yelled from the bedroom. Roberto, Kendra, and I cringed in unison and tiptoed to the kitchen.

"What's Morgan doing for Thanksgiving?" I whispered.

"Who knows? She and the other Gorgons are probably getting together so they can—" Kendra's sentence turned into another unintelligible yawn. When she finished, she shook it off, rubbed her right eye, then stared at us.

"I think she said she's going home," Roberto whispered.

"Morgan has a home?" I asked, forgetting to be quiet. I thought about canceling my trip so I could discreetly follow Morgan. Since they were fumigating the office, Bailey had said she might as well go home for Thanksgiving, but she never said where home was. If I trailed Morgan, maybe she'd wind up at the same place as Bailey. Then I'd know once and for all if they were related. I'd have to be careful and extra sneaky, but I knew I could manage it. I was very observant.

I was also obviously searching for any lame excuse to cancel my trip. Roberto knew me better than I knew myself.

"Of course I have a home," Morgan said from behind me, causing me to jump and drop my carry-on bag. "Do you think I came from Mars? You'd better not answer that, or I'll kick your ass."

"I didn't mean anything bad. It's just that you never talk about personal stuff," I said.

She pushed by us on her way to the coffeemaker. "That's because it's personal."

"Good point," I said.

"Who used my mug without washing it?" When nobody answered, Morgan nodded at me and asked, "Aren't you supposed to be at the airport?"

"I'm going! I love how you're all trying to get rid of me." I looked at Roberto and added, "Except for those who think I'm too much of a pussy to—"

"That's not what I said!"

"Guys, please don't argue," Kendra pleaded. "Be thankful he cares, Nick."

Morgan pretended to puke in the kitchen sink.

"All I'm saying is that if you happen to miss your flight, which is entirely possible if you hang out here much longer," Roberto said, "then you're welcome to spend the day with my family."

"Fine. I have to go. I hope you all have a great day."

Roberto and Kendra hugged me. Morgan grunted and waved without looking up from the coffee mug she was scrubbing. Outside, I hailed a cab and asked to be taken to LaGuardia.

"Are you going home?" the driver asked. His accent, and the fact that I could only see the back of his head, compelled me to glance at his medallion number. Next to it was a photo of a smiling man with dark skin and the name Samir Singh.

"Uh, yeah," I answered slowly. He made me nervous, which annoyed me. I didn't like it when people made assumptions when they learned that I was gay. I didn't want to be a hypocrite. "Where are you from?"

Samir Singh glanced at the rearview mirror. Somehow his eyebrows managed to look cautious. "I live in Queens."

"That's not what I meant."

"I know. I pull your chain."

"My leg," I corrected.

"I yank your leg?"

"Never mind," I said. "Where are you from originally?"

"Why is it that you are asking? Why is there so many people driving today? I will take a shortcut, yes?" Without waiting for my answer, he made a sharp right turn that flung me against the door. I should've listened to Eartha Kitt and buckled up for safety. "You are wondering if I am from Iraq. If I am, will you shoot me in the head?"

"No!" I exclaimed.

"For that, I am thankful," Samir Singh said. "We are similar, my friend, in that your color causes me fear, as well. Your people fear me and do not want me to drive them. Or they want to cause me harm when they think I am against them. I am not. I only want to drive this taxi, not harm people."

"I'm sorry," I said.

"Why are you sorry? Do you send people to hate me?"

"I meant, I'm sorry if I acted like them."

"No. You are right to be cautious. Better to be safe than dead, no?"

"You sound like my uncles," I said and smiled. I noticed that we were approaching the Triborough Bridge. "Do I pay the toll now or at the end of the trip?"

"Now."

I reached for my wallet and cursed when I realized it was missing. I ransacked my carry-on bag, thinking I might have dropped it into one of the compartments. It wasn't there, either.

"What is wrong? Give me the money."

"I don't have it," I snapped.

"You must!"

"I forgot my wallet."

Samir Singh said something foreign and suddenly I was flying against the door again when he yanked on the steering wheel. The U-turn, shortly before the toll booths, thrust us into the path of several oncoming cars and trucks, but somehow we lived.

"What are you doing? Are you crazy? We could've been killed."

"I will take you back to get your wallet," Samir Singh said, "but you will most likely be missing your flight, if it is to leave soon."

"I can't."

"You cannot board a plane without your identification. You cannot pay me. Unless you have cash in your pocket? If you do, I will most happily turn the car around."

"No, don't!" I didn't think my skull could handle another concussion. "I only have a couple dollars, I think. But I can't go home."

"Not if you do not catch your plane, no," Samir Singh agreed.

"I mean, I can't go back to my apartment."

"I am most confused. Where am I taking you, and how will I be paid? What have I done to deserve this?"

If I went back to the apartment, I'd have to face the humiliation of Roberto assuming he was right. Maybe he was. Maybe I'd subconsciously forgotten my wallet because I was still afraid to fly. But I wasn't ready to admit that to him. I didn't want to go home until after my roommates left for their various Thanksgiving destinations. That would take a few hours yet. I couldn't have Samir Singh circling the city and racking up a cab fare I could never afford.

"I don't want to go home," I finally said. "To either home. I was supposed to fly to my parents' house, but I'm still afraid to fly. And if I go back to my roommates, I'll feel ashamed."

"Fear is a wall. It is not your guide. There is no shame in following your karma," Samir Singh said. "You are not meant to fly home today. That is all there is to it."

"My family's going to be very upset with me," I said, dreading the call I'd have to make.

"Or they may not."

"They will. I don't want to see anybody."

"Close your eyes to what you do not want to see."

"Now you're just making fun of me."

"Karma brought me to take you to where you are supposed to go. Where would you like that to be?"

"I can't pay you."

"There are rewards greater than the American dollar. Where am I to take you, my friend?"

I asked Samir Singh to stop on the far left corner of Columbus Avenue and Fifty-seventh Street, but he let me out on the near right. I didn't care. I was thankful for his kindness and glad that someone jumped into the cab after I exited. Hopefully, she had money.

I entered Blaine and Daniel's building and waved at Stratos. "Hi. I know it's early, but I'm sure they're up. I have my key."

"They're up, all right. Upstate, that is," Stratos said.

"What?"

"Nobody's home. They left yesterday. All of them."

"Happy Hollow," I mumbled. It had never occurred to me that they would continue their tradition of spending Thanksgiving at Gretchen's retreat. "Did Gwendy go with them?"

"Yup. Emily, too. Kruger. Gavin. Like I said, all of them. Sorry, kid."

"No, that's fine. Thanks, Stratos," I said and forced a smile before I walked outside.

I figured there wasn't much chance of waking Sheila and Josh in their San Remo apartment. If they weren't in L.A., they were probably with Blaine and everyone else. I could go to their place and figure out what I wanted to do. Once the coast was clear at my place, I could go home. Or I could stay at Sheila's. Or call Adalla and spend the day with her, Isleta, and their extended family. I could swallow my pride and go to the Bronx for the Mirones Thanksgiving. Or to see Isaiah, and we could have a big feast at—

"McDonald's," I said, staring up at the giant Ronald McDonald that hovered over me. I abruptly changed direction, realizing that Central Park West would be crazy as participants gathered for the Macy's Thanksgiving Day Parade. No way did I want to be caught in a crowd of people.

Roberto was right, even if he hadn't said it out loud: I was a pussy. But at least I was a pussy that the San Remo doorman recognized as he waved me in. Just to be safe, I knocked before I used my key to go inside the apartment.

I ignored the view of the park and the parade preparations and looked around, admiring what Nigel had been able to do with the small space. He'd honored Josh's passion for antiques with Shaker furniture. Whatever storage system he'd designed had conquered Sheila's tendency to live in clutter and chaos.

I crossed the room and stared at photos hanging in black frames on the wall. All the pictures were black and white. Except for a few wedding photos that I remembered from their town house, all were Josh's work. I studied the photos: Uncle Blaine with Daniel and Daniel's three sisters. Emily sitting between Gretchen and me in the park. Sheila's brother Jake and his girlfriend, whose name I could never remember. Blythe and Davii with Adam, Jeremy, and somebody dressed in geisha drag. Martin and two cute guys I didn't recognize. Daniel and Gretchen, this time with their friend Ken, who'd died of AIDS.

I stared at Ken for a while, but instead of feeling sad, I felt okay. I was glad Uncle Blaine had escaped the Dunhills and found his real family in New York. Even if I wasn't with them today, they were my family, too. Knowing they were there made me feel better.

We weren't perfect. We were just family. I might stay away for months, but I knew I could come back any time I wanted to. That made the prospect of calling Wisconsin a little less daunting.

I took out my phone and called my mother's work cell. I couldn't believe it when my father answered. It was evident by his hoarse voice that I'd woken him up.

"Is Mom awake?" I asked.

"Do you know what time it is? Chuck? Didn't you come home—"

"Nick," I corrected him. "I needed to call and stop anyone from picking me up at the airport later."

"What? When? Who's driving you home?" he asked, still sounding disoriented.

"No one." Why hadn't my mother answered the phone? I could tell her the truth. But not him. "I won't be there. My flight got canceled." It wasn't exactly a lie. I hadn't said *who* canceled it.

After a long silence, he said, "That's just terrific, Nicky. This is so typical of you. I canceled a ski trip to Telluride because you said you were coming home. I lost my ass on the deposit. And now you're not coming."

"Mom told me you didn't have plans," I said.

"She didn't know. It was supposed to be a surprise for the whole family."

"The *whole* family? But not me?"

"Don't give me any crap, Nicky. You made the choice to give up your family three years ago."

I stared at the pictures on the wall. "Tell Mom I'm sorry I couldn't make it. I'll call her later."

He hung up without answering. I tried to figure out how he and Uncle Blaine could be brothers. Then I thought about Tony, and it didn't seem so weird.

I stared at my cell phone a minute before I snapped it shut. There was no point ruining my uncle's holiday with a pitiful phone call telling him that I was alone on Thanksgiving. It was a stupid holiday anyway: an excuse to eat too much before the following month of spending too much just so families could fight and be miserable at Christmas.

I was the lucky one. The day was mine. I didn't have to fake being happy or face the way I made other people unhappy. I didn't have to answer questions about what I was doing with my life or listen to criticism about all the ways I didn't meet other people's expectations.

All I had to do was wait until my roommates were gone, and I could do exactly what I wanted. As soon as I figured out what that was.

Josh and Sheila were the kind of people who threw their loose change into a bowl on their dresser at the end of the day, and I was the type of person who had no shame in grabbing a fistful of quarters so I could get back uptown. There was enough left over for a cup of coffee from the deli across the street from our apartment. I stopped there first after I emerged from the subway station. I was standing on the corner, waiting for the light to change, when I noticed Morgan leaving our building and stomping down the sidewalk across the street. I didn't think she'd seen me, but I ducked behind two old women and crossed the street with them, just in case.

Keeping a healthy distance, I followed Morgan for three blocks. I expected her to go to one of the nearby subway entrances, or wait at one of the bus stops, but she passed them all by, which fueled my curiosity. If she wasn't going home, wherever that was, then what was she doing? Was her home within walking distance of our apartment? And why hadn't I left my carry-on bag in Sheila's apartment? I switched the strap to my other shoulder and cracked my neck, then ducked behind a stoop when Morgan checked for oncoming traffic and crossed the street in the middle of the block.

She hopped over a river of slush that had gathered in the gutter, but slipped when she landed on the curb. Her arms spun in the air as she tried to regain her balance, but she landed on her ass in the puddle. I stuffed my arm into my mouth to keep from laughing out loud, but any noise I made would've been drowned out by Morgan's shrieks of annoyance.

She stood up and brushed the wetness and grime from her pants, but they were hopelessly sodden. I retreated even farther into hiding when she looked around to make sure nobody had witnessed her clumsiness.

She went into a shop and I hesitated, wondering if I should go in after her. I hurried across the street, careful not to mirror Morgan's misfortune, and tried to locate her through the storefront window. I couldn't see much of anything. Then I noticed the display—two mannequins, both encased in rubber, one paddling the other— and took a step back to read the store's sign: RUBBER RIGHT.

"Okay," I drawled. Finally understanding why Alice felt compelled to go down a rabbit hole, I entered the fetish shop. If I never found out anything about Morgan, at least I'd learn why Rubber Right was open on a holiday.

"Hi. Happy Thanksgiving," someone said as the door closed behind me. I turned to see a black woman in a red patent leather catsuit standing behind a counter. Her head was shaved and her lips were painted fire engine red. If I hadn't been shadowing Morgan, I probably would've begged to take pictures with my cell phone's camera, so I could draw her later. But since I was trying to keep a low profile, I smiled and put a finger over my lips in the international sign for *Shhh! I'm stalking my roommate.* Red Kitty nodded knowingly, pointed behind me with a riding crop, and said, "Ball gags are in the back, sweetie, next to the leather hoods."

I nodded and turned to creep away, jumping when I heard the crack of Red Kitty's riding crop connect with the counter. I turned around with wide, questioning eyes.

"You have to check your bag. Now!"

I practically threw my carry-on bag at her, which seemed to please Red Kitty. She clipped a playing card to it, stowed my bag under the counter, then handed me a corresponding queen of hearts. She arched a penciled eyebrow and said, "Proceed."

I crept past racks of harnesses, vests, and other leather gear and tried to find Morgan before she discovered I was there. At the same time, I tried to figure out what I'd do when I did find her. Maybe I'd pretend to casually bump into her, as if I always bought a new whip on major holidays. Didn't everyone? Or I'd leap out and ambush her. As far as she knew, I was on a flight home. The shock would make her let down her guard and she'd tell me every sordid detail about her life. Which was really what I wanted. It bothered me that I'd lived with Morgan for months and knew so little about her. How was that possible?

When I reached the back wall of the store without seeing Morgan anywhere, I stood up and grunted in disgust. How did she get out without being spotted? I didn't see a back door. As far as I could tell, the only way out was the front door. Then I noticed two dressing rooms in the back corners of the shop. Both had long red curtains that were closed and covered the entire door frame. I glanced behind me to make sure Red Kitty was occupied and carefully moved one of the curtains aside. The dressing room was empty. I turned around to check the other dressing room and ran into Morgan.

"What the hell are you doing here?" she asked.

"Me?" I said indignantly. "What about you? I thought you were going home to see your family."

"Oh no," she said, wagging a finger in my face. "No, you don't. That's my line. You're supposed to be on a plane to Michigan."

"Wisconsin."

"Whatever. You lied to us."

"No. I forgot my wallet. I missed my flight. It's been a shitty day,"

I said. It was then that I realized she was wearing a nurse's costume made of white PVC material. I pointed at her and said, "Back to you. What's going on here?"

She looked uncomfortable for a moment and crossed her arms over her midsection. But then she put on her usual defiant glare, adjusted her cap, and said, "I don't have to answer that."

"In that outfit? Yeah, I think you do."

"I don't have to do anything."

The sudden crack of Red Kitty's riding crop silenced us. "Quiet!" Red Kitty boomed. I stepped backward in fear, but Morgan only looked embarrassed. Red Kitty looked at her and said, "I take it this is one of your roommates? What did I tell you about bringing drama to work?"

"Work?"

"Mind your own—"

We were interrupted by another crack from the riding crop. Red Kitty massaged her temple and said, "I've got the worst headache. Why did I think it would be worth it to open on a holiday? I'm closing up and going home. Might as well close for the weekend, while I'm at it. Business has been so shitty. I should've done what my mama suggested and been a stockbroker. No, I had to sink my savings into this dump. 'Baby, sex sells,' Marcel said. That's right. Sold me up the river. Met some tramp and left me with nothing but this money pit. What do I got to be thankful for? Thankful for this? I don't think so! Shit. That's right. I'm going home. I don't need this. I don't need nothing from nobody no how, and don't you forget it."

We stared silently as Red Kitty wandered back to the register, talking to herself the entire way. Morgan turned to me and whispered, "Let me get my coat, and I'll meet you outside."

In Pathmark's produce section, Morgan held up two cucumbers and asked, "Which one is better?"

I couldn't help but laugh. Although she had her coat on, she was still wearing the PVC nurse's uniform. If I were a patient in a hospital and she entered my room with those cucumbers in her hand, talking about taking my temperature, I'd probably black out.

"They look the same to me," I said. "Does it matter?"

She looked annoyed. "Of course it matters. You're the artistic genius. You're telling me you can't see the subtle differences in these cucumbers?"

"I'm not an artistic genius, and they're just vegetables."

She made an obvious show of comparing the size, ripeness, smell, and feel of the cucumbers, then placed one in our cart. Walking ahead of me and pulling the cart behind her, she said, "They're not the same. I'm surprised at you. Aren't you supposed to be a twin?"

I grabbed the handle of the cart, jerking her backward. She glared at me, clearly annoyed, until I said, "Takes one to know one."

Her expression faltered, but only for a millisecond. It was enough for me to know I'd struck a nerve.

"Where am I? A playground? Can we just get something to eat and go home?" she said and stalked down the aisle toward the baked goods.

I followed her, maneuvering the cart to catch random items as she hurled them back at me: a loaf of Italian bread, a bag of ginger-snap cookies, a box of coffee cake. I missed the coffee cake and it broke open, flying all around me.

"Hey!" I shouted.

Morgan turned around, saw the carnage, and sighed. She selected another coffee cake and gently placed it in the cart.

"At first, I thought you and Bailey just looked alike," I said. "With millions of people around, it's always possible to see someone who looks like somebody you know."

"Most everybody I see looks like a Neanderthal," Morgan mumbled.

The man behind the butcher case looked affronted. He turned to the guy next to him and said, "You help them. I'm going on a break. Stupid holidays. They bring out the worst in everyone."

Morgan rolled her eyes and asked the other guy for two pounds of ground beef.

"Then I thought the two of you might be cousins," I persisted.

"Who?" Morgan asked.

"You and Bailey."

"This is the woman you work with, right?"

"Yes. Your sister."

"How did we get from being cousins to twins?"

"Ha!" I exclaimed. The guy behind the counter jumped in surprise and ground beef flew into the air, sticking to the ceiling. He swore in Spanish and started weighing more beef.

"Ha? What are you shrieking about?" Morgan asked.

"I didn't say anything about you and Bailey being twins. You just admitted it!"

"I admitted nothing. You said something in the produce department about my being a twin."

"Oh yeah," I said, feeling stupid. Today's karmic lesson was that I wasn't cut out to be a detective.

"For God's sake, Nick, get a grip," Morgan said. She took the ground beef, thanked the butcher, and pulled the cart toward the dairy section. I watched her select cottage cheese, grated Parmesan, and ricotta. I followed her through the store, trying to pretend Bailey was there instead. It was next to impossible. I couldn't imagine Bailey in a vinyl nurse's uniform.

I did my best to let it go. I stopped questioning her. On the walk home, we laughed every time one of us slipped and almost fell on the icy sidewalk. I confessed to laughing at her when she fell earlier, surprised when she admitted she'd have done the same in my place. I didn't think she was able to laugh at herself.

"I'm sure I looked like a water buffalo on skates," she said.

"No. It wasn't like that. It was like watching a movie where the high-and-mighty hot girl finally bites it and does something human."

Morgan paused on our building's stoop and said, "Did you just call me a hot girl?"

"I spoke without thinking," I said. "I meant to call you a horrible wench."

"That's what I thought."

"I don't know why you always hide your body under lumpy clothes. When we get upstairs, find a mirror and look at yourself in that outfit. You look good. Guys have been checking you out the whole way home."

"Shut up."

"It's true!"

"No, really. Shut up. There's a hot guy checking me out right now. Go up without me."

"I don't know how to make a lasagna. We'll starve."

"Fine. Nurse Boyardee to the rescue."

"If it makes you feel any better, I'm thankful."

"Like the man said, this holiday brings out the worst in everyone."

Upstairs, Morgan put away the groceries and prepared the lasagna while I washed vegetables and made a salad. I braved another question, asking her about the second job.

"Student loans," she lamented. "I hate being in debt, and I owe so much money. It's frightening. I don't have the winning personality required for waiting tables, or other part-time jobs in the service industry. I tried to work at a herp shop—"

"A what?"

"Reptile dealer. But people are so freaking stupid that I'd talk them out of buying snakes. Not exactly a path to success. When I saw the HELP WANTED sign in the S&M shop, I thought it might be a strange place to work—"

"But maybe the customers would be happy to take your abuse," I guessed.

"Exactly."

I put the bowl of salad into the refrigerator and said, "I'm surprised. I never thought you worried about anything. You always seem so in control. Of everything."

"That other cucumber? The one I didn't choose? Part of it was rotten beneath its skin."

"I don't think you're rotten. I know I've acted—"

"Let me finish," Morgan snapped, slapping a spoon on the counter as if it were Red Kitty's riding crop. "You don't know me. You make assumptions. If you'd taken the time, you'd have realized the one cucumber had a big soft spot. It's okay, though. I do the same thing sometimes. I know how I come across to people. I know I'm a hard-ass bitch. Whatever. I'm glad I got to see today that you're not the immature drama queen I thought you were."

I was about to protest the drama queen label when the door opened and Roberto surprised us both.

"What are you doing here?" we all chorused.

Roberto's mouth was actually hanging open. I couldn't tell if he was shocked to see us because we were all supposed to be somewhere else, or if he was amazed to see Morgan and me in the kitchen at the same time without brandishing weapons.

Or maybe it was the nurse's uniform, because Morgan was still wearing it. He stared at her, then at me, before he passed me a plastic bag filled with containers of food.

"Can you put this in the refrigerator? It's all stuff my mother made. Is that lasagna?"

"Not enough time to cook turkey," I explained.

"My mother made turkey. It looked really tender." He gestured to the fridge and said, "Help yourselves, if you want."

"Looked tender? Didn't you eat?" Morgan asked.

Roberto shook his head and said, "No. My stomach's been upset all day. It was too crazy at the house. Every one of my brothers has friends over. I came back here for some quiet."

"I'm sorry," I said.

"No, it's cool. I'm glad to see you guys. Make all the noise you want. I can sleep through anything."

That wasn't why I was sorry, but I kept my mouth shut.

"Go take a nap. Dinner won't be ready for a while. Maybe then you'll feel better, and you can join us," Morgan said.

"Doctor's orders?" Roberto teased.

Morgan looked down at her outfit and said, "I need to change."

"I've been waiting to hear you say that for months," I joked.

"Stick that in the oven and bake it for forty-five minutes," she ordered. When I picked up the pan, she added, "I was talking about your head."

Roberto looked better after his nap. The three of us had just settled around the table in the living room with the lasagna, the reheated Mirones food, and a bottle of Morgan's wine when we heard the door open, then a flurry of footsteps in the dark hall. Kendra stopped short in the doorway, stifling a scream when she saw us.

"She *says* they're harmless," I said, gesturing toward Lucifer and Hugsie, who were winding their way around the TV, which was off.

"They're not—you're not—what are you *doing* here?" Kendra demanded.

"Eating," Morgan said. She got to her feet, grabbed the snakes, and disappeared into their bedroom.

Kendra still hadn't moved when Morgan came back with another plate and silverware, so Roberto said, "We have a boatload of food. But you probably already ate with your family. Did you get there in time to make the salad?"

Kendra stared at the food. I could have sworn she was salivating. "Oh, come on," I said. "Eat. We know you didn't go home. We all got busted today."

"I went to the Bronx," Roberto protested.

"You went there long enough to pick up food," I said. "Morgan—well, never mind what Morgan was doing."

"They both know," Morgan said, spooning lasagna onto her plate.

"Know what?"

"They know where I moonlight."

"Everybody knew but me?" I asked, giving Roberto a dirty look.

"That's where I met her," Kendra said. She took off her coat and flopped down between Roberto and me. "I used to work there, too."

"Don't tell me, let me guess. With your excellent housekeeping skills, you were the Rubber Room's French maid."

"Rubber Right," everyone corrected me in unison, and Kendra added, "I was more the literary one of the bunch."

"You were a teacher? A nun with a ruler? A schoolgirl in uniform?" I speculated.

"Little Red Riding Hood. Heidi. Bo Peep. Goldilocks. I got my best sales as Puss in Boots."

"And then she got fired as Tinklebell," Morgan said.

"It's Tinkerbell," I said.

"Not for Mr. Pee-On-Me, it wasn't."

"I thought you were just selling the stuff," I said.

"We were," Kendra said, frowning as she picked cucumbers out of her salad. "He wanted more. When I turned him down, he threw a fit, accused me of a bunch of stuff, and I got fired." I stared at her so long that she shifted uncomfortably and said, "What?"

"I think that may be the first time I've heard the end of one of your stories. And it sounds like one of mine."

"So now you know our big secrets," Morgan said. "Let's move on."

"I don't think working at a fetish shop is the biggest secret at this table," I disagreed.

Before Morgan could respond, Kendra shrieked, "Okay! I lied! I don't have a family to go home to. My parents got divorced when I was a little kid. My grandmother owns a horse farm in Kentucky.

She paid my mother to move back to Trenton with me and stay away. My father got remarried to some Louisville debutante and they have three perfect blond daughters. My mother and her boyfriend usually start drinking early on holidays and they're passed out by dark. Now you know. Happy?"

We all gaped at her. I finally said, "Is that where you got the money to pay me back? From your father?"

"My grandmother," Kendra said. "All I have to do is threaten to come for a visit and she'll wire me money. I must not be allowed to ruin the *guhls'* opportunities."

"So your pot-smoking granny—that must be your mother's mother?" I asked.

"No. It's the one in Kentucky," Kendra said.

"Have you ever met your sisters?" Roberto asked.

"A few years ago. They're actually kind of sweet," Kendra admitted. "There's just no place for me in that world. Unlike the rest of you, I don't have a family to go home to."

"Am I not sitting here with you?" I asked. "It was just like Roberto said. I couldn't deal with my family, so I canceled my trip."

"At least you tell the truth about yourself to your family," Roberto said. "All I do is dodge questions from my brothers. 'When you gonna bring a girl home?' 'When you gonna get married?' Or my mother. 'When you gonna find a nice girl and make a *nieto* to call me *abuela*?' 'I'm only nineteen,' I say. 'You too ashamed to bring a girl here?' she asks. My family gives new meaning to the Spanish Inquisition."

"You should take Adalla to meet your mother," Kendra said. "She comes with a baby already."

"She's met Adalla, and I'm not making up shit about a girl-friend. But I can't tell her the truth." When nobody said anything, he went on. "It would kill her to find out I'm HIV-positive. And JC would kill me long before I ever get sick with AIDS."

"Ohhhhh," Kendra said in a long moan and dropped her head.

Roberto met my eyes, then looked at Morgan, who reached over, thumped his arm with her fingers, and said, "Nice try. I'm not get-ting back in the nurse's uniform for you."

He laughed, and Morgan looked almost coquettish as she smiled at him. It scared me, but fortunately she immediately turned to me with her usual deadpan expression and said, "I didn't know Thanksgiving was a day of confession. Must be some church I never heard of. Fine. Bailey's my twin."

"See, now I don't believe you," I complained. "You're humoring me. I'm starting to think you're my imaginary friends. You're each a projection of my own fucked-up life. Roberto has a secret from his family and no kids in his future. Kendra has a family that throws money at her to keep her away. Now *you* have an estranged twin."

"I never said we were estranged," Morgan said. "Bailey and I get along fine. We're just totally different people who live separate lives."

"You're not that different," I disagreed. "Otherwise, I wouldn't have known you were sisters. Chuck and I have similarities, too, like anybody who grows up in the same house."

"That's just it. We didn't grow up in the same house."

"I read a good mystery about twins who were separated at birth," Kendra said.

"We *weren't*," Morgan said. "God. You people have been nosing around my private life for months, and now I can't get a word in edgewise." She paused. When none of us mouthed off, she said, "When we were two, our mother had a fling with a musician. Yes, you would recognize his name. No, I'm not telling you. She ended up moving into his castle in"—she paused for a beat—"an undisclosed European country. At first, she had us with her. But I got asthma and it was decided that a drafty castle wasn't a good environment for a toddler with respiratory problems. So they split us up. I was raised in a farmhouse in Connecticut. Bailey grew up surrounded by rock stars."

"I thought she just slept with them," I said.

"It's like *Parent Trap*," Kendra said.

"Without the Disney ending. When we got older, they threw us together at holidays, but we had nothing in common. We didn't fight. We just didn't get all gushy about it. If we met each other any other way, we'd never be pals. Why should we pretend to be just because we're twins?" She noticed Roberto's frown and said, "You get it, don't you, Nick?"

"I guess," I said, not sure that I did.

"Don't you have *any* good memories of your siblings? Either of you?" Roberto asked.

Morgan's dark eyes got even smaller, which seemed almost like a smile. "It's fine, Roberto," she said. "There's nothing missing from my life. I probably had it lots better than Bailey, because our mother's so self-absorbed. I got along fine with my father and my stepmother. I also stopped having breathing problems after I moved back to Connecticut."

Roberto looked at me, and I did a desperate scan of my memories to find something for him.

"Sure I do. Like when my dad taught Tony to shave. Chuck and I sat on the edge of the tub and watched them. My dad put shaving cream on us, too, and we pretend-shaved." It was a lame effort, and Roberto didn't look impressed. "Saturday nights were okay, too, at least before we were teenagers. We played games. Shared popcorn my mom made."

"Microwave or regular?" Roberto asked.

"Real popcorn," I said.

"Did you ever have a Jiffy Pop accident?" Kendra asked. When we shook our heads, she said, "I wonder if my life would have been better with a twin." She looked confused when Roberto and I started laughing. Morgan sighed and took her empty plate to the kitchen for seconds.

Later, Kendra vanished when it was time to wash dishes. Roberto and Morgan swore I was getting in their way on purpose and kicked me out of the kitchen. I fell across the futon, realizing how many hours I'd been awake, and thought about what was going on at home. My grandparents would be gone by now. My mother was probably disappointed in me for not showing up. She'd have opened a second bottle of wine and would be staring from the kitchen window. I wasn't sure how much snow they'd gotten, if any, but it probably still looked bleak outside. That would make her mood worse.

Tony was either planted in front of the TV watching a game or getting ready for a date. And Chuck . . .

My day with my roommates had turned out better than okay, so there was no reason for me to feel depressed. Maybe it was Chuck who was sad.

"Suck it up and just do it," I muttered and reached for my cell phone to call him. As I flipped it open, it rang. I looked at the display: CHUCK/CELL. Morgan could deny it all she wanted; there was something to the twin thing. I braced myself to hear how I'd fucked up the Dunhill Thanksgiving and said, "Hello?"

"When we were seven," Chuck said, "what was that kid's name that stole your bike?"

I thought for a few seconds and said, "Joey?"

"Yeah. Joey. He was an asshole," Chuck said.

"I wonder whatever happened to him," I mused.

"I killed him," Chuck answered in a monotone voice.

I laughed and said, "You sound just like that movie—"

"With the dog who says he's going to kill his father," Chuck said.

"What was the name of that movie?" I asked and settled against the pillows. It was the best position for the trip I was taking to Wisconsin, with no help from Northwest Airlines or Samir Singh.

November 27, 2003

Dear Nick,

I warn you in advance that this letter may be emotional. I'm not feeling like my usual give-'em-hell-attorney self. It's Thanksgiving night at Happy Hollow. We put together a feast today. Emily has been well spoiled. Now everyone is tucked in, dreaming their dreams. I can't sleep, so I came downstairs and stirred up the fire a little.

Holidays stay hard, but Thanksgiving is like none other. Anyone who knew her would say this is the holiday when Gretchen went all out. It still stuns me that I had only one Thanksgiving with her, and you had none. This isn't the way it was supposed to be. We were supposed to have years and years to be part of traditions with her.

Today, we remembered a tradition of Gretchen's and told one thing each of us is grateful for. But really, for me, there are too many to name just one. What I've lost, what we've all lost, is beyond measure. But so is what remains. How can love and friendship and laughter and family be measured? They sustain us, lift us up, and help us go on.

When I looked around today, I felt a different absence. The absence of Nick. You were the most amazing person in those months after Gretchen's death, especially the way you took care of Emily. We all could deal with the things we had to take care of knowing she was safe with you. There was so much to do that it might have been impossible for Blaine, Daniel, Kruger, and me to find any time to be still and grieve. You helped give us that time. Thank you.

I worry about you. Maybe because so much time has slipped by without seeing you. I hear from other people that you're doing well. I want to think that this past year has been you giving yourself the space YOU needed to grieve and heal.

I would love to get together. I want Emily to see you. I'm not trying to push you. I just want to remind you that you're loved and we're very thankful that you're part of our lives.

Much love,
Gwendy

16

Happiness Is an Option

If Quentin Starch hadn't been a little bit crazy, I would never have made the discovery that left me reeling. Isaiah and I had a few deliveries on the Monday morning after Thanksgiving, and then I was scheduled to work in the office. Last I'd heard, I was supposed to help Nigel put together some drawings for a client. I didn't have any more details than that.

However, when I walked through the door, Eileen looked frazzled. I paused with my apple juice halfway to my mouth. When I saw her take a knitting needle from her hair and try to write with it, I wanted to run back to Isaiah. Nothing fazed Eileen, so her disarray promised a bad day in the office.

"Help," she said the second she spotted me. "I can't do this search and keep up with the phones and everything else. Especially not when I started my day with two bran muffins and a glass of prune—"

"Oversharing." I cut her off. "What search? A computer search?"

She explained. Quentin Starch, a major client, had heard a theory: *Don't buy cars built on Monday or Friday.* Allegedly, employees did sloppy work on those days because they were recovering from one weekend or eager to start another one.

"Mr. Starch has extended this theory to the purchase of anything mechanical, including the Organique Kitchen food processor that Bailey"—Eileen's voice became acid when she said Bailey's name—"has insisted that Mr. Starch have in his newly remodeled kitchen."

"You're trying to find a food processor that was manufactured in the middle of the week?" I asked.

Eileen nodded and said, "If you can believe it, this information is actually available. Because every Organique Kitchen appliance is treated like something rare and wonderful. At their prices, they should be. There are eight Organique Kitchen stores in Manhattan. I've called all of them. Although everyone I talked to was insulted by the implication that any of their food processors aren't flawless, they did give me the manufacturing information."

"So what's the problem? I can just pick up—"

"Every food processor in stock has a Monday or Friday date on it," Eileen said. "Which Mr. Starch will know, because each one comes with a—a—*birth* certificate, you might call it."

"Should I call stores in other cities to find a Wednesday baby?"

"Mr. Starch is giving a dinner party tomorrow night. He needs his food processor today." She gave me an apologetic look and said, "There are over two hundred other stores in Manhattan that carry Organique Kitchen's small appliances."

"How many have you talked to?" I asked apprehensively.

She scratched her scalp with the knitting needle and said, "Eleven. All painful. No one can believe I expect them to find this information. In fact, they're a little surly when I tell them why I'm calling."

"See? Mr. Starch is right. Employees suck on Mondays. Other than me." I took the list from her and studied it for a minute, trying to find stores near the office.

"You can use the guest office," Eileen said. "And close the door. I don't want to hear you whimpering after every call."

I went into the guest office, which was really nothing more than a closet with a chair, table, and phone. After I took off my coat and finished my apple juice, I ran my finger down the list of stores. Vance Kitchen and Bath on Fourteenth Street caught my eye. I thought about third-period English class in ninth grade, when our teacher, Mr. Vance, thundered at Shelley Creighton, "You don't think poetry is *important?* I'll only go to a doctor who understands poetry. If a surgeon doesn't read, I don't want him cutting me open! People who don't appreciate literature *have no souls!*"

I dialed the store's number.

"Good afternoon, Vance Kitchen and Bath, this is Anita. How may I help you?"

"Hi, Anita, this is Nick. By any chance do you have an employee in your store who loves poetry?"

Anita didn't miss a beat, saying, "Howard likes to recite dirty limericks. Does that count?"

"Maybe. May I speak to Howard?" After a few seconds of bad hold music, a man came on the line and identified himself as Howard. I gave him my name and said, "I hear you appreciate poetry."

"Okay," Howard said. He drew the word out to let me know he was mystified but not yet offended.

"I'm trying to locate something for a man who finds a certain poetry in kitchen appliances," I said. "He wants an Organique Kitchen food processor, but it has to have been assembled on a Tuesday, Wednesday, or Thursday. I'm told that information is available with every—"

"He's heard about hungover plant workers, huh?" Howard interrupted. "Let me check the computer."

A few minutes later, I emerged from the guest office, waved a sheet of paper at Eileen, and said, "Got it." Her mouth dropped open. "Of course, I can't actually pick it up, since I don't have a corporate credit card."

"Go, go!" she said, reaching inside her knitting bag for a handful of twenties to thrust at me. "This should cover it. Just be sure I get a receipt."

I wondered if it was pathetic that I took pride in such small accomplishments. But I felt good. Maybe because my Thanksgiving weekend had ended so much better than it began. The unpleasant phone conversation with my father, the sadness of not seeing Blaine and my big gay family, as Fred called them—even the absence of Fred from my life—had all been made better by my roommates and my painless phone conversation with Chuck.

Then on Saturday, Roberto and I were invited to a big family feast at Adalla's uncle's place on the Upper West Side. On Sunday, Adalla's mother took care of Isleta so that Adalla, Roberto, and I could have dinner with the Mirones family at their favorite Mexican restaurant in East Harlem. I'd ended up with three family dinners instead of none. My friends had made me feel like I was part of something, and that feeling lingered.

When I got to Vance Kitchen and Bath, Howard let me go with Julien to the stock room to find the exact food processor I needed. Julien pulled the ladder over, gave me a look with soulful brown eyes, and said he didn't like climbing ladders. I wasn't sure whether or not I did, but I went up three steps and reached for the first food processor. That was when I felt Julien's hand slide its way up my inseam.

I looked down at him with a frown and said, "Stop that."

"You don't like me?" His face looked pouty. "It's because I'm French, isn't it?"

"I already lost one job when a hidden camera taped me doing something I shouldn't."

Julien looked around anxiously and said, "You think there are cameras back here?"

I suspected his hand had gone up a few other inseams before mine. "There are cameras everywhere."

He dropped his hands, I brought down the food processor, and he opened the box and handed me the paperwork.

"Friday, damn it," I said, and climbed the ladder again. At least that time I went unmolested.

The third box I pulled down had a Tuesday food processor. Julien led me back to the floor, I paid for it with Eileen's money, and finally I was outside, hugging the box to my chest and hoping it would block the cold air. I walked toward Union Square, where I intended to spend more of Eileen's money on a cab back to the office. Then I realized that I'd forgotten to put on my gloves. My hands were freezing. I set the box on the ground and gripped it with my calves just in case thieves were lurking. When I took my gloves from my coat pocket, one of them fell to the ground. I angled myself to pick it up, and as I stood upright again, I scanned the area around me. Which was when I saw her, down a narrow alley between two buildings.

I must be crazy, I thought. *It's because last week was Thanksgiving, Gretchen's favorite holiday. But I swear, if that's not Gretchen . . . I* know *it's Gretchen . . .*

I finished pulling on my gloves, picked up the box, and checked out the storefront. It was covered by a pull-down metal door. There was no sign to tell me what business was on the ground floor, or even if the space had a current tenant.

I walked slowly down the narrow alley toward the spray-painted mural. Finally I stopped and stared at the woman in the painting: head thrown back, arms raised in dance, laughing face, chestnut hair with blond streaks . . . Someone had painted Gretchen on this hidden wall. I even recognized the fawn-colored shirt she was wearing, which had been one of her favorites. It tied at the collar. She'd always left it untied, then complained when the little tassels on the ends dipped into whatever she was eating. She stopped wearing it once Emily started putting the tassels in her mouth.

When I could tear my gaze from her, my heart pounded, because I recognized her partner in the dance. She was touching the brilliant wing of a giant bird. No, not just a giant bird. Gretchen was dancing with a quetzal, Roberto's signature muse and totem. This was his work, a perfect depiction of Gretchen's soul, her zest for life. I wanted to kiss the wall. To go home and rave to Roberto about how much I loved it, how good it felt to see Gretchen happy and alive because of his art.

Except . . . I looked around, realizing how the painting was tucked away. I'd never have noticed it if I hadn't stopped in the exact place that I did. I wasn't meant to see it. No one was. In spite of the cold air, and even though I needed to go back to the office, I stood there for a long time, trying to work things out in my head.

By the time he was fifteen, Roberto had been caught a half dozen times "defacing" buildings and subway cars. I had no idea how much it had cost his mother and older brothers to work out the deal that landed Roberto in art school. They'd paid fines, legal fees, and tuition. Roberto had been placed on two years' probation. That had ended the year before, and now that he was over eighteen, it was no longer illegal for him to have spray paint in his possession. But if he got caught in the act, things probably wouldn't go well for him. He was likely to lose his job, and with it, the health insurance he needed.

Creating graffiti was always an activity that required stealth. But once it was done, the whole point was to have it seen. Since Roberto had hidden his work, he knew what he was risking. The fact that he did it anyway . . .

He had to be so frustrated. It was like a sickness, his compulsion

244   *Timothy James Beck*

to create these huge splashes of color and form. Since leaving school, he'd had no opportunity, no space, no encouragement to do what he really wanted. He'd tried to channel his creative energy into his job at Drayden's, but it obviously wasn't enough for him.

I realized I was jumping to conclusions. Maybe this was just a one-time thing. Or maybe he'd done it a long time ago. Except the mural was only a little weathered. I leaned forward and located his tag, a subtle *BirdO* hidden in the quetzal's plumage, and the *9/03* beneath it.

"Fuck me," I muttered. "How am I supposed to pretend like I didn't see your gift to New York on a shitty anniversary?"

My gut told me that there were other gifts hidden on other walls of the city. How long could he tempt fate before he got caught? And could I really keep my mouth shut about it? Roberto and I weren't like Fred. We didn't keep secrets from each other.

I thought about the roommate confessional on Thanksgiving and reached up to lightly touch Gretchen's hair with my gloved hand. I was wrong. Roberto had been really good at keeping a secret.

If Roberto noticed anything different about me over the next couple days, he didn't question me. The holiday shopping season was in full force. Even though Roberto's retail job didn't involve selling, he was still constantly changing displays or creating new ones at Drayden's. He came home late, didn't talk much, and fell asleep quickly. Which was fine with me.

One thing I was sure of: There was no evidence of what he was doing in our apartment. There wasn't a place to hide paint cans, markers, nozzles, tips, and masks. Of course, he could be doing it with a crew, so somebody else might be keeping his supplies. But he'd always worked alone in the past, and I didn't think that would have changed.

Any other time, I'd have talked to Fred about the mural. Now that was out of the question. The last thing I needed was for Roberto to read about my discovery on baristabrew-dot-com. If I asked for advice, it would have to be from someone wiser. Older. Maybe Adalla or Blythe. Or Uncle Blaine.

When I got home Thursday night, I found a letter that seemed like an answer. My cousin Emily's mother, Gwendy, had written me to suggest that we get together. Gwendy was not only an attorney, but as Gretchen's widow, she'd understand what had driven Roberto to paint that particular mural in September.

I called her and arranged a time and place for us to meet on Saturday.

"Wow," Gwendy said. "That's . . . I don't know what to say. It's beautiful. It's so *her*."

Gwendy hadn't canceled our plans to meet at the Big Cup, even though a storm had dumped eight inches of snow on the city the night before. Although more snow was forecast, the air was clear when we walked from the coffee shop to the mural.

I held her hand and pretended not to notice the tears streaming down her cheeks. At least until she turned and hugged me for the tenth time. Except unlike before, she didn't let go for a while.

"Okay," she finally said and pulled away.

"Okay? You sure?"

"I'm okay. I'm glad you warned me. It must have been quite a shock for you to find it on your own."

"It was, but it made me happy, too. In a weird way."

"It's not weird," Gwendy said, turning again toward the mural. "Explain the parrot to me. What I know about art could be painted on the head of a pin."

What you know about birds, too, I thought. "The quetzal's a rain forest bird. Sacred to the Mayans. They called it the god of the air. To them the quetzal represented freedom. Unfortunately, it was such a symbol of wealth that it was hunted until it was almost extinct. Roberto's always been fascinated by the quetzal. One time he told me . . ."

When I trailed off, she returned her gaze to me, her eyebrows raised. "What?"

"Sometimes the female quetzal leaves her children, but Roberto said the male is just as nurturing, so he steps in to take her place."

Gwendy's mouth twisted in a reluctant grin, and she said, "Blaine would appreciate that part. I want to tell Roberto that I've seen it and it made me feel good."

"I haven't told him yet that *I* saw it. He's only been off probation a year. What if he gets caught? What if some building owner wants to press charges? What if his career goes down the toilet?" I stared into her untroubled eyes. "Am I making a big drama where there is none?"

"Oh, who doesn't do that? Maybe this was a onetime tribute. Or maybe Roberto's gone back to street art. I don't know. I can say that if he gets caught, or the next time you get caught with something like a fake ID, would you just call me? What's the point of having an attorney in the family if you don't use me?"

"Again with the freaking fake ID," I mumbled. "That was ages ago."

I realized my mistake too late when her eyes flashed at me and she said, "Which goes to show how long it's been since I saw you. Why have you stayed away from Fifty-seventh so long? Where have you been? What's going on with you?"

"Nothing. Nowhere. I'm just working. You know. But it's all good. I like my job. I like living in Harlem. My roommates are cool, and I've made other friends. That doesn't mean I don't miss everyone. I do. But I'm mostly just working."

"It wouldn't kill you to pick up a phone and call someone once in a while, you know?"

"Okay, okay," I said sheepishly. "I'm sorry."

"Don't be sorry, just don't keep giving me reasons to make you feel guilty." She smirked as if acknowledging a job well done.

"Did you bring the camera?"

"Yeah. I forgot I had it." She reached into her pocket and handed me the camera.

I removed my gloves and took photos of the mural. Roberto's color choices on the brick would look great with the snow providing contrast.

"The thing is," Gwendy said thoughtfully, "if it's been here since September, chances are no one's gotten too worked up about it. Who knows? Maybe he had permission—"

She broke off, looked at me, and we both shook our heads. Getting approval wouldn't be Roberto's style. It defeated all the emotion and intention behind street art.

When she took back the camera, we both stared at Gretchen for a while in silence. Finally, I asked softly, "How do you do it?"

She didn't pretend not to understand me. After a few seconds, she said, "I don't ever mind talking about Gretchen. Why don't we walk to keep warm?"

I fell in step next to her. I figured we wouldn't walk long before she'd catch a cab back to Midtown, if for no other reason than to get out of the cold. I wondered if I wanted to go home with her. I didn't think so. Not yet.

"You know I'm not one to mince words." She broke into my thoughts. "Was it our fault you disappeared?"

"I didn't—whose fault?"

"Mine. Blaine's. Did we heap too much responsibility on you with Emily? You basically took over, and we let you."

"I wanted to be useful. You'd lost Gretchen. You couldn't get back into the Tribeca loft and were stuck staying with us. You and Blaine had to deal with all those agencies and attorneys and people asking you questions. I wanted to help. So I took care of Emily. After you got your apartment in our building and Kruger moved in, you didn't need—I didn't—"

"You felt like you got dumped, didn't you?"

"No. I just . . . You know, I had school and friends and shit to do."

"Uh-huh." After a pause, she said, "There's something I never told you. I don't know if it makes a difference."

"What?" I asked anxiously. I tried not to panic over all the things she might be about to say. Things I'd worried or wondered about. Questions with answers I didn't necessarily want to hear.

"You helped me in a way that's hard to put in words," Gwendy said. "See, everyone else knew me or Gretchen before we were a couple. But for you, it was always Gretchen and Gwendy. Everything you did or said showed that you completely respected our relationship."

"You mean other people didn't?"

"Not always. Maybe it wasn't intentional. For example, it never crossed your mind that Emily wouldn't stay with me. To you, I was Gretchen's surviving partner. Emily's mother. But some people assumed Blaine would take Emily because he's her biological father, whereas I'm not her biological mother."

"Uncle Blaine didn't feel that way, did he?"

"No. Neither did Daniel. There was never a question that they saw me as Emily's parent. Just like there was no question in my mind that she and I needed them. That's why I used the first insur-

ance money to buy in their building. We've created our version of a
family, and it works for us."

"It's a lot healthier than what some people call normal families."

We'd walked another half block when she surprised me by asking, "When did you cry, Nick? You were only seventeen, just a kid
yourself. I was so lost in my own grief that I didn't think about
yours."

"It's okay," I said. "I promise. I'm fine."

"I want to know what happened. I feel like there's something we
missed. Something that pushed you to drop out of college. To
move out of Blaine's."

"I needed to figure some things out," I said. "You didn't do anything. Neither did Blaine."

She had on her attorney face, and I knew she was thinking back
to January. Her instinct was good, but her timing was off. I wasn't
going to pinpoint it for her, or remind her that I hadn't wanted to
go back to Wisconsin the previous Christmas. Gwendy hadn't really
wanted to travel by air, either, with Emily. In the end, we'd all been
flown there on a jet belonging to one of Blaine's bosses. Not going
commercial had been a compromise. But nobody had considered
that I might not want to stay at my parents' house, or deal with my
father.

*"Whatever it is, you need to snap the hell out of it," he said after my
grades came in the mail. "If this is about Blaine's—whatever she was—that
happened over a year ago. It's time that you—"*

"Gretchen," I said. "Call her by her name. She's the mother of your niece."

*"I'm not heartless. I don't blame that little girl for being the result of sci-
ence taken to an unnatural extreme. If you want to think of her as your
cousin, go ahead. But her mother was never a Dunhill. It's not like you lost
a relative. She's just somebody who used your uncle's sperm to get knocked
up because she wouldn't do it the normal way. And now she's somebody
you're using as an excuse to fuck up. Dunhills do not fuck up, Nicky. At
least not on my dime. Get it together."*

"Nick?"

"How do you do it?" I repeated my earlier question. "How've you
done it? It must've been impossible for you, all this time without
Gretchen. I miss her, but it has to be a million times worse for you.
I'm sorry. It's not like I'm making it better."

"Keep talking," Gwendy ordered.

"There are times I can barely walk down the street. I hear a noise that's louder than it should be, and I practically come out of my skin. A low-flying jet makes me freeze. You're so together. You, Uncle Blaine, Daniel, and Gavin. Everyone. Everyone has it so together and I don't get it. Sometimes I feel like I'm going crazy because this stuff still affects me so much. I feel like I'm living on another planet. Or like I'm invisible on this one. Like I'm standing there freaking out, and nobody can see me."

She reached for my hand, and we kept walking.

"Nick, the strong times, the weak times—they all come in waves. Trust me, none of us has it together. Just when I think I'm through the worst of it, I'll read something that sets me off. Or I'll dream about her. Last night when it started snowing—do you remember that blizzard we had right after Emily was born? It was the first time Gretchen let Blaine take Emily home with him. All last night, I thought about that day, how hard it was for her to be separated from the baby even for a few hours. And I sat by the window and cried my eyes out while I watched it snow."

"I wish I *could* cry," I said. "I've tried to make myself cry. It just doesn't happen."

"So you keep it all in? That's not good."

I shook my head and said, "Roberto. I can talk to him. Although I usually don't have to. He always just knows. Do you think I'm crazy? For freaking out over loud noises? Hating the subway? Not wanting to leave the island by tunnel or bridge? Even though sometimes I feel like the city's out to get me?"

She'd turned down Seventh, and we came to Greenwich Street. I wasn't sure if it was intentional. When I stopped, she looked around as if to figure out why.

"Oh," she said. "I don't know what I was . . . See? We're all a little crazy."

"What finally happened with the loft?" I asked, looking in the direction of the building where she'd lived with Gretchen.

"I sold it. I want to talk to you about that, too, but another time." She started walking again, leaving me no choice but to follow her. "I'd think you were crazy if you *didn't* freak out now and then. You're not alone. Lots of us don't want to go on subways, be in tall buildings, or do things that we used to consider no big deal. We work around it. We go about our business because we have to. But you don't have to deal with it alone. We're here for you. It's okay if you come home once in a while, even when you're not okay. Especially when you're not okay."

"When you don't see me, just assume I'm all right. 'Cause I am. It's been good, living on my own."

She stopped and turned toward me, and I smiled when she smiled. "I think you're right," she said. "You look good. It makes me feel much better to see you like this. I'm proud of you."

"You and Sheila are the only people who've said that."

"Really? I know Blaine feels the same way. The city's not an easy place to live, but you've managed to find and keep an apartment, get a couple of jobs, make friends. Are you in love?"

"No," I said, and my expression made her laugh.

"There's time for that. That's the thing you have to start believing in again. The luxury of time. You can't maintain the intensity that comes after a tragedy. I don't mean you personally. I mean all of us." Her eyes went past me, and her expression was thoughtful. "I can't step away from the reality that she's gone. The questions never end. My imagination . . . But the point comes when I have to stop driving myself crazy with it. I have to appreciate everything I had and still have. And the ways she provided for me and for Emily."

"Do you think Emily remembers her?"

"I have no idea what gets embedded in a child's brain," Gwendy said. "She doesn't seem to. We talk about Gretchen in front of her. She knows she had another mommy, Grandpa's daughter, who's gone now. Eventually there'll be questions. We'll deal with them then."

I took a deep breath and said, "I don't want to keep walking downtown."

"Me, either. I was thinking the snow would be nice in City Hall Park, but—"

"Yeah," I said.

"You know what? Let's go skating at Rockefeller Center."

"Really?" I asked.

"I love to ice skate. For just a little while, let's pretend the only thing crazy about us is that we're tourists who've come to Manhattan during the holidays."

"Aren't we lucky it snowed?" I asked and took her hand again as we turned to walk back up Seventh.

December 12, 2003

Nick,

 I'm glad we talked on Thanksgiving, since you probably won't be coming home for Christmas. Especially after the way things were last Christmas. They won't be any better this year. Maybe worse.

 Mom asked me to clean out some of our old stuff. I found this big box of blocks. You probably don't remember that Uncle Wayne gave these to us when we were about five. They'd been Uncle Blaine's, and Grandma was going to throw them away when she was on one of her redecorating binges.

 We used them to build all kinds of stuff. Cities. Bridges. None of the other kids who came over got it. They liked Legos and more exciting stuff that made noises or had flashing lights. We had all that, too. But it was the blocks we liked most.

 I don't know if girls like stuff like this, but I think our cousin Emily has a birthday sometime this month. I figured I'd send the blocks to you. You can decide whether or not to give them to her. I didn't think they should be thrown away. It's kind of cool to think of another Dunhill kid playing with them the way we did. I kept one block for myself. You remember the big green one we used to fight over? I win.

 Hope you have an all right Christmas, wherever you spend it.

Chuck

17

A New Life

Running into Dennis Fagan on the street was intentional. I didn't think he cared whether anyone at Cutter's knew I was hanging around there hoping to see him, but *I* did. I didn't want to look pathetic if he blew me off or acted like nothing had ever happened between us. I reminded myself of a high school girl, like I'd gotten knocked up and was looking for my baby-daddy.

When Dennis saw me cut across his path to Cutter's entrance, he didn't walk past me or turn and go the other way. His pale blue eyes crinkled into that smile that didn't exactly warm them but let me know I wasn't about to be kicked to the curb. He reached over and gripped the back of my neck, shaking me like a bear playing with its cub.

"I thought maybe you'd moved away," he said. "Or at least gone home for the holidays."

"Nope," I said. "This is home."

He nodded and said, "What'll it be? A beer or—"

"Or," I said.

Another nod from him and we started walking. Silent walking, since he made that comfortable. He also constantly scanned and assessed everything around him, leaving no energy for idle conversation. He wasn't checking out men, though, or even watching for danger to come hurtling out at him the way I always was. Again, he reminded me of a bear. One who walked through the forest like he didn't have much to fear and wasn't really hungry, but thought it was his job to keep watch.

The image made me smile, and he cut his eyes at me as if we shared a secret.

Later, we lay on his bed with my head in his lap, my knees pulled up to my chest, while we passed a joint between us. I spotted a duffel bag and a suitcase across the room and said, "Are *you* going out of town for Christmas?"

"For work," he said. "My dumbass brother-in-law won a contract in Georgia, and he can't hold on to a good crew. I guess Atlanta doesn't speak Atlantic Beach, so it's the Fagan boys to the rescue."

I didn't say anything while we finished the joint. When it got too small, he dropped it in an ashtray next to the bed. Then he rested his hand on my head.

"How long do you think the job will take?" I finally asked.

"Don't know." He played with the spikes of my hair, flattening them, then fluffing them up again.

"Oh," I said. I winced when I heard how forlorn my voice sounded. I'd morphed back into the high school girl. Any minute, he'd kick me out the door and tell me to come back when I grew a pair.

"People come and go," Dennis said. "If you're meant to see them again, you will." I decided not to say anything, in case it came out sounding needy. He ruffled my hair again. "I'll never live anywhere but this city."

"She has that effect on people," I said.

"The difference between me and most people? Manhattan's not a woman to me. What satisfaction could I get from that? My city's a man. His feet are downtown. Practical. Walking toward the future. His head's Uptown, exotic music filling him with crazy-good ideas."

"And Midtown?"

"The best part," Dennis said. He pushed my knees down and reached for the zipper on my jeans. "The heart and the soul and the gut and the sex."

"I'm in bed with the poet of the Ironworkers Local 40."

"Yeah. I write poetry with my tongue," Dennis said and dove for me.

I couldn't remember the last time I'd spent all night with a man other than my roommate. Dennis made me feel safe the way Roberto did, but Dennis definitely came with benefits. Even though we were up half the night fucking and eating and fucking again, he was awake early. He didn't say anything about me getting up. I grinned when he sang along to his CD player while he took a shower. Just like at Uncle Blaine's apartment, the Pet Shop Boys served as the great equalizer between dissimilar gay men.

I dragged myself out from between the covers, peed without flushing the toilet in case his apartment had the same water issues that ours did, then waited for coffee to brew while I stared at the office building across the street. When the shower stopped running, I went back inside the bathroom and flushed.

"I could cook breakfast," I offered.

"That'd be great," Dennis said, emerging from behind the curtain with a towel around his waist. He kissed my shoulder, ran his hand over my tattoo, then lightly smacked my ass and said, "Only if you want to. But if you do, you'd better get moving."

I hustled into my clothes. By the time I put scrambled eggs, bacon, and toast on his tiny table, he was dressed, too. As hot as he looked naked, he looked even better in his work boots, jeans, and layers of shirts.

"Hey, can I take a picture of you with my phone?" I asked before he sat down.

"Are you getting sentimental, young Nick?"

"I want to sketch you looking like this," I said. "It helps to have a photo."

"Fire away," he said, picking up a slice of bacon and biting it in half. He was unselfconscious about getting his picture taken, but I worked fast in case he changed his mind.

After we ate, he wouldn't let me do the dishes. He filled the sink with hot water and left them soaking. We walked downstairs together and paused on the street.

"Let me see the picture," Dennis said. I pulled it up and handed him my cell phone. "I guess I could have shaved," he said, rubbing his face. Instead of handing the phone back, he scrolled through the menus until he figured out how to add his number to my contacts. "That's my cell. Now no matter where I go or how long it is before you see me again, I'm just a number away."

"Are *you* getting sentimental?"

"Here's some more poetry for you," he said. "You've got a nice cock, a sweet ass, a kind heart, and a good head. You're one of my kind. My brotherhood of buddies. It's basic, but it lasts longer than everything else."

I nodded. He smiled at me and then started walking down the street. I went in the opposite direction. After a few seconds, I turned around to watch him, but he'd already vanished.

I looked toward the financial district. For the first time in so long, the empty sky didn't make my stomach hurt. I felt a little bit like a poet, too, when I thought of Dennis being there, rebuilding something. He was a witness to what was gone, he and the ghosts looking out for each other. Gretchen would respect him: a strong workingman like her father.

"See ya," I whispered. I jammed my cell phone in my pocket, pulled on my gloves, and started looking for a subway entrance. I had to get home and fight my roommates for real estate in the bathroom. I was going to be late for work for the first time since taking the job. I'd probably still beat Bailey in, and I'd get around Eileen by pretending to eat her culinary weapon du jour.

Jisella took off her safety goggles, rubbed the bridge of her nose, then tossed the goggles to the workbench, saying, "Let's call it a day."

"Good," I said. I returned the belt sander to its home with the other tools and massaged my arms. We'd been working at a frantic pace all day because of a new high-profile client Mr. Wamsley had acquired while on vacation over Thanksgiving. Jisella and I were ordered to construct a platform bed. Every time we'd start to cut the headboard, Bailey would run into the workshop and make us stop because she'd changed her mind about which type of wood we should use. After wasting perfectly good planks of rosewood, white pine, birch, and cherry, Bailey went back to her original choice of walnut and acted as though we were degenerate subordinates for being annoyed that our production schedule was cut in half by her indecision.

"The longer I work with Bailey, and the longer I live with Morgan, the more it seems like the two of them have switched bodies," I complained.

"I can't get over the fact that you live with her sister. It's so random," Jisella said. "It's like a plot twist in English literature. Or one of those fairy tales where a member of royalty switches places with a commoner, and they turn out to be siblings."

"Did you just call me a fairy?"

Jisella ignored me and said, "You're right, though. Bailey's getting more annoying every day. I think she's losing her *It Girl* status with the magazines and it's grating on her. Now she'll actually have to work and prove she's talented. Unfortunately, she doesn't have the best managerial skills."

"I figured that out after the seventh time I found Susan crying in the supply closet."

Jisella removed three drafting pencils from the knot of curls at the back of her head and shook the sawdust from her hair. She cracked her neck, then stared at me with a pensive expression. I avoided her eyes and started to clean the workbench. I brushed the wood chips and dust to the floor and brought out the broom. While I was sweeping, Jisella finally said, "Can I tell you something?"

"Can I stop you?"

"I'm serious. This is a secret." I stopped sweeping and waited. She glanced at the doors, making sure they were closed, then said, "In four or five months, I'm out of here."

"What?" I said. "You're quitting?"

"I'm moving on. I've been planning this for a long time. Putting it off, I suppose. It's easy to settle in to a job and get lazy. I've always wanted to make my own furniture and have a shop where I can sell it. My own place, my own terms. Ever since you came along, I've been wanting to get out of here more than ever."

"Thanks." I started sweeping again.

"That was a compliment," she insisted. "We're a great team. You've made this job fun again. When you learn something new, you come alive. I know it sounds corny, but I see myself in you. The way I was when I was just starting out. It's nice."

"Where's the dustpan?" I asked.

She found it where it had been kicked under the workbench and crouched down to hold it for me while I moved the pile of dirt and debris.

"I found the perfect space in SoHo," she continued. "It's expensive. I may have to sell my soul, as well as a kidney, but it's just right for what I want. I can live and work there. There's a basement with enough room to work, a store, and a loft apartment behind it. It's perfect. You need to join me."

"I already have a place to live," I said.

"I mean I want you to work for me," she said. Then she added, "With me. Don't say anything. Just promise me you'll think about it."

I leaned on the broom and tried not to get swept up in her excitement. Even though Bailey was revealing herself to be a bitch in lamb-trimmed designer clothing, I still liked my job. However, since Jisella's proposal seemed to be in the planning stage, I said, "Sure. I'll think about it."

Jisella stood up and grinned. She brushed sawdust from her jeans and said, "Great. I'll keep you posted. Want to grab a beer somewhere?"

"Maybe in a couple years."

"Right. I keep forgetting that you're"—she broke off and wrinkled her nose, as if she'd just smelled something foul—"substantially younger than me. I'll see you tomorrow."

As I was leaving, Eileen repeatedly rapped her knitting needles on her desk and called out, "Nick, wait! You need to see this."

"Come on, Eileen," I moaned. "I've had a long day. Can it wait?"

"No. Look at this blog entry. Isn't this about your uncle?"

I cringed, expecting her to show me baristabrew-dot-com. It was worse. Spread across the screen was the *LoDownBlog*, gossip columnist Lola Listeria's latest outlet for rumormongering. Judging by the various ads blinking and taking up space in the margins of the Web page, Lola was doing well for herself. I scanned the entry in the general direction of Eileen's knitting needle.

Next season's residents of The See-List House are set to be announced next week, but Lola's got the cast list! However, in order to maintain our friendship with the Music Media One channel, Lola can't name names. But I can tell you that you won't want to miss the excitement when everyone's secretly splendiferous soap sensation slaps Alison Arngrim! Oops! Lola didn't disguise that very well, did she? Let me try again. Jaleel White! Hahahahaha!

Instead of explaining the intricacies of my extended family to Eileen, I said, "Urkel isn't my uncle."

"No, not that one. I know that item's about your uncle's boyfriend. Isaiah and I used to watch *Secret Splendor* on our lunch break. Look at the next entry."

"All I want to do is go home, Eileen. Not read the meaningless meanderings of a mindless moron." I cringed. "See? Now I'm talking like her."

Eileen frowned, tapping the screen expectantly with the knitting needle.

"Whatever," I said and continued reading. "Holy shit."

"I thought so," Eileen said smugly.

"Thanks, Eileen, I'll see you tomorrow!" I yelped as I made a dash for the door.

"He just got home, so he should be around here somewhere," Gavin said when I rushed inside the first floor of my uncle's apartment and called Blaine's name. "He's probably changing."

"Yeah, that's what I heard," I said and headed for the stairs.

"Tell him to put his damned shirt in the hamper!" Gavin called after me.

The door to the bedroom my uncle shared with Daniel was open. His back was turned to me as he pulled a sweatshirt over his head. I watched, somewhat annoyed, as the sweatshirt covered his muscular frame. I wondered how we were part of the same gene pool. I knocked on the door frame. When he turned and saw me, Uncle Blaine made a big show of clutching his heart, gasping for air, and falling backward onto his Cottage-style bed.

I clapped and said, "And they say Daniel's the actor in the family. Do you need help getting up?"

"Yes," he said and held out his hand. I took it and he pulled me down next to him. I laughed when he pummeled me with a pillow while saying, "Where have you been? Why haven't I seen you for months, you ungrateful little bastard?"

"Drop the sham and I'll tell you," I said.

"The what?"

"The ruffled thing you're beating me over the head with," I explained. "Seriously, who decorated this place? Laura Ashley's gay brother?"

"Actually, it was her lesbian aunt," Blaine said as he leaned back on the mountain of pillows.

"I can't think of a comeback for that one," I said. "Is there a lesbian stereotype about home décor?"

"I don't know anything about lesbian stereotypes."

"I've got news for you, Uncle Blaine. You *are* a lesbian stereotype."

"How do you figure?" he asked, looking insulted.

"You artificially inseminated your best friend, a lesbian."

He grinned and said, "I've come a long way, baby."

"Gross," I moaned and covered my face with the sham.

"Speaking of babies, I was about to go downstairs to see Emily and Gwendy. Want to come?"

"Could you please stop saying 'come'?"

"We could grab a bite to eat later," he said. "I was supposed to have dinner with Violet to go over budget reports. But I can cancel. Unless you want to hang out with her, too?"

"Wait a minute," I said, sitting up. "Budget reports? I thought you got fired."

"Fired?"

"I read online that you got fired from Lillith Allure."

Uncle Blaine rolled his eyes. "What was the first thing I warned you about when you moved in with me?"

"The importance of using condoms when having sex," I stated. "I don't think the banana puppet show applies to this situation."

"No, not that," Uncle Blaine said, clearly annoyed. Then he asked, "But while we're on the subject—"

"Yes, always!" I interrupted.

"Good."

"God."

"Anyway," he said, looking amused at my embarrassment, "I meant what I said about the tabloids and how they always lie or warp the truth. If they say something about Daniel or me and you want to know if it's true, just ask us and we'll tell you."

"That's why I'm here," I said. "Is it true?"

"Of course not." He got up from the bed and returned his suit to its hanger in his closet. He closed the door, then looked at me. "If that's the only reason you stopped by, I guess you'll be going now."

"Give me a break," I said. "That's not the only reason."

"How would I know? I haven't seen you in months," he said.

"Nice try. You're from Wisconsin. Ethnic guilt isn't your strong suit."

"You're right. I just hung that in the closet," he said.

I picked up his shirt from the floor and tossed it to him, saying, "Gavin says to put this in the hamper."

I heard him muttering something about fastidious queens haunting him every minute of the day as he went back into the closet. When he came out, he said, "What's new with you?"

"Uh-uh. You think I don't know that Blythe, Sheila, and Gwendy have reported everything I do or tell them back to you? Why is Lola Listeria claiming that you were fired?"

"*Her*? That's your online source? Please." Uncle Blaine sat on the bed again. "The truth is that I resigned. Now that Sheila's moved on and Faizah's been established as the new face for Lillith Allure, the company wants to go in a different direction with their advertising. Frankly, so do I. It's been fun, but I want to do other things."

I was tempted to say that I understood, since that was how I'd felt about college. But I kept quiet.

"I originally took the job because running the advertising department at Lillith Allure was perfect training for opening my own agency one day. That's what I intend to do."

"What about Violet?" I asked.

"She's coming with me, of course. I couldn't do it—or much of anything, for that matter—without her. She'll be my business partner. Or vice president of accounts and creative services. Or . . . something. We haven't hammered out the details. But we did buy a loft in the flatiron district. It's great. Entire floor of an old warehouse. You should come see it sometime."

"Yeah, sure," I said. I thought about his boss, who was like another of Emily's grandfathers and who'd always looked out for Uncle Blaine. "What about Frank Allen? Did you tell him yet? Was he crushed that you're leaving?"

"Frank was the first person I told. I wouldn't make a move like this without getting his opinion first. Or his approval. He knows it's the right move for my career. He cautioned me about how risky it is to start my own business, then turned right around and described how the benefits outweigh the risks. I've got some talented people lined up to work with me. I've already got clients waiting to hear that I'm open for business. I'll probably have a better opportunity to make time for Emily, for my family. It may sound sappy, but I feel like I'm creating some sort of legacy to leave behind."

"That's cool," I said.

"I'm sure the Dunhill Group will have an opening for a bright and talented individual like you," he said.

"The Dunhill Group?"

Uncle Blaine blushed and looked down at his hands. "I'm still playing around with names for the agency."

"It sounds like an English rap group," I said.

"Point taken."

"With nothing but white people in it," I added.

"Sipping tea and eating crumpets. I get the idea," Blaine barked.

"Where was this job offer when I left school?" I asked.

"You're still joking, right? You would've declined and accused me of trying to interfere in your life. Or you would've thought I didn't have any faith in your ability to make it on your own. I was your age once. I remember what it's like to go against the grain. When everyone in your family has your life mapped out for you, and you suddenly reveal to them that you're perfectly capable of deciding for yourself how you want to live. I knew better than to step in and start yelling at you the way my father did to me," he said adamantly.

"Daniel told you to butt out, huh?"

"Pretty much, yes," Uncle Blaine admitted. He stretched out on the bed, patted the space next to him, and said, "Get comfortable. Talk to me."

I flopped down next to him and sighed. "Go ahead. Get the interrogation out of the way."

"You're such a brat." He rested his jaw on his fist, and I noted the affection in his bright green eyes. With a pang, I realized how much I'd missed him and how many months had passed since I'd seen him.

"I haven't consciously avoided you," I assured him. "I got busy with life."

"We all do," he said. "I'm not pissed at you. I'm curious. I just scored a twelve-page advertising spread in *Vanity Fair* called 'Nick: 2003.' Describe the February photo."

I grinned and said, "I'm sitting on a fake white bearskin rug. I'm dressed for the cold, but the man with me is shirtless. He's got one of those doctor bags next to him. I'm wearing his stethoscope and pressing it against his bare chest."

"Did I say *Vanity Fair* or *Genre?*" Uncle Blaine asked. "What's the name of the scent you're advertising?"

"Polar Melt."

We continued in that vein for a while, until he asked about September. We exchanged an uncomfortable glance; then I said, "The anniversary wasn't the worst part of the month. My *Vanity Fair* wardrobe choice was emo, and my fragrance was Betrayal." I explained the drama over Fred's blog and finally said, "I was worried that somebody would tell you about it. Or you'd find it and think the stuff he said about you or the rest of our family came from me."

"What did I just tell you?" he asked. "If you want the truth, go to the source. Fred's selling something just the way Lola Listeria is. I don't need to hear about you from Fred. Or from Blythe, Sheila, and Gwendy, for that matter. I've always known you'll tell me what you think I need to know. Maybe even what *I* think I need to know."

"I guess if my *Vanity Fair* layout has a theme, it's that people aren't always who they seem to be. Some people that you trust will fuck you over. People you barely know will come through for you. People you think you know really well can . . ." I frowned. "Actually, I think 2003 has taught me that everything and everyone is constantly changing."

"Is it hard for you to deal with change?"

I looked him in the eye and said, "What I really wanted was for everything to stand still so nothing else bad could happen." I paused, but he didn't say anything. "I thought I was mad at you for trying to control my life. Maybe I was really blaming you for not doing a better job of it. I guess that does make me sound like an ungrateful little bastard, doesn't it?"

Blaine laughed and said, "It sounds like we're a typical father and son."

"Yeah? Which one are you?"

"Smartass."

I talked to him about my job, avoiding any discussion of how it wasn't the one I'd had when I moved out. I had to show him my tattoo, which he pretended to like, even though I knew he was covering up his dismay that I'd gotten one. He was curious about my mother's visit and seemed glad to hear that we'd begun talking regularly on the phone.

"I think they're splitting up," I finally said. "She doesn't say so. But I'm getting the vibe."

"How do you feel about that?"

"I feel like it should be a relief."

"But it isn't."

"It makes me sad. It's like they wasted all those years, and now she's old and it's too late for her to be happy."

"Trust me, she's not too old for a fresh start. She's not much older than Gretchen would be. You just see her as old because she's your mother."

I grunted, unconvinced, and said, "Didn't you want to go downstairs?"

"Are you going with me?"

"Sure."

He followed me from the bedroom, then surprised me by dropping his hands on my shoulders and pulling me back against his chest. It made me think of Roberto, and I smiled.

"I'm glad you're here," he said. His voice sounded fierce when he added, "I love you so much."

I choked up and waited to see if the tears would come. When they didn't, I answered quietly, "I love you, too."

"I'll bet Emily's changed a lot," Roberto said after I caught him up on what I'd been doing.

We were bundled under the comforter on the futon. The heat in our apartment was for shit. On mornings that none of us had to work, nobody wanted to be the first roommate up. That unlucky person had to brave the chill to turn on our array of space heaters, which were probably a threat to take out the Tri-State power grid.

So far, Morgan and Kendra hadn't emerged from the Snake Pit, and Roberto and I were waiting them out.

"Yeah," I said. "In my head, Emily's around Isleta's age, but a year makes a big difference. Plus she's a Dunhill."

"Right. She's already years beyond the average child her age."

"Exactly. She remembered me, too. Without laying any guilt on me. Kids are in the moment, you know?"

"Aw, was Uncle Blaine rough on you?" Roberto asked in a tone of mock pity.

"It was horrible," I said, and he brought his hand out from under the covers long enough to make the international *you're-jerking-me-off* motion. I yawned. "This year, instead of a big Christmas thing, they're planning a low-key gathering on the last day of Hanukkah. Not just for Kruger. Gwendy and Blaine want to start introducing Emily to her Jewish heritage. I think it'll be cool. You're invited, of course. Anyone I want to bring. I figured you'd be all right with it because it wouldn't interfere with the Mirones Christmas."

"Yeah, that's chill," Roberto said.

"You and I also have something to do today."

"It's my day off. It's cold. I'm going nowhere," he said.

"All those Saturday mornings you've dragged my ass out of here to run errands with you? Payback time."

"Kendra!" he yelled. "Phone!"

It took about a minute before she emerged and stood in the doorway squinting at us. She was wearing thermal underwear, a sweatshirt, and several pairs of socks. She clumsily pushed her bangs out of her eyes and looked around. "Whose . . . which . . . what phone?"

"Oh yeah," Roberto said. "We don't have a phone, do we? Hey, could you turn on that heater?"

"Okay." She turned on the heater and headed for the bathroom.

"Like taking candy from a baby," Roberto said.

"Shooting fish in a barrel."

"What a stupid phrase. Who shoots fish? And what if you shot a hole in the barrel? It just sounds like a bad idea all around. Much like leaving the apartment with you. Where are we going?"

"I'm not sure," I said. "All I have is an address from Gwendy. She wanted us to meet her around one. That's the extent of my information."

"She probably wants something heavy lifted," Roberto said.

"That's so sexist."

"I know. Just because I'm a guy—"

"I mean that you'd imply Gwendy couldn't lift shit for herself."

"Stop dodging the subject," Roberto said. "Jisella offered you a job. But your uncle said you can work for him, and you know he'd pay you better than Wamsley & Wilkes, and probably better than Jisella. It'll be a while before she's making good money. Not to mention that a huge percentage of new businesses fail. Why aren't you jumping at Blaine's offer?"

"What makes you think Uncle Blaine's new business won't fail?" The look he gave me made me say, "Right. He's like his ugly cat, Dexter. He'll always land on his feet. I don't know if I want to leave Wamsley & Wilkes. I like my job. I've learned a lot from the designers and the craftsmen. Craftspeople," I corrected myself. "What would I do for Blaine? I'm not qualified for more than what I'm doing with Isaiah. Blaine'll expect me to go back to school, get a degree in something. But I'm happiest when I'm working with Jisella. Making stuff. Maybe it's not art the way you or Blythe or Melanie create art. I guess it's closer to what Dennis Fagan does. A trade."

"Then take the job with Jisella."

"But maybe I *should* go back to school. Maybe there's stuff I need to learn that Jisella can't teach me. I don't know. I don't feel like figuring it out right now."

Roberto stared at me, like he was trying to decide if I was holding something back. I'd been asking myself the same question. I should be excited about all these opportunities coming at me. I wasn't sure why I wasn't. Maybe it was a simple case of not wanting to let Blaine down, but also not wanting to work for him. I wondered if my father or Uncle Wayne disliked working for my grandfather. I couldn't work for Grandpa Dunhill; he was a bastard. Blaine was nothing like that, but if I ever worked with him, I'd want to be on equal footing. Which meant my options were a degree in advertising or business. Either possibility made me want to run screaming in the other direction.

"You're right. There's no reason you have to decide now," Roberto conceded. "You've got a job you enjoy, working with people you like. That's basically where I am."

I'd have believed him except for the Gretchen mural. I wondered if he believed himself.

Roberto yawned, swung himself over me, and said, "Sweet Jesus, it's cold. I hope Kendra remembered to turn on the bathroom heater."

"Are you sure this is the right place?" Roberto asked.

The two of us stared at some kind of institutional building a couple stories tall. Weeds were growing through cracks in the sidewalks around the building. There was razor wire on top of the chain-link fence that went around the property. Nonetheless, vandals had found their way in. The yellow brick was tagged with gang graffiti. Most of the building's windows were broken.

I looked at the slip of paper I was carrying and said, "This is the address she gave me."

There were apartment buildings in the area that looked occupied, but other than a few delis and some pawnshops, there weren't many open businesses. I wasn't sure if they were closed permanently or because of the weekend. It should have been a busy day for Christmas shopping. I tried to convince myself it was just cold weather keeping the sidewalks empty.

"Maybe I should call her," I said. "She could have written it down wrong."

As I reached for my cell phone, Roberto said, "Too late. I don't know who you pissed off, but Tony Soprano's here."

I whipped around to see a black Cadillac Escalade with darkly tinted windows stopped at the curb. Gwendy jumped out of the back, saying, "I know. I'm late. I'm sorry."

But I was already moving past her toward the man who climbed out after her. He grabbed me in a big hug and said the same thing he always said. "Are you taller? You seem taller."

I held on like a drowning man until I heard Adam say, "Do you two want to use the backseat?"

Jeremy and I pulled apart. I hugged Adam, then glanced past him to Blythe as she lit a cigarette and said, "Nice digs, Gwendy."

"Yeah, what do you guys think of my new place?" Gwendy asked, looking from the building to me and then to Roberto.

"You gave up legal aid to become a crack whore?" Roberto asked. "Is this your pimp's car?"

"It's my uncle Mario's car," Jeremy said.

Blythe took a long drag off her cigarette and rattled the gate. "Do you have a key for this?"

Gwendy tossed her a key chain. As Blythe began working at the padlock, Gwendy said, "This was originally an elementary school. It was built in 1935, when people knew how to construct buildings that lasted."

"Too bad," I said, giving the building a critical look.

"Over the years," Gwendy went on in a cheery tone, "it was also repainted with lead-based paint. There's asbestos in some of the plaster, too."

"Bought yourself a Superfund site, huh?" Adam asked with his killer smile. Roberto smiled, too, as he looked at Adam.

"How come even straight guys fall all over him?" I muttered.

"Bitterness doesn't go with your hair color," Jeremy said. "Men, women, children, dogs, and Mary Tyler Moore. I've seen him melt them all."

Blythe finally won her battle with the lock. The others seemed to know where they were going, so Roberto and I followed them after exchanging a clueless glance. Adam took the keys from Blythe and opened a lock on the front door of the building.

"Don't expect much," Gwendy said, as if she needed to let us down gently. "Except for vagrants, the building hasn't been used for fifteen years."

The sun, muted by filthy windows, provided the only light. But it was enough to see the grime and debris of years of neglect. Some rooms were empty. Others were piled high with broken or scarred children's desks.

While Adam and Gwendy talked, using phrases like "adaptive reuse" and "smart growth," I listened in mystified silence. Blythe wandered in and out of sight as she looked around, sometimes nodding or talking to herself.

"Fortunately, it's not really a Superfund or Brownfield site," Gwendy commented as she began leading us down a hallway. "It took me over a year to negotiate a price and establish a timeline that included tax deferrals. Now we're finally ready to start. Beginning with the removal of the asbestos and lead paint. Some of the rooms will have to be gutted down to—"

"You're restoring the building?" Roberto asked.

"Restoring, reclaiming," Gwendy said with a nod.

"What are you going to do with it?" I asked.

Gwendy stopped and turned back to us. "Do you remember a school project you two did with Melanie? You had to design a Manhattan-themed mural for a fictitious hotel lobby." Roberto and I nodded. "You were working on it at Blaine's one night when Gretchen was there with Emily. When she came home, she told me she'd figured something out while she was watching you."

"What was that?" Jeremy asked. The sadness in his dark eyes reminded me that like Daniel and Martin, he'd been friends with Gretchen long before the rest of us met her.

"She said there are always organizations to try to meet the physical needs of kids. Immunization and school lunch programs. New mentoring groups are developed all the time to fill in educational gaps. Churches take care of kids' spiritual needs. But that night made her think there was something she called a *soul hunger* that went neglected. A child's need for a creative outlet. Whether it was painting, acting, dancing, writing, culinary arts—which was Gretchen's hobby—she thought directing kids' energy that way would keep more of them from falling through the cracks."

"I'm proof of that," Roberto said.

"It's the basis for my work," Jeremy said.

Gwendy looked at him and said, "I think what you do for gay and lesbian teens is great. A huge percentage of the homeless kids and runaways I've helped through legal aid are kicked out by their families because of their sexual orientation. Unfortunately, they're not the only marginalized children. Even little kids are victims of poverty, language barriers, or racism."

"And disease," I said. "I remember when I used to go with Gretchen to rock babies who had AIDS."

"She had a genius for making money, but children were her passion," Gwendy said. She waved her arms. "This is the future Gretchen Schmidt Center. It's going to feed that soul hunger she saw in children. Much like your high school, it's going to be a place where creativity is encouraged and developed. At low or no cost, because it will be fully funded by the Gretchen Schmidt Foundation."

"How long can that last?" Roberto asked. He seemed to think his question sounded bad and hastily added, "Your intentions are good, but it sounds like something that will take a lot of money."

"I understand why you'd ask," Gwendy said. "I'm not depending on only Gretchen's money for this. I've got donations and sponsorships from individuals and corporations. I've been working on this for two years."

"A center like this wouldn't just serve children," Adam mused. "It could help revitalize the neighborhood."

"That's what I'm hoping," Gwendy said. She looked at me. "It was great hearing you talk about how much you like living in East Harlem. I stopped thinking I could save the world a long time ago. But I look at you and your friends, and it makes me believe that you've got what it takes to make things better."

"I think anyone who knew Gretchen will want to help with this," Blythe said. "I know I do. I'll be glad to paint or teach. Anything."

I saw Adam and Jeremy exchange a glance, and Adam said, "I wonder if it's safe to check out the second floor."

When he nudged Blythe toward a set of stairs, Gwendy motioned for Roberto and me to stay back with her. After the others were out of earshot, she said, "I had a reason for wanting you two here today. I have a good legal mind and a great team of experts advising me. But I don't have an artistic bone in my body. I need the two of you. It can be as long as two years before the building is toxic-free and ready. Nick, I know you have contacts through Wamsley & Wilkes who could manage this project correctly. But I want to start connecting with the surrounding community, too. I want the highest possible number of neighborhood people helping get this off the ground. That's where you come in," she said to Roberto.

"What can I do?" he asked.

"Can I be completely honest?" Gwendy asked.

She made me nervous. I wondered if she was going to say something about the Gretchen mural we'd found. I felt like I should have talked to Roberto about it first.

When he nodded, she said, "I don't want people in the neighborhood to think this is just a bunch of guilty white liberals coming in and trying to dictate things. This is primarily a Latino community. I want a hands-on liaison. From the time the construction fence goes up around the site, I want someone to engage kids, teens, old people, or anyone else in painting it. Considering your talent, your love for street art—"

"My rap sheet," Roberto said.

Gwendy laughed and said, "When the building's ready for cosmetic work, I want every hall, every wall painted in murals. Somebody will need to plan and manage that. To provide creative input. To figure out ways to make it reflect and involve the community. I think you're that person."

"I have a job," Roberto said. He gave Gwendy an intense stare and said, "With benefits. I can't give up benefits like my health insurance."

The expression that crossed her face—a mixture of comprehension and sadness—disappeared so fast that I wondered if I'd imagined it.

"I can more than match whatever Drayden's package is," Gwendy said.

Roberto stared at the floor a minute and said, "I'm interested. I need to think about things. Also, there's somebody I'd want to bring with me. An illustrator who could help with the art design now and probably work with kids later."

"I knew you'd be perfect," Gwendy said. "You're already out-negotiating me. Right now, it's me, my board, and an assistant. Trust me, if either of you knows good people for me to interview and hire, I want to talk to them. Or Violet does."

"I don't know why I didn't guess that Blaine and Violet would be involved in this," I said.

"It'll be a wonderful memorial to Emily's mother," Gwendy said. "I wouldn't dream of doing it without Blaine and Daniel's input and help." She looked around with a bemused expression, as if she were trying to imagine Daniel and Blaine in such a dump. "Let's go find the others before Blythe burns the place down with her chain-smoking."

As she walked toward the stairs, I held Roberto back to whisper, "Who were you talking about? What illustrator?"

"Morgan, of course." He laughed at my dumbfounded expression. "All these months, and you still know almost nothing about her."

"I know enough to question whether she should work with children. I've always figured she probably eats them."

"Then maybe you shouldn't have been stealing food from her, *mijo*," he said, laughing again as he followed Gwendy.

18

Here

I'd gotten a call from Uncle Blaine the day after Christmas. He'd decided at the last minute to throw a New Year's Eve party and invited me to come with as many guests as I wanted to bring. I didn't have firm plans, so I gave him a noncommittal answer. When a few of my friends were at Cutter's trying to make plans for the holiday, I tentatively mentioned Blaine's invitation. I didn't think anyone would want to attend a party thrown by an advertising executive who was in his "thirty-something" era. But other than Adalla, who would be in Texas on New Year's Eve, they surprised me by agreeing wholeheartedly.

When I mentioned my surprise on the way to the party, Morgan cynically stated, "They're all hoping to rub against models and famous people."

"And you're going because why?" Roberto teased.

"Someone has to keep you kids in line," she answered.

"You borrowed Red Kitty's riding crop?" I asked.

"Very funny," Morgan replied. She turned the cab's rearview mirror toward her and reapplied her lipstick.

Our driver turned the mirror back into place and loudly said, "Don't touch the mirror. Don't touch anything. Do not make me put you out of my cab."

"Do not pass 'Go.' Do not collect two hundred dollars," I mumbled. I wondered how Samir Singh was celebrating the new year.

"Sorry! Gosh," Morgan muttered. "You don't have to be such an asswipe about it."

"I freely admit I'm going to this party so I can meet famous people," Kendra said. "If I'm going to be a producer someday, I need to start networking."

"Don't producers usually have money?" Roberto whispered in my ear. I elbowed him in the ribs.

"I've never met anyone famous before," Kendra continued. "Unless you count Ellie Waltham from Trenton."

"What about that party for Hugh Jackman?" I asked.

"Who's Ellie Waltham?" Roberto asked.

"She did the weather report back in Trenton," Kendra explained. "But that's not all she did!"

Roberto, Morgan, and I watched the cabdriver. He was glancing expectantly at Kendra's reflection in the rearview mirror, obviously waiting to hear what else Ellie had done. I finally added to his misery by pointing at the corner of Broadway and Twenty-third Street and saying, "You can let us out here."

Uncle Blaine's party was in the loft he'd purchased for his ad agency. It took up the entire floor of a converted warehouse. We stepped off the elevator into a cavernous and raw space. Christmas lights had been wound around a balcony that ran the perimeter of the space. They provided just enough light for me to see that the place was packed with people. The only person I immediately recognized was a DJ from Club Chaos, who was spinning from a makeshift stage made out of packing crates.

"Do you see Melanie? Blythe?" I shouted to the others, trying to be heard above the music and noise. "Isaiah and Luis?"

Kendra and Morgan both shook their heads and shrugged. Roberto snapped his cell phone shut and said, "I can't get a signal. Let me try yours."

I handed him my phone. He motioned to a window across the room and wandered toward it while dialing.

"We're going to find the bar," Kendra said.

"There's no bar, baby," a woman next to us said. She pointed with her beer bottle and said, "There's trash cans filled with beer on ice by the DJ booth, and a table with the hard stuff next to that. Mix your own."

"Thanks," Morgan said. She looked at me. "Do you want anything?"

"Not yet," I answered.

I went in search of Roberto and overheard someone saying, "I can't stand this shit!"

"That's *exactly* why I want to sell the club," a familiar voice answered. I pushed forward through the crowd and saw Andy Vanedesen talking to a gigantic drag queen who was dressed in a kimono.

"What? You smell a shrub?" the drag queen asked. "This place could use some greenery. You'd think Daniel would've—"

"No!" Andy interrupted. "The club! I'm *selling* the *club*."

"You're selling Club Chaos?"

"Keep it down!" Andy shouted. "It's not public knowledge yet."

"What's not, honey?"

"That I'm selling the club!" Andy screamed. "Honestly, Brenda Li, you've got to stop huffing the Aqua Net."

Brenda Li patted her wig. Then she spotted me. Suddenly I was surrounded by folds of printed silk and my cheeks were being pinched. "What a shayna punim! Look at the doll face on this one."

Andy pulled me free and hugged me. Brenda Li pouted before gliding into the crowd. I leaned toward Andy's ear and asked, "Why are you selling Club Chaos?"

Andy's mouth fell open. "Who told you?"

"I overheard you yelling at what'shername. Brenda Li."

"Oh. Don't repeat this to anyone, but I'm getting up in years. It's time to try something new. Something quieter. Running a club is *such* an aggravation. The drama, the payoffs, the *noise*—I've had it. Let someone else deal with it. What about you? What's new with you?"

"Nothing much," I answered. "Have you seen my uncle? Or Daniel?"

"They're somewhere in this sea of filth. I don't know. Do you know what time it is?"

"Another hour until midnight."

Andy groaned and said, "Oh, dear Lord. I need another drink."

After Andy walked away, Roberto materialized out of the crowd and handed my phone to me. "Here. Melanie got stuck in traffic. On the plus side, I got some choice photos of that drag queen kissing your forehead."

"Thanks," I said. "Is there lipstick on my face?"

Roberto spat on his thumb and wiped it above my eyebrow. "Not anymore."

"Gross," I said, batting at his hand.

We avoided the center of the loft, where everyone was dancing, and wound through the crowds, looking for Kendra and Morgan, as well as anyone else we knew.

"I see your uncle invited a thousand of his closest friends," Roberto said.

"I've never seen half these people before in my life," I replied. "But I guess if everyone you invite brings a friend, then—" I broke off when I saw Blythe and Daniel huddled in a dark corner of the loft. Blythe was passing her cigarette to Daniel, who took furtive puffs from it every so often. I snuck up behind him and said, "Busted!"

He jumped and dropped the lit cigarette on Blythe's hair. She screamed and swatted at her head, causing the cigarette to bounce off a nearby woman's ass and onto the floor. Daniel stamped it out and brushed off the woman's butt. When she turned around, he said, "Honey, your ass is smokin'!"

She wasn't amused, but Roberto and I were. We laughed openly at Daniel.

"If you tell Blaine I was smoking, I'll tell him about that time I walked in on you and—"

"Okay!" I yelped.

"Is my hair on fire?" Blythe asked. "I don't do performance art."

"You're fine," Daniel said.

"I heard a rumor that Andy's selling Club Chaos," I said, hoping to change the subject.

"Oh, please," Daniel said. "At the start of every year, it's the same tired story from him."

"Maybe this year, that dinosaur will actually retire," Martin said, wrapping his arms around my chest from behind. When I turned to look back at him, he said, "Hi."

"Hi," I said and grinned.

"Stop molesting my . . . nephew, son, or whatever he is," Daniel said.

"We're not related," I said.

"Oh. In that case." Daniel stepped forward with a lascivious grin and outstretched arms, then turned away and said, "Ew. No. Can't do it. So wrong."

"Where's Blaine?" I asked.

"Speaking of so wrong," Martin said.

"He's over there," Daniel said, pointing to the center of the room. I saw my uncle in a deep discussion with his assistant, Violet Medina, who was nodding at whatever he was saying while taking notes on her BlackBerry. "The life of the party, as usual."

"How do you feel about all this?" I asked, gesturing to the loft.

"It's going to be great for him," Daniel answered. "Whatever he wants, I'm behind him all the way."

"That's not what I heard," Martin said.

Daniel said, "Just because he looks like a top—"

I put my hands over my ears and loudly sang "Mary Had a Little Lamb." Roberto pulled my hands down and said, "I'm getting a beer. You want?"

"I want," Martin said, linking his arm in Roberto's. As they walked away, I heard Martin say, "You look just like a roommate I had once."

"When are you going to L.A.?" I asked Daniel.

He gave me a blank look and said, "To see Sheila?"

"No. I heard you're going to be a resident in *The See-List House.*"

He smiled and said, "I already did that. Last fall. It airs in a couple of months."

"Oh. I didn't realize. Did you really slap Alison Arngrim?"

"Wouldn't you slap Nellie Oleson, if you had the chance?" he asked.

"Who's Nellie Oleson?" Blythe asked.

"You," he said, pointing at Blythe, "leave this party. Now."

"I can't believe you slapped someone," I said.

"It was scripted," he explained. "It was the producers' idea. Alison and I pretended to get into a fight. I slapped her, which caused major drama and got me kicked out of the house. It'll get good ratings. In return, the producers agreed to let Alison and me do a series of specials for their network about AIDS. Everyone wins."

He had to move closer to me to let three drag queens get by us. He took in every detail of their appearance as they walked away; then his expression turned to one of approval.

I watched them, too, and finally said, "How does anyone know what's real?"

"Sweetie, they are *people*," he said with a frown.

"Not them. You didn't seriously slap Alison Arngrim. Blaine didn't actually get fired. Andy won't really sell his club." I thought about my roommates and then, in a sudden moment of sadness, about Fred. "Sometimes you think you know people, but they're carrying around all these secrets. How does anyone know what's real?" I repeated.

Daniel looked at me, and then his gaze went back to Blaine. He smiled. "It's all real. The beauty and the grime. The truth and the lies. What we have, and what we're missing. When life throws shit at you—"

"I know," I interrupted. "Use it as manure in your garden."

"I need new lines," he grumbled.

"Do you ever worry?"

"I'm a Virgo," he said. "I always worry. About what in particular?"

"Like when the soap bought out your contract, did you worry you wouldn't work again?"

Daniel nodded slowly, giving it some thought before he said, "Sometimes. No matter what you're doing, whatever profession, you create your own opportunities in life."

"Sometimes opportunity knocks," I said, thinking about Jisella's offer.

"That's true, too," Daniel agreed. "No matter how badly things can suck—and they will, from time to time—the thing to remember about life is that it's always full of possibilities. As long as you're not hurting anyone, you can do anything you want to, Nick. Don't let anyone tell you otherwise."

"I'll keep that in mind," I said.

"I'm going to get a drink and save your poor roommate from Martin's wandering fingers. Need anything?"

I declined. Daniel gave me a hug and wished me a happy new year before waving to someone and walking away. I climbed a staircase to the balcony and looked at the mass of people below. I finally located Isaiah and Luis in animated conversation with a group of people I didn't recognize. Then I spotted Gavin and Ethan slow-dancing in the center of the room. Ethan's head rested on Gavin's shoulder as they swayed to the music, until Gavin said something and sent Ethan into a fit of laughter.

Near them, Kendra was dancing with a man I'd never seen before. He was tall, strikingly handsome, and looked like he'd been shipped in from Italy for the party. His hands never left Kendra's waist as they danced. She looked as though that Ed McWhoever guy had just showed up at her door and handed her a giant check.

Morgan was sitting on a window seat alone, her back to the room so she could frown down at Manhattan. Every time someone sat next to her, she slowly moved her head and stared until they became visibly uncomfortable and left. Then she went back to looking out the window. But when Roberto walked up and offered her a beer, she actually smiled and accepted it. They clinked the necks of their bottles together, and she moved over so he could sit next to her. Roberto pointed toward the crowd and mimicked someone dancing badly. The two of them began laughing. It was strange to see her laugh. It was even stranger to realize that I'd come to find her adorable even when she didn't laugh. She'd be repulsed to hear that description of herself.

Someone leaned on the railing next to me and said, "Want to dance?"

Without looking at him, I said, "That's okay. I'm fine."

"Are you sure? I'm a great dancer."

"Really. I don't think so," I said, wanting to be left alone so I could watch my friends.

"Want to go back to my place? I'm easy, and I give great head." That caught my attention. I turned to see Davii grinning broadly at my horrified expression. "Ha! Made you look."

I grabbed the waist of his jeans, taking note of the fact that he was going commando, and said, "Come on. Let's go."

"Whoa. Wait a minute," he protested. "I was kidding."

"You mean you don't want to dance?"

"Oh, okay," he said.

"Try not to look so relieved," I muttered.

We pushed our way to the center of the dance floor and started moving to a Garbage remix. Davii put an arm around my waist and pulled me against him, grinding his pelvis against my ass. A few people around us egged us on. I was in the mood to give a good show, and Davii seemed to be a willing partner. I turned and pulled his shirt over his head, stuffing it into my back pocket. Then I took off my own shirt and tucked it into the waist of his jeans. Davii laughed and ran a finger down my chest, making me quiver when he passed over my stomach. Then he pulled me closer.

"You're a brat," he said, nuzzling his lips against my ear.

"I saw an opportunity and grabbed it," I said.

"That's not opportunity you're grabbing," he said.

"Sorry."

"I'm not."

He kissed my neck, my chin, and finally, my mouth. His kisses were delicious. I was glad I hadn't had any beer, or anything else that would've left my breath less than Colgate fresh. When he pressed his forehead against mine and smiled, I said, "It's not midnight yet."

"Couldn't help myself. I've always wondered about you."

"Wondered what?"

"Whether you look as good horizontal as you do vertical," he teased.

"Who's the brat now?"

"I'll be serious for a minute," he said as the people began counting down from ten. "I wondered if you'd like to have dinner sometime."

"I've been known to eat," I said.

Everyone started shouting and confetti rained down from the balconies around us. Davii kissed me again, then hugged me. "I've been known to be impatient," he said. "How about breakfast, instead?"

"I'm not that kind of boy," I said. When Davii smirked, I added, "Okay, I am. But I like you. We're friends. I'm not sure that I—"

"Hey, Nick. Hang on," he interrupted. "I'm just talking about having a meal."

"Oh, right," I said, embarrassed.

"In the middle of dinner," he continued, "if one of us suddenly feels like saying, 'Know what? This feels like a date,' then we'll deal with that as it happens. No pressure. Sound good?"

"More than good," I agreed.

"I know the big new year moment has passed, but—"

I kissed him again.

* * *

What obviously never crossed anyone's mind except mine, and possibly Roberto's, was that I hadn't left the island of Manhattan for the last year. Once I'd dropped out of Pratt, there was no reason to leave. My job as Isaiah's copilot had never required taking a bridge or tunnel. And I hadn't gotten as far as the Triborough Bridge before I backed out of my Thanksgiving trip to Wisconsin.

After saluting the new year at Blaine's party, a few of us gathered at the Renaissance Diner. I was still floating from Davii's kisses and thinking of Daniel's wisdom about possibilities. I finally forced myself to focus on Jeremy, who was making everyone laugh with stories about a group of his cousins that he called "the Guidos."

Jeremy's grandmother was getting rid of her stuff and moving in with his parents, and most of his relatives were fighting over her antiques. Since Jeremy was her favorite grandchild, she was giving him whatever he wanted. The plan, as originally conceived by Jeremy, was to get two of his cousins to drive the furniture to Wisconsin in a truck belonging to his father's business. One after another, Jeremy began to lose faith that even one of his accident-prone and directionally challenged cousins could find his own ass, much less Wisconsin.

As I listened, it struck me that a change of scenery might help me make the decisions about my future that I'd been avoiding. I meant to speak privately to Jeremy while everyone was laughing. But one of those weird moments happened when it got quiet for no apparent reason just as I said, "I'll drive the truck to Wisconsin for you."

Every head turned my way, and Uncle Blaine said, "What about your job?"

"My job and I are on a break."

"Oh no, you didn't get fired again, did you?" Kendra blared.

"Again?" Uncle Blaine repeated in a surprised tone.

"Hey, thanks, Kendra," I said.

"Did Bailey fire you, or was it Mr. Wamsley?" Morgan asked.

"Nobody fired me," I said. "I'm still on the payroll."

"Then how can you just take time off—"

"Excuse me," Jeremy said. "I think he was talking to me, if the rest of you would like to piss off." Adam laughed as my uncle glared at Jeremy. "Would you take somebody with you?" Jeremy asked, ignoring Blaine.

"I don't think so. There's no hurry, is there? Can I take my time driving?"

"Absolutely," Jeremy said. "You'll be doing me a huge favor. I'll pay you, too, in addition to all the expenses."

"You don't have to do that."

"Of course I do. I was going to pay some idiot cousin. I'd much rather pay you. At least then I know my Edwardian mahogany bed, Chinese cabinet, and antique bedwarmer won't end up in Saskatchewan."

"I slept with an antique bedwarmer once," Brenda Li said in her raspy voice. When we all turned her way, she looked down at her omelet with a demure expression.

"God," Morgan muttered. "Brenda, have you met Kendra? I think you may be long-lost twins."

"There's a lot of that going around," I said. I looked back at Jeremy. "How soon do I leave?"

It was just after six on a Tuesday morning when I pulled the Caprellian Brothers Architectural Salvage truck into a loading zone and ignored the guard who started waving at me. I wasn't even at the Lincoln Tunnel, and my palms were sweating and my heart felt like it was exploding. All I could see were white spots, as if I'd been in a room where somebody was shooting pictures with a flash.

"He's having a panic attack," Ethan said, sitting next to me on the bed.
"Deep breaths," Gavin ordered. "Focus on your breathing."
"Don't tell Uncle Blaine," I gasped. "He's got enough—"
"Just breathe."

The guard tapped on my window and boomed, "You okay, son?"

My vision cleared and I nodded at him. Before he could tell me to move the truck, my cell phone rang. I rolled down the window.

"Getting directions," I lied. "Give me just a minute." He nodded and walked away as I answered the phone.

"Yo," Roberto said. "You left the iron on."

I smiled. I didn't have an iron, but I did have a best friend. "I remembered to stop the newspaper delivery, right?"

"Yeah, but you didn't put the cat out or arrange for the neighbors to water your plants."

"Why the hell are you calling me?"

"I'm feeling very codependent, Nickito. Can you come back and hold me?"

"You sick fuck. I can't talk to you and deal with traffic."

"Don't forget the way home."

"Which home?" I asked. "Eau Claire or Harlem?"

"Either."

"Not likely," I said. "Go to work so you can pay my bills."

"Translated, that means Kendra's bills. Drive safe, *hermano*."

He hung up. I dropped the phone on the seat, took a deep breath, and maneuvered my way into the lane for the Lincoln Tunnel. When I exited the tunnel on the Jersey side, I was grateful that traffic kept me from doing more than glancing in the rearview mirror at the Manhattan skyline. It was better to keep moving forward without looking back.

I put in the earbuds of the iPod that Daniel and Uncle Blaine had given me the night before. They'd made me promise to wait until I was on the road before I started critiquing their song selections. As soon as I heard the beginning of the Pet Shop Boys' "It's a Sin," I accelerated. It was going to be a good trip.

Blaine and Adam, of a single mind in the control freak department, had planned my itinerary to the smallest detail. I agreed to their scheduled stops in exchange for Uncle Blaine's promise that he wouldn't tell anyone in Wisconsin that I was coming. Even though I could have made a quicker trip of it, I'd given my word to stop for the night just across the Ohio state line.

I checked into a motel room and lay down for a few minutes, trying not to see the road every time I closed my eyes. Even though I'd planned to spend my drive time weighing my options for my future, I'd passed the hours reliving my three-plus years in Manhattan. I made a game of picking a person and remembering key moments in our friendship.

It was inevitable that as I started getting tired, my defenses went down and I thought about Fred. I'd been trying not to because of Davii. Fred had lusted after Davii for so long, and I didn't want my anger at him to be part of my interest in Davii.

I wasn't even sure that I was still mad at Fred. Sometimes I wondered if I was being too unforgiving. Like Uncle Blaine pointed out, Fred was selling something, and it wasn't necessarily meant to be the truth.

I missed him. We'd shared a lot of good times. Even though we were different, he'd been the gay friend my age that I was closest to. I wondered if he missed me. Or all of us, really. I wasn't the only one who'd broken off contact with him. Roberto definitely never talked to him. Which reminded me of why I was still mad at Fred. Whatever else he was selling, he shouldn't have sold out Roberto's right to privacy.

I tried to wash Fred down the drain with my road dirt when I showered. There was a café next to the motel, so I grabbed the novel I'd been reading, a Christmas present from Daniel, then bundled up and walked to the café. It was clean and warm. At my request, the host put me in a quiet booth away from everyone else.

Breakfast was always a safe bet, and after I ordered, I started reading. I was vaguely aware of noisy teenagers coming in and sitting at a nearby table. I gave them a quick glance to determine that it was a group of girls before I went back to reading.

After a while, one of the girls called, "Hey. Excuse me."

I looked over to see if she was talking to me, and found all four of them staring at me.

"Hi," I said.

"You look like that guy. The guy in that band? That sings the song about the friend and the girl?"

I had no idea who she was talking about, so I said nothing. Another of the girls said, "Are you him?"

"Nope," I said.

"See, I told you," a third girl said. "Why would anybody famous be in a place like this?"

"He could be going to the Rock and Roll Hall of Fame," the first girl said.

I smiled and said, "You caught me. I'm being inducted."

The fourth girl, who'd been rolling her eyes through most of the exchange, said, "You're a little early."

"Sound check," I said.

"It's two months from now. In March."

I was given the snubbing a liar like me deserved, which was all I'd wanted in the first place. When I went back to my room later, I called my uncle to assure him that I was alive, the truck was intact, and I was going to bed.

Adam had recently converted a barn on his property into offices and moved his business out of his house. That meant that I wouldn't be in the way of anyone who worked for Adam's AdVentures, and I'd have all the privacy I needed. After I helped a couple of his employees unload Jeremy's antiques into a storage room, I was a free man. My stay on the farm was open-ended. Adam had reminded me of where the car and truck keys were kept and told me to use whatever I needed.

I spent my first afternoon and night in Eau Claire on Jeremy's computer. I'd forgotten how easy it was to spend hours looking up obscure information. I opened a free mail account and e-mailed people whose addresses I knew: Uncle Blaine, Jisella, and Adalla. I typed in baristabrew-dot-com, then quickly hit the red X before I could get myself worked up over Fred again.

On my second day in Eau Claire, I spent a few hours driving around in Adam's pickup truck, trying to adjust to the wide-open space, the quiet, and the postcard-perfect look of the countryside. I took a spin by Dunhill Electrical and my grandparents' house, but I avoided my parents' neighborhood, the area around the mall where Drayden's was, and UW–Eau Claire. I had the uneasy feeling that if I got too close, my mother and my brother would sense my presence. I wasn't ready to face them yet.

It wasn't until my fourth morning, while drinking a cup of hot tea and staring at the snow-covered blankness outside the kitchen window, that I finally picked up my cell phone and called Chuck. "Where are you?" I asked.

"Leaving English class," he said and yawned. "Why are you calling so early?"

"Do you have another class now?"

"No, I'm done until an afternoon lab."

"Do you know where Adam Wilson's farm is?"

After a pause, he said, "Is that the one with the webcam in the front yard? The white farmhouse?"

"Yeah. Don't tell anybody, but that's where I am. I wondered if you could drive out here."

I held my breath during the long silence before Chuck said, "Is everything okay?"

"What would be wrong?" I asked.

"I don't know. It's just weird that you didn't tell anyone you were coming."

"We can talk about it when you get here. I mean, if you get here."

"I'm on my way."

I couldn't believe how nervous I was as soon as the call ended. I went to the guest bathroom and washed my face and brushed my teeth again. Then I spiked up my hair, freshly blue thanks to Kendra's cut-rate colorist. I took off the ratty shirt I was wearing and put on a sweater. I decided I looked too geeky and put on a long-sleeved, black T-shirt and a different pair of jeans.

"Why?" I asked, ignoring my reflection as I pulled on a pair of thick wool socks. "Like he gives a shit what you're wearing?" I went back downstairs, brought the fire back to life, and threw more logs on it. "I'm acting like it's a fucking date."

I was staring out a front window when Chuck's Jeep came up the drive. I had the advantage of being able to see him first. Or I would have, except he was hidden under a wool cap pulled nearly to his eyes, a down vest over a hoodie, gloves, and hiking boots. Apparently, my mother was still dressing him out of the L.L. Bean catalog.

I opened the door before he could knock. We stared at each other, but neither of us made a move.

"It's not exactly balmy out here," Chuck said.

"Sorry," I said, wondering why everyone in my family turned me back into a gawky kid.

I stepped aside so he could come in, then watched as he peeled off his layers. When he took off his cap, I saw that he had a buzz cut. He looked like a Marine. A Marine who could kick my queer ass if he felt like it.

But he also looked like the right kind of Dunhill, just the way Blaine did. Even if he was my brother, I could acknowledge that he was what Adalla would call wicked handsome. The only thing we had in common was our light blue eyes. He made me feel too tall, too thin, and totally inferior.

When he took off the hoodie, he was wearing a long-sleeved black T-shirt almost identical to mine. Except his hadn't come from a resale shop in the Village and mine definitely wasn't accentuating the body of an athlete.

Neither of us seemed to know what to say, so we stared at each other. I kept thinking of the tentative steps we'd taken on the phone and in letters. It was like meeting in person undid all that. I couldn't tell by his expression if he wanted to play nice or fight with me.

He started things civilly by asking about my job. I asked about his classes. We got quiet again. Then he asked how Blaine was doing. I told him about the new business. I felt a little anxious when I realized we were almost at the end of safe topics and said, "How's Mom?"

The forced pleasant expression left his face and he said, "She's all right." His tone made a lie of his words.

"How bad are things at home?" I asked.

He flinched at the noise as a log broke, and I stayed still when he reached for the poker to mess with the fire. I knew he was buying time.

"I can't believe they're still together," he finally said. "They sleep in separate rooms. They never speak to each other. At least not while I'm around."

"So you don't have to hear them fight."

"No, Nick, I don't hear them fight. That makes everything okay. You can go back to New York with a clear conscience because I'm living in a quiet house."

"Where's that coming from? Why are you so hostile?"

"Sorry. I forgot that you don't like conflict unless you cause it."

"Me? Wasn't I the one who moved away so you'd stop beating me up? All I wanted was to be left alone."

"Give me a break," Chuck said. "I never beat you up, and you usually antagonized me into taking a swing at you."

We glared at each other.

"Why are we doing this? We're not kids. In two weeks, we won't even be teenagers anymore. I didn't come here to fight with you."

"Why did you come here?" he asked.

"I don't know. I was just delivering some stuff for a friend."

"Am I supposed to keep it a secret? You planning to slip out of town without seeing Mom or Dad?"

"I definitely don't want to see him," I said. Chuck turned back to the fire. I stared at him, wondering how such a familiar face could belong to a stranger. "Chuck."

"What?"

"I lied. I do know why I came. I want to fix this." He still didn't look at me. "I don't give a shit about him or Tony. They wrote me off a long time ago. But you and me . . . It shouldn't be this way."

"Maybe you should have thought about that before you took off."

I felt the first flicker of anger come to life inside me. "Before I took off? You make it sound like I abandoned you. Do you remember what things were like for me when we were sixteen? When I had to make sure I didn't run across the wrong assholes at school in case the fag got his ass kicked? When Tony would come home from college and say the same shit I heard at school? And he'd get Dad worked up and yelling at me. After years of trying to be invisible, I had a target on me. Mom had no control at all over either of them. But did you stand up for me? No. You gave me more of the same. So I found a way out. A place where I could be safe, because I couldn't be safe in my own home."

He was finally looking at me, and I stepped back from the anger in his eyes.

"You think I'm going to hit you? I'm not going to hit you." He lowered his voice and said, "That's not how it was."

"Why don't you tell me how it was, then?"

"It's not worth it," Chuck muttered. He twisted around like he was going to pick up his stuff and leave.

I didn't get mad as quickly or as easily as Chuck, but all of us had what Uncle Blaine called the Dunhill temper, and mine was escalating. "Just say it," I snapped.

He turned toward me again. "Dad's an asshole, Nick. He was always an asshole. Maybe he doesn't like getting old. Maybe he didn't like seeing three sons who reminded him that he wasn't hot shit anymore. He cheated on her and bullied us to make himself feel like a big man. Tony and I found our own ways to stay under his radar. Tony made himself into a duplicate. With Tony, it was always, 'That's right, Dad.' 'Can I go, too, Dad?' 'Teach me how to do that, Dad.' 'You're the best, Dad.' Like a puppy jumping up and down, trying to get a pat on the head. Just the opposite of you."

"I tried to stay away from him," I said.

"No, Nick, you didn't. You constantly challenged him. Talked back to him. Argued with him. Defied every one of his rules. You always brought him down on us with that mouth of yours. Or by getting in trouble at school. Do you honestly believe that you tried to be invisible? With your constantly changing hair color? Your pierced ears? Your black fingernail polish and bracelets and eyeliner? *Invisible?* Right. And there she was, always trying to come between the two of you before it got too bad. Trying to keep peace. Then you fucking announced to the world that you were gay. If you had a target on you, you're the one who painted it."

It was the most he'd said to me in years. I was surprised to realize that my anger was gone. I wanted him to keep talking. "What did you do to stay under his radar?"

"I tried to do everything right so he wouldn't get mad at me. Got good grades. Did my chores. Didn't talk back. Pushed no buttons. Made sure I was always just a little better than average at the things he respected, like sports, but never quite as good as Tony."

"Why not?"

"When Tony excelled, it was a reminder to Dad that his glory days were behind him. You and Tony were like opposite ends of everything that irritated him. I tried to . . . I don't know what. Be in the middle. Just escape his notice."

We were quiet for a while. I mentally replayed his words and finally said, "I guess you were the one who was invisible. Not me."

"That's one way of describing it." He put the hoodie on. "I won't tell anybody you're here. You do whatever you want. Like always."

I felt the same kind of panic I'd experienced when I was trying to drive out of Manhattan. I didn't want him to leave.

"Why didn't you stand up for me, Chuck? I don't mean at home. Even she couldn't stand up to him there. But why didn't you stand up for me at school? We were brothers. You were my twin."

He gave me an annoyed look. "Tell me something, Nick. Who beat you up at school? Who shoved you into a locker? Or threw rocks at you in the parking lot?"

"You know nobody did that," I said. "It was just threats. But it was enough to keep me scared and on edge."

"You have no idea how much you intimidated our classmates, do you? With that in-your-face attitude and your stupid black coat, they mentally voted you Most Likely to Take Them Out, and I don't mean on a date."

"That's crazy. Nobody ever felt threatened by me."

"Whatever," he said.

"So, what were you voted? Most Likely to Sell Out Your Brother?"

"No. I was Most Likely to Be Gay, Too. While you were hanging out with your arty friends who'd take up for you, or going to those stupid meetings to be told that you were here and queer, I was catching shit in the locker room. On the field. Everywhere I went. 'Hey, Dunhill, your twin's a fag. That must mean you're a fag, too.' Along with graphic descriptions of what we probably did together."

"Gross. Did it get better after I left?"

"It took a while, but of course it did. I swear to God, if you tell me that's why you left, to make things easier on me, then I *will* hit you."

"No. I should have been voted Least Likely to Be Noble," I said.

"Actually, you're Least Likely to Stick Around," Chuck said. He picked up the down vest and said, "Hope you heard what you needed to hear. Have a safe trip back."

I caught him as he moved past me, putting my arm around his chest from behind the way Roberto so often grabbed me. He was rigid at first, and I remembered that unlike Roberto, most straight guys didn't know how to hold or be held by another man. They didn't understand that when we embraced, it wasn't always as lovers. We held each other as friends, as brothers, sometimes even as fathers and sons.

It made me sad to realize that no man had ever held Chuck that way. Like the brotherhood of buddies that Dennis Fagan talked about. Like Roberto and me under the same blankets without awkwardness. Like being hugged by Blaine and Daniel, or Gavin and Ethan, or Jeremy and Adam, and knowing their only intention was to make me feel safe and loved.

I wondered who made Chuck know that he was safe and loved, and I felt like my heart was breaking open.

"Nick, let me go," Chuck said.

"No. I don't want you to leave."

"I won't leave. But you're crying down my neck."

"I don't cry," I said even though I realized he was right.

"You're either crying or drooling, and I truly would rather it be tears," Chuck said. He dropped the vest on the floor next to us and managed to turn around without dislodging my arm. He slid his hands behind my back and our foreheads touched for a few seconds. Then he pulled his face away from mine.

"Sometimes I feel like we don't know each other at all," I said. "Like we're strangers."

"Sometimes when we don't see each other, I feel like neither of us exists," he said. "Do you think things would've been different if we'd been identical?"

"Yeah, I'd get a lot more dates," I said.

"Shut up. At the beginning, didn't we see each other, even though we were on opposite sides of the womb? Do you think I ever put my hand out"—he moved his right hand from my back and held it near my face—"and wished you could touch it?"

I lifted my hand and pressed my palm against his. Our fingers clasped.

"I don't want to be afraid anymore," I said.

"I don't want to be alone anymore."

His eyes filled with tears, but he smiled at me until I smiled back, so that we were both smiling and crying as we stared at each other.

We'll be fine.

I know.

We'll always be brothers.

We'll figure out how to be friends.